For my mother and two beautiful daughters, M and D.

EZEKIEL KING

FROM INNOCENCE
TO ARROGANCE

AUSTIN MACAULEY PUBLISHERS™

LONDON • CAMBRIDGE • NEW YORK • SHARJAH

A CIP catalogue record for this title is available from the British Library.

ISBN 9781528918763 (Paperback)
ISBN 9781528918770 (Hardback)
ISBN 9781528962438 (ePub e-book)

www.austinmacauley.com

First Published (2019)
Austin Macauley Publishers Ltd
25 Canada Square
Canary Wharf
London
E14 5LQ

A special thank you to Dr C Bassiri and Deborah B for always believing in me.

Foreword

To my beloved readers.

I would firstly like to extend my gratitude for the time you will spend reading the following pages. I hope they will provide every emotion I experienced writing this incredible book.

Please do not attempt to replicate, modify or undertake any of the activities depicted in this novel. This book is not a 'how to' book.

I wrote this book to show the world how 'intellect' as great as it may be can go nowhere if it is misdirected and does not have positive adequate mentoring.

I hope this novel will allow the world to see that there are millions of children around the world that have the qualities to succeed but are instead wasted engaged in negative activities. My quest is for these children to be enlightened as to what they should be doing to achieve and how to achieve – that, of course, being the polar opposite to some of the things depicted here. I hope bringing this lifestyle to the attention of the wider public and providing a deeper understanding will help us combat the problems we face within our communities globally.

This book has been written for you to reflect, contemplate and live the best lives you can.

I say this to any person stuck in a life of crime, the problem is not your willingness to work, your intelligence or anything else that you have tried to change. The problem is where you are expressing your energy, if you decide to put all your energy without respite into positive endeavours, you will succeed and achieve your objectives in business.

If an action is not positive for all parties involved, both present and vacant, then it is not the right action to undertake. Proof of this is being many an action is done in haste, lacking consideration for the future. These actions are often reflected on in the years that follow as futile.

I hope you enjoy the most-revealing, -authentic crime story ever written.

I love you all, all nations.

Ezekiel King – 2019

Prologue

I never could understand why people called me 'Big CY'. I'm only 5'7", so it isn't because I'm tall. Maybe it's my heavy build?

I could remember the time people had started calling me Big CY though. It was around five years earlier when I was 21. I was ruthless. Hurting people had become normality for me. I didn't enjoy it; to me it was purely part of the job.

I liked to run and maintain a tight ship, so anyone unlucky enough to be in the way of my smooth sailing was dealt with the only way I knew how—violence.

As extreme and calculated as the person on the receiving end needed to cure them of their stupidity of crossing me again, as long as god graced them with the blessing of life, my anger for anybody disrupting my work life or my personal life held no discrimination. 'Shoot him' and 'shoot her' were identical phrases to me. Why should I care if she has a vagina, and he has a penis? 'Fuck them both' was my attitude.

My life had been one big roller-coaster ride for the last ten years. It had been one big blur of cars, clubs, clothes, money and women amongst other things.

They say 'everything has a price'. I had never agreed with that.

I would park my car outside my friend's house and beep the horn of whatever car had tickled my fancy that month.

Nine times out of ten, I'd spot a slight twitch of a curtain before the house door would open. I'd watch whoever I had arranged to meet run to my car as I would wind my window down. I'd be given a double-bagged quantity of money, anything from £6,000 to £100,000 plus.

So, what was the price of that? Breathing air?

I would stare out of my hotel window at these lifeless ants rushing to work, like the death penalty awaited if they were ten minutes late for work. I'd think to myself, *you really don't have a clue, do you?*

Robots, rushing to spend a lifetime breaking their backs to make a managing director they don't know richer than he already is.

I used to laugh at the fact that if this doughnut with his Costa coffee running to his office job was to unfortunately drop dead, the rich MD they work for would be pissed off that he will now have to replace him at short notice. It probably wouldn't even cross his mind to send a card to this doughnut's family. How misguided is this twat, practically running for a guy they'll never meet at 7:30 in the morning? I'd close my hotel room curtains to stop looking at the hundreds of lost ants, pushing other people's dreams without even knowing it, before they made me anymore pitiful of their pathetic existence.

Premiership football players are among the few people that earn enough money to be running around at 7:00 in the morning, I thought to myself as I sat on the corner of the bed. I was careful not to sit on last night's conquest's feet who was sleeping off being shagged half to death.

"Baby," I said softly to wake the sleeping fake-tanned brunette in my bed. I called her baby, because for the life of me, I couldn't remember her name. When she told me the night before, I obviously hadn't been listening. The loud music inside the club combined with the fact I was probably thinking what to say next to manipulate my way into her knickers made her name a 'need to know', and I didn't. I wanted to fuck her, not marry her, but right now I needed to wake this bitch up so I could get her a taxi home.

Time was ticking. I needed to call my worker, Chris, and tell him to get the money from the stash house, so I could drop it to my friend Bob to pay for the cocaine. We were sure to be sold out by the time I left the hotel.

"Baby," I said again in a kind and caring tone. I felt like throwing her out of the hotel window if it would speed up the process of her leaving. I gave up, I had to go. Plan B was to get dressed quietly, wash my face and leave without saying goodbye. The room had female clothes here and there. Thin knickers on the floor, a dress flung over the chair, a flat shoe here and a heel there. My jeans and T-shirt were folded in a neat enough pile. I never treated my expensive designer clothes like these sluts treated their cheap dresses and shoes.

I left the hotel room without saying goodbye.

I waited until I was back inside my car to call Chris. He'd been out with me the night before, but I knew he'd be awake. I'd punch his fucking lights out if he wasn't.

I'd treated that girl sleeping upstairs like a fucking princess last night, just long enough for her to give me what will one day be her husband's most prized possession; and more importantly, the hole that will bear her children.

The fucking idiot, I thought to myself as Chris' phone rang in my ear.

"Cyrus?" Chris said as he answered trying not to sound hung over.

"Go get it, Chris, and make sure there is 130 grand there, all right? I'll be with you in 30 minutes," I explained.

I spoke quickly and slightly mumbled. A kind of slang I had developed to make a listening device struggle to have any clarity, also to make transcribing a nightmare.

"Wait, before you go. Did you take that sexy girl with the brown hair back to the hotel?" Chris asked.

"No, I went home and had a wank, you idiot. The silly bitch is sleeping in the Ramada Hotel in town. I left her there. Go get the money now, I'm on my way," I replied.

"Big CY!" Chris shouted in a playful tone, paying homage to my immoral actions.

I'd arranged to meet Bob at ten o'clock sharp in a graveyard car park on the outskirts of town. I had just enough time to go to my favourite café and eat my poached eggs with hollandaise sauce before a big glass of fresh orange juice. Then I'd have to jump back in my expensive German jeep, drive to Chris' house to collect 130 grand, then go straight to meet Bob to pay for the cocaine that would be delivered to Chris an hour or so later.

Yes, I guess I was 'Big CY'.

What I'm about to tell you is how all this came to be, and how my innocence turned to arrogance.

Chapter 1

My dad never could stand my Aunty Delma. She saw straight through the façade that was him being a 'changed man'. She knew he would always be a firearm-wielding thug that was quick to cheat on my mum.

My feelings towards my aunty were quite the opposite. I was 15, and she treated me like the rebellious 15-year-old son that she'd never had. More importantly to me at the time, this allowed me to be the rebellious teenager I was with no adult intervention.

When I was with my Aunty Delma, her only contribution in terms of authority or rule-making came in the form of her bright smile displaying her perfect teeth, and the look of contentment in her eyes as she observed whatever mischievous rule-breaking I was engaged in at the time. She didn't care about what I did; as far as Delma was concerned, my dad had made the rules, so she took pleasure in seeing me go against them.

Delma's daughter, Tanisha, on the other hand, had rules. Tanisha is an only child, very well behaved, and nothing like me.

It was a Saturday afternoon in the middle of July. As can be expected in England at this time of the year, the weather was not blistering hot, rather a warm affair that was T-shirt weather but not quite warm enough for shorts. I had just got home after walking my girlfriend, Olivia, home. I knew everyone on our estate. I had lived there for 15 years and spent the last six of those years running around the housing estate doing anything from having water fights to playing football against the side of someone's house which drove them crazy.

I had planned to spend the rest of the afternoon visiting one of the older kids' houses, sitting in his garden smoking weed while he drank beer. He would almost most certainly end up wanting to fight whoever was unlucky enough to be there when he'd had one too many. Usually, there would be four or five drunk people in 'Mick the Prick's' garden, which gave me decent odds of not having to directly absorb the brunt of his drunken rage. The five-to-one odds in Mick's garden were far better than the guarantee of my dad coming home and being the harsh critic to my every move. Plus, my older brother would still be out at his friend's house where he would probably end up spending the night.

My older brother, Daniel, is three years older, and those three years came with a lot of desired freedom.

I opened the poorly constructed gate that my dad and his out of work friend built from some sort of wooden panelling he'd probably stolen from work. Credit granted, it was a gate, but the wood warped due to exposure to the rain, so it took a nudge to open and a little swing to shut it. I actually think it made the gate sturdier. Opening our front door, my mum was in the kitchen cooking; the smell of onions and garlic frying hung in the air. She would always start cooking around 5:30 in the evening in anticipation of my dad's 6:30 arrival home.

"Hi, Mum," I said cheerfully as I walked into the kitchen and gave her a kiss on the cheek.

I loved my mum dearly and always will. That kiss was payment for all the stress I'd put her through, and the stress I knew holding our family together put on her shoulders. She deserved a noble prize for the services rendered at home if the world knew.

I stopped in the doorway that led out of the kitchen and asked her the first question anyone with a brain asks when entering our house. "Where's Dad?" I said in a tone that gave the impression I wanted to hear he was in the living room or upstairs. I used the cheerful, inquisitive tone purely for my dad's benefit. I didn't want him to think I was checking if he was out, which I definitely was. "He's not back from work yet, and Daniel is at Lee's house before you ask," my mum replied as she lifted her head and looked at me in the eyes as if to say 'there you go, you've got all the information you wanted, Cyrus'.

Without there being time for the next thought to enter my head, I heard the door knock and open almost simultaneously. "Claire?" bellowed a friendly female voice above the sound of shopping bags hitting the thin hollow walls in the narrow corridor that led from the backdoor to the kitchen.

My mum's younger sister walked into the kitchen vibrantly and placed whatever she had brought with her on our dining-room table.

"Hi, Delma," I said happily as I proceeded to give her a kiss on the cheek—a kiss only the most important women in my life warrant. "I'm staying at your house tonight," I said before she had even had time to put her car keys down. Delma smiled widely as she looked to my mother to pass her verdict. My mum and I didn't have to speak to understand each other. A simple look from her would tell me chapter and verse most of the time, or occasionally I would get a mixture; meaning she'd say something while giving me the 'look' as well.

This occasion was a mixture. "Well, I don't mind," she said as she gave me the 'look'. "You know your dad might have something to say about you staying out, and you should ask him really," was what the 'look' meant. I acknowledged that and gave it the full respect it deserved by reassuring her. "Dad won't mind. If he gets back before we leave, I'll ask him," I said as I proceeded swiftly with another kiss to my mother's cheek. I hoped I would be gone well before my dad returned home. He would only come home and make up some sort of excuse for why I couldn't stay out. I could just feel him coming back to say something, like I need to give him a hand cleaning out the garage, or he needed help fixing the fence, or gate which he'd built broken.

Delma reached into a plastic bag she'd put on the table and took out a bottle of Alcho-pop. It explained the clanging and banging noise she'd made as the bottles hit the thin cardboard walls in our hallway. I left the two of them to talk while I went upstairs to get a pair of shorts and a T-shirt that were the closest thing I had to a set of pyjamas. Also, I had one cigarette I'd hidden in my room with some rolling papers that I had borrowed from my dad without his knowledge or consent. I filled a carrier bag with my make shift pyjamas and went back downstairs to linger in the kitchen. Delma knew exactly what this meant, as did my mum. Putting me out of my misery, Delma took the last sip of her drink before placing the bottle in the bin. I watched attentively as she picked up her car keys. "Claire, I'll see you tomorrow then when I bring your little monster back," Delma joked as she gestured me to leave. Little did the three of us know that I'd soon become a monster in my own rights. More precisely, the years that would follow would make me society's worst nightmare.

As we walked outside, I still had visions of my dad pulling up. I got into Delma's car feeling a sense of achievement mixed with freedom. Delma had a navy blue expensive German saloon with a grey leather interior. I was sure it was a present from her long-term partner, Mervin. Delma was a care nurse for the elderly. I don't know how much money she earned, but I was sure it wasn't enough to afford the car she drove. Mervin, however, had a really well paid job. I didn't know exactly what his job title was, but he was incredibly intelligent. He always wore suits and spoke very good English. He and my Aunty Delma had been together for as long as I could remember. Mervin doted over Delma; her wish was literally his command.

While Delma drove the ten-minute journey to her house, I began to think. Firstly, about how it felt nice to no longer have rules to follow having left the confines of my house. Secondly, that I wasn't going to have to listen to my dad nagging at me over something or another, and it was that which led me on to my final thought, *I need a permanent solution to my problem of being rule bound.*

At the tender age of 15, my understanding was that problems are solved with money. I had a problem, so logic told me I needed money.

Staring at my aunty as she drove, I evaluated her financial situation. Delma had a nice car, a decent house and a good standard of life. But then again, she had a full-time job and a borderline-rich boyfriend.

I can't clean old peoples' arses and get a rich girlfriend, I concluded silently.

"Do you want me to get you anything?" Delma asked as we arrived at her house.

"I would really like a spliff of weed, but I don't have any. I just have some rolling papers that I stole from my dad," I replied reluctantly. Delma smiled; we had just pulled on to her driveway. She hadn't even opened the front door of her house, and she was already catering to my every need. I loved my Aunty Delma. She reached for her bag and took out her purse.

"I don't know who you can get weed from, but I will pop to the shop to get you some cigarettes. The guys that live across the road will probably be able to get you some though," Delma said as she handed me a crisp 20-pound note.

"I know them; and yes, they'll be able to get me some," I assured her. Delma smiled and gave her usual look of approval.

I got out the car and walked across the road. I knew a few people on my auntie's street. We had another relative on the street that my mum would visit every Sunday. My grandmother's sister was old though.

While my mum would visit her, I'd go to Delma's across the road, or I'd hang out with the guys that lived on the street. One of the lads was called Jason. He was 23 and had a reputation for being a 'hard guy'. He didn't take any crap from anybody. I don't know why, but Jason had always seemed to really like me. He would always nod at me as a sign of respect and go out of his way to say hello to me. The way Jason treated me made me feel respected; also, it made me feel like I was one of the boys.

I knocked Jason's door and waited. A blonde girl came to the door after no more than a few seconds. "Is Jason home?" I asked while trying to act cool.

"Jaasonnn, door!?" the girl bellowed toward the staircase that was a metre behind the front door.

"Who the fuck is at the door?" Jason said in an angered tone as he walked down the staircase. Jason's frown turned into a smile as he saw it was me.

"Yes, Cyrus, what's up, pal?" Jason asked as he joined me in the doorway.

"I'm staying at my auntie's house tonight and haven't got any weed to smoke, so I thought I'd ask if you could get me some," I explained while taking out the £20 to hand it to him. Jason took the £20 note from me. He told me he would have to pop down the road to get my weed, so I should go back to my auntie's and come back in 15 minutes. He would then be back home and have the weed I wanted. "Okay thanks," I said as I gave him a fist pump and started back across the road.

I never knocked my auntie's door, I just opened it. I felt more at home here than in my own house. My Aunty Delma had always seen to that. She was sitting on the sofa in the living room with my younger cousin, Tanisha. I gave Tanisha a nod and said, "Hello, Tan." She returned the gesture.

"Get your cousin a drink, Tanisha! And he's hungry; warm him up some dinner, could you?" I smiled as Tanisha rolled her eyes as she got up adhering to her mother's request. I sat in Tanisha's seat which was still warm. Aunty Delma told me to put what I want on TV as she is going to the shop. I told her I had to go across the street to see Jason, but I'd be straight back.

"Okay," she replied. "Tan is going to make you some food, I'll be back in ten minutes."

After my aunty left, I ran back across the street to knock Jason's door. The same girl answered, but before she could shout Jason again, he appeared and signalled for her to go into the room she had just came from before giving me my weed. I offered him some for himself, but he refused as he already had some, he said.

Back at Delma's, my food was ready; roast potatoes, roast chicken, veg, gravy and some fruit juice that was neither cordial nor fruit juice. It was delicious, as was the food. I thanked Tanisha as she sat back down looking unappreciated. Mervin walked through the door next. A very slim man who looked very unsure of himself. He was no fighter—that was for sure. I felt like the man of *this* house; plus I knew my aunty called the shots, not Mervin.

Mervin greeted me, "Hello, Cyrus, nice to see you." He was surprised more than anything else, but he instantly accepted the fact I was there and clearly had no issue with it. Delma came back and slid my cigarettes and rolling paper under the cushion I was leaning on. I thanked her by giving her a raised eyebrow and cheeky smile.

I sat back as my food digested, feeling very contempt. I had no dad here to nag me, no mum to check I wasn't doing anything to trigger my dad nagging or getting annoyed. No big brother here, and this gave me time to think. I took out the cigarettes, peeled off the protective plastic and took out a cigarette. As I lit it and took a pull, my mind thought of home and the fact that this feeling of satisfaction would be short-lived. I began to think how I could change that. *Money,* I thought. I worked out my expenses to be carefree. I needed £20 every day. £10 to buy some weed, and £5 to buy cigarettes and rolling paper, and another £5 to buy drinks and snacks from the shop. *But how could I guarantee to secure this money every day? I could rob the post office near the estate I lived. I'd get a year's worth of £20 at least. It was definitely achievable*, I thought as I smoked my cigarette. I had never robbed anywhere before though, but I knew it couldn't be too difficult. I had been involved in fights quite often and had become a fairly good fighter, plus I loved weapons, knifes, bats and guns. My dad had a gun under his and my mum's bed. He didn't know I knew where it was, but I did, and I knew he kept the bullets in his bedside drawer. Little gold shells with 9mm written on the bottom in tiny writing.

The gun was black, metal and very heavy. My big brother, Daniel, and I would take it out and show it to the other kids on the estate when our mum and dad were out. My dad brought me an air rifle with little led pellets. On Sundays, he would take me and usually four or five kids from the estate that would follow us to the field to shoot cans or bottles, or anything that wasn't each other. So, I considered myself to be well accustomed to the use of weaponry. Some of the older boys on the estate would wind me up, calling me fatty and making fun of me, so I had got mad and got a knife from the kitchen drawer. The older kids had ran for their lives.

Once, I even got my air rifle and chased 'Mick the beer drinker'. He ran to his house and locked the door. I had even taken my dad's gun out the house. I knew he'd kill me if he found out, but for my year's worth of £20, maybe I could make an exception. I had to do something, and I *was* going to do something.

The weed in my pocket was releasing a strong deep stench that hit my nose, like foul smelling body odour, almost like it was demanding my immediate attention. I adhered to this by taking it out of my pocket and examining the contents of what looked like a miniature sandwich bag filled with a bright light green vegetation that almost looked illuminous. Two balls of bud that were perfectly trimmed of its leaves to present the fruit of the female cannabis plant in all its glory. *Stinky,* I thought to myself as I took the smaller bud out and placed it on my lap.

Jason had given me a good deal. I'll thank him next time I see him though, I thought as I began to construct a joint by breaking a boulder of a bud into smaller pieces. I had always had big plans and now was the time to start implementing them.

My auntie's house was a lot nicer than ours. It was a corner, semi-detached and positioned at a 60-degree angle on the end of a row of houses. Delma had a double-tarmacked driveway with a small garden next to the driveway. This was only a two-bedroom house, but it was the size as my mum and dads' three-bedroom house.

I would be sleeping in the living room tonight as Tanisha would be in her room that was her little sanctuary with teddy bears and pink and white thing everywhere. Her room was at the top of the stairs on the left, and her mum's room on the right with a bathroom in the middle. The staircase was a metre back from the front door, the same as Jason's across the road. Thick grey carpet ran its way up Aunty Delma's staircase and into the two bedrooms. Downstairs had laminate flooring throughout.

I liked the fact that I'd be downstairs. I have always liked my own space, a luxury I very rarely had the privilege of enjoying. Sleeping on the sofa was a small price to pay for feeling like the king of a castle.

The gas fire was on and gave the air a thickness that made the room feel all the more cosy.

Leaning forward in an attempt to almost stay sitting, I stretched forward to adjust the setting on the heater from the second to the lowest.

My cousin Tanisha was on the single-seated sofa, and I was sitting on the three-piece sofa. The room wasn't extraordinarily big. It only had the two sofas and a brown wooden coffee table with a glass top, and some sort of flowers etched around the edges where the glass met the wood. A fine coffee table, as far as coffee tables went.

My feet rested on a thick beige rug as I had kicked my trainers off upon entry to the house. Tanisha sat playing some application she seemed to be obsessed with on her iPad, and I sat back in the sofa, like a fat kid with a full belly that was just about to smoke a joint and chill out. That was exactly what I did. The weed almost took my breath away as I inhaled my first puff as if my lungs were protesting its presence. "That stinks, Cyrus," Tanisha proclaimed as she scrunched up her face and made a gesture to cover her nose. No argument from me—she was right—the stuff was potent. The smell and taste had over-taken my senses at the first puff. That's when it hit me. Well, in actual fact, two things hit me. The first was the fact that I was now high, but the second thing that hit me would be the factor that would have a lot more of a long-lasting impact on my life and would change it forever. I was going to sell drugs, and sell drugs in a major way!

The weed really started to take full effect as I swivelled my legs 'round to put my feet up. The cold leather felt soothing as I rested my head against the arm of the sofa. There was something on the big flat screen TV suspended on the wall, but I wasn't watching it. I was still in deep thought. Forget robbing the post office and getting money once. I'd get money every day if I was a drug-dealer.

The time was about 9:20 as the sun started to withdraw its light, leaving a calmness in the sky. *It's still light, but definitely going to be dark in the next half hour,* I thought.

"Tell your mum I'm just popping across the road if she asks where I am, okay, Tan?" I asked.

It was a rhetorical question, more of a statement as she just looked up at me and raised her eyebrows to confirm. I put my white sports trainers on; they made me feel about a foot taller. They had an air bubble around the back of the heel, and a smaller one on the side with a little white tick where my ankle sat when I had them on. I had to absolutely beg my mum to buy them for me.

"One hundred and twenty pounds, Cyrus?" I could still hear the calling of her voice in my ears, even though a full week had passed.

I walked through the garden and started back across the road. Jason lived almost directly opposite my Aunty Delma's, but slightly to the right. The street made a giant 'T' shape with my auntie's house at the start of the vertical on the corner, and Jason's house was on the long row of houses that made the horizontal at the top, making my auntie's house half on the same street as Jason's and half on a street that turned off Jason's road.

I suppose if Jason looked out of his window, he would be able to see down the side street opposite him that broke the long row of houses that faced his house. Delma's house would have been to the left of that break looking from Jason's.

I knocked Jason's door as the cool summer's breeze swept over the short hairs on the top of my head. A high-pitched 'clink clink' sound that seemed louder than could be expected came from his letterbox as I flicked it open twice, letting the spring mechanism slam it shut. I could see flashes of light coming from the TV in the living room; as the room was in darkness, it would flicker from lighter to darker as the TV lit and then dimmed the room. The door opened as Jason's slim figure appeared in the doorway. He had short brown hair that looked recently cut. The sides were bald, almost to a shine, like hair had never grown there before. Jason's blue eyes gave him a menacing look in the twilight of the sun setting, and the pink glaze over the white of his eyes immediately told me he had been smoking the high-quality cannabis he had gotten for me.

"What's up, pal?" he asked as if he had no clue what my second unannounced visit of the day could be about.

"Jay, could I have a quick word with you?" I said a lot quieter than I imagined it would come out. Jason stepped out into his garden. He was wearing German designer beach sandals with a blue matching T-shirt and shorts. He was well dressed for someone wearing sandals and a T-shirt which made me feel a bit scruffy, even though I had on my best tracksuit and trainers.

"Cyrus, what's up?" Jason urged me.

"Basically, I'm 15 now, and I leave school next month, and my dad is always on my case. I need some freedom and need to start making my own money. I've had a good think about it; long story short, I'm going to start selling drugs, Jay, and was wondering if you could help me?"

Jason smiled; his face said shocked and happy at the same time as his eyes lifted in thought.

"Cyrus, in order to sell drugs, you need to have people to sell them to and money to buy the drugs to sell." Jason let out a sigh. I remained silent and just looked at him.

"My uncle sells weed in big weight, but I don't know how he'd feel about a 15-year-old buying drugs from him. What I'll do is, I'll call him and tell him my friend wants to graft and see what he can do for you."

I smiled this time. It was a natural reaction to the news, and it was a big smile as I felt my cheeks rise. Jason bought me back to reality with his next and final statement.

"Cyrus, I wouldn't do this for anybody, so don't let me down; you're a good kid, so stay a good kid. If he says yes, don't fuck it up! My advice to you is if you can't swim, stay out the fucking sea, Cyrus; and there is definitely sharks in the water you're talking about diving head first into, little man." The smile had faded from my face as Jay's eyes stared deep into mine with the most serious facial expression I had ever seen.

I knew advice when I heard it.

'Cyrus, wear a coat today, it's going to rain' or 'Cyrus, have some breakfast, or you'll be hungry when you're out'. That was advice. What I had heard was closer to a death threat rather than advice.

I was lost for words and just nodded at him, probably with the same gormless look I get when my dad is telling me off.

"Cyrus, if you're not serious, I won't ask him because I like you, and I don't want to have to show you the other side of me. If I vouch for you with my uncle and you mess up, he'll fuck you and me up. Then I'll be forced to fuck you up as well, and I don't want that, little man. This can go two ways, well three, actually. One, you do business with my Uncle Jabber. You make loads of money and become best of friends. Two, you do business with Jabber, mess it up, and he'll come to find you and beat you, and whoever is with you, to death. Or three, you tell me right now; Jason, this is not a good idea, let's just stay friends; and thanks for the weed you got me, and I'll see you soon."

He stared at me with widened eyes as he allowed my options to be deliberated.

Shit just got real, the voice in my head screamed.

"Jason, your Uncle Jabber and I are going to do business and become the best of friends. I'm going to put my all into making that a certainty," I finally said with as much confidence as I could have wished for.

The slim 23-three-year-old with the slightly glazed eyes and skin fade, in his matching, German-designer beach outfit, stared at me for a few seconds. As I stared back, I didn't know if he was going to tell me to fuck off or throw a party. I had absolutely no idea what was going through this guy's head.

Eventually, his face brightened with his smile as he shook his head in a movement that said no.

"Cyrus, you're a fucking nutter, and that's why I've always liked you. Definitely not a normal 15-year-old, and that's why I'm going to call my uncle and tell him I've got someone who wants to work."

The sun had completely fallen, leaving the street in darkness and a lot cooler in temperature. I was leaning against the waist high fence that ran five metres from Jason's gate to the front door.

"Okay, cool," he said. "Go back to your auntie's, and I will come knock the door quietly when I've spoken to my uncle. Don't tell anybody about this, okay, CY?" he added.

"I won't, and I won't let you or your uncle down. See you soon," I reassured him, and I meant it.

I walked back across the quiet residential road towards the house on the corner opposite Jason's house; slightly to the right and into the garden, this time in the dark. I opened the door slowly; the golden handle was cold in my hand. The door made a kind of suction noise, like a strong fridge. Like the white UPVC door was fitted with millimetre precision.

I kicked off my sports trainers and entered the living room after locking the front door. Tanisha had gone to bed when I returned. I sat down and thought to myself, *Are you fucking serious, Cyrus?* "Yes, I am fucking mad," I told myself back.

This was and is how it's going to be from now on; I'm a drug-dealer now, I reminded myself. The room had cooled.

Chapter 2

My face was stuck to the cream leather on my auntie's sofa as my now open eyes told my brain it was morning. A mixture of eggs frying and the smell of toasted bread filled the air in the living room as I moved my head from left to right to unstick my cheek from the arm of the sofa.

"Morning, Cyrus," my aunty said cheerfully as she peered in from the kitchen doorway that joined the living room. I gave Delma a conservative smile and reciprocated.

"Good morning, Del." Delma smiled before disappearing back into the kitchen momentarily. Delma reappeared with a plate in one hand and a mug in the other. She placed the two pieces of dinning ware on the table in front of me while saying,

"Breakfast is the most important meal of the day, and you should eat your breakfast every morning."

Truth be known, I had never been a big fan of breakfast, but I wasn't about to tell my Aunty Delma that. Instead, I just tried to look as stoked as possible before saying, "Thanks," as I showed my appreciation by nodding. "I usually eat breakfast every day," I lied.

Where the fuck was Jason? I thought as I stared down at this large dinner plate sectioned off with scrambled eggs, plum tomatoes, mushrooms and toast that did nothing for me other than turn my stomach.

Jason couldn't have come back last night, or I would have heard him; surely I would have heard him? I contemplated.

My aunty had sat down on the single seat sofa next to me. She was very carefully sipping what looked like a fresh cup of coffee. "Do you have anything planned for the day, Cyrus?" she asked.

"No, Del, I've got no plans today. I'm just going to chill out for a while until I have to go home when you want to get rid of me," I joked. Delma smiled at me and shook her head. We both knew that I was as welcome at Delma's house as welcome could be. My aunty was wearing a knee-length dressing gown, dark grey in colour, made from a kind of soft fury material. The gown had flowers etched into it in a slightly darker grey that made them almost invisible. Her hair was curly and shining as it sat just below her shoulders. It amazed me how her facial features were all in such perfect proportion with each other. Delma's immaculately groomed and shaped eyebrows made her light blue eyes seem even brighter than they were.

"Tanisha has gone to town with Mervin to get groceries for dinner, and I'm going to get ready because I've got an appointment at the nail salon," Delma said as she continued to sip her coffee.

"Oh, okay," I replied as I sat still thinking about Jason; his uncle and the cannabis I wanted.

"You're welcome to come with me if you want? I'll be there for about half an hour, or you can just stay here until I get back. It's totally up to you," Delma said as she began to get up. I thought for a second as I stretched my arms out left and right while trying to muster up a natural-looking yawn.

"I'll just chill out here if that's okay?" I replied as I fell back into the sofa after stretching.

"Yes, that's fine," Delma replied as she started towards the staircase to get ready.

I had planned to run across the road to Jason's house the second she left. I hoped he hadn't knocked the door after I'd fallen asleep. This would not have been a good start as far as me not letting him and his Uncle Jabber down. Remembering what he'd said to me the night before, I recalled his exact words, *you need people to sell drugs to, and you need money to buy drugs*.

I knew a lot of people that would buy weed from me—that was for sure! My dad smoked weed. Also, my dad had about ten friends that I'd seen smoking weed at various times. I would smell it slowly working its way upstairs as I would sit in my room playing on my computer. A strong skunk-smelling weed that I had become so accustomed to that I actually started to like it. Additionally, I had at least ten neighbours that bought cannabis, and all my friends either smoked or knew people that smoked weed.

The next part of what Jason had said was a major problem. I didn't have any money to buy the drugs I wanted to sell. I knew I would have a lot of money and a nice German saloon, like my aunty's, one day. After all, that was my motivation behind wanting to become a drug dealer, but this information was not going to act as currency to pay for my initial start-up costs.

I had a problem that needed a quick fix. On reflection, I was glad Jason hadn't woken me up if he had knocked the door last night.

"Think, Cyrus," I told myself impatiently. *Where could I possibly get a large quantity of money from in the next ten minutes?* The voice in my head asked impatiently.

My trail of thought was broken as my aunty came back down the stairs and into the living room. "Bye, CY, I'll be back in 40 minutes. Help yourself to whatever you want, okay?" Delma said as she left.

I sat for the next 60 seconds in complete silence while in deep thought. Absolutely no idea sprang to mind, which was rare for me. I could have asked my aunty for the money, but it was a humongous request; also, I didn't want to involve Delma in case she tried to talk me out of my plans. Twenty-five minutes later, I concluded that I had no other option other than to tell Jason. After all, I did say I wanted him to help me. I didn't even know how much money I needed, so he couldn't seriously expect me to just have a large unknown quantity of money just laying around.

I got up from the sofa which now had an indent from where my large ass had been. I started up the stairs to freshen up. I had taken my tracksuit bottoms off at some point during the night, so I had only my boxer shorts and my T-shirt on. I weighed about ten stone, and most of that was made up by my thighs, legs, chest and shoulders. I was a chubby lad, but I was also fairly stocky too.

I found my toothbrush amongst the four that were in the toothbrush pot in the bathroom. My Aunty Delma's bathroom had tiles around the bath and sink. She had a thick black-tiled floor with a type of glitter embedded in the granite. The bathroom was spotlessly clean with a big mirror above the sink. The smell of bleach was faint but still noticeable to my acute sense of smell in the morning.

I had my own toothbrush here, as I stayed at my Aunty Delma's at least once a month. She had bought it for me when I had accompanied her grocery shopping sometime before.

I finished freshening up by drying my-now clean face on one of the three towels that were hanging on the chrome-heated towel rack behind the door.

Back downstairs, I picked up my tracksuit bottoms from the end of the sofa where my legs had been as I slept. I expected them to be a lot more creased than they were. While putting them on, well practically, as soon as I picked them up, a tremendous waft of cannabis hit my nostrils. It was the culprit that had put me to sleep the night before. I put my tracksuit bottoms on before making my way to the doorway to put my trainers on. The day was a lot cooler than it had been the previous day. The air was crisp and fresh. I had been awake the best part of an hour, but I still felt a little drowsy, like I hadn't woken up properly.

The morning air made me feel rejuvenated instantly. The time was roughly 11:30, I had estimated. I walked back across the road towards Jason's house. The street was still quiet in terms of being populated, but it was now bright under the suns light; the street looked very different to how I'd left it the night before. Most of the cars had now moved from there kerbside parking spaces outside of their owners houses. My auntie's house was one of the few houses on her street with a driveway. I walked through Jason's waist-high gate and down his five-metre slender pathway to his front door.

'Clink, clink, clink' was the high-pitched sound made by the metal letterbox as I flicked it open thrice. A few moments passed before I heard a key turn in the lock. The girl I had seen the day before stood in the doorway. She was wearing a pink belly top that left almost nothing to the imagination. I could see her sparkling belly button piercing as I looked down to avoid her captivating gaze. I felt my heart skip a beat as I looked at her beautifully tanned skin where her short top left her stomach visible. She had huge breasts that bulged at the top of her bra; like the belly top she wore was suffocating her tits, and they were trying to escape.

Wow, the voice in my head whispered quietly as I was scared she could hear me thinking. She had skin-tight pink shorts on, identical in colour. She was stunning.

"Hiya, is Jason there, please?" I said finally as I tried to make out her appearance was nothing out of the ordinary.

"No, he has gone out; he said he'll be back this afternoon."

"Could you tell him Cyrus knocked for him? If I'm not at my auntie's across the road, then I'll be back to see him soon," I said while trying to speak calmly and confidently. On reflection, it was a nervy attempt at best.

"Okay, I will do," she replied as she closed the door after giving me a warm smile.

She had long blonde hair, with light brown bits, and the most beautiful eyes. I had tried not to stare at her in the face too much;

the nerves I had felt at the first sight of her in the light of day told me I had an instant attraction to her. I giggled to myself as I walked back across the road.

I reached Delma's front door not even a minute later, pressed the handle in a downward motion and let myself in. I hadn't locked the door; I simply walked back to the lounge and slumped down on the sofa. The indent my ass had made in the sofa had completely vanished, leaving the seat a shining creaseless cream leather cushion. I had only walked across the road and back. It felt like I had run a marathon due to my lack of exercise.

I imagined my aunty would take me home at around 6:00 p.m. that gave Jason approximately six hours to get home with an update for me. Also, it gave me time to figure out how I would pay for the drugs I wanted to sell.

I sat back with the knowledge that I could do nothing more to further my objectives.

The smell of weed in my pocket grabbed my attention again. It seemed to let off the same deep stench. Every time I moved my leg, the smell was seeping out from my tracksuit bottoms.

I might as well smoke it because I've got a big day ahead of me. I'll need a clear head later, I told myself.

Sitting there in my auntie's living room in complete silence gave me time to think. As I began to roll a joint, I told myself that I would only smoke weed at night from now on. I can't be high on cannabis and expect to run a successful drug-dealing business. Money was going to be the focus of my life from now on.

I took out one of my rolling papers before placing it on a book that my aunty had been reading. Next, I ripped a tiny rectangular shape from the cardboard packet the papers came in. I rolled the tiny piece of card into a cylinder and placed it onto the left-hand corner of the rolling paper. Next, I reached in my pocket to take out the small re-sealable bag that my weed had been given to me in. I took out the perfectly trimmed light-green boulder of bud and broke it in half.

The crystals in the core glistened against the almost yellowish centre of the bud. I carefully broke the bud into tiny pieces before I mixed the tobacco from half a cigarette with it. Lastly, I transferred the tobacco-and-weed mixture into the rolling paper and rolled it into a perfect cone shape.

As I licked the thin line of gum at the top of the rolling paper, a strong smell of weed hit my nose. Fresh and concentrated, like the strongest smell known to man.

This is going to be the last joint I smoke in the daytime, I told myself once more.

Smoke bellowed from the spliff as I lit it, like I had set fire to a bale of hay in the middle of the living room. I inhaled deeply, which made me choke as the thick potent smoke filled my lungs. The weed tasted nice, but it was so strong it had made my eyes start to feel heavy after no more than a few pulls on the joint.

I mustered up the energy to get off the sofa. I walked into the kitchen to get a drink and some sort of ashtray. The little circular ashtray I'd used the night before had been cleaned. I found it sitting on the kitchen work surface.

"Cyrus?" I heard Tanisha shout as the front door was opening.

"I'm in here," I replied while thinking, *Shit! Mervin's going to walk into a house that smells like someone has been growing weed in the living room, then changed their mind and set fire to the whole harvest.*

Tanisha and Mervin joined me in the kitchen. Both of them were holding different colour carrier bags. They placed the groceries on the dining table. I was already in the process of opening the backdoor that led from the kitchen into the garden. It was a pointless exercise to get rid of the smell.

"That's some strong stuff you've got there, Cyrus," Mervin said as he raised his eyebrows in astonishment.

"That's exactly what I thought when I lit this," I replied to make light of the situation. I stepped out into Delma's modest back garden.

The garden was not huge. It had three metal garden chairs near the door and a wooden shed at the back on the left. Only a small square of grass starting two metres from the door where the concrete slabbing ended.

I sat in one of the lightweight metal chairs to finish my joint.

The next few hours consisted of me going back into my auntie's house very high, eating crisps and chocolate. My Aunty Delma had returned home, equipped with a new set of acrylic nails that had made her very happy.

I looked out of the living room window occasionally towards Jason's house to no avail. Mervin had been busy in the kitchen with Tanisha cooking dinner.

Roast beef, parsnips, Yorkshire puddings and roast potatoes amongst other things that they had told me about enthusiastically.

I received my first phone call of the day around 4:30 p.m. It was my girlfriend, Olivia.

"Hi, babe," her high-pitched excited voice had bellowed in my ear as I accepted the call. Olivia and I had been in a relationship for six months. She was pretty attractive. A light-skinned, mixed-race girl, about 5'5", with thick legs and a bum worthy of winning Brazil's Miss Bum Bum Pageant.

Olivia had large round eyes that made her face look exotic and attractive as I would stare at her.

I thought Olivia was sexy, but nothing like the girl that had answered Jason's door, but still a great piece of ass. Olivia was a year older than me, nearly 17. Her birthday was going to fall in the following month. She didn't know, but I had planned to break up with her for no apparent reason. I liked Olivia, but I didn't love Olivia.

"Hi, gorgeous," I replied in a low and uninterested tone.

"What are you doing today, Cyrus? You haven't called me, so I was starting to get worried," Olivia explained. She was right; I hadn't called her, and now that I thought about it, I hadn't even thought about doing so.

"Oh shit, sorry, angel face. I'm just at my auntie's house. I stayed here last night. I'll call you when I get home; we'll meet up and do something if you want?" I replied in the same tone. Of course,

I was lying; I didn't want to call her when I get home. I didn't even want to go home. Money was what I wanted. After all, if I was going to become a successful drug-dealer, what the fuck did I need her for? With money, I could buy sex if I wanted it. And buy sex off someone that looked like the girl that answered Jason's door. Not her! Plus, I'd had sex with her loads of times; and quite frankly, it was getting boring to me.

"CY, please don't forget to call me because I miss you," Olivia said emotionally.

"How can I forget to call you, ya nutter? I miss you too and will call you the second I get home. I love you," I replied as I lied for the third time in less than two minutes.

"I love you too," Olivia replied.

The phone went dead as we both hung up. I knew Olivia and I were never going to last together. It felt like a chore to speak to her. I liked the chase. The catch and conquer just meant the end for me. It was like some sort of immoral animal instinct that had been imbedded within my DNA passed down from generations of womanisers.

To my knowledge, womanising in my family could be traced back as far as my family tree could be traced.

I let out a big sigh of trivialisation. The display in the bottom-left corner of the TV hanging on the wall read 17:37, as the news reporter reeled off tonnes of irrelevant information.

"CY, dinner is ready," Tanisha called through to me from the kitchen. I calculated that I would be going home in the next half an hour without hearing from Jason by the look of things.

I hadn't replied to my younger cousin telling me dinner was ready; instead I just joined my aunty, Mervin and Tanisha at the large wooden dining room table. My place had been set opposite Mervin.

Mervin had strong cheekbones that were clearly visible due to him having minimal body fat. Quite the opposite to me. Mervin was white, but he had a deep tan. He had short black hair combed forward. At 6ft tall, he was a lot taller than me; it bugged me that I could never work out why he always seemed nervous and unsure of himself.

"All right, Merv?" I said cheerfully as I pulled my chair out to sit down.

I looked down at the huge plate of Sunday roast that my cousin and Mervin had spent the last few hours perfecting. It looked delicious. The combination of meat and vegetables that mainly came on Sundays. I imagined that eighty percent of the houses throughout the country would be sitting down to a similar meal. A glass of the same red juice I liked had been poured for me. I had figured out it was some kind of guava juice. It was thick and sweet which would leave a lasting taste that was slightly chalky.

"Thanks, everyone. This smells and looks amazing!" I said genuinely as I dug in.

The beef was succulent. It fell apart with ease as I effortlessly sliced a small piece to put inside one of my three Yorkshire puddings.

On top of the beef, I put a quarter of a golden brown roast potato with a splash of gravy and a dollop of horseradish. A kind of roast dinner, Yorkshire pudding sandwich.

My Aunty Delma sat in front of me to my left with Tanisha opposite her. Tanisha was telling us all about her English teacher at school. About how the teacher had lost her temper at one of the pupils. I found the story interesting because I was usually that pupil. It was nice to know I wasn't alone in making the teachers lose their rag.

Tanisha was 13. She was very intelligent for her age. She was slim with pale skin. Her hair was usually tied back behind her head in a ponytail. It made the front of her hair flat and shiny as her tight ponytail pulled every hair in her head tightly back.

I finished my dinner, and my aunty began to collect our plates.

Delma had a beige valour tracksuit on which the words 'Juicy Couture' were written in fancy writing made from crystals on the back.

She collected my plate, adding it to the others on the side near to the sink. I could feel the grain of wood as my hands rested on the table. It was smooth under my fingertips with a hint of texture that only sanded wood had.

"Cyrus, I told your mum I'd bring you back after dinner. She said your dad had been asking where you were; if I don't take you home, they'll only moan next time you want to stay," my aunty said sympathetically. She knew I didn't want to go home.

"Okay, you're right," I said as I sighed heavily.

Back to my dad's castle tonight. Well, back to our cardboard house on a shit council estate was a more accurate description.

"Merv will take you home when you're ready if you get your things ready," Delma said as I walked back into the living room feeling disgruntled.

I hugged my cousin, Tanisha—well, kind of patted her on the shoulder.

"Merv, I'm ready when you are," I called through to the kitchen.

My stuff was ready. It was a carrier bag next to the sofa I had slept on. It had sat there since I had arrived, containing navy shorts I had brought with me to sleep in.

Mervin appeared from the kitchen with a single key in his hand. "Ready, mate?" he asked as he signalled he was ready.

"Yes," I muttered back. "Love you, Del, see you soon," I said calling through to the kitchen as I walked in the opposite direction towards the front door.

"Bye, Cyrusss," a voice said behind me as I left my auntie's house.

Mervin's car was parked next to Delma's on the driveway. It was an expensive black German car. It looked new and clean. It had little numbers followed by a single letter on the back that read 435D. I knew enough about cars to know this was the model of the car.

I got in the posh BMW besides Mervin. The car smelled of new leather mixed with a hint of air freshener.

This car is better than my mum and dad's house, I thought as he started the engine that growled before calming to a gentle purr.

We were back on my council estate in less than then minutes. Mervin had driven slowly, but the car felt as though it wanted to go fast.

We turned left, off the main road, and drove straight down past the only right turn which was a dead end, before turning right at the bottom to stop ten houses later on our right. My house was the last house on the right. A giant kerb with concrete stumps prevented cars going any further.

"There you go, Cyrus," Mervin said as he turned to face me.

"Merv, what do you do for a living?" I asked inquisitively as we sat staring through the windscreen.

"I'm a web designer," Mervin replied looking a little bewildered.

"Oh, okay, I just wondered. Thanks for the lift, mate," I replied as I jumped out of the shiny black saloon. I stood watching as Mervin carefully reversed to turn around before turning left and then out of sight.

Turning to face my house, I stood for a few moments. I was preparing myself for the act of being happy to be home. Only delaying the inevitable, I walked to my gate, grabbed the handle and used my thumb to press the metal button above it to release the lock on the other side.

Using the ball of my foot, I kicked the gate open gently to avoid the risk of scuffing my best trainers. I had become so used to having a broken gate. I habitually used a special technique to open the gate without even realising I was doing it.

I swung the gate closed behind me. As I approached the front door, I could see my dad in the kitchen through the large window that overlooked the front garden.

I opened the door which I'd expected to be locked considering my dad was home. I entered the kitchen.

"You all right, Cyrus? I see you've remembered where you live then?" my dad patronised.

My dad was a big Jamaican man. He wasn't ridiculously dark in skin colour but not that light-skinned either. He was more of a perfect median between the colour of milk and dark chocolate. Like a strong brown if that makes sense.

"Of course, Dad. Are you all right?" I replied in a light cheerful tone.

"Yes, I'm cool. I'm just frying some fish; your mum is in the living room," my dad added as he continued cooking.

"Smells nice," I complimented.

My dad had done a lot of things badly in his life, but one thing he had always done well was cooking. He had always cooked great Caribbean cuisine going back as long as I could remember.

I guessed that had contributed to my heavy build, that combined with his genetics.

My father, Calvin, was six-foot tall with broad shoulders and a bald head the size of an impressive black bowling ball. We have the same jet black eye colour. To me, that added to his seriousness of his resting facial expression that came effortlessly to him.

My dad was a very scary man to look at. The type of man that could say 'don't fuck with me' without uttering a single syllable.

Our kitchen had a white-tiled floor with a large rectangular window above the sink facing the front garden that I had just came through. The kitchen had another window facing the back garden at the opposite end of the room. Both had a ceiling-to-window frame blinds that were a dark nude pink colour.

If you took the blinds down from both windows and stood in the garden, you'd be able to see straight through the house. At the back of the kitchen, we had a large circular brown dining table with matching chairs. We didn't have many luxury items in our household, but the few nice things we had were of high quality. For instance, we had a large flat screen TV in the living room.

My dad had an expensive stereo and a few diamond calls he would always show off, and that was about it. Everything else in our house was purely 'fit for purpose'. For instance, our fridge, it was a fridge, but it didn't dispense ice or anything. If you wanted ice, that could be found in the bottom section of the freezer. Ice would be kept on the top shelf in a tray if you were lucky enough for someone to have put water into the little tray with twelve sections that made individual cubes of ice.

We had a cooker and an oven, but they were not state-of-the-art appliances as was our washing machine and dryer. All cheap, white Chinese appliances that were simply fit for purpose. I wasn't ungrateful; I just wanted the best things in life. After all, someone had to have the biggest and best, I just wanted that someone to be me.

I found my mother in the living room, with her feet folded underneath her thighs on the sofa, captivated by the television. She had always loved to watch the soap operas. *EastEnders*, *Coronation Street* and so on. I couldn't stand them. I think I was permanently scarred from the years gone when I had wanted to stay out playing in the street, but I wasn't allowed; so I'd have to sit and endure the soaps while my mum would sit fascinated by every word of the shite. I slumped down on the sofa next to my mum who hardly afforded me a sideward glance.

"Hi, Claire," I joked. She turned her head almost 90 degrees to look at me long enough to see her smiling at me. I called her Claire sometimes as a joke; she was 'Mum' and a great mum at that.

Calling my mother Claire occasionally had become a running joke between us that had never gotten old, provided I didn't overdo it.

"Did you have a nice time at Delma's?" my mum asked without even looking at me. My mum loved the soap operas, and no one in our house could deny her watching them. She had two full-time jobs away from home, and then she'd have to keep the house tidy on top of that.

She'd have to put up with my dad's random mood swings and anger; she'd deal with me getting into mischief which was more often than not and deal with the house finances.

I think it would be fair to say they were another four or five full-time jobs. So, for this reason, my mum watching the soap operas was accepted collectively. Even my dad knew where to draw the line. This was the line.

When the soaps are on TV, 'leave Claire the fuck alone' was the general consensus in our house.

"Yes, I had a good time… or escape," I said while smiling widely as I leaned over to kiss my mum on her cheek before heading upstairs.

The alarm clock on my bedside table read 7:20 p.m. I was still holding the carrier bag, I'd gotten out of Mervin's car, within my hand.

My bedroom had a paper-thin blue-bobbled carpet on the floor. My single bed frame was made from hollow poles, like a cheap farmers gate had been reconstructed into a bedframe just for me.

As I sat down on my bed, the springs in my mattress compressed to exhaustion with almost no resistance. The mattress had been my older brother's; and before that, no doubt it had been another relative's mattress. It wouldn't have surprised me if it had been my dad's mattress from when he was a child, knowing the corners he would cut as long as it didn't affect him.

Looking around my room, I told myself, *you won't be in this situation for long, Cyrus. Things will soon get better.*

My room didn't have much in it. I had floor to ceiling blinds, a bed and a brown chest of drawers that was chest-high, as I would stand next to them. They were backed into a cupboard in the corner of my room that had no door on it towards the back left-hand corner of my room. The chest of drawers fit inside the cupboard almost perfectly. I think it had been done to save floor space.

I had a small TV unit with an old TV and my gaming computer. I also had a small black bedside table, an alarm clock, and that was it.

The best thing about my room was that it was my own space. My TV hadn't come with a remote control. I had to turn it on manually at the side using the power button which I did whilst standing.

I turned my gaming computer on and picked up the control pad. I spent the next 15 minutes shooting tiny computer-generated police officers.

"Cyrus," my mum shouted up to me from the bottom of the staircase.

"One sec," I replied as I put the control pad down and hurried down the 13 steps.

My mum stood at the bottom of the staircase, holding her phone towards me.

"For you," she said as she gave me her phone. I took the phone from her while looking slightly confused.

I had a phone. It wasn't as good as my mum's phone, but it was a phone. It worked; it was fit for purpose. I held the phone to my ear.

"Yes, pal." My eyes gaped as my heart almost stopped beating in shock.

"Mum, it's my mate from school. I'll bring your phone back down in a minute," I said as I started back up the 13 steps. The phone was still by my ear, but I didn't speak until I was back in my room.

"Cyrus?" the voice on the other end said.

"Hi, mate, how did you get this number?" I asked with a stomach filled with butterflies.

"I'll get to that in a minute, little fella. I need to ask you something first."

"Go on, mate. What's up?" I said urging the man to continue.

"Can you speak?" the man asked.

"Yes, I'm in my room alone," I explained.

"Well, I spoke to my uncle, and he's given me something for you," Jason said. I smiled to the point that my back teeth would have been visible. Then I remembered my problem. *Money!* I thought.

"Jason, I do want the stuff, but I don't have the money for it. I don't even know how much money I will need to pay for it," I explained while wishing I had any alternative solution. The phone fell silent as I held it firmly against my ear.

"Cyrus, do you want to let my uncle and me down?" Jason asked.

"No, of course not. I've known you since I was about 12. You've watched me grow up, and you've always been good to me. You're the last person I want to let down," I replied. It was the truth.

"So, come and get your weed then; but when I call you to collect the money, do not let me down. I'm back at my house now, and I've got it here for you," Jason said.

"Okay, I'll be half an hour because I'm back at my house now," I explained.

"I know you are. Your aunty gave me this number," Jason replied. He was clearly taking pleasure in the fact I had no clue what was going on.

"Oh, okay," I replied as the penny finally dropped.

"Cyrus, how are you going to get here?" Jason asked. It was a good question. I knew my neighbour would give me a lift, but a lift right this minute was unlikely. It was a Sunday night and nearly 8:30 at night.

"I'm standing…" Jason stopped speaking mid-sentence as I heard a female voice talking to him in the background.

The voice was familiar—it was my Aunty Delma. She was talking quietly, and Jason was listening, saying the odd 'okay' and 'yes'.

"Cyrus, I'm standing outside your auntie's house on her driveway.

I'm calling from her phone; she said she will bring me to you. Pick you up so that you can come to my house and then take you home. You can't tell your mum or dad. She said you need to walk to the shop at the top of your estate because she can't pull up outside your house. Okay?" Jason explained.

I knew I had a 10:00 p.m. curfew at the very latest, and the time was now 8:25 p.m. I couldn't tell Jason that, but luckily I wouldn't have to because I had enough time, just.

"Okay, mate, I'll be at the shop in ten minutes," I answered. The phone went dead as Jason hung up. This was real. I couldn't believe what had happened in the last 24 hours. *I must be mad,* I told myself as I stood in my room stiff with shock. My mum's phone was still in my hand as my arm hung by my side. I was smiling with a mixture of emotions as the happiness, shock, confusion and anticipation coursed through my veins. Two minutes passed before I realised I had not moved a single inch. They comprised of me standing perfectly still, with my jaw open, deep in thought.

Eight minutes left, the voice in my head said urging me to start moving.

I pulled my tracksuit bottoms down to my ankles and stepped out of them using one foot to stand on them as I pulled the other foot out, freeing both feet from them. Pulling my collar over my head, I used my right hand to take off my T-shirt in one smooth fast motion.

Stepping forward to my chest of drawers, I opened the top drawer to take out my grey sports T-shirt, closed that drawer and opened the third of the five drawers to get out my matching grey Nike tracksuit bottoms.

I spun on the spot to pick up my mum's phone from the bed where I had threw it before changing and started back downstairs. *Six minutes left.*

"Mum, here's your phone; I'm just going to pop up the road to borrow a new computer game from Lee," I said to my mum anxiously.

"Cyrus, there's some fried fish, it's snapper with rice, yellow yam and green banana. Come and get some," my dad called through from the kitchen.

"Thanks, Dad. I'll have some in 15 minutes. Lee has a game I want to borrow from him. I know I've hardly been at home in the last day and a half, but I have no homework to do," I said calmly as I tried to explain why I was going to be leaving the house again so soon. My dad just looked at me for a full five seconds. I could read nothing from his facial expression. It was as plain as a garage door.

Finally, he spoke,

"Cyrus, you think I was never 15. I was 15 before you was a twinkle in my eye. You go where you are going to go, but it sure as hell isn't to get no computer game. Just make sure you're safe, and you aren't getting into any trouble. Go on," my dad said in his slightly faded patois accent.

How the fuck did he know I wasn't going to get a computer game? And what the fuck is a twinkle in his eye? My dad is a psychopath.

Three minutes left.

I didn't reply to my dad; doing so would have only drawn more attention to the fact he knew I was lying. Instead, I left the kitchen to get my grey hoodie from the back of the cupboard door in between the staircase and living room.

Unlike my Aunty Delma's, our gold handle squeaked as I pulled it down to exit the house using the same door I'd came through earlier.

I walked through the garden slowly, trying not to alert my dad to the fact I was in a rush, yanked open the partly stuck closed gate and closed it quietly. Then I sprinted as fast as I could. Left past the ten houses that made up the row I lived on. Then I turned left, running past the side of my row, followed by the side of another three rows that were parallel behind the row my house was on. A line of roughly 20 houses on my left made a row leading to the main road which was the end of our estate.

I turned right at the main road; my pace had slowed to a gentle jog due to my poor endurance. The local shop was roughly 20 houses to my right across the road from the top of our estate. I could see it.

One minute left, I thought as I slowed further to a relaxed power walk. I turned left to walk along the concrete path that led to the entrance of the shop. I thought it would be best to wait there. The shop was a general convenience store that had about ten isles. They sold essentials such as bread, milk, cigarettes, alcohol, chocolate and a variety of household items. A big square brick building with a car park twice its size in front of it that could park roughly 30 cars. The shop had bright lighting outside on the concrete walkway that ran the length of the front of the shop. I stood just out the reach of the electric door sensor as I didn't want to repeatedly set the door to open as I waited. Scanning the car park, I couldn't see my Aunty Delma's car which was a good thing. I had rushed to get to the shop as I didn't want them to have to wait for me; but now I was here, I wanted them to hurry up. I was on a budget for time.

The night air was cool and soothing on my face, but my body was hot having just run more than I had in the last two weeks at least. The odd customer would walk past me, holding carrier bags before they'd disappear around the corner on foot or into a car from the car park.

Minutes later, I spotted my auntie's electric blue German saloon indicating to turn right. It did so and then took the immediate left into the shop's car park. I could see a slim white figure was sitting in the passenger seat as I began to jog over to the car to get into the back seat.

"I wasn't expecting to see you so soon, Del?" I joked as I closed the back door and tried to make light of the situation.

"I wasn't expecting my neighbour to knock my door for you either, Cyrus," Delma replied in a tone that meant that she wanted an explanation from me. Jason was in the passenger seat. He hadn't said a word.

"Jason, I've always been able to trust my aunty, so I'm going to explain what I spoke to you about last night if that's okay?" I said not wanting to drop myself in any more unwanted problems. Jason swivelled in his seat to face me in between the drivers and passenger seats. He just stared at me with a cheeky mischievous smile, like we were two young kids that were about to be told off.

He didn't give a toss; instead he just found the whole thing funny.

"Yes, of course, I don't mind; your aunty is spot on. She brought me here to see you, didn't she?" Jason said before turning back around in his seat to face the road.

"Del, I've had enough of my dad bossing me around. I'm 16 in 20 days, it's time I started making my own money. I'm not even old enough to work; and if I do get a job, it will be a shit one. I want to make a lot of money, so I've decided to sell drugs. I've asked Jason to point me in the right direction. He told me to think about it, and I have; it's my choice," I said careful not to rant but let her know it was a thought-out decision.

Delma turned to face me. She had on the same valour tracksuit she'd worn to dinner earlier. Her zipper was just low enough to see her white vest top underneath and the tanned top of her huge chest which was now more visible due to her turning in her seat as Jason had.

"Are you sure this is a good idea?" Delma asked as she pointed at me with a face full of concern. I could see her perfectly manicured red nails that matched her red lipstick subtly.

"Yes, Del, I'm sure," I replied as I looked her in the eye.

"I guess we better make a move now then," Delma said as she turned to start the car by pressing the start button with the small of her index finger. I knew it was to preserve her new nails, but it looked elegant nevertheless.

We turned right out of the car park, then left.

"Cyrus, be careful please, will you?" Delma said expressing her worry.

"Don't worry, Del, I'll be fine," I replied.

"And Jason, make sure you look after him, please," Delma added.

"Don't worry, I will," Jason replied confidently. I sat in the back of the car, looking out into the night, wondering what would be the outcome of my venture.

"Listen, you two, if anyone ever asks, I don't know anything about this, so I definitely didn't give you a lift to sort this out; did I, Cyrus?" Delma asked.

"No, you never," I replied as I laughed slightly.

"I'm being serious, you two," Delma said as she smiled.

"I'm going to drop you two at the bottom of the road where I picked Jason up from. If Mervin knew I was doing this, he'd hit the roof; you know what he's like," Delma explained.

"Where did you tell him you were going, and what did you tell him Jason knocked the door for?" I quizzed.

"I told him Jason knocked the door because you left your computer game at his house when you were over his last night. Isn't that right, Jason?" Delma said as she tried to cement her alibi. She looked at Jason as if to say 'tell me what I want to hear'.

"Yes, that's right; Cyrus left his computer game at mine," Jason replied before chuckling.

Delma tutted and shook her head. She had clearly appreciated his humour.

"And I've drove to your house now to return your computer game, haven't I, Cyrus?"

"Yes, you have, Del," I replied. I had always had a cheeky nature, combined with being fairly funny, but I knew when to push my luck. Things were going well, so I toned down my playful nature as I didn't want to unnerve my aunty.

We stopped just before the turning to my aunty and Jason's street.

"How long are you going to be doing this?" Delma asked. I didn't even know what we had to do, so I left Jason to answer that question.

"Fifteen minutes max," said Jason.

"Okay, I'm going to drive to the supermarket; I need a glass of wine when I get home after all this," Delma said as she shook her head. I could tell that our criminality had excited her, but she was still airing on the side of caution.

"My treat," Jason replied as he put a note of some sort on the seat he had just got up from.

Jason smiled and shut the car door.

Chapter 3

I heard the low rumble of my auntie's German saloon as Jason and I turned to walk along the road towards his house. His legs were longer than mine. I struggled to keep up as he stepped quickly, slightly ahead of me. Dusk was starting to display the change in the colour of the sky. It was around nine o'clock in the summer months.

"Open the door then!" Jason demanded as he knocked his door twice in quick succession. He acted as though he was annoyed that no one had been looking out of the window waiting for him to arrive.

I heard the lock in the door turn, making an unmistakable clunking noise before the door opened, and we entered Jason's house.

I followed him through the living room to the kitchen. Sweet smelling marijuana lingered in the air practically as soon as the front door had opened. The blonde girl who had answered the door earlier was sat alone in the living room. Her eyes were fixed on her phone as we walked passed her through to the kitchen. The living room was well furnished and decorated. It had oak flooring with white walls covered in black swirly patterns. The girl I assumed to be Jason's girlfriend was sitting on a big corner-piece sofa. She had her feet resting on a matching poufe, and a large flat screen TV was suspended on the wall in front of her.

"Grab a seat, we need to talk," Jason said as we entered the kitchen, and he closed the door behind us.

The 'nicey nice' tone he had used in my auntie's car had gone from his voice completely. After all, there was no attractive woman here that was concerned for my welfare.

"Cyrus, I'm going to give you four-and-a-half to start with. When you've sold that, we'll do some more. I usually just help my uncle doing the odd errand; but after you saying you want to do some work, I told him to give me some weed to sell to you," Jason explained.

"Okay," I replied. He'd spoken quickly which had left me slightly confused.

"How much money do I have to give you for four-and-a-half?" I asked while not quite sure how much four-and-a-half was.

"It's the same stuff I gave you last night. I'm going to let you have it for £670," Jason answered while staring at me waiting for my reply. My instincts were screaming at me, telling me to ask questions. Things like: 'How much does a four-and-a-half cost usually? Isn't £670 too much for me to take on?'

What amazed me was what I actually said, "How much will I make off that?" I had said it on impulse. I couldn't help but ask the question the second it entered my mind. My greed had overcome every other emotion in my body. Fear, contemplation, uncertainty. Fuck them all, I was involved.

I had never seen myself as a pussy. I wasn't scared of anybody or anything. My dad had made sure he'd installed that in me. Truth be known, I consciously knew I wasn't scared of Jason or his uncle; because when push came to shove, they were both made of flesh and bone. The same as everybody else.

"If you think you can't win with your fists, use a knife. If you think you can't win with a knife, use a gun." This had been the lesson my dad had taught me. It was around the time other kids my age were being taught to ride their pushbikes. Like their dad's, mine had made sure I understood the lesson as clear as day.

Jason stood in front of his square wooden dining table, clicking buttons on his cheap black Nokia phone. He was muttering numbers under his breath that made no sense to me.

"Well, it's not as simple as what you would make, because that would depend on how you sell it," Jason explained.

"What do you mean?" I interrupted.

"Well, at £10 per gram, would bring you back £1,260, minus the £670 for me would give you a profit of £590," Jason explained while making calculations on his phone.

"Oh, okay," I replied. *Nearly £600 profit,* I thought. Jason had my full attention.

"Or…" he continued, "you could sell it in ounces at £190 per ounce. That would give you a profit of…erm… £180," Jason explained.

"Why is there such a big difference in what I'd make?" I asked without thinking; using my lips before my brain had got me into trouble in the past. My dad had head-butted me while on holiday for doing exactly that.

"Think before you speak, you fucking idiot." I could still hear him grunt for dropping him in it at a family meal. The lack of thinking didn't earn me a head-butt this time; instead I just got a look from Jason that said, "Are you seriously asking such a stupid question?"

"Cyrus, if you sell it in ounces, it's a maximum of five transactions. Ounce, ounce, ounce, ounce and then sell the half ounce. I get paid, you get paid. If you sell it in grams, it's more transactions, more work, but you earn a lot more," Jason explained reluctantly.

"Okay, I understand," I replied as I nodded.

"Nobody gets weed on credit, and it has to be paid for in seven to ten days at the most, okay?" Jason said with raised eyebrows.

"Okay," I replied.

Jason reached under the dining room table and retrieved a black bin liner. This was the source of the smell that had the air in the house to the point of saturation with the sweet odour of powerful unburned skunk. He opened the bin liner and threw one, two, three, four and a half full sandwich bags containing the potent weed he'd given me the night before. I looked at the bags sat on the table in front of me.

That's a lot of weed, the voice inside my head said as I realised the enormity of what I had decided to do.

"Have you got scales?" Jason asked in a more relaxed tone, compared to when he'd first spoke.

"No," I replied realising I'd made a schoolboy error.

"Have you got bags?" Jason asked. This time I thought before speaking. I was glad I did because I probably would have said yes assuming he meant plastic bags, but the extra thinking-time bought me to the conclusion he meant little re-sealable bags that most drug-dealers put the individual deals inside of.

"Nooo," I replied, realising I was about as prepared as a skydiver with no parachute. Jason sniggered as though he found my lack of preparation slightly funny. He turned his back to me, opened one of his kitchen drawers and used both hands grabbing items in each hand before turning to face me. Jason threw two clear plastic packets containing small re-sealable bags on the table in front of me before placing a set of black digital weighing scales next to the bags.

"There's 110-pound weed bags in each packet, and you can have the scales for free. Think of it as an early Christmas present," Jason said while smiling.

"Where are you going to keep your weed, mate? I'm assuming that you're not going to take it home?" Jason asked curiously. He was right to be curious. I couldn't take the weed home; my dad would probably shoot me if I was lucky enough not to be beaten to death slowly and painfully.

"Oh, at my neighbour's house," I replied. I had always been smart enough to be able to think fast.

"One second, I'll give her a call to let her know I'm coming," I added.

I took out my phone, contacts, Trish, call.

"Helloooo," a low hoarse female voice said as the call was accepted.

"Hiya, Trish, it's Cyrus. I've got a bit of weed here with me; do you mind if I bring it to your house please?" I explained.

"What?" Trish replied.

"I've got a bit of weed here with me, and I can't take it home; you know what my dad is like. Could I bring it to your house please?" I explained. I needed the answer to be yes.

I had made my best effort to disguise the fact I hadn't prearranged this with my neighbour, but it was a poor effort. I felt nervous, and I was sure Jason could hear the desperation in my voice.

"Yes, okay, but you will have to get here quick because I'm going to bed in half an hour," Trish replied. Jason's facial expression told me he knew I was lucky to secure such a last-minute fix to what could have been a major problem.

"Okay, let's go, your aunty will be back at the end of the road in a few minutes," Jason said as he began to throw my drug-dealing kit into a carrier bag.

"Scales, resalable bags, four-and-a-half ounces of bud," Jason said as he listed the items as he bagged them, like an inventory clerk.

Jason handed me the carrier bag before I followed him out of the kitchen and through the living room. The beautiful blonde girl sat alone on the sofa, watching what looked like some sort of reality TV Show.

"Bye, babe," Jason said as he opened the front door. We stepped back outside into the summer night's cool air. I could see Mervin's shiny German coupe parked on my auntie's driveway across the road. I could tell someone was watching TV in my auntie's living room, as a light was illuminating the big square window at ground level.

I put my head down and followed Jason back towards the end of the street. I held the carrier bag containing my drug inventory by my side as I walked making no attempt to conceal it. The excitement that coursed through my body gave me a spring in my step to the point it blocked any paranoia that I should have been feeling, considering I was walking down a residential road holding a bag of drugs. It didn't feel as though anybody could see me under the cover of darkness.

"Your auntie is proper cool, isn't she, CY?" Jason asked as he broke the silence.

"Yes, she's always been cool. I can't believe she picked me up to do this," I replied. I actually could believe it, but it seemed like the right thing to say.

"Yes, I didn't know how she'd react when I spoke to her. It's not often that you meet a woman as good-looking as her that doesn't have their head up their own arse," Jason stated.

The street was very tidy; it had medium-priced cars here and there outside of people's houses as they settled in for the night. We got to the end of the road to find my auntie's electric blue German saloon parked up waiting for us. The car looked a lot darker in colour at night, as though the lack of sunlight had taken away the brightness of the blue, leaving only the shine from the paint.

I opened the backdoor to climb into the car while Jason got back into the front passenger seat. Almost as soon as the car pulled off, the smell of potent skunk started to make its presence known.

"Cyrus, that stuff really hums," Delma said. She was right; even I was shocked by the extent of the deep concentrated stench.

I spent the ten-minute drive back to my estate thinking about my drug-dealing journey that would start with the sale of the weed sat beside me. As I looked out of the window towards the calm night's sky, my subconscious was telling me, *this needs to go smoothly.* I could not afford to fuck this up!

"Are you okay, Cyrus?" my aunty called into the back of the car as we approached the shop I'd been picked up from.

"Yes, I'm good," I reassured.

"Cyrus, I'm going to pull into your estate and turn around at the top of the road, just in case there are people outside the shop. I don't want them to smell that when you walk past," Delma smartly added.

I hadn't even thought about that. Delma indicated into my estate and turned left before stopping immediately.

"CY, give me your phone number, mate, and take my number," Jason said. We exchanged numbers before I said goodbye and took my drug-dealer starter kit. Silence fell as I heard my auntie's car pull off behind me. I walked down towards the bottom of the road.

My estate was grubby. It had the odd piece of litter on the ground. Wind or decomposition where the only two things that removed litter from my estate's paved walkways.

In order to get to my house, I'd walk down to the bottom of the road and turn right. I didn't do that; instead, I walked down the road and took the only other turning on the road—the first right.

Turning right, but looking to my left after doing so, were a row of houses that were directly behind my house.

I entered the gate—last but one on the row. This was Trish's house.

Trish's gate was flimsy, made from thin dark wooden slacks. Her garden was small with square concrete slabs on the ground. Trish's house had single-paned glass windows which must have made the house freezing in the winter months.

I tapped on the big square piece of glass in the middle of the front door. She had a white plastic door which didn't match the rest of the house, as this was double-glazed.

Her landlord must have needed to replace the old door and done so, neglecting the fact that the whole house needed new doors and windows.

"It's open," Trish shouted from the living room signalling me to come in.

In through the front door, you had a door immediately on your left which was a toilet. Just past that, the living room was on your right.

To your left would be through to the kitchen with a cupboard on your right just before the kitchen entrance. The house stunk of cigarette smoke.

"Hi, Trish," I said innocently. My tone gave the impression that I was there to bring her a gift or check on her welfare. Not that I was there to use her house as a narcotics storage facility.

I joined the overweight 50-year-old woman in her living room.

She was sat in front of the TV, watching something that looked like it would bore any sane person to death. I stood staring at her for a few seconds to make sure I had her full attention.

"Trish, I've got some weed here. I've got to pay almost £700 for it, so it has to be kept safe. I'll come and pick it up tomorrow after school if that's okay?" Nothing much seemed to bother Trish. I had seen her with bruises or black eyes over the years. She'd been given them by various men she had been in brief volatile relationships with. Years of alcohol-abuse combined with her ADHD-suffering son being in care had long since taken Trish past breaking point. Trish wasn't living. She was 'existing'.

Her short, badly bleached blonde hair looked thin and brittle and poorly maintained—she had given up. To me, Trish was perfect—a loner that lived almost directly behind my house. My bedroom window gave me a direct view of Trish's house, but on the opposite side, I had entered it. If I had looked out of my window, her house was one house to the right, directly opposite.

"You said you had a little bag of weed, not a bloody carrier bag full, Cyrus," Trish said lethargically. Her voice was hoarse and dry, clearly the effects of excessive smoking.

"Trish, it's not a carrier bag full, it a carrier bag half-full," I replied while giving her my very best cheeky smile.

Manipulation was a trait I'd had to learn early growing up in my household, and I knew just how to take advantage whenever possible.

"Put it in the cupboard near the kitchen," Trish replied as she smiled and shook her head.

"Thank you, Trish… Is everything okay with you though?" And how's your day been?" I asked. I didn't care how her day had been. It was purely common courtesy.

"I'm okay. I've been at the hospital this morning to see my mum. She's getting better slowly. She's just old," Trish explained.

"That's good. I'm glad she's on the mend," I replied again out of courtesy. I turned around to leave the living room. Walking through the open living-room door, I opened the cupboard door on my right, just before the entrance to the kitchen. The cupboard was cluttered with bin-liners full of old clothes and boxes containing general household junk. I moved a few things out of my way to allow access to the back of the cupboard. I opened a box towards the back of the cupboard and carefully hid my bag of weed under the contents. Once hidden, I threw one of the bin-liners on top of the box before stepping back over the jumbled mess and closing the door.

Job done, I thought to myself as I felt the relief of weight being lifted from my shoulders. I now had drugs to sell, and I had then stashed in as safe a place as I could have wished for. The only people that knew about my illegal venture was Jason, Delma and Trish. I was happy.

"Trish, I'm going to go to mine now, but I'll be back just before four o'clock tomorrow to pick my carrier bag up, okay?" I said in a meaningful tone. I couldn't afford for Trish to be back at the hospital when I needed my weed to sell, so it was crucial for me to tell her when I expected her to be home.

"Okay, Cyrus, say hello to your mum when you get home for me," Trish replied as she took her eyes off the TV to say goodbye.

I left Trish's house using the same door I had used to enter. I could have used the door on the other side of her house, but that would run the risk of my dad seeing me come out of her house. The excuse of needing to get a computer game would have been dead in the water completely if my dad saw me leave Trish's.

There was two ways to get back to my house from Trish's using the door I left through. I could turn right and walk back to the road, and then right and right again, using the same route a car would take. Or I could come out of the gate, turn left and left again. This route would take me walking along a small footpath. The footpath route would take less than a minute. The route towards the road would take roughly two minutes, give or take a few seconds. I chose the longer route. I needed the time to consider my next moves. Jason had told me that the £670 I now owed him needed to be paid in a maximum of ten days. I worked out if I sold £70 worth of weed in a day, I would be well on target. I had school in the daytime though. I wished I hadn't. My time needed to be spent selling drugs from now on. Our school would break up for the summer holidays on the following Friday. It would give me six weeks to run around the streets doing as I pleased.

My estate was quiet as I walked slowly towards my house. In my neighbours' windows, I could see lights shining through the various window coverings they had used as curtains.

As I got nearer to my house, I could hear our next-door neighbour's dogs clanging the empty metal container around that they received their food in; it was like they were pleading with their owners to put food in them

The gardens on my estate were no bigger than a small garage; my next-door neighbours' garden must have had at least 60 pieces of dog faeces on the floor. That, combined with the ammonia in the dogs' urine let off a smell that I was sure was toxic. It would take your breath away as the putrid smell would hit your sense of smell like a train.

I opened my gate and knocked the back door, it couldn't have been later than 10:00, so I wasn't late home. *No nagging for being late,* I thought to myself, as I was expecting my dad to open the door. Anybody other than my dad would have been a bonus.

Life had taught me to always expect the worst outcome in everything, to always expect disappointment. Always expect the person you are relying on to let you down. With that mentality, there was never any shock, pain or disappointment. Alternatively, if somebody did keep to here word, then this was joyous on the rare occurrence it happened. I had long since become accustomed to applying this to my everyday life.

My dad answered the door and stood looking me square in the eye. He was giving me an on the spot drug and alcohol test visually. I stared back at him deep into his eyes as I let him study my pupil dilation for long, silent seconds. I hadn't even walked through my door without being criticised.

My dad turned and walked back to join my mother in the living room. I locked the back door and walked through the kitchen towards the stairs and living room. Before going upstairs, I peered into the cosy-lit living room to find my mother and father sharing the big sofa watching a film.

"You's okay?" I asked.

"Have some food before you go up," my dad replied.

"Okay I will," I said. I wasn't hungry; my appetite for food had been taken away by the excitement of starting my drug-dealing venture.

I went into the kitchen to get a snack rather than a meal before going upstairs to my room. I placed crisps, chocolate and a drink on my bedside table. My brain was moving at 100 miles an hour as I sat down to think things through. If I'm going to make a substantial amount of money, I'm going to need help. My dad is not going to allow me to be in and out of my house every five minutes to serve customers. Likewise, he would never allow people to knock my door to buy weed either, but who could I trust? I contemplated. *My brother had more freedom than me. Although he had his own friends, he was my brother, and he loved me. I could trust him to an extent,* I concluded. Also, I had a few trustworthy friends I could ask, but involving more people would mean I'd have to share my profits, wouldn't it? Then again, if more people were helping, I'd be making more money, wouldn't I? I could have sat on my bed and asked myself questions all night.

"Time will tell," I told myself.

"It always did."

Chapter 4

I woke up the next morning at 8:00 a.m. sharp. The high-pitched beeping of my little digital alarm clock pierced the morning silence violently. I hated being woken up, but still set the alarm religiously.

My mum would only start shouting at me to get me up if I didn't. I got up and turned my annoying alarm off. I had no intention of going to school though, my plans were to get the ball rolling as soon as possible. In fact, I wanted to collect my weed from Trish's house before she went out, not at 4:00 p.m.

My dad was at work, so I'd get no hassle from him until late in the evening. My mum wouldn't wake up until 10:30.

I put my shorts on to go and check if my brother was in his bedroom. He had his own key to the house, so he'd come in late most nights. I found him in his room wrapped up in his quilt like a cocoon.

"You want to make some money, Daniel?" I said softly as I rocked him gently by his shoulder to wake him up. He moved and opened his eyes sluggishly, looking annoyed at the fact I had woke him. "Do you want to make some money?" I asked again. Now he was half-awake.

"What? What you on about?" Daniel asked. Now looking at me puzzled.

"I've got some weed I need to sell. I'd like you to help me, and I'll pay you," I whispered, not to alert my mum in the next room. Danny's eyes widened as his brain interpreted the information I had given him.

"What do you mean? How much weed have you got?" he asked. I took my dad's advice and thought before I answered.

"I've got about £600 worth in ten-pound deals." This was just under half of what I actually had; and in the event of something going wrong, it would still leave me enough to pay Jason.

"Where did you get it from, and is it any good?" Danny asked looking surprised.

Daniel was taller than me and had a darker complexion. He was slimmer than me; Daniel was six feet tall and known to be reserved and quiet, unlike me, but also that he wouldn't take any shit from anyone.

"I got it from one of my mate's uncles. I've got to pay for it in seven days though…it's potent. I'm not going to school today, so come with me to sort it out if you want."

Daniel had always tried to keep me doing the right thing and behaving; so under normal circumstances, he would have had a problem with me saying I was going to truant or wag it, but this wasn't normal circumstances.

Daniel earned about £60 a week. He had a job cleaning the car park of a shop at the top of our estate. He also had a paper round that he did in the afternoons in our area; however, I was proposing a far more lucrative offer.

"Cyrus, I'll help you when we get out of the house; we'll talk more. If it's as good as you're saying, then I'll be able to sell it." Daniel was wide awake and as on board as I could have hoped for.

"Meet me in Trish's back garden in ten minutes," I told him before going back to my room to throw on a tracksuit. I brushed my teeth, washed my face and was at Trish's front door in five minutes.

"It's me, Trish," I said as I knocked on the big piece of glass in the back door impatiently. She opened the door in her dressing gown—it was grubby and worn. Her face was wrinkled with loose skin that was discoloured. "I've come to get most of that stuff. I'll take the rest in a day or two if that's okay?"

I was bubbly and cheerful. She was slow and drowsy as if she was still feeling the effects of the sleeping tablets she had probably taken the night before.

"Yes, okay, it's where you left it," Trish told me as she returned to the kitchen.

In through Trish's front door, I turned left and then opened the cupboard on my right. As soon as I did, I could smell the skunk that had saturated the air in the cupboard with the same potent stench it seemed to leave wherever it went. I rummaged through the clutter, moved the box on top and retrieved my bag. I counted out two-and-a-half ounces of Skunk, leaving two ounces of weed left in the bag. I took a packet of little plastic seal bags containing one hundred clear bags and my brand new digital scales. Then I hid the bag back where I had put it the night before.

"Have you got an empty plastic bag, Trish?" I asked with both my hands full of my illegal contraband. Trish opened the drawer in the kitchen and handed me a carrier bag. "Thanks," I said as I put the weed, drug bags and scales inside the plastic bag. I asked Trish about her plans for the day, purely to pass time while waiting for Daniel. I said goodbye to Trish and went back into the garden to wait for my brother.

As I stood in the cold morning air, the best idea hit me. I needed my own shop that I would sell my weed from. The idea I had was to go to Tom and John's house who lived about a ten-minute walk away from my house in a nicer newer estate. I would turn Tom and John's house into my shop.

I took my phone out of my pocket and scrolled through my contacts to call Tom, hit the call button and waited. No answer, so I repeated the call twice more. "Hello," a male voice said on the other end of the phone. "Hi, it's Cyrus, is Tom there?" I said pleasantly.

"Hi, mate, it's me, John. Tom is in bed, but he'll be up soon, Cyrus; what's up?"

John was Tom's older brother. Tom was 16, and John was 18. They came from Irish background and had the most relaxed household I had ever seen. Their mum was a nurse, and their father worked for some company that had him out the house from seven in the morning until seven in the evening. Tom and John had absolutely no rules at all apart from the obvious, like don't 'burn the house down'. John and Tom were very similar in nature and appearance. They both had soft dark hair, they both were very slim and loved to smoke weed. They were also two of the few friends I had that were allowed to smoke weed in their house.

"John, can my brother and I pop 'round for a joint? I've got some strong weed. I also need to talk to you and Tom," I asked. I thought it best to save my business proposition for a face-to-face talk.

"Yes, we're both at home, I'll see you in a minute," John replied. I hung up as my brother joined me in Trish's garden.

"Yes, Cyrus, you little bastard, what have you been up to? You've been busy, haven't you?" Danny said as he gave me a fist pump in acceptance. I smiled back at my brother and told him we would walk and talk.

As I started to lead the way to John and Tom's house, I explained the thoughts I had been having about our dad and about money and freedom. I explained how that thought process had led me onto my decision to start selling drugs. I told my brother how I had spoken to a friend to source the weed that I now had in my hand. I decided to leave Jason's name out. I chose to keep my contact to myself exclusively.

Daniel knew who Jason was, but he had no clue he was who I had done business with. He didn't need to know, so I didn't tell him.

We decided to talk profit after we had sat down, and Daniel had seen the quality of the product I had.

The roads were busy, parents walking children to school, buses filled with spotty kids going to school, and hundreds of cars containing people on the way to start a fresh week of work.

We blended in; two mixed-race kids walking down a busy road with a carrier bag in the direction of my school. I didn't feel as though anybody expected or suspected the carrier bag I was holding to be half-filled with drugs and scales.

All the morning, commuters had made me feel hidden, just like the darkness of night had previously when Jason and I had walked to meet my aunty.

'Morning', the odd person would say to either of us, or both of us as they walked by completely oblivious.

We arrived at John and Tom's house ten minutes after setting off. I knocked the door to be let in by John. He was topless as he was halfway through getting dressed.

The McBride's house was made of brick, unlike my family house. My house was very 'lived in', not dirty so to speak, just untidy, with clothes piled in a corner, waiting to be ironed on a sofa and in need of a 'spring clean'. As soon as you walked through John's front door, it brought you straight into the living room. The McBride's had a big, black three-piece leather sofa with two single matching sofas, a small black coffee table and a TV on a stand in the corner of the room. The McBride's had an open-plan dining room behind the living room that had a big brown table heavily varnished to the point it seemed to have a thick shiny layer on top of it, with about six dining chairs. The kitchen was to the left of the dining room. Their carpet was thin, green and looked grubby, like it had been walked on a thousand times and had spent years having drinks and ashtrays spilt on it.

As soon as you enter the house, the stairs were in front of you. Their living room to the right and a small second sitting room through a door immediately to the left.

This second small sitting room was John and Tom's 'chill out room' in the years that would follow, it would become one of the area's most successful drug dens. The McBride brothers would always have people at their house, either skipping school in the day, or just chilling out at night, but almost certainly smoking weed. They had the coolest parents any kid like me could wish to have.

"Yes, mate," I said to John as I sat down on the single-seated leather sofa.

"How come you aren't going to school, Cyrus?" John asked after saying hello to my brother.

"Because I've got this, mate," I replied as I opened up the carrier bag to take out the smallest bag I had, containing the big nuggets of buds the size of the top half of a big thumb. I gave one to Daniel, and another to John. The mini boulders of lime green buds were perfectly trimmed, bone dry and absolutely stinking.

"It's Big Buddha Cheese," I said remembering what Jason had told me.

"It's absolutely killer weed," said Danny.

"This looks banging," John said.

"Go and show Tom," I said feeling proud of my endeavour. John started to walk up the stairs, leaving my brother and me in the living room. Everyone seemed happy, so now it was time for me to be happy. The only way I could be happy was to pay Jason and have my profit in my pocket, so my attention had switched almost instinctively back to the job at hand.

I had done some calculations before I went to sleep the night before, so I called John and Tom downstairs to discuss my plans with them and my brother at the same time. That way, it would prevent me repeating myself. I asked them all to come to the big, brown, shiny dining table, which they did. I sat at the head of the table with the three of them sitting around me, like a business meeting with the managing director of a large company. I explained to them, "I'll give you all two ten-pound bags each for free, I'll give John and Tom £60 each cash, and I'll give my brother £100."

I had their full attention. Three sets of eyes and ears fixated on my every syllable. "But in order for me to do that, I need help from all of you!" I said.

"What do you need us to do?" Tom said eager to know what his role would entail. "Every time I sell 120 ten-pound bags, I'll pay everyone. To begin with, I'll give each of you one ten-pound bag; then when we've sold half, I'll give you all another ten-pound bag. I'll give John and Tom £60 each and Daniel £100." They all looked at me a little confused. "So, here's what I want everyone to do. I've got 70 ten-pound bags in this carrier bag, which I want to leave here in deals for you to sell. John and Tom, you serve people I send here and anyone that you can get to buy weed from us. Friends from school, people from the local area, family, just anyone and everyone you can."

I studied their facial expressions to see if they were on-board. I had explained it as if to say 'this is what's going to happen', not 'is it all right with you if this happens?' That's how a mug conducts business. I was no mug, and this was my first day of my new job, and I was the boss.

I sat at the head of the table, and I was calling the shots. The three of them sat nodding their heads, like puppies, waiting to be patted on the head and given a treat. I was in business.

"You're a nutter," said Daniel, "you didn't say what you wanted me to do," smiling at me with a face that told me that he was impressed.

"Dan, I want you to help me by giving John and Tom more weed when they need it and by picking up the money from their sales. I also need you to get 100 people minimum from the local area to come and buy weed from here, starting as soon as we finish bagging up the weed." I placed the scales on the table and all three sandwich bags of weed with the clear packet containing the little empty deal bags. I weighed the individual bags to make sure they were the correct weight. I then emptied all the weed out on the table, made sure my digital scales were set to grams and started weighing gram, gram, gram, gram, gram, gram, gram, gram, gram... all the way to the 70th gram. I got pretty fast at it. Towards the end, I would estimate the amount needed by filling the bags by eye; then I would put the bag on the scales, and it would be dead on a gram.

My brother, Daniel, John and Tom struggled to keep up the pace, ramming the stinking herb into the little bags. When we had finished, I told the three of them to each pick a ten-pound bag of weed for themselves, leaving 67 bags which would bring me £670. This was the exact amount I needed to pay Jason. The two ounces hidden in Trish's cupboard would be all for profit. I didn't even think about them. For now, my only concern was paying Jason, and I didn't want to let him down. I told John and Tom to half the 70 bags, putting 35 in a pot to be sold and 32 upstairs. When all 67 were sold, I told them to call me so I could tell my brother to bring the rest and pick the money up. Everyone agreed to do as I said, which made me over the moon inside. I didn't show them I was happy by being excited or smiling; instead, I kept an emotionless facial expression to let them all know if they messed up, I would go absolutely ballistic.

My brother, John and Tom all picked the biggest juiciest bags of ganja they could, out of the 70 there were. They collectively decided to build a joint each to celebrate our new venture.

When the three of them realised I weren't building one for myself, they said they'd give me a piece of theirs so I could roll myself one. I made a deal with myself not to smoke in the day. A deal I would adhere to. For me, it was business before pleasure. In fact, until I had enough money, it was all business—pleasure could wait.

I sat at the dining table while my brother got high with our two friends. They told me how great the weed was and about how it stunk more than any weed they had smoked, also how it tasted beautifully sweet to inhale. They were right, all this was true. But I didn't give a fuck; I wanted £670 to pay Jason as soon as humanly possible. Nine times out of ten, I would get what I wanted. Sometimes, I'd use my cheeky smile or my great sense of humour, or if that didn't work, I'd get angry. Failing that, I'd swiftly result to violence. I sat deep in thought in the smoke filled room, at the big, shiny, brown dining table, twiddling my thumbs while the three of them smoked. Now I had a shop, but it was about as busy as a horse with no legs. I needed to market my product and do it quickly. I got my phone out, called and texted every contact that wasn't my mum or dad or going to tell my mum or dad. When I had finished, I'd gotten some good feedback. I'd given out Tom's number to people that scored cannabis at least 20 times. People had also told me they would pass on the number to their friends to score as well. When I had finished that, I was filled with optimism. I sat back in my chair with a slight sense of achievement, without even a minute's rest, "Daniel, call every person in your phone book and tell them to take John and Tom's number to come and buy some of the most potent weed in England. It's been imported from Amsterdam," I said. It was a lie, but it sounded good. I hadn't graduated from school yet, but I had a PhD in bullshitting, and I intended to earn more from my experience in bullshitting rather than any dickhead with a PhD in astrophysics or chemical engineering.

The feeling I had watching the three of them making call after call to promote my weed-selling business was strange. I had never felt it before. I felt fully in control. I felt in charge as I sat there sober as a judge, listening to them tell everyone they know to come and buy my drugs, that my drugs were the best. I felt powerful, there and then. I knew I wanted that feeling more than anything in the world.

I let the three of them finish making their calls and chasing people up, then checked their progress in turn. Tom, who was the youngest and the same age as me, told me that most people were at school, so he had sent about 30 text messages to people that would definitely want to buy weed later.

John told me that most of his friends were at work, he'd said they would 'pop around' when they finished to get two ten bags each if it's good. Which we all knew it was. Best of all though, one of John's friends worked on a building site where about 20 men would go out on lunch together, and John's friend would collect everyone's money and buy weed for them, usually on a Monday or Thursday. He had planned to do so today.

After John had told him how good the weed was, he'd said he'll be down at 12:30 on his lunch and would want maybe £200 worth. "John, call him at 12:15 to make sure he comes, mate; we need that sale," I told John to try and cement the transaction.

Daniel told me a few lads want to see the stuff, so he said he would take the ten-pound bag I had given him for free to show some people; anyone that wants some, he'd send to the McBrides to score. "Okay, good, we all know what we're doing then. And Dan, are you going to show people now?" I said enthusiastically in an attempt to get everyone as motivated as I was.

I had never understood people saying things like 'I've got to go to work'. Yes, I understood that people have to pay bills and life costs money, for me it was the point of 'having' decisions being made for you that ate away at me. 'Got to, have to', these small but powerful phrases meant fuck all to me. I ain't 'got to' do anything, and the days of people telling me I 'have to' are long gone. It wasn't that I was lazy; I was prepared to walk to the end of the earth to make my drug-dealing business a success. If it meant making proper money, then I'd work 24 hours a day, seven days a week, including Christmas and birthdays. What made the difference between accepting and refusing something in my eyes was all down to this: is it 'my' choice? Or am 'I' benefitting? Or is it for 'me'? If the answer to any of these phrases is no, then there's almost no chance of me playing ball… well, not without kicking or screaming. From now on, if I don't want to do it, then in order to get me to do it, they'll have to drag my rotting corpse to make me do something I don't want to.

My brother had left John and Tom's after saying goodbye to go and get some customers. I was meant to go to school, but I didn't want to go, so I wasn't going to. Instead, I planned to go near to the school with three ten-pound bags of weed to show people and give John and Tom's number out. The best time to do this was lunchtime. All the kids who were lucky enough to be spoiled by getting enough money to go to the local chip shop instead of the school cafeteria would be outside the chippy. "John, call your mate from the building site," I said at 12:14 exactly. John rang his builder friend that he had known from school. Some ugly guy called Paul that I hadn't met before. Paul confirmed he'd be leaving in 15 minutes and needs £220 worth if it's good, and the emphasis was on 'if'. He had said if it's shit, he won't want it.

At this, I told the McBride brothers I'm going to go out to try and sell three bags and get customers before leaving their house.

I spent the lunch break shoving an open bag of weed under more kids' noses than I'd dare to remember. "Smell this, lad, it's potent," I said followed by, "take these numbers, my mates selling this 24/7 around the corner in the new estate." Sales pitch over.

It was successful as well. I sold two ten-pound bags to a guy that lived near the chip shop ten minutes after getting there. I sold the last ten-pound bag to two school kids that went 'halves', paying £5 each. The chip shop was a five-minute walk from the McBrides' house, and a two-minute walk from one secondary school and a five-minute walk from another secondary school. *Prime hunting ground to secure cannabis deals,* I thought as I walked back towards John and Tom's house. There was a butcher's, a hair salon, three corner shops and a chippy there. People would stand outside the shops after school, or sometimes older lads and girls would hang about there from time to time; but at lunchtime on a school day, there would always be 60 to 100 kids there. I planned to take full advantage of this every day. If I could, I'd get someone standing there wearing an A-Board with the McBride's number to buy drugs. I'd be arrested in a day or two though, so that was fully out of the question. My brain was working overtime as I paced back to John and Tom's house. I was walking faster than usual that it hadn't even occurred to me how quickly I was walking. I'd always walked slow, just like my dad. I hated being rushed, I preferred to do things in my own time. I guess walking slow was my subconscious rebelling against having to be anywhere quickly. Walking slow and comfortably at ease was my way of saying I don't rush for nobody. I walked quickly because I was walking for my own gain. I was rushing because I wanted to get somewhere quickly. I was walking quickly for me.

Chapter 5

I knocked John and Tom's front door full of excitement. I had sold three ten-pound bags, but more importantly, I had spread the word really well considering my shop had only been open a few hours. John's little brother, Tom, let me in—his eyes still red and glazed. The house still had a sweet smell of weed in the air. I plumped down on the sofa next to John, the coolness of the leather on the big black three-piece sofa felt soothing against my warm body. "My mate's been and gone," John said. He wasn't smiling, so I expected bad news. Maybe he wasn't happy with the size of the deals; maybe the stuff he could get elsewhere was better?

"Did he buy any?" I asked feeling deflated. "Cyrus, he bought 30 bags, mate," John said as his poker face changed to a bright smile. I nearly jumped off my seat in excitement.

I dived at John and gave him a big hug. This was the best news of the day. I put my hand in my pocket to take out the £30 I had got from the deals I had sold at the chip shop. "So, we've got £330 so far. When we've sold another 34, my brother will bring the last 56, and we can all get paid."

"Yes, that's great, Cyrus. I think we'll need the other half either tonight or tomorrow; this stuff is the best I've ever seen. My mate said if you keep it as good as this, he'll buy 50 a week at least," John said filled with optimism.

"I hope so, mate. I'll call Daniel and see how he's getting on. Did your builder mate's work friends like it then?" I took my phone out and started to call my brother.

"Yes, they loved it," John replied as Daniel's phone rang in my ear.

"Yes, Cyrus, are you at John and Tom's," Daniel asked.

"Yes why? What's up?" I replied.

"I need to come and pick up seven ten bags; my mates are giving me a lift to the McBride's. I'll drop them off to people and bring the money back to the McBride's."

"Yes, that's cool with me," I said. I didn't care how they were getting sold or who to, as long as they were getting sold.

I sat in the McBride's house for the rest of the day. I planned to go home just before 6:00 in the afternoon before my dad would get home. By 4:30, my brother had come and left three times and had just left to drop off another two bags. More of John's friends had been to buy the odd ten bag, and there was now £490 in the pot. People had told my brother they would come after work. Some of John's mates said they'd come after work to score as well. It had been a good day, but I know that a bunch of builders weren't going to buy 30 bags every day, so I was not going to start counting chickens just yet. The three of us sat playing on the computer in the smaller living room which was what we would usually do at the McBride's, but I had lost all interest in futile indulgence. My days of being stimulated by computer games were over.

I felt restless, like I should be doing something constantly. My instincts were telling me I could be doing something to improve business, but what? I was eager and ambitious.

At 5:30 in the afternoon, it was time for me to leave the McBride's to go home. My brother had been back for the last hour, so I gave the three of them one last team talk and told them to call every person they had already called in the morning before I go home, which they did. It paid dividends as well, because a few people said they would be on the way soon. I wanted to wait to see the deals take place and make sure things went smoothly, but I couldn't. It was time to go home.

As I walked back home with my brother, the journey felt different. The feelings I had in the morning of anxiety and anticipation had completely gone from my body. They had been replaced with a sense of achievement. It felt good. I still felt powerful, I felt like somebody. We took the turn for our estate and walked towards the bottom of the road to take the right turn towards our house—the last house on the right. As we did, I looked down the first and only right turn towards Trish's house. Her battered old car was parked outside her house. I didn't say anything out loud but told myself, *my stuff is safe and sound.* Walking into the house with my brother would take a bit of attention off of me. Skipping school was easy, getting away with skipping school was the hard part. My mum wasn't too bad though; even if she found out, she'd most likely have a little nag at me but not tell my dad. If someone puts him in a mood, we'd all feel the brunt of it, so she didn't want an unhappy house no more than I did. Plus, I only had three days left of school before I would be leaving school for good. Six weeks of school left, I couldn't wait. I worked out that on Thursday when my school breaks up, I'd still have six days to pay Jason; so if I needed to, I could work flat out to make sure his money was all there. Obviously, I hoped it wouldn't come down to that, but I was thinking of the worst-case scenario. Life had taught me to always plan and anticipate for the worst—anything else was a bonus.

Daniel let us in the house using his house key. "Mummm?" he shouted to check where she was to help me sneak to my room. No answer; she wasn't in.

I ran to my room.

I sat on my bed imagining that this is how someone must feel after a long hard day at work. I kicked my trainers off to lie down for five minutes. *Shit!* I thought. I hadn't called Olivia back. I told her I'd meet her to spend some time with her. I hadn't even remembered I had a girlfriend; my brain had been so focussed on selling weed that I'd forgot she existed. I didn't care though; she was of no use to me now. I had got with her because she was a conquest, but I had slept with her now, so the excitement had passed. I had stayed with her to pass the time when I was bored— basically just female company. I knew I wasn't going to be bored anymore now I was a drug-dealer. Plus, I had a new conquest, so I didn't need her anymore. I didn't feel like calling Olivia or spending time with her. As I lay on my bed, eyes closed in my shithole of a room, my thoughts raced. I wanted to be out doing stuff, but I knew it would be better to stay at home. At least when my dad came home, I'd be there. That would make him happy, giving him no excuse to nag me or try to put restrictions on my movements whenever I *had* to be out.

John and Tom knew exactly what they had to do, and my brother was helping them, so there wasn't much I could do right this minute anyway.

I convinced myself to relax eventually, only with the knowledge that the McBrides were doing my bidding as I did. The rest of my evening consisted of my dad coming home, me having dinner, then pottering around the house. Instead of leaving the house, I decided to call the McBrides to see how things were getting on. As I sat on the thin mattress on my bed, the little digital clock on my bedside table read 9:15 at night; it was starting to get dark. I was eager to know if my brother, John or Tom had gotten any more sales. John's phone rang in my ear as I sat in my room, with the TV providing some background noise to muffle the sound of my voice, so my dad couldn't hear me on the phone. "Yes, Cyrus," John answered.

"You all right, mate? How you getting on?" I asked.

"Well, mate, there's about six people here chilling at the minute. Everyone is loving the bud, we've sold a bit more."

"Oh yes, that's good. How much money have we got in the pot now?" I asked to know where we stood in terms of paying Jason.

"We've got £590 in the pot; we'll need the other half tomorrow, I reckon." John sounded a little disappointed. I, however, was over the moon. It was our first day selling, and we were only £80 short of paying Jason. I was contented with that. "Oh, yes, Cyrus, why don't you come down? Chris is here. Chris, he wants to talk to you."

Chris was probably my best friend. I had a few close friends; John and Tom were really close to me too. Chris and I had been friends for the last year; he was my brother and John's age. He lived around the corner from the shop at the top of our estate. His mum and dad had their own business and would spoil him rotten. The whole household was overweight from eating fast food takeaways almost every night. Chris was 5'8" and must have weighed about 14 stone, mostly of soft bouncy fat. He had dark blonde hair that was a kind of a blondie brown colour, big cheeks and big blue eyes. He seemed innocent to look at, but we shared the trait of being mischievous. I think that's what our friendship had stemmed from. We both were different from most of the other kids. Other kids knew where to draw the line, they knew when to stop doing something out of fear of getting in trouble, whereas Chris and I didn't give a toss. If they didn't benefit us, rules and regulations went out the window. It would be fair to say we were partners in crime before we knew what crime was. "John, could you just put Chris on the phone, mate; I'm going to stay in tonight, but I'll be down tomorrow."

I could hear people in the background laughing and talking. I would have liked to have went down to the McBride's, but I knew I'd have to be out a lot from now on; so the more I could stay at home, the better. I didn't want to raise the suspicion of my dad until whatever I had to do, made me not give a shit about my dad's suspicions, and this wasn't it. "Yo, Cyrus, you forgot about your good mate Chris now, haven't ya?" Chris' bubbly voice joked. "Don't be silly, mate. I've just been busy trying to make some money, need to sort some stuff out. I'm sick of having to rely on my mum and dad for everything." It was true. I was doing this for independence as much as anything else, and money was the product needed to enable me to buy my independence.

"True, mate. I'm sick of asking my mum and dad for everything too. I need to start making my own money too," Chris said in a more serious tone. I hadn't even thought that Chris might have been feeling the same. I had heard it in his voice; he meant it.

"Shall I come and see you so we can have a chat? If this is the weed you can get, I want to get involved," Chris asked.

"I'd like you to; but I've been out the last two days, and you know what my dad's like. Shall I meet you straight after I finish school tomorrow?" I replied trying to compromise.

"Yes, definitely, I'll come and pick you up from school, walk down to the chip shop; I'll be there waiting for you," Chris said. "Okay cool," I said before hanging up. Chris had been driving for about two months. His parents had bought him a newish small two-door car to get to college, even though the college was only a 15-minute walk from Chris' house; and he could have definitely done with the exercise. I planned to go to school in the morning only because I didn't want school to call my parents. That would only put my actions under scrutiny, that's the last thing I needed. I wanted to be under the radar, at least until I had enough money to do whatever I wanted.

My birthday would be in three weeks. *As soon as I'm 16, I can legally move out,* I thought to myself.

Phone still in hand, I called Olivia. I wanted to start to distance myself from her; so I concluded, the earlier I start to do it, the better. I didn't want to use up precious brainpower thinking about her.

"Hi baby," I said trying to sound a little under the weather. She almost instantly noticed the groggy and ill tone of my voice.

"What's up with you, CY?" Olivia asked sounding concerned.

"I'm not very well, sorry, I haven't called. I've got a bad stomach bug, I think." I lied while trying to sound poorly without over-doing it.

"Oh baby, I hope you're okay? Is there anything I can do?" Olivia asked. Knowing Olivia couldn't get me any weed sales, I literally had no use for her other than sex.

"No, babe, I'm okay. I'm just going to rest. I'll meet you on Thursday though. My mum says it should take at least three days to pass. I don't want you to catch it." I was a great liar, and she bought it without a seconds' thought.

"Okay, babes. As soon as you feel better, call me. I miss your kisses," Olivia said keen to comfort me.

"Okay gorgeous, I love you," I said. Happy to have convinced her, I had a valid reason not to see her for the next three days.

"Love you too, Cyrus. Bye, babe," I put the phone down feeling relieved.

Darkness had fallen outside on our estate. My room had gone from light to dark, peering through my blinds without me even being noticeable. Trish's living room light flickered, as her TV changed the brightness in the room. I felt at ease knowing I could just peer through the bedroom window to see my stash house.

I worked out that after paying Jason, my brother, John and Tom, I'd have £300 profit for myself. It wasn't the £590 Jason had told me I'd get because I wasn't doing the work. After all, I had never expected them to sell weed for me for free, plus I wouldn't have wanted them to. It wouldn't have been fair. The money they made was their motivation; that's the way I looked at it.

I went downstairs for the best part of half an hour to physically show my dad I was still in the house, so he couldn't moan the next day. I was already planning to be out. Before returning to my room to get my stuff ready for school and the day ahead, it crossed my mind to call Jason to give him an update, but I fought back the urge. I wanted to wait until I had £670 in full before I spoke to him.

Having nothing to do for the rest of the night, I got undressed and climbed into bed. The little green digits on my digital alarm clock read 22:26; this was earlier than I'd usually go to bed. My body was tired though; my brain was still active, running over possibility after possibility, working out calculation after calculation. Eventually, I wore myself out and fell asleep.

My alarm woke me up at 08:15, still feeling tired. I felt like I could sleep for another eight hours at least. It was light outside as I rolled out of bed to start the day. I completed my usual routine of teeth-brushing, face-washing, dressing and having no breakfast before leaving for school. Before I left, I glanced into Daniel's room to find him sound asleep, wrapped up like a cocoon, exactly as I had found him on the morning before.

I walked the same route towards John and Tom's to get to school. The same amount of traffic and commuting people filled the roads and pavements. Mothers with brigades of children and pushchairs looking half-asleep, completing their maternal duties by taking their young children to school and nurseries.

My slow walk was relaxing as I observed everyone around me, living there lives by having decisions being made for them. When at school, I said the usual hellos to the kids, most of which had no real concept of life—a bunch of fucking idiots really. Then I had the luxury of learning about things like human anatomy. Why? I'll never know. We had the NHS (National Health Service) that provided free health care; they were human anatomy specialists, so why a bunch of 16-year-olds needed to know how a kidney works is beyond me; unless of course, I wanted to be a doctor, which I didn't.

The day continued to be wasted until 3:30 in the afternoon when I was released from school. Hundreds of different aged children with bags strapped over their shoulder, all disappearing in different directions, like ants. The noise of hundreds of unbroken voices filled the air outside the school. The day was warm and bright as I said, "Bye, lads."

Chapter 6

The next month seemed to fly by as my status in the drug game grew from strength to strength. My shop was thriving. Everybody in a four-mile radius knew where to get the best weed from—thanks to my brother and the McBrides. From middle-aged builders and factory workers in their 40s and 50s to spotty 15 and 16-year-old kids, everybody came to score from the McBrides. At times, I would sit around the house for an hour or two in the chill out room. John would rarely get ten minutes to himself before either the door knocked or the phone rang or both. I would sit and watch with no expression on my face, almost as if I was oblivious to what was going on. I would sit, talking to Chris or whoever I was with at the time, almost pretending I couldn't see the droves of people that would keep arriving at the McBride's house to buy drugs.

I was very aware of what was going on, and inside I was bubbling with excitement. I was happier than I had ever been internally. The problem with always wanting more means that you will never be content; I definitely wanted more.

I was making more money than John and Tom put together, it was important that I kept a shrewd poker face. If I started dancing every time I paid them their wages, then they may start to wonder why I was so happy. The way I saw it was that they were happy to sit at home and get paid £200 a week each to answer the front door or phone; and as far as they were concerned, smoking free weed all day was the best bonus they could have wished for. I didn't feel guilty; technically, I was providing a pothead's paradise. However, I was making a 'killing'. I was getting through three batches every seven days, and this was netting me £900 a week, which was the same as a senior manager in a moderately successful business. In fact, I earned more than the man in the suit with a briefcase, because the taxman had no idea I existed, and this meant he kept his grubby fingers out of my pockets.

I had just turned 16; my blue and red National Insurance card had arrived in the post sometime last week. "You can get a job now, Cyrus," my mum had said happily, knowing I was now eligible to work. I had to summon up every ounce of deception in my body to smile at her and look happy that I could now get a job. I had a job, and a job I liked; my job paid better than my mum and dad's jobs put together. As far as I was concerned, the piece of plastic called a 'National Insurance Card' was irrelevant to my life, I intended to leave that in a drawer in my room forever.

Chris would come and pick me up every morning without fail. It was the summer holidays, so my dad didn't ask where I was going. "Do you want some money, Cyrus?" my mum had asked as I was running out the door on a few occasions.

"No, I'm okay," I had called back to her as I was leaving the house. I knew this rose her suspicions, but I didn't care. I started selling drugs for independence, so having to take pocket money from my mum defeated the object. Mine and Chris' venture had taken off since picking up our first 40 ounces of cannabis. We kept our weed in a safe that Chris had been given for Christmas; God only knows why Chris' mum and dad brought their 18-year-old son a safe. I imagined it was because they gave him so much that they assumed he would need a safe to hoard his accumulated wealth. The safe provided us with a secure location to keep our weed. Even if Chris' mum and dad suspected he had drugs in the safe, they couldn't open it; and there was no way that they would call the police on their golden child—we could guarantee that much.

Chris lived a five-minute walk from my house on the estate. It was across the main road. Along the main road to the left a short distance, before turning into a residential side street, the crossing of that main road marked the division between the houses on our estate, and the houses that were double the price across the road where Chris lived. Chris' house was a big, red-bricked corner house with a perfectly paved driveway. Tall conifer trees were planted around the house either side of the driveway. The house had posh dark-brown window frames with lead patterns on the glass. The house Chris lived in was more suited to my taste than the cardboard thing I had the pleasure of living in. Chris had kept to his word in fine fashion since our first conversation in the fast food restaurant's car park. He had asked me to get 40 ounces which I had done. A month had passed since then, we were now getting 50 ounces every five to seven days, depending on the demand. Chris' cousin was a good customer, as were some friends his cousin had. Also, some other dealers from the local area brought their cannabis from us to sell. All of the dealers tended to be a lot bigger and older than Chris and me, and this did worry me. I knew exactly what I was capable of, what worried me is the fact that they might not. If they thought I was a pussy, they might want to 'fuck me', and I couldn't have that. I planned to do something to ensure everybody would know exactly what I was made of as soon as the opportunity arose. The person that steps out of line will be the person I used to make an example out of. I didn't know who this person would be. I didn't want it to be anyone, but at 16, I was wise enough to know the world is not made of daisy chains and buttermilk. I had already made plans to beat whoever crossed me half to death with a baseball bat or stab them or worse, depending on what the violation would be.

I had spent the last week or two in the passenger seat of Chris' car. From the ounces of cannabis Chris was selling for me, I had saved nearly £500. Added to the money I had made from my shop, I had saved nearly £2, 400, which meant I had gone from broke to having £7,150 in just over a month. Saving almost every penny made had its benefits; the money stashed at my aunt's house, combined with the money hidden in my room meant if the worst were to happen, and Chris and I lost 50 ounces for any reason, I'd have enough money to pay Jason and Jabber and start again. Every time we picked up a new batch, it worried me sick. I wasn't worried about the police or the risk of being court. It was just knowledge that the money I had saved was at risk. That was where the worry stemmed from. Fifty ounces of cannabis cost me £7,500. I had nearly saved enough money to cover that. My big brother and I had spoken about me giving him a little bonus. He was running the shop really well. Daniel made sure the McBrides never had to wait in between collecting a new load of merchandise to sell. Daniel picked the money up on time without fail and kept me up-to-date as and when I needed to make sure I had more cannabis to give him for the shop. It was only fair my brother reaped a fair reward for his hard work. Daniel was happy to make £300 profit a week tax-free. I had given him direct access to Trish's house, which in turn gave me less work to do. It didn't make sense me having to go there every time the McBrides needed cannabis. Trish knew my brother just as well as she knew me, so it wasn't a problem for Daniel to go there. I surmised me doing my own dirty work wasn't logical.

It was a Saturday afternoon. I rolled over as I began to wake. I loved to wake up naturally, it felt unrushed and relaxing. For me it was the complete opposite to the sharp, noisy bleeping of my digital alarm clock. Waking up naturally suited my love of doing what I wanted to do perfectly. I rolled over and stretched gently as I prepared mentally for the day ahead. I didn't have much on the agenda for the day, just the usual or what had now become the usual. I would wait to be picked up by Chris, after satisfying his forever need to eat. I would spend the rest of the day marketing my new drug-dealing enterprise. After I had made two trips to my shop (the McBride's) and got my brother and Chris to call all of their contacts and customers, my day's work was done.

My time was now my own, with no school to go to anymore. Also I had successfully dumped Olivia, which made me a free agent, I was happier than ever. I lay in my bed wide awake just savouring the feeling of contentment before my phone rang. I had put it on the floor next to my bed and turned the call tone volume down, so my dad wouldn't hear the fairly frequent calls I now became accustomed to receiving. The calls I received mainly came from either John or Tom, my brother, or the odd customer that was still calling me even though they knew I would just send them to the McBride's or Chris. A few drug-dealers would call me to send Chris with two ounces here or five ounces there, but that was practically it. So, the name flashing on my phone came as a bit of a surprise to me. 'Jason' flashed on my phone which was unusual. *What did he want at 11:30 in the morning?* I had cannabis at Trish's for John and Tom to sell, and Chris had about 30 ounces hidden at his house. He can't expect his money yet, as I still had seven days before our usual ten-day deadline, so I had no idea what he could want. "Yes mate," I said as I answered.

"Yes, Cyrus, you okay, mate?" Jason asked. I knew Jason had not called me to see if I was okay. Jason wasn't the type of person that gave people welfare calls.

"I'm good, mate, what's up?" I asked eager for him to get to the point.

"Are you busy today, Cyrus?" Jason asked.

"No, why?" Jason didn't seem annoyed, so I wasn't worried.

"Cyrus, my uncle wants to meet you, so he said he's coming to pick me up; and then we are going to come pick you up, and then we'll go and get some lunch?" Jason asked. I had seen Jason's Uncle Jabber outside Jason's house when I had visited my auntie over the years; he had a kind of army style haircut. Jabber was definitely overweight, but he had an equal mixture of fat and muscle. He had a kind of powerlifter's physique.

Jason's Uncle Jabber had tattoos on his arms and wore a thick gold bracelet. Jabber looked mean and intimidating, big fleshy cheeks and a big red head. I didn't mind buying the guy's drugs. I appreciated the fact him and Jason were happy to give me cannabis on credit, but why would he want me to come for lunch? I concluded it would be rude to say 'no', and the fact I had told Jason I wasn't busy meant I couldn't exactly make an excuse up now. "Yes, I will come for lunch if you's want; what time were you thinking?" I said reluctantly and purely not wanting to rock the boat.

"My uncle will be at mine in half an hour, so we will be at yours in 45 minutes," Jason explained.

"Okay, pick me up from the shop at the top of my estate," I said as I wondered if Jason actually knew where I lived. Jason knew a lot of people that were sure to know where I lived, but I had used this little bit of psychology to test Jason to see if he had done his homework on where I lived.

"You mean the shop at the top of your road," Jason said after a slight pause. He was letting me know he knew exactly where I lived. I did owe him just under £8,200, so I couldn't blame him for finding out my address. It was the nature of the game I was in. If somebody owed me that sort of money, I'd camp outside their house and follow their every move. In any event, Jason had given me a subtle warning, it was also a warning I understood clearly. The only problem with what Jason had said to me was that it had been said to me. If Jason had said that to anybody else, it would have been perfectly reasonable. I knew I had read into what could have been said innocently. I knew that I had derived conclusions from something that could have been innocent. 'You mean the shop at the top of your road', I ran it over in my mind as I lay relaxing in my cheap metal bed.

"Definitely a threat," I concluded silently. I would have respected Jason a lot more if he would have said, "Cyrus, you owe me eight grand, of course I know where you fucking live." I switched the shower on and started a leisurely morning procedure of washing, deodorising, creaming my face and getting dressed. My dad had left the house before I had woken up. He had disturbed my sleep slightly, and I had heard him pottering around before leaving while I was half-awake and half-sleep.

"Morning, Cyrus," my mum said as she heard me coming down the last few steps of our creaky staircase.

"Good morning, Mum," I replied.

"Cyrus, I'm going to your Auntie Delma's if you want to come?" my mum asked.

"No, I'm going for lunch with Chris," I lied. I turned right at the bottom of the staircase which took me straight into the kitchen. My mum was left of the bottom of the staircase in the living room, most likely polishing or doing cleaning of some sort. Getting ready as slow as possible, I had wasted half an hour; a slow walk to the shop would leave me five minutes to wait for Jason and his Uncle Jabber. Jason called as I open my front door on the side that faced Trish's house. This was the side of my house that was closest to the shop. One thing for me about being lazy was that I always tried to ensure a minimal amount of physical labour is required to complete any given task.

I stood outside the shop with mixed emotions, part of me wanted to meet Jabber. After all, it was him who gave the cannabis to Jason to give to me. Maybe I could negotiate a better price? The other feeling was the same resentment I had for having to do anything I didn't want to, and standing outside the shop was not my choice. The shop car park was empty; there were only a few cars parked in the 30 or 40 spaces provided, and I felt like this made me stand out to any passing pedestrians. I leaned against a stump outside the shop in an attempt to look like a random kid waiting for some other random kid to go and do something random. I didn't want to look like a drug-dealer waiting to go for lunch with some other drug dealers, and that's how I felt standing outside a shop on a main road with an empty car park. To my relief, a car indicated off the main road to come towards the entrance to the car park to the shop. The driver had a big white head the size of a football that was slightly off circular. A skinny white guy was sat in the passenger seat; my suspicions were confirmed when the car pulled into the car park and flashed its headlights at me. It was a finely crafted luxury German car. I guessed Jabber's car was six or seven years old; nothing like my Auntie Delma's boyfriend's car, but it was still a nice car. I walked slowly and confidently towards the car. Both Jabber and Jason gave me a smile as I walked past the front of the car to get into the back. Climbing in the back of Jabba's car, I sat behind Jason; the immaculately clean car seemed spacious. The car looked a lot better from the inside. Everything seemed to be covered in cream leather.

"Cyrus, this is my Uncle Jabber," Jason said as he had flipped down the sun visor and opened the mirror, so he could see me without turning around.

"Nice to meet you, Jabber," I said as relaxed as I could act. I had loads of questions to ask, but I had no intention of asking them yet. I decided to let Jason and Jabber dictate how our conversation was going to go. I would only interrupt to ask questions if and when the opportunity arose.

"So, Cyrus, you're the young lad my nephew has been telling me about," Jabber said finally without taking his eyes off the road.

"I guess so," I replied trying to hide the fact I felt slightly uncomfortable. We had been travelling about ten minutes when my phone rang—it was Chris.

"I'm outside," Chris said. How could I have forgotten? Chris picking me up in the morning had been routine since the day I had left school.

"I'm not at home, mate. I'll be home in an hour or two, so come pick me up then if that's all right?" I explained.

"Okay, mate. I'll pop to John and Tom's, and then I will come and get you later," Chris said before putting the phone down. Jabber's driving technique made being a passenger very comfortable. He didn't accelerate too quickly or break too sharply. It felt like I could put a cup of coffee on the seat next to me without the worry of it spilling. The spacious German car was smooth on the road, and Jabber negotiated corners elegantly. Just short of 15 minutes after setting off, we pulled into a posh-looking restaurant with its own huge car park. The restaurant's logo was displayed on a big red sign practically everywhere I looked.

"Have you been here before?" Jabber asked. Still looking at the newspaper-sized menu.

"No, I've never ate here," I replied as the car came to rest in a space outside the restaurant. I watched as Jabber's wide forearms reached for the handbrake.

"Well, you don't worry, Cyrus; this is my treat," Jabber said as we all reached for our door handles to get out of the car.

"Cyrus, I've got a spliff here. Smoke some of this with me outside, and my uncle will go and get us a table," Jason said waving the white cone-shaped spliff while smiling. Jason and Jabber were both wearing designer jeans and T-shirts. As Jabber walked off towards the big brown entrance doors, I thought he must weigh at least 19 stones. He had rolls of meat on the back of his head above his neck.

"Jason, hurry up with that crap because I want to order," Jabber said as he turned around to face us before opening the restaurant's door. Jason acknowledged him with a nod and a wink. The restaurant had glass windows at the side. I could see people eating inside through the large glass windows. It looked posh, and so did the people inside. They reminded me of Chris' parents, business owners; people with money to waste. Jason and Jabber were dressed appropriately in their expensive jeans and T-shirts. I felt out of place in the grey tracksuit I was wearing. Jason and I sat on the chrome garden chairs that were on some wooden decking at the side of the restaurant. As I looked around at my surroundings, I realised that this was the other side of the tracks. This is where the crabs were that had gotten out of the barrel or had never been in the barrel. The cars in the car park were all new and shiny; the building looked like no expense had been spared on construction or design. *This was why I started dealing drugs. I wanted to be part of this side of life,* I thought. Jason chugged on his big spliff.

"Here," Jason said passing me the spliff. It was absolutely stunk, even outside. The mid-day weather was warm with almost no breeze. The air was almost stagnant, which made the smell linger in the air longer than could be expected outdoors.

"I'll only have two puffs. I've stopped smoking cannabis in the day," I said as I took two pulls on the blazing cone. The thick potent smoke hit my lungs like a bulldozer. I had to strain not to choke as I exhaled the smoke, much to the relief of my lungs.

"Let's go inside," I said to Jason as I handed him back his joint. I was eager to see the inside of the building, also I wanted to get to know Jabber a little better. In all truth, I was feeling a lot more relaxed than I had first been, I had changed my mind. Lunch was something I wanted to do. Jason threw his joint in one of the ashtrays while it was still alight. His mannerism would have led me to believe that he owned the restaurant. I smiled as I followed him over towards the entrance doors. As we stepped inside, there was music playing in the background, and a very attractive girl wearing a red and black uniform was standing at a little station, presumably to greet and seat customers.

"My uncle has already got us a table," Jason said to her as he walked past her without even stopping to hear a reply. Out of the entrance and into the restaurant, the place was beautiful to look at; dark wooden floors with spotlights and gold metal trim everywhere. It had red leather booths, seating couples and small families. The restaurant was all open plan, except a glass conservatory section that had been visible from where Jason and I were smoking. There was a raised area in the middle of the room which housed a big square bar. It had a motorbike suspended in the air, and spotlights running around the top of the bar. The room felt warm and alive; the atmosphere in the restaurant was similar to that of a Christmas morning. Jason and I found his uncle seated at a booth taking up the best part of two seats on the phone. As the two of us slid in opposite, Jabber put the phone down and extended his hand to shake my hand.

"How do you like it here, Cyrus?" Jabber asked clearly aware I had been scanning this new and exciting environment.

"It's very posh in here, Jabber," I said still taking in what was pleasing to the eye wherever I looked. Jason was clearly stoned as his eyes had glazed over. He looked through a newspaper-sized menu. His uncle peered down at his menu on the table as a beautiful girl approached wearing a short black skirt and red polo shirt tucked in at the waist.

"Hi, guys. Are you ready to order, or do you want a few more minutes?" the waitress asked cheerfully with a bright smile. I hadn't even realised that I was just sat staring at her.

"Yes, I know what I'm having, are you two ready to order?" Jabber asked turning his gaze to Jason and me in turn.

"Yes," Jason said. I hadn't even looked through the menu. I had spent the five minutes I had been sitting down looking around. "Do you like steak, Cyrus?" Jabber asked me realising I hadn't a clue what I wanted.

"Yes, that's fine," I replied nervously sensing the beautiful waitress was looking at me.

"I'll have a mixed grill, with corn and mash potato and special sweet glaze. Can I have a fillet steak medium for my friend here with special sweet glaze on the side, with chips and roast corn and three Bahama Mamas, oh, and whatever he wants," Jabber said as he pointed to Jason while handing the oversized menu back to the waitress. I watched as she tapped away on what looked like a mini tablet device.

"I'll have a surf and turf with peppercorn sauce, please, and chips," Jason added to his uncle's order as he looked the waitress straight in her eyes and smiled at her confidently.

She smiled back before nervously asking Jabber, "Are the three cocktails for you? I don't care personally, but if my manager knows that I didn't ask, he will have a go at me," she had said it as though she had meant it. I could tell she didn't want to ask but had to.

"Yes, lovely, all three cocktails are for me; and could I have them all large," Jabber replied sarcastically. I didn't know what a 'Bahama mamma' was, but thinking before speaking allowed me to conclude it wasn't worth asking as I would soon be finding out. The waitress left our table after smiling at Jabber's blatant sarcasm. Just looking at Jabber and Jason, it was clear they were drug-dealers. Jabber was huge but well groomed. He sat with a cold look in his blue eyes that looked tiny in comparison with the size of his body and head. His hair was shaved at the side and dark on the top, like a military cut. Jabber had a presence about him that told anybody that looked at him he was his own boss. His thick gold bracelet glistened under the lighting inside the restaurant. His dark grey designer T-shirt was the size of a single bed sheet.

"I'd definitely do her," Jason said as we watched the waitress work the dining room floor. She had black leggings on that disappeared under her skirt and shiny black dolly shoes. She was stunning.

"So, Cyrus, you are doing quite well selling weed, mate, considering you've only been doing it a month?" Jabber asked feeling totally at ease.

"Yes, I'm pleased with how things are going, and I'm happy with the quality of the cannabis," I replied. Jabber sat looking at me with his hands resting together on the table, like a schoolteacher.

"Yes, the cannabis I gave you is strong; people tend to like that one. I should have a better one in the next three weeks," Jabber said in his deep and low tone, even though he was clearly making an effort to speak softly. "Jason tells me you're getting through 50 ounces a week. Cyrus, I've been in this business long enough to know potential when I see it, or in your case, hear about it, which is why I invited you to lunch," Jabber continued as I sat listening and taking in what he was saying. "I want you to continue to work with us, Cyrus. If anyone gives you any trouble, I want you to tell me straight away, and I'll sort it; but take my advice and save your money and box clever, stay under the radar. You are doing a good job, so just keep it up," Jabber extended his hand to shake my hand for the second time. His hand felt at least twice the size of mine, big and fleshy, like the bones in his hands were hidden under inches of meat. He gave me a smile and leaned back relaxed as though he had finished talking for the afternoon.

Our food arrived moments later. The same waitress brought it over swiftly, followed by three small fish-bowl-sized cocktails with small paper umbrellas on sticks in them. She listed our orders back to us as she placed the food on the table before placing all three cocktails in front of Jabber and smiling at him.

"Enjoy your meals," she said before turning to continue working the dining-room floor expertly.

"Lads, try these cocktails, these are for you two for being top lads," Jabber said sliding Jason and me each a large heavy glass. I didn't know where to start or to look. If this is how the other half have lunch, then from this moment on, I am in the other half. I took Jabber's advice and took a big gulp through the straw of my cocktail. It was sweet and fruity with a pungent alcoholic kick; it was a very nice alcoholic fruit cocktail—pineapple and mango with some sort of syrup and strong rum made ice-cold by the boulder-sized cubes of ice. Absolutely delicious.

"That's a winner," I said smiling at Jabber in approval.

"It is a great cocktail, but after you've had a few, they get you smashed. Bring a girl here, fire a few of these down her neck; when you get her home, her knickers will fall off," Jabber said as he laughed to himself. Jason and I laughed at his suggestion equally.

We all started to attack the large plates of tender steak, mini chrome buckets of perfectly fried chips and shrimp. "Cyrus, cut a bit of that steak and dip it in the special sweet glaze source," Jabber suggested. I obliged by slicing my fillet steak and dipping it in the small black ramekin of sticky sweet glaze.

"Umm," I said as my taste buds went crazy. *This is what life is about. I'd soon get to Jabber's size if I ate like this every day,* I thought to myself. We finished our food as we sat and joked mainly about the waitresses and business; we washed our food down with the Bahama Mama cocktails. I felt a little lightheaded and bloated as I sipped the last bits of alcohol from between the boulders of ice. Jabber signalled the waitress to come over by nodding and raising his hand subtly. A minute later, she re-joined us at our table and put a black leather book on the table before collecting our plates.

"That was nice, wasn't it, lads?" Jabber said as he reached in his pocket and pulled out a wad of cash that was more suited for buying a car then lunch.

"Let's go then, lads," Jabber said as he threw a series of notes into the leather book and began to get up.

I felt ready for bed with a belly full of fillet steak and rum. If they had beds here at this restaurant, I would have definitely suggested having a nap. Jason was right; the cocktails tasted sweet and led me into a false sense of security. I definitely felt giddy as I got up and followed Jabber and Jason to the door. Jason retrieved his joint from the ashtray outside before joining his uncle and me back at the car.

"I'm glad I got to meet you, Cyrus. You are a good kid, and we are going to make a lot of money together," Jabber said as he fired up the car's engine.

"Yes, it was nice to meet you too. And I hope we do make loads of money together," I replied, now feeling totally at ease in this monster of a man's company.

As I said goodbye to the two of them back in my local shops' car park at the top of my estate, I felt like we had built a strong bond in just under two hours we had spent together. Jabber had made me feel welcome, and like I was part of their team even though I was my own boss, it was nice to know he had my back. I planned to take a nice slow walk to John and Tom's. It was a nice day, and my full belly made me feel like I needed a nice slow walk to digest the food and alcohol; also, it gave me time to think. Seeing first-hand how the other half lived made me in no rush to get to John and Tom's to carry on with the not-so-great standard of life I was living.

Chapter 7

A week had passed since meeting Jason's Uncle Jabber. I had paid my debt to him on time for the batch of weed he had given me. I had sold my last batch in half the time Jason's Uncle Jabber had expected. Also, I had picked up a new batch which I was told was going to be the last batch of the same stuff; this made me worry when I thought about it. Things were going so well, I didn't want anything to change. The weed I was selling had everybody going crazy for it. The 50 ounces I gave Chris weekly were flying, to the points we chose who to do business with and had no worry of not being able to meet our deadline.

The McBride's house had become everyone's port of call for their £10 or £20 bags of cannabis, and John's older friends were spending £500 a week plus; practically all of the lads on the building site brought their weed from the McBride's. I was worried that with the change of product would come the change of progress for the worst. I had called Jason on numerous occasions, telling him I want the same stuff. He fobbed me off, saying things like 'Don't worry. It will be as good as this stuff' or 'Are you still on about the change of weed, Cyrus, chill out, little man'. Jason had given me his uncle's number, and I had called him to voice my concern.

"Cyrus, how are you, little fella. The weed I'll have will be better not worst, don't worry," was basically what Jabber had said.

As I left my house to start a slow walk to the McBride's out of boredom, I turned right out of my back gate, walked between the stumps that prevented a car from taking the same route and started my journey. Taking this route was the shortest way to get to the McBride's. It wasn't a major shortcut, but a shortcut nevertheless. As I walked through my estate, I looked around at all the shitty council houses occupied by families on benefits and single mums. Nearly out of my estate, I saw one of two brothers at their gate. He was a heroin-addict and crack cocaine-smoker; it was common knowledge on our estate. I had known Luke all my life; the change

81

in Luke had come as a shock to the other kids and me on our estate. One day he was smoking weed and had clear skin and fairly decent hygiene; the next day he had lost his mind through drugs and had the worst hygiene known to man. His fingertips were black; and for a white kid that stood out like a sore thumb, he was always sweating and grubby. Yes. Heroin and crack changed Luke's life completely.

Luke would shout and bully his mum's last penny out of her purse to buy heroin. At times, he'd be violent and aggressive to get her to part with her cash for food and bills. Other times, he'd complain of stomach cramps and withdrawal symptoms, promising her in tears if she provided money for drugs to make him better, he'd get the help needed to kick his drug habit. I would still say hello to Luke in passing, but the days of us hanging about in his garden smoking weed were long gone.

"Hi, Cyrus, I heard you're doing well for yourself now, mate," Luke said trying to look and act as normally as he could, considering his situation.

"Yes, mate. If anyone wants weed, go and see the McBrides," I replied quick to promote my business at every opportunity. Luke was standing in the gateway of his garden where the gate would be if it was closed. He was just standing there looking out at the street, scanning his surroundings, like a bird of prey on its perch. As I got closer, he stepped out of the gateway to come closer to me.

"Cyrus, did you know at the bottom of this road some Turkish people or Kosovans have moved in?" Luke asked.

"And?" I said, not quite sure what that had to do with me.

"Well, yesterday, my mate, Doyle, seen them unloading of van full of big brown boxes into their garage. When they saw Doyle was watching, they started acting really nervous," Luke explained. I understood exactly where Luke was going with this. Luke was suggesting I steal the brown boxes, and I can honestly say I loved the idea.

"What was in the brown boxes though? I asked, trying to sound disinterested, but still wanting and needing valuable information.

"I don't know, you will have to get in there to know that," Luke said.

I thought for a minute before saying, "Fuck it, I'll rob it. And you don't tell anybody else that we've had this conversation!" I reached in my pocket and gave Luke £20 which he accepted without a murmur. We both knew his situation. The fact he didn't even ask me for any money made giving it him justifiable to me. I didn't expect a thank you, and Luke didn't give me one. If Luke weren't a drug-addict, he probably wouldn't have accepted it. If he wasn't a drug-addict, I probably wouldn't have given it to him. We both knew this, so there was nothing to speak about. It was a conversation that need not be had.

I kept walking to the McBride's house without further interruption. Life was getting boring for me sitting around in John and Tom's or driving around delivering ounces with Chris. I had money now, but I didn't do anything with it. Even with all these people around me, I felt lonely. I missed having a girlfriend. Olivia had liked me for who I was, and I had dropped her, like a hot potato to sell drugs. I didn't regret it though. I knew sacrifices had to be made, and Olivia was my first of many more to come.

All the people around me seemed to have things to do. John and Tom took turns answering both their phones and serving customers. So when either of them were working, they had two phones that rang to the point it was actually ridiculous. Then they had a house phone that would call quite frequently, then answering the door, serving people and locking the door after them kept both the McBrides busy all day. My brother would be busy with his friends getting more customers. He would also have to pick money up once or twice a day from the McBride's, then sort out their batch for the next day, make sure they had enough little empty drug bags and weigh up bags for John and Tom when they were too busy to do it themselves. Chris would drive around all day selling ounces when he wasn't eating, sleeping or smoking cannabis, which seemed to be his favourite pastime, but me, I was bored because my job was to get paid when the job was done and commission the next job. In essence, I only had to work for one hour a week. I felt like something was missing. I had a void in my life that needed filling. I was too young to know that the void I had was greed!

I got up from the sofa in the McBride's chill-out room at about 9 o'clock at night. I had been sitting there for hours. Chris had gone to his house to get ounces of cannabis to drop to someone. I had decided not to go as Jason and his Uncle Jabber had told me to avoid being in a car when people are dropping off drugs, which gave me even less things to do with myself!

"Stay under the radar," Jabber had said. Understanding his point, I took his advice on self-preservation; therefore, I decided to only accompany Chris on certain sales when I deemed it safe. I said goodbye to the McBride brothers and the few stoned teenagers that John and Tom liked enough to let them stay and smoke weed in their house and left. The ten-minute walk back to the estate was quiet—I liked the quiet. At only 16, it felt like I had spent two lifetimes listening to people. The sound of human voices in general grated on me. Sometimes, I just liked to hear nothing. The setting of the sun left the sky cool and tranquil as I started the walk back towards my house. The sun had almost disappeared by the time I got back to the estate.

A few of the older lads in their early 20s were in the street opposite my house listening to the music playing out of a car one of them had. Not wanting to go in so early, I went over to talk to them for a while. I had nothing better to do.

"Hi, Cyrus," one of the lads said respectfully. I had noticed the change in the way the group had spoken to me since I had started dealing drugs. They now treated me like one of their peers instead of just the little mixed race kid that lives in the street. *It's about time you fuckers started giving me the respect I deserve,* I had thought. If I hadn't started dealing and earnt that respect, one of them would have overstepped the mark one day, and I would have had to stab or shoot one of them so things hadn't worked out too badly.

"How are you lot? Are you lot okay?" I asked to make conversation.

"We're good, just hanging out. Have you heard about them Kosovans at the bottom of the estate?" the same lad asked.

"No, why? What about them?" I lied to see what other information I could get.

"Apparently, crackhead Luke's mate. Doyle seen them unloading boxes into their garage," one of the group said.

I had a think for a split second before saying the same thing I had said to Luke, "Boxes of what?"

"I don't know, but we are going to check it out," the same lad said. I knew the lads that dossed around the estate, a few of them had dabbled in crime. Although they were older than me, they were not hardened criminals. They were more talk than action, but as they had said they planned to rob the garage, I thought it fair game to give them the first bite of the cherry. After all, the boxes could have old clothes in them for all I knew.

I stayed in the congregation for ten minutes before going home, feeling neither here nor there about the Kosovans' garage. I was making good money, so I wasn't bothered either way.

It was my greed that gave me the restlessness that would never leave. It made me feel like I was always missing something. It was my subconscious that wanted to hoard all the money and women in the world away for myself, and I would not be content until I did. If the last woman had the last pound, I wouldn't feel content until I owned her and that pound exclusively. I didn't understand the constant feeling I had as I walked into my room feeling tense.

I waited until I was sure I was alone upstairs before I slid out the last draw of my big unit of drawers. I took the draw completely out so I could see the carpet underneath the cupboard. Then I took the money I had stashed there out and counted it. '£3,520'. I took my wages from John and Tom's and added it to the pile. They had just paid me another £300. I took £20 out for spending money and put the rest under the set of drawers, slid the bottom drawer back into place quietly and sat down on my bed to relax. Purely out of boredom, I made a few pointless phone calls. Chris asked me if I wanted to come to meet some girls with him. Chris liked me to come to see girls with him as his weight made him nervous. He knew bringing me would be sure to lighten the atmosphere, as I knew how to have a laugh with girls. Although I almost always wanted to go and meet girls, I declined the offer.

"Tell them we will meet them on Friday, mate, I want to go and get some new clothes on Friday. After, we will go and meet them looking fresh! What do you reckon?" I had asked the question spontaneously.

"Yes, that sounds good to me," Chris replied sounding happy about the idea.

It was a Wednesday night. I didn't feel like going out, and I had already decided to try to sleep off the restlessness and anxiousness I had been feeling for the last few weeks. It didn't occur to me that the feelings of anxiety and restlessness had started around the time of my criminality.

I hadn't planned to go shopping before I had spoken to Chris, it just came out in conversation; but after I had said it, I had looked forward to it instantly. I planned to buy some dark blue Italian jeans, similar to the kind I had seen Jason wearing. A designer T-shirt, similar to the one his Uncle Jabber had worn with some designer trainers. I had the money to do it, so I might as well. I imagined the jeans would probably cost £150 and T-shirt and trainers may be £300; an expensive outfit for a 16-year-old. If I could pull girls in a tracksuit, wait until they see me after my shopping trip. I'll have them queueing around the block.

The prospect of pulling a new bird and a hotter one than I had ever thought would look at me lifted my spirits. Deciding to call it a night, I switched off everything electrical except my phone and went to sleep.

Reggae music playing downstairs in the living room told me my dad was at home as I rolled over feeling well rested the following morning. My dad had a great taste in music; he'd listen to anything from jazz to reggae. My dad is definitely eclectic when it comes to his taste in music. The music my dad was playing gave me a nice feeling as I woke up. I got out of bed to start the usual routine of washing, brushing my teeth, creaming my hands and face. I needed a haircut, but I had planned to do that after my shopping trip on Friday. After getting ready, I joined my dad who was now in the kitchen in his dressing gown and slippers. "I'm making you some breakfast before you rush out, Cyrus," my dad said in the most pleasant tone he'd use when doing a selfless act. My dad was a man of many moods. One day, he'd be as nice as warm apple pie and ice cream; the next day, he could be the most miserable nightmare anyone could hate to meet. It just depended when you caught him. At his age, you would have thought he would have learnt not to take his moods and problems out on other people, but he hadn't. It was common practice for my dad to come home after a bad day at work. Come home in a foul mood; then mum, my brother and I would have to bear the brunt of his bad mood. I stood to watch my dad finish frying fish on the stove which was the breakfast he was making.

My dad was born in Jamaica in the coastal town of Negril, growing up in the Caribbean; so near to the sea meant he had grown up eating a lot of fish, him doing so also meant I grew up eating a lot of fish. I didn't mind as it was always so very tasty. "What are you up to today, Cyrus?" my dad asked as I stood next to him receiving a silent cooking lesson.

"Not much really. I think I'm going to meet Chris for lunch and then probably meet some girls and chill out with them," I replied trying to justify being out the house all day innocently.

"Oh, okay, just stay out of trouble," my dad replied. The fish was dry fried and had turned a kind of reddish. It was 'red mullet', a very meaty fish that has a slightly salty taste and leaves a slightly sweet aftertaste. It was one of my favourites. My dad had given me a piece of fish with some 'hard food' yellow yam and cassava.

I sat down at our dining room table to eat. It was the kind of breakfast that was packed full of nutrition and taste. My dad left the kitchen to go upstairs, which allowed me to finish eating a little quicker than I would have had he still been there to tell me to take my time. Placing my plate in the sink, I started out the door. "Thanks, Dad, that was lovely," I said as I pulled the squeaky door handle to leave. Outside the back of my house, I could see two of the lads that had been in the group, drinking beer and listening to music the night previously. I wondered if they had found out what was in the Kosovans' garage.

I did not want them to know that I had a direct interest in the matter, so I used my knowledge of manipulating to get the information I wanted. "Hi, lads," I said to start conversation. I knew although these lads were older than me, they were light years behind me in terms of intelligence, so I used this to my advantage.

"Yes, Cyrus, what are you up to today?" One of them asked.

"Nothing really, mate, you seemed to be having a good night last night. What did you lot and up doing?" I asked innocently, as though I was just making conversation with no ulterior motive.

"Nothing, we just had a few beers and went home about 1:00 in the morning," the same dumb guy told me.

Great, I thought. I knew these mouthpieces didn't have the brains or the balls to carry out anything that didn't involve killing brain cells with cheap alcohol.

"Oh, yes, I will catch up with you guys later. I am just going to start work," I said as I started walking in the direction of John and Tom's. I smiled to myself as I walked. People are so easy to manipulate if you know how.

If I wanted to know if somebody had eaten their dinner. I didn't need to say 'have you had dinner?' I could simply ask 'are you hungry?' If you ask the right questions, it's amazing the information people offer up without a thought in the world. *Fucking idiots.* Taking my phone out of my pocket, I searched for Chris' number in the phonebook and pressed call.

"Cyrus," Chris said as he answered.

"Fatty," I joked in reply.

"You idiot, what's up? Where are you?" Chris asked.

"I'm walking at the top of my estate on the way to Tom and John's," I replied.

"Cyrus, I only have five ounces left, so we are going to need more tomorrow, mate," Chris explained, quick to bring me up to speed on business matters.

"How much money have you got there now then?" I asked as that was my primary concern.

"I've got £50 under £8, 500," Chris replied. We only owed £7,500 for our 50-ounce supply, but I liked to finish selling it all before paying everybody at once. Me, Jason, Jabber and Chris, all got paid together, then we would start a fresh batch. It saved the confusion or anybody having to wait for their money all wages longer than anybody else. "What's your plans for Friday then?" Chris asked.

"We will get paid tomorrow, then we can go shopping out of our wages and get fresh haircuts if you want?" I said, letting Chris know I had already mapped out our plans for the day.

"Yes, that's fine with me. I've got to go out for a family meal later today, so I will call you after that if it's not too late. If not, I will come and pick you up first thing tomorrow," Chris said.

"Okay, I will see you later or tomorrow," I said before putting the phone down. Next, I called Jason. I liked to use my phone as I walked down the road, it made me feel important, like a businessman tending to his financial affairs.

Using my phone while walking down the main road would give anybody that saw me the impression that I was busy and important—I liked that.

I strolled leisurely down the main road on the footpath; arriving at the McBride's house, I tapped the letterbox loudly. John and Tom's mum and dad owned the house, but to me, I had an equal stake in this place as it was 'my' place of business.

When the McBride parents were not at work or in the pub, they would either be drunk from the pub or tired from work. This combination mixed with their excessive-relaxed attitudes made them never a problem for me when negotiating the running of my business from their front door. I had told John, "Meet people at the top of your street when it's really busy. I don't want you pissing your mum and dad off, mate'. We had spoken about this on a few occasions. John answered the front door looking hungover from the night before; he had on his shorts and no T-shirt.

"Morning, mate," John said sounding like he had just crawled out of bed.

"Morning mate," I reiterated as I stepped into the house. It wasn't morning; it was 12:10, but I chose not to get on John's case. Under normal circumstances, I would have, but I had come to know when I pay John and Tom, they liked to have a knees up, drinking beer and smoking weed until the tiny hours of the morning, so I wasn't surprised to have to wake them up on the morning after payday. "Where is Tom?" I asked anticipating being told he still in bed.

"Sleeping, I will wake him up in a minute," John replied.

No shock there, I thought to myself. "Still asleep? The lazy bastard," I joked as I pretended to be surprised he wasn't up.

I plumped down on the black leather sofa in the living room. There was something about sitting on a cold leather sofa that I had always liked. It was the same feeling as getting into bed and putting your head on a cold pillow. I just found it soothing to my senses. I had spoken to Jason during my slow walk to the McBride's and told him I would need another 50 ounces for my bulk cannabis sales, and most likely another nine ounces for my shop at the McBride's. He had told me he would have it ready, but it would all most certainly be 'the new stuff', much to my distress. I didn't really have nothing planned for the day other than what I had already done, which was wake John and Tom up to make sure that my shop was open for business. As my mind wandered, the same sense of restlessness returned. I sat in the McBride's and watched people start to arrive to score cannabis with the same regularity I had seen standing outside my local convenience store. I thought about Friday. I planned to wake up and call Chris. There was a designer clothes shop in the city centre. Jason had told me about the shop when I had told him where I had brought sportswear from in an attempt to impress him. He had frowned and said, "Cyrus, those shops are okay for sportswear, but you cannot get decent clothes from there. You need an up-market designer clothes shop."

When you don't know what to say, it is best to say nothing, so I did not reply. I just took his advice on-board while feeling stupid for offering shopping tips to someone that dressed better than I did. I would definitely be visiting the suggested shops though, then I'd get my haircut before going home to get showered up. My final plan being to find some girls were worth going through the effort I would have gone through to look good for them.

Hours passed as I sat down doing absolutely nothing. I served a few customers personally, purely out of boredom. I had two puffs on John's joint reluctantly and walked to the chip shop with Tom.

The shop had taken £460 by the time I decided I had been there long enough. It was about to start getting dark as I said my goodbyes to everyone, John's mum and dad included.

"Bye, Cyrus," the McBrides' mother had said as if it was a pleasure to have had me turning her home into my own personal drug den. *Surely, one of the loveliest women you could ever wish to meet,* I thought as I started up the street in the direction of my estate.

The sky was left incomplete darkness by the time I entered the scruffy council estate I called home. The night air was cool and fresh as I took deep breaths in to wind down after the 10-minute walk. Sitting down all day had given me the worst stamina ever, so I was slightly out of breath after my walk. The air felt clean and pure in my lungs as I inhaled deeply through my nose. A few of the younger kids were still hanging out near their houses, their parents obviously not caring that the 12 or 14-year-old kids were on the street at nearly 10:00 at night. It was at this stage I'd always think, I can't be bothered to go in; but after five minutes and having no alternative, I would just give up and go inside my house.

Tonight was different.

Tonight, I had a great alternative.

Tonight, I would rob the Kosovans.

Tonight, I would rob the Kosovans or Turks, or whoever the fuck they were.

I was different from them idiots who sat around drinking cheap beer, congregating around parked cars, telling stories; reason being, as soon as I remembered about the 'Kosovans', if that's who they were, I wasn't going home until I had seen what was in those boxes. That is of course if: A) Luke was right, and B) I didn't get caught in the process.

To decrease the risk of getting caught, I thought it best not to attempt getting inside the garage alone. The two 12 or 14-year-old kids were the only people that I could see that were out on the dark estate. "You two, come here," I said as I approached the two kids.

"Hi Cyrus, what's up?" one of the two asked—the younger kids on the estate liked me. I think they looked up to me because the older lads had respect for me, mainly because everyone knew I had a bad temper and wouldn't take any shit.

"Will you two be able to stay out for an hour to help me do something? If you do a good job, I will give you both £20 each?" I asked, knowing if there was any possibility they could help, they would do so knowing they'd earn more than two weeks' worth of pocket money.

"Yes, we can stay out, what do you need us to do?" Callum asked excitedly

"Come with me, I'll show you exactly what I want you to do," I said as I started to march towards the house that Luke had told me was occupied by the Kosovans.

The house the Kosovans lived in was right at the bottom of our estate; it was about a two-minute walk from my house on the edge of the estate. The house backed onto a field and was the end house on its row. The street was pitch black with darkness around the houses and bushes and trees to the point it made the setting eerie. Truthfully, I found comfort in having the two younger boys with me; not that they could protect me in any way, but at least if these foreigners caught me trying to steal from them and killed me, at least my killing would be witnessed. One of my main motives behind taking the two young kids with me was, if we had to run away, it increased my odds of getting away. This way, whoever would follow us would have three people to pursue instead of one. Another example of manipulation, but I didn't care; for me, 'self-preservation' was key.

The house the Kosovans lived in was bigger and better then the house I lived in, it looked as though its owners had spent a lot of money on the house at some point. It was probably the best house on the estate. It had an extended garage that looked different to every other garage.

The doors of this garage were huge wooden doors that met in the middle, thick wooden slacks painted white; the garage doors had four arm-length, huge, heavy-duty hinges towards the top of each door on the right and left, and two more hinges towards the bottom of the door symmetrically. The hinges were painted black and shiny.

I knew the Kosovans hadn't extended the garage themselves or put this garage door on because I had seen it over the years when I had been running around the housing estate playing. The giant wooden doors painted white with the giant hinges painted black made the garage door look almost Victorian.

The house was in complete darkness which was good from one point of view, but it was also bad from another because I couldn't tell where these Kosovo/Turks were. To the right of the garage door was a dull brown gate—a far better constructed gate than the one my dad had built. Then to the right of the gate, there was a garden wall that was brick and the same height as the gate at above my head height. The garden wall led to the corner of the house, then turned on a right angle left towards the side of the house. The whole place was in darkness.

The entry that pedestrians could use to walk around the back of the house worried me. I hoped whoever lived in the house wouldn't sneak around the side of the house under the cover of darkness and ambush me. The two 12-14-year-old kids had no idea what I was up to, as I stood looking at the house and garage.

"Cyrus," one of the kids said.

"Ssshh, stop talking... I need you two to be quiet," I said to stop the kid talking before he said another syllable.

"We are going to rob this garage. Keep your mouth shut, and do what I say when I say it, and I will give you both £20 each if it goes well," I whispered. I was sure to look both of the kids in their eyes, so I knew I had their full attention.

I stepped closer to the garage to inspect the lock. It had a keyhole in the middle of the door that would open and close what looked like a heavy duty and sturdy lock. Also, the doors met perfectly in the middle, so there was no way of trying to pry them open. The silence was piercing. It made the atmosphere seem so calm and safe in one sense, but also unnerving and charged at the same time. The silence was interrupted only by the occasional rustle of leaves as the wind passed through the trees and bushes around us. *Shit, how the fuck am I going to get in here?* I thought eager to find the solution.

I studied the construction of the garage doors. The hinges. Almost in disbelief, I realised that the bottle-cap-sized rivets holding the hinges in place were actually giant flat-point screws! There were four of these giant screws inserted into each of the four hinges, holding the four corners of the garage doors in place. "I need a screwdriver," I whispered to my two youthful accomplices.

"Where are you going to get one from?" Little Callum asked. I shined the light of my phone onto the head of the screws. The screw heads were huge and covered with what looked like at least two or three coats of thick black paint.

"Follow me," I said to the kids as I marched quickly back towards my house—right, left, right, left—I turned through the little entries and walkways that led back towards my house.

I opened my wedged closed gate and knocked my door quietly, hoping it would be my mum and not my dad that answered the door. The light in the kitchen flicked on as a figure reached the door to let me in. "Hi, Cyrus," my mum said. "Is that you in for the night now?" My mum asked.

"In half an hour," I said quietly. When my mum had walked back through to the living room, I walked into the kitchen and opened the drawer that seemed to just have bits and bobs in it, like a draw dedicated just to clutter. I had seen a screwdriver in their before; and luckily for me, I found the sturdy black rubber-handled flathead screwdriver exactly where I thought it would be.

Back outside my house, I found the two young boys waiting right where I had told them to wait. The estate was silent as I closed my gate. The gate squeaked loudly as the two pieces of warped wood rubbed together as the gate closed. The two young boys were leaning against the side of my house looking lost, like they had no clue what was going on. Callum, the kid I knew better out of the two was small and skinny. His little body clearly not fully developed. He had a small frame and straight soft hair. As I looked at Callum, it became apparent to me that he should be at home drinking hot chocolate and getting ready for bed, but the combination of poor-parenting combined with me needing to take advantage of him had the poor little fellow waiting beside my house to commit a burglary. "Come on, let's go," I ordered the two kids as I walked body full of determination in the direction we had come from. From my gate, the three of us took ten steps right of my gate, then turned left 30 steps, then right through our little entry between houses, then left through another entry between more houses; then right another 30 paces, and there we were, back outside the big Victorian-looking double garage doors.

The house and street was exactly as we had left it. Still in complete darkness, still in complete silence.

Screwdriver in hand, I knelt down and tried to unscrew one of the big circular screw heads holding the hinge in place. It was impossible. The black shiny paint allowed my screwdriver no grip whatsoever. I tried again, this time applying as much pressure to the screwdriver to keep it in place. Still no joy. "For fuck's sake," I whispered as the two kids looked on nervously. Their facial expressions told me that they both wanted to leave. They knew better than to even suggest leaving as they could see I was determined and would by no means allow them to leave. I took the screwdriver away from the hinge and assessed the situation. "How the fuck can I open this?" I asked myself silently. Then it came to me. I put the screwdriver back in the groove of the screw head, but this time I used the corner of the flat sharp side to scrape the paint out of the grove.

The shiny black paint came away almost effortlessly, revealing the steel that was underneath, I scraped the paint away until a flat line of steel was visible in the middle of the screw head.

Then I put the screwdriver in place as I had before, applied a fair amount of pressure and turned slowly but forcefully. 'Crack', the paint around the side of the oversized screw broke away, making a distinctive but not too loud noise as the screw finally gave way.

My body filled with excitement as I turned my head to look at my little apprentices in the eye and gave them a menacing smile and wink as if to say 'we have lift off!' None of us said a word as I unscrewed the giant screws from where they had sat for probably the last five years undisturbed. When the first screw was out, I pulled the screwdriver away and repeated the whole procedure. When I had disconnected the hinge completely, I pulled it slightly away from the garage door to ensure it was totally detached.

The hinges at the top of the garage door were too high for me to work on effectively. I was too short to apply the pressure needed to scrape the paint away or turn the giant screws. There was no merit in asking one of the two younger kids to help as they were smaller than me. Using my resourcefulness, I improvised, one of the Kosovan/Turks neighbours had a big, square-shaped bin outside of their gate. Stepping away from the big garage door, I walked to the bin, tipped it back onto the wheels that allowed it to be moved easily and wield it quietly and slowly towards the garage I was breaking into. I put the big, square-shaped, government-issue bin on its side underneath the hinges.

Standing on the bin, I was now at the optimum height needed to work on the higher hinges. Implementing the same procedure to the letter, I removed the remaining hinges slowly and methodically. Effectively, this left the garage door not connected to anything on the left side or the right side. The only lock on the garage door now was in the middle keeping the two doors together. The worry of being caught had completely gone since the first turn of the first screw. As long as my surroundings stayed as quiet as it had been, I would not have a care in the world. My only concerns were (A) If there were any boxes in this garage? In which case if there was not, I would go straight to Luke's house and break his nose. (B) What was in these boxes? I had been standing by this garage door for the best part of an hour. My greed and boredom had seen to that. I had no intention of leaving until the job was done.

After a moment's thought, I wedged my screwdriver in between the wall and the disconnected garage door. Forcefully but quietly, I pried the door between the wall and the door.

At first, it moved a millimetre, then a centimetre, an inch; the door was made of thick and solid wood. It must have been just shy of three-inches thick. Eventually, I made a gap big enough for me to peer inside. It didn't make sense opening the door any further. The gap wasn't big enough to stick my head or body through, but it was big enough to enable me to see inside. I took my phone out to turn on the little flashlight on top. I shined the light inside. "Oh my gosh!" I said to myself as a new and fresh load of excitement mixed with adrenaline coursed through my body. It is a feeling that only a robber can explain. The excitement of attaining something significant for nothing mixed with the emotions of doing wrong.

Huge brown boxes stacked almost to the garage roof. The garage was huge inside, and there were too many boxes to count by glancing inside. Boxes in front of boxes stacked on boxes on top of boxes. They were rectangular-shaped and about a metre in length and probably 500cm in width and height. "What could possibly be inside all of these boxes?" I asked myself as the excitement turned to curiosity. I had enough of a gap to use my hands to pry the garage door open further. I had created a gap big enough to get inside the garage and get the boxes out if their contents warranted being stolen.

I took the first step inside of the garage. Clear pieces of plastic crinkled noisily under my feet. The noise was not loud enough to deter or worry me. I walked slowly and cautiously to the nearest box. I recognised the manufacturer's logo almost instantly. I opened a loose flap on the top of the box. I couldn't believe my eyes or my luck. *There must be over £1, 00,000 worth of goods here,* I thought to myself. Two hundred cigarettes in one box, and more sleeves than I could count in one box without opening it properly and at least 40 boxes. I picked up the same box I had looked inside and started for the gap in the garage door.

"Grab this," I told one of the two young kids as I pushed the box through the gap in the garage door. Picking up another box, I checked its contents; another box full to the brim of the same goods pushed through the gap in the garage door quickly, this time leaving the garage to join the two younger kids outside. "I want you both to grab that box and follow me," I whispered as my heart rate began to increase to the point I could feel it beating in the top of my throat. Acting on instinct, I started back towards my house.

I couldn't take these stolen goods home, I concluded. Desperation had my brain working overtime. *Trish's house,* I thought instantly. It must have been a little after 11:00 at night as I banged Trish's door to get her out of bed and let me in her house. The two younger kids and I stood waiting with what must have been 15,000 cigarettes in the two boxes we had stolen. "Cyrus, what's going on? And what the bloody hell have you got there?" Trish asked with a face full of concern.

"I've got Christmas here, that's what this is," I said as I practically pushed past her to place the box on her living room floor, quickly followed by the box the two young boys had carried. "Trish, have a look in these boxes, but keep your back door open because I will be back in five minutes," I explained while slightly out of breath. "Come on, you two, hurry up," I said as I barked orders at the two younger children to follow me.

Back at the garage, I had a look inside to check the scale of my job. I saw a box with a different logo.

Expensive, I thought to myself. Knowing that this box may potentially yield the most profit, I rammed it through the gap in the garage door to the children outside. Picking up a box that was identical, I followed the two younger children back to Trish's with our second haul. I opened Trish's aluminium and glass door to find her now sitting in her living room wide awake.

"Cyrus, where have you got all of these from?" she asked as she sat puffing on one of her own cigarettes.

"I will explain when I come back, don't worry though; just keep your back door open," I replied while placing two more boxes on her living-room carpet.

Ten trips later, I could see the change in the sky colour—it was almost light. It had felt like I had been doing this for ten minutes due to excitement and adrenaline, but as it was practically daylight now. The sun beginning to rise allowed me to work out I had actually been stealing these boxes for hours. Putting the last load in what very little space there was left available in Trish's living room, I decided to quit while I was ahead. Her living room was full from floor to ceiling of boxes of cigarettes and loose sleeves we had collected from the housing estates floor when two of the boxes had split. This was the most cigarettes I had ever seen. From wall to wall, width and length-ways, the living room was rammed of boxes. They took up more room than her three-piece sofa, her single seat sofa, TV and TV-unit combined.

"If you two tell anybody about this, I will kill you both," I warned the two children.

"We won't tell anybody, Cyrus, we promise," they replied as they looked at each other. Putting my hand in my pocket, I took out £60 and gave them a £20 and a £10 note each.

"Okay, go home now, you two, you both have done a good job, but I mean it! Not a fucking word to anybody!" As I said it, I glared at the two children, seriousness was an understatement.

The two young children looked back at me with their eyes full of fear. I had quite obviously scared them, which was my objective. They nodded as they whispered, too scared to speak normally, "We won't, Cyrus," as they turned and left £30 richer each.

The second the two children were out of the door, I locked it swiftly behind them. There was no way I would be losing my haul easily. I sat back down to look around the room at the size of the boxes of cigarettes.

"Where did all this come from?" Trish asked again in amazement. She could see my brain was working overtime.

"I stole them from a garage," I told her as I turned to face her smiling. I took my phone out, feeling the need to tell someone and called my brother, Daniel. His phone rang, almost to his voicemail before he answered it. "Danny, I just robbed about £50,000 worth of cigarettes," I told him boastfully. I knew the value of my haul was much more. I was taking into consideration stolen goods being worth half the actual value.

"Are you being serious?" Daniel asked as though what I had said to him just made him sit up out of bed.

"I'm being serious. I have," I confirmed.

"Where from? And why did you not call me?" Daniel had asked the question sounding annoyed to my surprise.

I then explained exactly what I had done to the letter. "Is there any left?" Daniel asked after hearing chapter and verse.

"Yes, there are about five boxes left in the garage," I replied. I had totally forgot about the boxes I had left. The two children and I had made so many trips, seeing the light come back to the sky had left me with no choice but not to risk losing what I already had by chancing my luck any further.

"I'm on my way," Daniel said as I could hear him now out of bed and active.

"Cyrus, nobody is going to come here looking for these cigarettes, are they?" Trish asked as the half of conversation she had just heard made her worry.

"No, nobody is going to come here," I reassured as my brain continued to race. Not being able to risk anyone bringing any more stolen cigarettes to Trish's house, I thought about my brother. There was no way he was not going to take the last five boxes. *What if he gets my cigarettes caught by bringing his cigarettes here,* I thought as I stood standing amongst the giant towers of boxes of cigarettes. I decided to call my brother back. "Yes, Daniel," I said as I heard my brother answer the phone. I could hear him running in the background. As he ran while on the phone to me, Daniel's main concern was confirming the exact location of the garage. When I had told him everything he wanted to know, I explained my reasoning behind calling him back.

"Daniel, rob whatever you want from that garage, but do not bring it to Trish's, okay?" I said firmly.

"Oh! Why can't I bring it there?" Daniel asked sounding annoyed.

"Because I don't want to lose the 30 boxes I've stolen because you want to steal five more now when the sun is up!" I explained sounding more annoyed that he had made me have to explain myself.

"Okay, call, I'll take them somewhere else and then come and see you with no cigarettes," Daniel said accepting what I had told him.

I put the phone down, leaving my brother who was now a man on a mission. "What are you going to do now, Cyrus?" Trish asked as she looked at me bewildered.

"I'm going to sell these cigarettes tomorrow, and I'm going to give you some money," I said as I stood staring at the cigarettes and walking around the towers and stacks of loose sleeves. I had answered her question for mine and her benefit. I hadn't planned that far; so from here on out, I was acting purely on impulse, making decisions on instinct after using whatever time I had to reach an educated decision.

My brother joined Trish and I in her living room. He had knocked the big square panel of glass, and I had seen his outline through the glass; plus who else is going to knock a 50-year-old's door at 5:00 in the morning. Daniel had entered the house, panting like he had just ran a half-marathon.

"What happened?" I asked not even waiting for him to catch his breath.

"I got them and stashed them in a safe place until the morning. No fucking way!" Daniel said as his eyes lit up and nearly popped out of his head as he scanned the room, realising the scale of what I had stolen.

"I have made a killing tonight, haven't I?" I asked with a big grin, putting my fist out to fist pump him, wanting praise.

"Yes, I just robbed loads myself, but no way near what's here," my brother explained. He was doing exactly what I had done, walking in between the towers of boxes and looking exactly what was there.

"How much money is worth do you think?" I asked, coming to terms with the fact I had hit it big.

"There's got to be at least 40 or £50,000 here, Cyrus," Daniel said, eyes still wide and continuing to scan the room.

"You all have to tell your mum, Cyrus. She will be able to sell these for you," Trish said, still sitting on the sofa where she was an almost permanent fixture. The thought hadn't even crossed my mind to tell my mum, but when I thought about it, it wasn't a bad idea.

The idea had loads of advantages: it would explain me having money, it would stop my dad getting on at me; and most of all, it would gain me respect in my house. If my mum sells some or all of the cigarettes for me, I would be one of the main breadwinners in our house; or if not a breadwinner, I would definitely have the most money.

I was only 16, but I knew if you had the most money in the house you live in, you automatically have the most or at least some respect from the occupants of that house.

"Yes, I'll send her over in the morning," I replied calmly and confidently. I had said it like that had been my plans all along. "All right, I'm going to go across to bed now then," I said to Trish as I looked at Daniel to signal it was time to leave. "Lock this door, my mum will be over in the morning," I said as Daniel and I left to go to our house. The morning was bright but motionless. It looked like midday, but it was pitch silent. Everybody was still sleeping, apart from the birds who were tweeting and whistling. The two of us crept into our house and up the stairs to bed. "A job well done," I said to myself as I took my clothes off and slid silently into bed.

The walls in our house were paper-thin, so my brother Daniel and I had perfected the art of being quiet. We'd had to, especially if we wanted to avoid World War III if we pissed our dad off. I was asleep in record time, considering I had felt so awake in Trish's living room, looking at my stolen stash. My body must have been worn out, my head hit the pillow, and I was out like a light.

I awoke the same morning to the sun shining through my floor to ceiling blinds. Instantly I remembered my shenanigans from the night before. I shot out of bed, like a bullet, threw shorts and a T-shirt on and went to Daniel's room to wake him. *No Daniel*. His bed was empty. I returned to my room to see my little digital clock reading 1:10 in the afternoon. Feeling as though the world had started without me, I got ready quickly and left my empty house to go to Trish's. *Where was everyone? No Mum, no Dad, no Daniel? Where are they?* I wondered as I opened the back door. Two steps out of my back door, I saw my brother was standing with his friend, Lee.

"Are you alive now, Bro?" Daniel joked with a big smile.

"Yes. Is everything good? And where is Mum?" I asked feeling puzzled. The night before, I had been running the show, but my morning started with me feeling like I had slept through the show.

"I'm good, look at this," Daniel said as he pulled out a pile of notes that was too thick to even attempt to fold. The pile of notes Daniel held in his hand was thicker than the garage door I had broken into the night before ironically. Daniel's friend Lee also brandished a thick folded pile of cash. Daniel had to have had at least £7,000 and Lee at least £3,000, I estimated. "Mum is at Trish's house," Daniel said looking pleased with himself.

"Where the fuck did you get that money?" I asked, now definitely feeling like I had missed the boat.

"I sold all my cigarettes. Lee sold them for me for just under £10,000," Daniel replied.

"I want a little cut, it's only fair as it was my job," I said, now frowning at the fact even Lee was now better off than me from my own job.

The two of them gave me £1,500 between them which made me feel a lot better as I marched around the corner towards Trish's house.

My mum answered Trish's door with a lot less of a surprised look on her face then could be expected. She had always known I was going to be a bad boy. Everyone knew I was going to be a bad boy, it was more a question of how and when it was never a question of 'if'.

"Cyrus, this is a lot of cigarettes, are you sure there is going to be no repercussions over this?" my mum asked which I had anticipated. It was the most important question that anybody with a brain would need answering.

"No, Mum, there is going to be no trouble, the people I stole this off were asleep and didn't wake up," I explained; she looked at me and fought hard not to smile. My mum didn't smile; instead she got down to business.

"Trish and I will sell as many as we can, but we can't sell them for full price. People will want to make money, how much do you want for a sleeve containing 200 cigarettes?" my mum asked.

"How much are they to buy usually?" I asked with no idea what the reply was going to be.

The most cigarettes I had ever brought was a packet of 20. "I think it's about £70 for a good brand, and most of these are good ones," my mum told me while confirming with Trish. I had at least five of the major cigarette brands, and a few small quantities of some less common brands; in all fairness, I had a good inventory. My mother picked up a sleeve of cigarettes and gave them to Trish. "These are from Cyrus, Trish," my mum said as she gave them to her friend.

"I will be happy with £40 per sleeve if they are usually sold for £70," I replied setting a price for sale. My mum looked at Trish for her opinion on price. She nodded to say yes, signalling it was a fair price.

"Okay, we will start selling them, Cyrus. Trish has a friend called Pete who sells cigarettes at a few social clubs. We will get him to buy some, and we've got a few other people that will want some," my mother explained as she let out a big sigh about to start the daunting task of selling this colossal amount of cigarettes. "Will these cigarettes be safe here though?" I asked making sure this wouldn't all just slip through my fingers.

"Yes, Cyrus, don't worry," my mum said.

"Okay then, I love you both, and I will pay you both for your help. I'm going shopping now," I said as I smiled at them both mischievously and headed for the door.

My brother and Lee were still leaning on the wall at the side of our house as I walked back towards my house. "Is everything good," Daniel asked; happy his business with me was concluded fully.

101

"Yes, everything is good, just keep an eye out for me, please, Bro," I asked.

"See you guys, later," I said to his friend as I walked back into our house to finish getting ready properly.

Pulling my best tracksuit from the chest of drawers and placing it on my bed with fresh boxer shorts and socks, I took out the £1,500 my brother and his mate had given me and threw it and my phone on the bed next to my tracksuit. *No need for hiding money now,* I thought, as the sight did everything for me visually. *Cheap drug-dealing phone sitting next to a pile of cash and a fresh set of clothes. A great sight!* I jumped in the shower and took a long relaxing soak, as though I was trying to rid my skin of the dirt I had been doing all night. I took time to meticulously wash my body. The hot water beating against my tired muscles in the shower left me feeling rejuvenated.

Chapter 8

"So, how long are you going to be then, Chris? I'm ready to go shopping now," I nagged.

"I'm going to leave my house now. Plus, I've got £8,750 here for you. I will bring it with me," Chris said. It was the money to pay Jason's Uncle Jabber, and £1,250 of it was my profit.

"Okay, bring it to my house, mate," I told Chris. My pocket was already bulging. There was no way I could carry that sort of money around with me. Chris put the phone down as I stood up off my bed to go and stand outside my house to wait for him.

"What are you up to today, Cyrus?" my brother asked as he seemed to be content to just stand outside the house with probably all of his pockets full of money.

"I'm just going into town to get some jeans with Chris," I replied as I stood facing the corner of the street that Chris would be driving around any second.

"Okay, if you need anything doing, call me," Daniel offered.

I walked slowly to Chris' car as he pulled up. "Yes, Cyrus! The money is on the floor by your feet," Chris said as he pointed to the brick-sized bag of tightly wrapped money on the passenger-side footwell.

I trusted my brother and his mate, Lee, but I still didn't want anybody to know I was picking up this much money. "Give me ten minutes to run inside to count this money. In fact, come inside my house and roll a joint while I sort this money out," I told Chris. We got out the car after I stuffed the big bag of money under the front of my tracksuit bottoms and pulled my tracksuit top over it to conceal it. We walked into my house. "Roll that joint on the kitchen table, I'm going upstairs for five minutes, Chris."

Back in my room, I ripped the bag open to reveal the bundles of banknotes arranged into individual thousands. I counted out £7,500 as quick as my little chubby fingers could enable me—that was Jason and Jabber's money. I slid my bottom drawer out completely from the big chest of drawers. There was just over

£4,000 under them. I put the £7,500 in the opposite corner under the drawers to my personal stash of money and placed the £1,250 I had remaining from the bag from Chris next to the money I had saved under the set of drawers. *I will count that later,* I thought to myself as I slid the draw back in place silently.

Chris was sat with a giant spliff, smiling at me sitting at my kitchen table when I re-joined him downstairs. It was the joints width that made it giant; the thing looked like a miniature baseball bat. "Come on, let's go," Chris said as he got up, looking like it took more effort than it should have because of his weight. Chris wore a grey tracksuit almost identical to mine; both grey, both made by the same manufacturer, both had a hood and a zipper. Chris had short, soft, light brown hair and looked chubby and friendly in the face. The wooden chair he had sat on had been totally concealed by his abnormally large body, especially for his age at 18. He was a big lad, not obese, just significantly overweight.

"Lock the door if you're leaving the street, Daniel," I said as I looked him square in the eye to let him know it was an order, not a request.

"Where do you want to go first then?" Chris asked.

"To that designer clothes shop in town," I said confidently, like I had been there hundreds of times before.

"Hello, Mum," I said after reading her name on the screen and answering my phone.

"Cyrus, do you want to sell 127 sleeves for five?" My mum asked, hearing half of what she had said.

"Five what?" I asked.

"Five thousand pounds… for 127 sleeves?" my mum asked, this time being heard clearly.

"What does that work out to per sleeve?" I asked, happy at the prospect of earning £5,000.

"It's £40 per sleeve, but you're giving him two extra sleeves for free," my mum explained.

"Can you do that for me now then, please; and keep the money safe for me, please, mum," I replied more than happily.

"Bye, Cyrus," my mum said as if I had patronised her by thinking I needed to tell her to keep the money safe.

We parked the car in the main shopping centre's multi-storey car park. The tinny car door slammed as I swung the door to shut it. As the two of us walked through the fairly busy shopping centre, I felt like more of a man then I had ever felt. My well-built best friend Chris by my side, who was also my partner in my drug business, a pocket full of money, wearing my best clothes had me walking with my head held high, not to mention I had made £5,000 profit during the 15-minute drive to town.

I am sure it was the fact I was no longer broke that had me walking with a little 'swagger'.

My Auntie Delma had £5,000 put away at her house for me, I had £5,200 under my drawers in my room that was mine, and I had £1,500 in my pocket that was causing a big bulge in my tracksuit bottoms; also, my mum now had £5,000 for me, and soon to be a lot more.

Sixteen thousand seven hundred pounds, I had worked out was my own money. I had tallied it up as we walked towards the designer clothes shop. Mannequin in the shop windows wore expensive Italian leather jackets and designer jeans and trainers. I walked into the shop and felt the difference in atmosphere instantly. Outside the shop in the shopping centre had been noisy, with people talking and rustling bags and goods as they walked, noisy children and scruffy-looking people as well as well-dressed upper-class people, but everyone was moving wherever you looked. Inside this shop was a different atmosphere completely; it was quiet and tranquil. Music played low in the background; the floor was a shiny dark-coloured wood that looked luxurious and expensive.

Perfectly folded T-shirts presented on angled, individual, square wooden blocks. All of the hanging rails were organised perfectly—jeans in one section, jumpers in another and a little section dedicated just to footwear. Everything in the shop was designer and top of the range. "Do you want some help, mate?" one of the two lads asked. He had a head full of gel and a face full of spots. His skin was tanned, like he had been over using sunbeds.

"Yes, mate, I'm looking for a pair of dark blue Italian jeans, and a grey, designer, German polo T-shirt," I said calmly and confidently to disguise the fact that I had never shopped in a shop of this quality before. Chris looked at me with a facial expression that told me he wasn't expecting me to say what I had said to the shop assistant. Yes, I was a chubby, mixed-raced kid from a shit-hole council estate, but I didn't have a little chubby, mixed-raced kid from a shitty council estates mentality. The quicker people started to realise that, the quicker they would save themselves the shock of my unexpected endeavours.

"The jeans are over there, mate," the half-spotty, smartly dressed assistant said showing me a table with six different designs and colours of jeans, all donning little metal badges on the back. I saw the pair Jason had worn.

"Them one's, mate," I said as I pointed at the ones I wanted.

"What size are you, mate?" The shop assistant asked. *Shit,* I thought; now he was going to know I don't shop in a place like this.

"Can I try some on, please?" I said as this was the best I could say given the circumstances.

"Yes, of course, mate. I will give you a 32" and 34". I think the 32" will fit you but try them both on," the assistant said as he passed me two pairs of the designer jeans and pointed towards the changing rooms.

"Could you bring me some T-shirts to try on at the same time, so I can see what they look like together?" I asked not wanting to have to try things on twice.

"Okay. They are just over here." I followed the slim assistant over to the T-shirts hanging on the rails. I looked through the different designs. I quickly spotted the one Jabber had worn to lunch, but there were much better designs here. I chose two before heading to the changing rooms.

I picked up the jeans to try them on and read the tiny tag hanging from the belt fixtures, '£185'. *Shit,* I thought. *£185! For a pair of jeans?* I unfolded the size 32 and tried them on, and they fit perfectly. They sat snug just below my waistline. Then I tried on one of the medium-sized T-shirts, which fit perfectly too and made my shoulders look broader. Sliding the curtain on the dressing room to the side, I looked in the full-length mirror on the wall. *This is how I need to dress from now on!* I told myself as I looked back at my reflection. I looked like a proper boss in the drug game now. I was out of my tracksuit.

My appearance had changed completely. I looked older, I looked more accomplished and more importantly to me. I looked more dangerous. Looking down at the bottom of my jeans, my trainers looked out of place. They were only just over a month old but looked grubby at the bottom of the immaculately cleaned and ironed Italian jeans. I had loved my trainers when my mum had brought them for me, but now they were an eyesore. They ruined my outfit; they were good trainers, and they cost nearly a £120, but they weren't in the same league as the jeans and T-shirt I was wearing. After putting my tracksuit back on, I found the spotty,

20-something-year-old just outside the changing rooms, standing near the till.

"Mate, I'll have the 32" jeans and these two T-shirts, but have you got any trainers to go with this outfit?" The assistant took the clothes I wanted and placed them on the counter near the till. There was an older man behind the till. He was short and in his early 40s. He looked like he had a lot of money; tanned with a short-sleeve shirt on and a very expensive-looking gold watch, it was plain to see this man cared about his appearance.

I chose some navy-blue trainers that the shop assistant had suggested. They matched my outfit perfectly, and I was very happy. I had chosen my outfit so that I would be wearing all my clothes made by the same designer. Chris was at the till buying a T-shirt and some shorts as I stood next to him to wait for the assistant to bring the trainers I wanted from the storeroom; he returned after a minute or two.

"Jeans, trainers and shirts," the assistant said to the older-looking guy behind the till as he passed him the box containing the trainers.

The older man looked at me a little confused as he said, "You all right?" As he started scanning little tags that were handing or stuck to the items of clothing. "That will be £610, please, mate," the older man had said when he finished tallying up the clothes I wanted.

"Yes, okay great, mate," I replied calmly as I pulled out the wad of cash that was so thick that it was a struggle to manoeuvre out my tracksuit trouser pocket. I watched the older man's face change behind the till as his eyes opened wide at the sight of my thick wad of cash.

"Have you got enough money there, mate?" he joked as I started to count the £610 he had asked for.

"Yes, I've just got a little bit of my pocket money here," I joked back as I glanced up at him from counting with a smile.

"Here you go, mate," I said as I gave him a small wedge in comparison to what I had left after paying.

Back in the shopping centre precinct, but now holding several bags of designer clobber, Chris and I stopped at the food court to eat. The food court was a big open area that had 10 to 12 places selling food. It had a big section in the middle to sit down and eat with all of the major fast food chains available as well as healthy options like baguettes and so forth.

After Chris and I had eaten our fast food and had our fill of unhealthy E numbers, we returned to find the car in the multi-storey car park. "How much did you spend in that shop?" Chris asked as he turned to observe my shopping bags I had thrown on the back seat.

"Just over £600," I said acting like it wasn't a significant amount of money.

"Big spender!" Chris joked as he started the car.

"I'd like to spend £5,000 in there if I could afford it," I said very seriously. I had no intention of doing that, but I would have liked to. The reflection I had seen of myself in the full-length mirror did something to me. It was the same thing that happened to me when I had looked inside the first carrier bag full of money I had ever had in my possession. It stimulated my ego, leaving me feeling content for a brief moment.

We stopped at my barbershop. It was the only place I liked to get my haircut. A short, dark-skinned Jamaican man who was usually high as a kite but an absolute artist when it comes to performing the only haircut I would have—'a skin fade'. He would make sure the sides and the back was as bold as a baby's bottom. He would perfectly blend it in to the hair on the top of my head while singing and even doing a few dance moves! My barber would shake his head to his music as he would step back to look at his progress before continuing. He was a character, but as I said, an artist with a set of hair clippers and a cutthroat razor.

"Hi, Mum," I said as we started our journey back towards my house from the barbershop. I wondered what she wanted now.

"Cyrus, will you sell 128 sleeves for £5,000? It's the same guy as earlier; you will just be giving him one extra sleeve for free," my mother asked.

"Yes, of course, but tell him to stop trying to bump up the freebies," I said, only half-seriously.

"Okay," my mother replied, about to hang up.

"Wait, Mum, have I got many sleeves of cigarettes left?" I asked as I realised I had sold £10,000 worth already. If I'm honest although, my brother had guessed that there was a lot of value in the boxes I had stolen. It was still just a load of boxes of cigarettes to me, plus I had earned it by unscrewing a garage door and carrying boxes that weren't even ridiculously heavy, so £10,000 for what I had done meant in my mind I had already had a major success.

"Cyrus, you are fucking joking. The two loads I've sold when this guy comes to pick this second load up has not even touched the surface! We haven't even hardly sold any!" my mother explained as she came to the realisation that I had no idea of the amount of money I had stolen.

"Okay, that's good, tell that guy to buy more then," I suggested.

"Bye, Cyrus," my mum said before hanging up.

I sat looking out the window, looking at the passing cars as I added another £5,000 to my personal bank balance in my head.

"What was that about, Cyrus?" Chris asked hearing half of my conversation. I chuckled to myself realising he had no clue what I had done. Then I proceeded to tell Chris everything that had happened. Chris drove with his jaw practically on his lap hearing how audacious I had been. Wide-eyed and opened-mouth, listening to my every word. "You jammy bastard, no wonder you're spending £600 on clothes like it's 50p, you lucky bastard. Why didn't you call me?" Chris asked feeling as though he had missed the boat.

"I would have, but I wasn't even sure if anything was going to be in there, it was a spur of the moment thing, plus, you were at your family meal, remember?" I explained.

"Oh, yes, shit," Chris said realising I had a valid reason for not involving him. "Cyrus, let me see if my uncle will buy some. If he does, give me a nice sorter for getting you the sale," Chris pleaded.

"Yes, of course, mate," I said without a second thought.

We parked outside the back of my house, facing the concrete stumps. We arranged to meet back up in an hour-and-a-half to go meet the girls that Chris had arranged for us to meet.

"Grab me a sleeve of them cigarettes, Cyrus, so I can go and show my uncle before I come back," Chris suggested. I nodded to say yes as I got my designer clothes bags from the back seat of the car and walked past my house to Trish's, knocking the big square piece of glass in Trish's front door to get her attention she let me in. My mum was right was my first thought as I looked at the living room full of cigarettes. Whatever they had sold had made the amount look untouched.

"Chris is going to ask his uncle if he wants any cigarettes. I'm trying to get them sold as quick as possible," I said to Trish as she picked up a sleeve and threw them into one of my designer clothes bags. "Where's my mum?" I asked Trish before leaving.

"Over the road, at your house," Trish replied as she sat smoking a cigarette, watching TV as normal. Trish's living room looked like someone had put the TV and a sofa in a cigarette warehouse. I left Trish's house to take the sleeve of cigarettes 'round to Chris who was waiting parked behind my house. I knew there was a chance someone could break in and steal my stolen stash, or the kids could have been seen stealing them with me and gave up the location of the cigarettes, or somehow the Kosovo/Turks could find the stash. I didn't care about Trish's well-being; my main concern was selling the stolen stash and getting paid. I just hoped I finish the job of turning the cigarettes into money and carrying on my life hassle-free.

"Here, mate, I've been selling them for £40 per sleeve, no cheaper, I've got about 1,000 sleeves left," I told Chris as I threw the sleeve of cigarettes onto the passenger side floor and closed the door.

"Hi, Dad," I said as I walked past my dad in the kitchen. I had made it almost through the kitchen to the door that led to the staircase before he stopped me.

"Cyrus, your mum has told me what you have done. Watch what you are doing. If somebody catches you stealing from them, they could kill you." My dad said firmly, but not angrily. It was a warning more than anything else. *That could have been a lot worse,* I thought as I walked upstairs towards my room.

"The last 24 hours has been hectic," I said to myself as I took my phone out to call Jason. "Yes, mate, I've got £7,500 here for you and Jabber," I told Jason before he could even say hello.

"Okay great, are you going to drop it to mine?" Jason asked.

"I will call my Auntie Delma and ask her if I can give it to her. She could come to my house and collect the money and then bring it to you," I suggested after trying to think of a solution.

"Yes, okay, let me know what she says then, mate," Jason said.

"Oh, shit, I forgot to tell you. I've got £10,000 worth of cigarettes. Ask your uncle if he wants to buy them. I've got every make of cigarettes for sale," I told Jason remembering I had a new business venture I should be promoting.

"What? Where did you get £10,000 worth of cigarettes from?" Jason asked sounding intrigued.

"I've just got them. I can't say where they've come from. But try to help me sell them, please, I will call you later, okay mate," I said before hanging up.

It was at that precise moment that I finally understood the all well to known saying…'*there is no rest for the wicked*'. Since my eyes had opened in the morning, I had been on the go all day. "Hi, Delma, I've got £7,500 here for Jason. If I give you £20, could you come and get it from me and then drop it to him, please?" I asked sounding as though I was pleading for her to provide a quick and easy solution to my problem.

"Yes, that's fine. I'll be at yours in 20 minutes. I'm going to come to see your mum, so just bring it downstairs to me," Delma replied. I loved Delma, always prepared to help me when I needed her.

"Okay, thanks, Delma," I said before hanging up to tell Jason she would be dropping money.

"Yes, Cyrus, my uncle said drop a sleeve off; and if the cigarettes are proper, he would buy the lot," Jason said before I had chance to explain what I had called him for.

"Okay, I will give a sleeve of cigarettes to my auntie, and she will give them to you when she brings you your money. She will be at your house in the next hour, I should imagine," I explained.

"Okay, make sure she brings the cigarettes, please," Jason stressed.

"I won't forget, mate," I said before putting the phone down. Before I even had chance to take my new clothes out of their bags, 'Chris' was flashing on my phone screen as I looked at my phone that had been sitting on my bed less than ten seconds.

"What's up now, mate?" I said as I answered my phone.

"Cyrus, my uncle said how many sleeves would you sell for £15,000?" Chris asked. I had no idea where to begin calculating how many sleeves I would give for £15,000 while on the phone.

"I'll give him £15,000 worth at £40 per sleeve. Obviously, I will give him a few extra because he's your uncle, Chris, maybe ten for free or something like that?" I replied.

"Okay, work out exactly how many, and he will buy them tomorrow. I'm coming to pick you up in 40 minutes anyway," Chris said. "If he does buy £15,000 worth, I want a nice sorter!" Chris added.

"Don't worry, I will give you a nice sorter, mate; see you soon," I reassured him and put the phone down. The phone calls I received had increased tenfold, in a way I didn't mind, as it made me feel important—I had a purpose. The receiving of so many calls and the need to make so many calls made me feel important, especially because the majority of my phone calls were related to money.

I put the change that I had left from the money my brother and his friend, Lee, had given me on the bed next to my phone. I started to take out my new clothes from their bags. They looked out of place in my room, almost like they were lost. Everything in my room was of poor quality and old; everything apart from some of Italy's and Germany's top-line designer clothes that were just laying on my bed next to £1,000 cash and my £20 burner phone. I looked around at the rest of my room and told myself, "It's me that is lost." The clothes are in the right place, it's me that should be somewhere else.

I needed to upgrade my surroundings. I decided to get a shower to wash off all the tiny hair that were starting to irritate my neck on my collar line from getting my haircut; plus, I didn't want to get hair on my new expensive clothes. While in the shower, I heard the elevated female voices laughing and talking, which told me that my Auntie Delma had arrived. When I had washed the soap off my almost bald head, I got out the shower and started getting ready. I de-tagged the clothes to put them on. My jeans felt rigid and stiff as though they wanted to keep their shape. Even though I now had them on, I took my trainers out of their smartly presented blue box and put them on.

I didn't even know expensive jeans needed to be broken in. Feeling like a thousand dollars, I joined my mum and Auntie Delma downstairs. "Look at you!" my Auntie Delma said as her face lit up in surprise at the transformation designer clothes had made to my appearance. The smile on her face remained as she scanned my body from top to bottom.

"You like these," I said showing her the sides of my trainers with tiny letters displaying the designer's logo.

"Yes, Cyrus, you look great and all grown up," Delma said still smiling and admiring my attire. My mum's face was full of shock. I think the realisation that her baby boy had come of age had left her almost speechless.

"Where are you going, Cyrus?" My mother finally asked when she had picked her jaw up from the kitchen floor and reattached it to her face.

"Oh, Chris and I are going to meet some girls," I replied smiling and feeling awfully proud of myself. My mum tutted and shook her head. Nothing I could say or do would surprise my mum, especially after the day she'd had. "Mum, could you do me a favour, please?" And grabbed two sleeves of cigarettes to give to Delma. I asked with the facial expression I always used, which was slightly frowning but with an element of pleading. I needed it doing, which from experience usually achieved the results I was looking for.

"Yes, okay, I will grab them in a minute and give them to her before she goes," my mother replied as she sighed in defeat of always giving into my every need.

"Delma, could you come with me for a minute, I want to show you something," I said as I used my hand to gesture that I wanted my auntie to follow me out of the living room. I walked up the stairs and into my room with my Auntie Delma following me. "Have a seat," I said to her as I pointed to my bed as that was the only place to sit down in my room.

Delma looked weird in my room. She looked like a footballer's wife. She had on light brown boots that looked fresh as though she had only wore them today. Her jeans were dark-blue and skin tight. She had a pastel peach-coloured top on with short-sleeves and an expensive-looking watch. She looked far too pretty and well dressed to be sitting in the room she was. Her curly light brown hair was held up on the back of her head in a type of donut-shaped ball. It made her face bright and showed off her perfectly formed facial features. She had clear skin with big blue eyes bright and light, like the clearest morning sky.

"Ssshhh," I said as I knelt down in front of my big brown chest of drawers that was backed into the cupboard with no door in the back of my room. My Auntie Delma just sat watching what I was doing silently. I slid the bottom drawer out completely to expose the piles of money I had left in individual stacks underneath. Reaching inside, I grabbed the biggest pile—£7,500. This was the money for Jason and Jabber. I carefully slid my fingers between the carpet and the note at the bottom of the pile and pulled the stack of money out from under the drawers. I placed it on the bed next to my auntie. Her eyes were telling me that she wanted to say something, as she frowned slightly in disbelief. "One second," I told her, letting her know I wasn't ready to talk yet.

I knelt back down in front of my missing bottom drawer and removed every note I had stashed under them. I had £4,200 that I had saved up over the last few weeks. In addition, I had the £1,200 that was my wages from mine and Chris' ounces sales over the last six days. I took the two separate heaps of money out and sat on the bed next to my auntie to count my wages. "Delma, I'm going to give you this £7,500 to give Jason," I said quietly.

"Okay," she whispered in reply.

"And I want you to take this £5,000 and save it with the £5,000 that you already have saved for me, so that makes £10,000 you will have saved for me, okay?" I asked to make sure we were on the same page.

"Yes, okay, Cyrus," she whispered in reply once more, but now looking down at the stacks of notes that were now lying on their sides due to toppling due to their height.

"Cyrus, what are you going to do with all this money?" Delma whispered as she looked at me like I was absolutely mental.

"I don't know," I said now giggling at her. It was the truth. I didn't know what I was going to do with all of this money. All I knew was I wanted it; and if need be, I was prepared to kill or die for it.

"Let me go and get a carrier bag, because I can't just carry that downstairs," Delma whispered before getting up and going downstairs.

Giving Delma all the money I had saved under my drawers with the money I had left from shopping didn't leave me broke. I still had nearly £1,400 left, £1,400 that I didn't exactly need for anything in particular; plus, my mother now had £10,000 for me, and so did my Auntie Delma. She was now filling a medium-sized carrier bag with more money than it was designed to hold. I gave her a kiss on the cheek and £80 for herself, which rounded the money I would have left to £1,300 exactly. "Cyrus, I'm okay, I don't need any money," Delma said adamantly as she tried to refuse taking any money from me.

"Just take it, please, I want you to get yourself something from me for all the help that you have given me," I said as I got up to go back downstairs.

Chapter 9

"I love you both!" I called through to my mother and auntie as I walked out of the back door of my house to meet Chris. He was already waiting for me. I noticed I was walking more upright as I approached Chris' car. I didn't know whether it was the new trainers I had on or just how I felt within myself, but I definitely felt a new demeanour.

I was walking a lot prouder. My back was straight. It almost felt as though I was pushing my chest out slightly as I walked. "Yes, Cyrus, what do you look like then mate?" Chris said as I got into the passenger seat, and he scanned my attire from top to bottom.

Trying not to smile and keep the composed 'bad boy' image I was now becoming accustomed to, I replied, "I don't know. What do I look like, mate?" I replied looking a bit puzzled as I said it.

"You look like a 16-year-old gangster," Chris said smiling as he extended his fist-to-fist pump me.

"Good, let's hope these girls think the same then!" I said now smiling profusely.

As we started to drive, Chris explained that his mum's brother had friends with market stalls and shops that did a lot of buying and selling. He gave me £80 for the sleeves of cigarettes I had given him to show his uncle. "My uncle will either want £20,000 or £15,000 worth," Chris said.

"Yes, okay, sound. I've got them for him," I replied.

"But what will be my cut for providing the sale?" Chris asked with the same facial expression and tone he always used when asking for something.

"If he buys £20,000 worth, I will give you £2,000; and if he buys 15 grand worth, I will give you £1,500, okay?" I replied as though he was lucky to get that much.

"That's fine with me," Chris replied happily.

We drove back in the direction of the city centre, the same way we had drove to go shopping. I knew we were going to some girl's house that Chris had met through his cousin. Chris' cousin had introduced Chris to the girls, and Chris had took one of their numbers and had arranged to meet the girl and her friends with me. Chris was 18 and almost 19, so he was two and a bit years older than me, that meant whoever these girls were, were also going to be older than me. Chris' cousin wasn't going to be at the house.

"What are these girls like then, mate?" I asked trying to get some sort of insight into what I would be walking into.

"They're proper gorgeous girls, mate, about my age. Their mum and dad are on holiday, so there are three of them at a nice house on the edge of town, having a drink alone," Chris explained like we were onto a winner. The part of town Chris referred to was the richest area in our city, I knew that much, I didn't know one person from this area. As far as I knew, they were all posh people that would have probably went to private schools, and their mums and dads were probably doctors and barristers.

"Sounds good to me, mate; at least we are dressed for the occasion," I said as I fist pumped Chris. I was confident at least I wouldn't look like a scruff from a council estate.

The area in question is a few miles from the city centre, away from the built-up hustle and bustle of city life. "Cyrus, I've got some weed on me. Shall we stop to get a drink to take and cigarettes and rolling papers?" Chris asked.

"Yes, of course, stop at a shop then," I replied agreeing it was a good idea. Almost at the girl's house, we stopped at a decent-sized shop.

"Chris, you go in on your own. I can't be bothered with some dickhead shopkeeper not serving you because I don't have identification with me," I said as the car stopped in the car park. I reached in my pocket and gave Chris £50 out of the £80 he had just given to me for the cigarettes. "I want change," I said while smiling and giving him way more money than he was expecting. As I sat in the car park, I decided to call Jason. I figured out it was a good time to call him as Chris wasn't with me. I didn't want Chris to know who gave me my weed, so calling Jason in front of Chris would almost certainly lead to him asking questions.

"Yes, Cyrus," Jason said as he answered his phone.

"Hi, mate, did you get your money from my Auntie Delma?" I asked trying to speak clearly, so he could hear me. It sounded like he was in a bar or restaurant.

"Yes, I've got it. Thank you, mate, I will get the new batch to you tomorrow; and before you ask, it is better than the last stuff, so don't worry!" Jason had spoken loudly, like he was talking into his phone so I could hear.

"Okay, see you tomorrow, J," I said before hanging up. He was right though; all week I had been so worried about the change of product that I would be selling. I had called him to talk about the new cannabis that I'd have to sell at least ten times; but since I had robbed the Kosovans/Turks, I hadn't even given it a second thought. I was more interested in Chris' uncle buying my cigarettes, and Jabber doing the same. If Jabber wanted to buy cigarettes, I'd get my next load of cannabis for free in theory, so that would be a major, major bonus.

Chris joined me back in the car, bottles clanging against each other. Chris had a big cheesy grin as he passed me a fairly heavy double-bagged carrier bag that must have had at least four bottles inside. "I've got a bottle of expensive vodka, coke and lemonade; oh, and I got was a bottle of champagne… Each!" Chris said with a big smile.

"Champagne?" I asked, not quite sure why he had brought champagne.

"Yes, champagne, Cyrus, girls love that sort of shit… oh, and you owe me £20 because it came to £140" Chris said.

"You spent £140 in a fucking off-licence?" I replied in disbelief.

"No, I didn't, we spent £140 in an off-licence, and you are the dumb one for buying cigarettes when you have already got one million for free, you fucking nutter!" Chris joked. I just smiled instead of replying—there was nothing I could say in reply to that. While driving, Chris took out his phone to start calling someone. "Hi," Chris said in a soft and polite voice that told me he must be talking to the girls we were going to meet. He sped up as he started to take directions, turning left then straight, then right through little but expensive-looking residential streets. I felt the anxiety start to set in as I began to feel nervous. Just the area alone was enough to make me feel out of my depth. We turned left through a little gateway that led into a driveway; stones crunched under the tyres as we started up a tiny driveway towards a house that was humongous.

The driveway was made of tiny yellow-looking stones. The driveway opened out into a big open area in front of the house. The garden around the house had perfectly trimmed grass with trees around the edges. You couldn't tell what the house looked like or the size of the house from the road, but as soon as we turned off the road, Chris and I were speechless. To the left and right of the house was the lawn, with the trees at the back of it that made the house private. The building was easily the size of six or seven houses on my estate. "Chris, who lives here?" I asked remembering I had a voice.

"Cyrus, this house is something else," Chris replied, not answering my question, instead still scanning the building and landscape gardening around the house and driveway.

"Whose house is it, mate?" I asked again.

"Holly's house; she is my cousin's girlfriend's friend," Chris explained as he parked his car.

"Why does Holly live in a house like this?" I asked; my brain was going ten to the dozen. I could have sat and asked him questions all night, but Chris isn't the type of person to entertain that.

"Let's go find out," Chris replied as he opened the car door to get out.

"Who's here?" I asked Chris as he knocked the front door.

"This Holly chick and her mates," Chris whispered realising he had already pressed the doorbell.

The big oak front door opened, and a short blonde girl answered the door. She looked even smaller because of the size of the doorway. She was slim and about 5'5" or thereabouts. She had pretty green eyes and a cute smile. "Hi, I'm Charlie, follow me. Holly and Daisy are in the sitting room," Charlie said in her very well spoken voice. Chris and I didn't say anything; we just looked at each other as if to say 'she's cute, let's follow her then.' Inside the house, it was very spacious. The floor had shiny white tiling, as we turned left from the doorway was the best staircase I had ever seen in a house. The stairs had thick red carpet and a bright chrome handrail. We followed Charlie through to the living room to find two more girls that were dancing in front of a wall-sized TV that was playing music videos. As they saw Chris and me enter the room, they stopped dancing; and the girl I was looking at blushed as she turned to pick the remote control up from the sofa to turn the music down. The music was fairly loud; not that her neighbours would mind as she didn't have any. She was probably an inch shorter than me, but her body was curvy. For her size, her chest was huge. As soon as I walked into the room, she had caught my eye. She was gorgeous.

"Hi, nice to meet you," the third girl said. Her friend had walked in the opposite direction to retrieve the remote.

"Hi, nice to meet you too. I'm Cyrus, what's your name?" I asked her more interested in talking to her friend.

"I'm Daisy," she replied as Chris and I smiled at her and gave her a slightly awkward hug. She was slimmer than the girl she had been dancing with. She had dark straight hair and wore jeans that were tight and came down to her ankles. She had on a white top that just covered her cleavage and came down to her waist; a type of vest top. The other girl joined Chris and me who were just standing in the middle of the living room where Charlie had left us. When we had seen the two girls dancing, we had stopped in our tracks. Charlie had gone over to a table on the other side of the room.

"Hi, Chris, glad you could make it," Holly said as she gave him a hug. "Who is your friend, Chris?" Holly asked as she gave me a once over looking at me from head to toe.

"Oh, sorry, this is my friend, Cyrus. Cyrus; Holly, Holly; Cyrus," Chris said as he made the introductions; as Holly looked at me, I felt an instant connection, like we were meant to be; staring Holly in the eyes made me feel warm inside.

"You want a drink, we brought some champagne?" I asked. She had on grey shorts with a matching top. Her hair was light brown and curly.

"Yes, of course, who is going to say no to champagne?" Holly replied as she smiled; she had dimples in her cheeks which made her even more appealing to me.

The living room had a TV on the stand in front of you as you walk in. It was positioned in front of the slightly to the left. It had thick cream carpet which had a big black fluffy rug, probably half the size of my living room floor home. It had what must have been a black, seven-seater, corner leather sofa positioned in an 'L' shape. Holly and Daisy had been dancing on the rug in front of the TV. On the wall, further in the living room was a giant mirror. It was on the other side of the fireplace that was in the middle of the wall facing where the sofa finished, and in the back of the room was a glass table with black leather-covered chairs. The carpet stopped just before the table and a wooden floor started; they looked expensive like everything else about this house. Chris and I followed Holly over to the table at the back of the living room where her friends Daisy and Charlie were now sitting, having a kind of girly consultation.

"Chris and his mate, Cyrus, have got us some champagne. Daisy, could you grab some champagne flutes from the kitchen, please?" Holly asked as I placed the bag on the table and started taking the bottles out.

"You guys brought vodka as well?" Holly asked when she saw me pull out the expensive vodka from the bag.

"We wasn't sure if you girls liked champagne, so we got two bottles of champagne and a bottle of vodka just in case," Chris added. "Holly, do you mind if Cyrus and I roll a joint?" Chris asked. Chris loved to smoke weed and must have spent half his adolescent life either eating or smoking weed.

"You can roll it in here, but you have to smoke it in the back garden," Holly replied.

Chris and I sat down to take in our new surroundings and roll a joint; just behind the glass table were some glass doors leading into the back garden. "That stuff stinks," Holly said, practically as soon as Chris opened the bag of weed he had. Holly had a matching tiny top to her shorts. Both had the emblem of a famous French designer on them in little shiny sequins that looked like diamonds. Daisy returned with five champagne flutes and placed them on the glass table.

"Help yourselves to some champagne. We are just going to pop outside to smoke a joint; come outside if any of you girls want some," Chris said before he opened the glass doors behind the table, and we stepped outside into the garden.

It was late evening. The sun was starting its retreat in the sky, and the air was now cool. I stepped out to look at Holly's garden—it was ridiculous. There was a hot tub to the right. It was a big square tub with a giant leather-looking cover on top of it. There were trees in the distance, and a soothing sound of water trickling coming from a water feature that was in the middle of a small pool-sized pond. We sat down on two of the five garden chairs that were around a wooden garden table on the pavement outside the back door. "Chris, this house is fucking amazing, mate," I said. It was the first thing I had said feeling relaxed since we had pulled onto Holly's driveway.

"I know, mate; the girls are really sexy as well, aren't they?" Chris replied.

"Which one do you like?" I asked Chris as I had a big pull on the joint, hoping to relax my nerves further.

"Well, I've been texting Holly, but I only met her once when her friend and she came to my cousin's house. This is the first time I've met her properly. Which one do you like?" Chris asked realising where this conversation was going.

"I am not going to lie to you, but I think Holly is gorgeous, mate," I said. I was not going to lie or beat around the bush. Chris sighed as I gave him back his joint.

"They are all sexy, Cyrus; what's wrong with the other two?" Chris asked hoping I would change my mind, but my mind was already made up. I was not even going to waste my time answering the question.

"Chris, here's what to do; text Holly and ask her which one of us she likes. If she says you, I will just chat up one of the other two girls? Okay?" I asked Chris trying to find a solution that would benefit me and not piss him off at the same time.

I watched attentively as Chris took out his phone and began to send the message. I stood enjoying the view of Holly's garden— perfectly trimmed grass, little garden lights illuminated a path that ran through the garden; and along the perimeter, the hot tub and the statue of the angel in the middle of the pond pouring water constantly into the pond from its mouth; everything was appeasing to the eye. Chris put his phone back into his pocket. "I have sent the message," Chris said as the door behind us opened; we turned to see Holly standing there with two glasses of champagne in her hands.

"Here you go, lads, and the girls said thank you. They are loving you two for buying us champagne, so thank you so much," Holly said as she smiled and placed the two glasses down on her garden table. "Do you like the garden? The pond is my dad's pride and joy," Holly said as she stared into the distance that was her garden.

"Why is the pond his pride and joy?" I asked without thinking. I could have slapped myself for speaking without thinking, especially to a girl as beautiful as Holly.

"Oh, because he loves his… Coy Carp. I think that's what they're called; he collects them," Holly explained as the breeze caught Holly's hair and moved it back gently. She looked angelic, like a model; I had thought as I stared at her. "Anyway, guys, comeback inside when you have finished. It's a bit cold out here for me," Holly said as she turned to go back in through the glass doors.

"Holly, you've got a text message, go inside and read it," I said as confidently as I dared. Holly went back inside as Chris turned to face me.

"You are funny, Cyrus," Chris said as he looked at me in shock.

"I want to know what she is going to say. If she don't like me, I'm going to drown myself in that pond," I joked as Chris finished his joint and laughed at me. We picked up our champagne flutes and made a toast; while in fact, I made a toast 'to the finer things in life' before we 'clinked' our crystal flutes together and took a big sip of our champagne.

"Errr… Chris, why do rich people drink this shit… it's too fizzy and taste too sharp," I said in disgust.

"I don't know, probably because it's expensive. We spent a £100 on it, so we might as well drink it," Chris replied.

"You can say that again!" I agreed.

We got up from the garden chairs, ready to go back inside, when Chris' phone 'bleeped'. Chris took the phone out from his pocket. "Is it a text message?" I asked eagerly.

"Yes, it's a text from Holly," Chris replied showing me the screen. We both peered at Chris' phone screen as he pressed 'read' to open the message.

"I like Cyrus; and my mate, Charlie, likes you, Chris," we both read at the same time. I was ecstatic that she liked me. I was also happy that the little blondie with the green eyes liked Chris.

"You jammy bastard, that Charlie is okay though, she's cute," Chris said as we walked back into the living room to join the three girls. When we got back inside, I felt nervous again. I wanted Holly to fancy me and not Chris, but now I knew she did it made me feel really nervous. I didn't know what to do with myself. In through the doors leading back inside the house, I sat down at the glass table. One of the girls were sitting at the table texting or clicking something on her phone. I couldn't help but think how beautiful Holly was; she was over the other side of the living room sat on the big corner piece sofa, talking to the short blonde girl that had let us in—her name was Charlie. I guessed they were talking about Chris and me; it was the little blonde one that Holly said liked Chris.

"Chris, I might have a vodka and coke, mate; I'll have some champagne later," I said to Chris, purely to make conversation. I wanted to talk to Holly, but I didn't know how to go about it.

"Cyrus, drink the champagne. We have had a good month, and we are celebrating; plus we've got some gorgeous girls here," Chris said as he leaned over to me so Daisy couldn't hear a word of what he'd said. The girls had turned most of the lights off in the living room by the time we had come back into the house. The dimly lit living room, combined with the music playing in the background provided the perfect atmosphere. The short blonde girl got up from the sofa and walked towards me, leaving Holly sitting on the sofa alone. "Cyrus, do you want to go and speak to Holly?" Charlie asked.

"Yes, of course," I replied as I got up; holding my champagne flute and walked over to the sofa.

"Hi, Holly," I said as I sat down beside her.

"Hi, Cyrus," Holly said as our eyes met.

"I'm so glad you didn't say you liked Chris," I said, thinking I should get that out there as quick as possible.

"Really, Chris is lovely, but I don't like him like that. When I saw you, I thought you are hot," Holly explained confidently.

I was flattered. "When I saw you when I came in, I thought the same about you; especially when I saw you shaking your bum in your little shorts," I said flirtatiously. Holly giggled instantly.

"I know. How embarrassing. Charlie didn't even tell us that she was answering the door," Holly explained.

"Cyrus, you are a bit younger than me, aren't you?" Holly asked. *Shit,* I thought to myself as I realised this could be a deal breaker. *Think fast,* I told myself.

"What makes you say that? How old are you?" I asked as I tried to deflect her question as best I could.

"It's nothing bad, you've just got such a cute baby face that it makes you look young, but I can tell you are a bad boy! And I am 18," Holly explained.

"What makes you think that I am a bad boy?" I asked liking the fact she could tell I was different.

"Well, you are wearing all designer clothes; and when you got rolling papers out of your pocket, you had a ridiculously huge pile of cash on you. I saw it when you took it out to get the rolling papers," Holly explained.

Holly and I sat talking for hours about everything from our families to school to close friends and about our dads. We seemed to get on so well, it was like we had known each other for years. We sat drinking champagne for the first hour until the bottle was empty. "You are really beautiful, Holly," I had said before leaning in to kiss her. Holly's lips were soft as I slid my tongue into her mouth as I held her by the back of her neck and slid my hand through the back of her thick, soft dark hair. We stopped kissing and sat back and smiled at each other—the attraction was mutual. Holly liked the chubby, mixed-race drug dealer, and I liked the well-spoken, curvy, tanned posh girl with the big tits and matching house.

"Cyrus, I want to show you something," Holly said as she got up and grabbed me by the hand. As I followed Holly, she led me back towards the front door that Chris and I had come in through. While getting up, I could see Chris and Charlie were sitting at the glass table talking. They both looked a little bit drunk and in deep conversation while he was rolling a joint. I followed sexy Holly towards the front door.

"You have to take your trainers off," Holly ordered as she started up the luxurious red staircase.

"Shall I come with you?" I asked, just to make sure I had the right and of the stick. I had to pinch myself to make sure that this stunner actually wanted me to follow her upstairs.

I felt like the cat with the cream as I followed Holly upstairs, eyes fixed on the back of her tiny shorts. At the top of the stairs, she turned and opened a door and switched the light on. The bedroom was fit for a king—a big king-sized bed that almost came up to my chest in height, a mirrored-wardrobe opposite the bed and big oak bedside tables with a big-screen TV suspended on the wall. "Come on," Holly said as she walked through the room to open a door that was in the room to the left. I followed her in the room to find it was an en-suite bathroom with what must have been a five-person Jacuzzi in it. "Cyrus, I would have took you in the hot tub in the garden, but it's not private enough with them downstairs. I want us to be alone," Holly said as she started to kiss me again passionately. The bathroom was as big as my living room in my house. When I first looked into the en-suite, I could have just stood there and looked around, but Holly didn't give me chance. "Cyrus, put the Jacuzzi on while I run downstairs. I'll be back in a few minutes," Holly said before leaving the room excitedly.

I was left in the bathroom, feeling tipsy while staring around at the spotlessly clean, white-tiled room. The floor tiles were speckled with tiny pieces of gold. The bathroom had a walk-in shower at the back to the left that was enclosed behind big glass doors. In front of the shower was a toilet. Right of the door when entering the en-suite was the sink with a mirror above it, which had lights built into the frame. In the back of the room on the right was the giant tub that was the Jacuzzi. I walked over to the tub, leaned inside to push the chrome circle down that was a slightly raised drainage hole to make sure it would hold water I was about to put into it. Turning the first oversized tap, water gushed out into the tub, like a small power waterfall pounding the base of the tub. I checked the water temperature to see if it was warm.

I heard Holly as she came through the bedroom, and I turned to greet her. She was holding a pink-coloured bottle of what looked like wine and two glasses. "I brought these up, so we can have a glass of rose together if you want?" Holly asked as she rejoined me in the bathroom.

"Why not?" I replied. I was tipsy and in her house; it was the nicest house I had ever been in. I probably would have agreed to anything she would have suggested.

"You didn't put any bubble bath in there, did you, Cyrus?" Holly asked as she put the bottle and glasses on the side that housed the sink.

"No, just water," I answered, not quite sure why she'd asked. It did cross my mind to put some bubble bath in, but I didn't want to start touching stuff. It seemed cheeky.

"That's good because if you put too much in, it will cover the whole of upstairs in bubbles when I turn the jets on. I wanted us to soak in the tub with a glass of wine, Cyrus," Holly said as she switched the lights off in the bathroom, just leaving the light coming from the large frame around the mirror and open doorway.

The room looked so romantic. Holly opened a bottle of some lavender bathing oil and poured some into the Jacuzzi which was now full. As I poured us a glass of wine each, Holly slid her shorts down to the floor. I couldn't help but to watch as she took her shorts completely off and her small matching belly top to which left her standing there in her matching peach-coloured bra and thong. I was left lost for words. Her tanned skin looked so soft and firm, her hips were curvy, and her chest looked even bigger now that she had taken her top off. She put her hair to the side in front of her and climbed into the tub elegantly. "Cyrus, get in here with me," Holly said softly. After giving Holly her glass of wine, I got undressed, leaving only my boxer shorts on. "Cyrus, have you got another pair of boxer shorts?" Holly asked as she saw me about to get into the hot tub in my underwear.

"No, why?" I asked.

"So, you will get them wet; you might as well take them off," Holly suggested coolly—she had a point. Having wet boxer shorts when I got out the tub wouldn't be the smartest thing I had ever done, so I took them off, covering myself slightly with my hands as I climb into the Jacuzzi. Now under the cover of the lavender-smelling water. Holly leaned across and pressed a button that made the hot tub start to vibrate quite fiercely. The powerful jets caused eruptions of bubbles on the surface of the water. *This is the life,* I thought as I looked across at Holly. The lighting in the room was perfect; it was dim and low-lit, so was the beautiful girl across from me. She had gorgeous eyes and hair and the most perfect smile. Being massaged by the powerful jets, Holly and I sat and spoke while drinking rose.

"I could get used to this," I said as I started to feel more relaxed.

Chapter 10

I awoke the following morning with a sore head from all the wine I had drunk the night before. I rolled over to see Holly was still asleep next to me in the giant queen-sized bed in the room we had come through to get to the Jacuzzi. I wondered where Chris was. The night before was a blur as my brain started to wake up properly. I remembered bits of what had been said between Holly and me. I had images in my head of what had happened before we had fallen asleep. I was in need of a glass of orange juice and some breakfast. I planned to find Chris and go for breakfast with him. The night before had been great, but today was another day.

I hoped Chris' uncle would buy the £20,000 worth of stolen cigarettes he had ordered. Also I hoped Jabber would buy the £10,000 worth if Jason had sorted it out with him. For me, that was better than anything. "Holly," I said in a soft voice to wake her. Holly moved slightly and rubbed the side of her face. Clearly she had awoken with the same sore head and hangover that I had.

"Good morning, Cyrus," Holly said as she lifted her head from the pillow.

"I'm going to go and find Chris. I'll leave you to rest, okay?" I said as Holly put her head back down on the pillow. I found my clothes hung over the ottoman at the bottom of what I can only guess was her mum and dad's bed. I put my clothes back on and started down the thickly carpeted staircase.

I found Chris asleep on the big, black corner-piece sofa in the living room. He was spooning the blonde girl that had answered the door to us. The glass table in the back of the room was a mess; champagne flutes and empty bottles of vodka and coke scattered on top of it. "Chris, it's time to get up, mate," I said in a far-sterner voice than I had used to wake Holly. I nudged him by his shoulder to wake him. "Chris, get up, mate; we've got a big day today," I said again in the same tone. Chris woke up, looking groggy. I watched as he scanned the room as I had not quite sure where he was.

"Cyrus, what time is it?" Chris asked as he squinted and stretched. The girl in front of him was still sleeping as he got up, trying not to disturb her too much, which he didn't achieve due to his size. She stirred slightly and clearly didn't know what was going on.

"Chris, let's go, let's go get breakfast and start work," I said, keen to get the ball rolling in terms of business. Along with the sale of my stolen cigarettes, I also had to get a new batch of cannabis from Jason and his Uncle Jabber.

My itinerary for the day meant that I did not have the time to be lounging around with the girls, regardless of how prestige they were. "Okay, let's go, mate, is Holly still asleep?" Chris asked after making sure he had everything.

"Yes, mate, I would be as well if I didn't have so much to do," I replied. Back in the car, we sat exchanging stories about the events of the night before. Chris told me he had an interesting night, but it wasn't quite as interesting as mine. We laughed and joked about the finer details of our intimate encounters. I told Chris that after our Jacuzzi together, Holly had showed me her dad's watch collection. He had solid gold Swiss, German and French watches, some of them were diamond encrusted, but all of them were pristine and housed within a case sitting on individual cushions. "He's a senior aircraft engineer," Holly had told me.

We carried on talking about the night before, talking about possible future outings to Holly's house over breakfast. Our topic of conversation changed to business quickly.

"Ring your uncle, Chris, and see how much he wants to spend, so I can get the cigarettes ready," I said as we finished our breakfasts. We were in a decent café near town, the type that has plastic tablecloths and middle-aged women with hairnets whizzing around the tables with full English breakfasts and tea and toast. It wasn't a dump of a café, and the place was clean and tidy. I decided to call Jason even though I was sitting next to Chris. I figured he was still a little groggy from the night before; and I was going to be talking about cigarettes, not cannabis. Plus, Chris was busy trying to call his uncle. We both sat there with our phones pressed against our ears with empty breakfast plates in front of us and half-empty cups of tea. "Hi, mate," I said as Jason answered his phone.

"Are you okay, Cyrus?" Jason asked in reply.

"Yes. I was just wondering if you have sorted the new stuff out. And if you have spoken to your Uncle Jabber about the cigarettes?" I asked speaking slightly mumbled and cupping the phone with my hand, so Chris couldn't hear my every word.

"Yes, it's sorted, you can come and pick up your weed in the next hour, and my uncle wants £10,000 worth of cigarettes," Jason said as though he had just remembered.

Yes! I thought to myself.

"Okay, I will bring them to yours when I come to pick up my stuff," I said before hanging up the phone. I was already feeling giddy inside with the morning's productivity so far. I had only been awake an hour.

"Cyrus, you better give me £2,000 because you love me, and I introduced you to Holly, because my uncle said he wants £20,000 worth of cigarettes at 2:00," Chris said, now off the phone and smiling as he leaned back in his small wooden chair contentedly.

Chris and I looked out of place in the café. We were still wearing our new designer jeans and T-shirts that were made by the same designers, but different colours and patterns. I still had my new jeans and trainers on. There were mainly old people in the café reading newspapers and drinking tea. I liked to go for breakfast whenever Chris and I were together early enough, which wasn't often.

Back in the car, we headed back towards our side of town.

"Chris, drop me at mine. I'm going to get a shower; then I'll have them cigarettes ready for your uncle for 2:00, and I will give you £2,250, not 2,500; we will meet in the middle," I said as I smiled at Chris and puffed on my cigarette. It was at this time that I felt the first feelings of my standard of life improving. My skin felt soft and smelled of lavender. I felt well rested from sleeping in the quality of bed I had slept in. I didn't feel hungry anymore as breakfasts had seen to that—I generally felt good within myself. My agenda for the day was to serve Chris' uncle his batch of cigarettes, then Jabber his batch of cigarettes and pick up the cannabis and give it to Chris and Daniel. Then I planned to get an early night after working out how much money I had to the nearest pound.

The weather was cool and windy for a summer's day as I stepped out of Chris' tiny car to go into my house. "Bye, mate, I'll see you in about an hour," I said as I peered in through the open door before closing it. "Back to normality," I said to myself as I opened our poorly constructed back gate. The place looked small and depressing as I walked into our garden. I knocked on the back door by tapping on one of the nine pieces of glass in the top of the door. The door was wooden at the bottom and had individual square pieces of glass in the top. My brother, Daniel, answered the door.

"Good morning, Cyrus. Where did you sleep last night? Mum's been asking where you were; she said you went to meet some girls with Chris," Daniel told me as we walked through the kitchen.

"Come upstairs to my room," I said as Daniel followed me upstairs.

We sat down on my bed constructed from hollow tubes of metal as I explained what I had done the night before. "I'm coming next time you go there," Daniel said at the point I was telling him about the hot tub in the garden, and how pretty the girls were. I continued to tell my brother what I had done all the way up until walking through our back gate. "Where did you get your new clothes from, and your trainers are really nice?" Daniel asked before doing what everybody had done I had seen since I put them on—looking at me from top to bottom, then bottom to top.

"I got them from town," I replied, "where is Mum?" I asked quickly to try and get a handle on where my business stood in terms of selling my stolen cigarettes.

"She is over Trish's house," Daniel said as he stood up and left me alone to get changed and ready for the day. The feeling of restlessness had returned to me much to my distress. It was almost a stomach-churning feeling of missing something, like a slight anxiety that I could never get a hold of. I concluded it was because I had £30,000 worth of cigarette sales to do. On top of that, I had to get a new load of cannabis for my workforce to supply.

"Hi, Mum, I'm back home now," I said in a happy and cheerful tone.

"Okay good, Cyrus, we have sold another £5,000 worth, and the same guy will have another £5,000 worth later," my mother informed me as I could hear her stop counting money and Trish's voice in the background.

"Are there many cigarettes left?" I asked still finding it hard to believe I had generated so much cash in from them.

"Cyrus, there is absolutely loads, it's going to take a while to shift all of these," my mum replied as if she thought I was being sarcastic asking if there was many left.

"Chris' uncle is going to come and buy £20,000 worth at 2 o'clock, then my mate is going to come for £10,000 worth later, will I have enough to supply their need?" I asked, hoping the answer would be yes.

"I will count them out, but I am sure there will be enough and a lot more," my mother confirmed.

"Brilliant, can I give them your phone number to sort it out? They will bring the money with them, and can you sell them from our house as I don't want anybody to know where they are being kept?" I asked and suggested.

"Okay, as long as they are not dodgy or idiots," my mother replied. I always had a talent for delegating jobs.

"Mum, I will sort you out a nice chunk of money for helping me when these are sold, okay?" I said feeling very grateful for what she had done for me.

"Okay, Cyrus," my mother replied in her 'stop patronising' voice. We both put the phone down, and I called Jabber directly. It didn't make sense calling Jason to call Jabber. I only still called Jason about the weed because that was what I had always done. So, it made sense to just keep doing it; plus, he had gone out on a limb to get me cannabis when I had nothing, so I didn't want him to think that I had just forgotten about him.

"Hi Jabber, how are you doing, my friend? It's Cyrus," I said in a solid and confident tone that demanded respect.

"Oh hi, Cyrus, I was just thinking about you, and you called me. Have you seen the new stuff yet?" Jabber asked assuming that was why I had called him. It was the only reason I had called him before, so he had fair reason to assume that was what this call was about.

"No, not yet, I'm getting it in the next hour, but I was calling you to see what time you wanted to come and buy these cigarettes as I have got them here for you?" I said in the same tone that demanded to be treated as an equal. Jabber paused for a few seconds while thinking.

"Have you got them there now?" Jabber asked in his deep and bass-filled tone.

"Yes, I've got them here," I replied.

"I will come and get them now. I've got £10,000 here, so I will leave now. Your house is the first left after that shop on the main road, isn't it?" Jabber asked.

"Yes, take the first left after the shop, then go straight down to the bottom of the road and turn right, and it's the last house on the right," I replied, with no care in the world that he'd know where I lived.

"Mum, bring 256 sleeves over to the house, please. My mate is going to be here in ten minutes," I said as soon as my mother answered the phone.

"Okay, is he going to call me, or are you going to sort it out?" my mother asked. Trish's house was directly across from the front of our house, and one house to the right if you are standing in front of our doorway.

While waiting for my mum and Jabber, in that order hopefully, I decided to have a shower. I was in and out in under five minutes. Two more minutes later, I was dry and mostly dressed. Back in a tracksuit, I felt comfy feeling the soft material against my body. The jeans looked nice, but they felt rigid, like they restricted movement slightly. *Shit,* I thought as I heard my dad's voice downstairs.

"Cyrus," my dad called to see if I was home.

"I'm up here, one second, I'm coming downstairs now," I called down the stairs to my dad. I put my tracksuit's jumper on and started down the thin creaky staircase. As I neared the bottom of the staircase, the front door opened that was directly at the bottom of the stairs. My mother and Trish came in holding giant bags. They put them down in front of the cupboard next to the stairs and went back out of the house. *Why did my dad have to come back now and not in half an hour?* I thought as I walked into the kitchen to see what he wanted.

"Good morning, Dad," I said trying to act happy to see him.

"Are you all right? I've just been to the market. I've got papaya and honey mangoes, and I'm going to cook some curry mutton with rice and gungu peas," my dad was suspiciously happy. (Papaya is a fruit from the Caribbean, and honey mangoes are bright yellow mangoes that grow mostly in the South East and are very sweet. Curry mutton is lamb curry with Jamaican spices, and gungu peas are little peas otherwise known as black-eyed peas.)

"It sounds lovely. I'm going to be pottering around the house today. I'm just waiting for my mate buy some cigarettes," I explained to my dad. It was better for me to tell him instead of it surprising him. If I told him, he would have less grounds to start moaning and nagging.

I expected Jabber to arrive any minute, so it wasn't like I had much of a choice. No sooner had I thought that then my mum and Trish re-entered the house with the last bags of cigarettes. My phone rang, with Jabber calling me. "Is it all right if my mate comes in to buy these cigarettes?" I asked my dad. He seemed to be in a strangely good mood, which would have made me an idiot not to take advantage of it. "Hi, Jabber," I said sounding pleasant and innocent because my dad could hear me.

"I'm outside, mate," Jabber replied.

"Okay, I will come out to show you which house it is," I said purely for the benefit of my dad's ears.

I put the phone down, started out the back door. I wanted to tell Jabber not to mention weed in front of my dad because he would drop me in the shit. I met Jabber as he opened our warped back gate. "Mate, my dad is in, don't mention weed," I whispered trying not to lose too much face.

"No problem, Cyrus, I won't," Jabber replied as he manoeuvred his wide frame through our gateway. Jabber followed me through the back door and around the corner into the kitchen.

"Fucking hell, son," Jabber said as his eyes lit up at the sight of my father. My dad smiled at Jabber; no way near as happy as Jabber was to see him, but that was my dad's nature—reserved and cold personified.

"Long time, no see, Jay," my dad said as the two of them shook hands and gave each other a manly hug. It looked like a polar bear hugging a grizzly bear. Jabber's big gold bracelet jingled as they shook hands.

"I can't believe Cyrus is your son. Now that I look at him, I can see it as clear as day," Jabber said as he stared at me; then my dad in turn while shaking his head in disbelief.

"I know, small world, hey, Jay? Cyrus told me his friend was coming to buy some cigarettes, I didn't expect that friend to be you," my dad said. Jabber was standing there with a carrier bag that looked heavy due to the amount of money inside of it. The money was concealed in the bag though, due to being wrapped up in plastic and then put inside the carrier bag Jabber was holding.

"Cyrus knows my nephew, little Jason, that's how I know him, Calv," Jabber lied; well more accurately told half of the truth.

"Cyrus, why didn't you tell me Calvin is your dad—he is the real deal," Jabber said while looking at me. I was still standing feet planted to the spot they had been when I realised they knew each other.

"Just cool," my dad said to Jabber. Letting him know blowing his trumpet was not needed. "Jabber, if you ever hear his name, let anyone know this is my little boy, and tell them 'don't fuck about', all right, mate? I'm off the streets now, but I want you to watch out for him, okay?" my dad said to Jabber with the same stern look he gives me when I'm getting a warning. I knew my dad had been dodgy years ago, but I could never have imagined him giving Jabber a direct order. Jabber was about 18 stones and about 6'0" with a bald head; he wasn't the type of guy you'd tell to do anything. I left the two of them talking and went around the corner into the hallway to get Jabber's cigarettes that my mum and Trish had left outside of the cupboard by the stairs. Making two trips, I put them on the floor near the wall where Jabber was standing.

"How many sleeves are there, Cyrus?" Jabber asked, softer-spoken than ever before.

"There is meant to be 250, but I've gave you six extra sleeves for free, Jabber," I said it like I had never done business with him before or had a decent conversation with him.

My dad was watching us out of the corner of his eye as he was putting things in the fridge and pottering around the kitchen. "Okay, looks good to me," Jabber said as he flicked open the bags to give his goods a quick inspection. "Here is the money, mate," Jabber said as he put the carry bag he was still holding on the dining room table which made the sound of a phonebook dropping on the table as it rested on the hard wooden surface.

"Cyrus, will you give me a hand putting these in my car?" Jabber asked. I hadn't said much since he had come into my house; the fact him and my big black dad had known each other had put me on the back foot from the get go. "Calvin, nice to see you, pal. I'll give your Cyrus my number. If you need anything, don't hesitate to give me a call," Jabber said as he picked up three large bags with ease and started around the corridor towards the back door. He placed the bags on the floor to get his car keys out to open the car. I wasn't sure what to say to him if anything, and there was a slight awkward silence between us.

"Cyrus, I can't believe that is your dad. He is one of the most feared men in this city," he said as he threw the bags on to his back seat.

"Really?" I asked shocked he thought so highly of my dad.

"Cyrus, he's a gunman and had been for years. I heard he got married and settled down years ago, I would have never guessed it was your mum he got married to," he said timidly. His whole persona had changed in ten minutes—he looked smaller and weaker. Almost deflated, he generally had a respect for my dad that was verging on fear.

I wasn't scared of my dad, so if Jabber was scared of him, then I wasn't scared of Jabber, seeing him act like a scared puppy in front of my dad made me lose the little bit of respect I did have for him. "I knew he messed around with guns in the past, but I didn't know he had major street cred," I sympathised with Jabber.

"Cyrus, your dad is a fucking warrior on these streets, it wouldn't surprise me if he had a gun on him when he was in the kitchen cooking. He's a fucking gangster!" Jabber said seriously as he climbed back into the driver's seat of his car, which looked like a tight squeeze even though the seat was almost certainly all the way back.

"Nor me, to be fair," I replied thinking well. I know he had a gun upstairs, so it was hardly impossible for him to have it in the kitchen, was it?

"All right, Cyrus, you take care, and call Jason when you're ready to grab your new cannabis; and if your dad ever finds out, then this has got fuck all to do with me, okay? And tell Jason the same," Jabber added before closing his door. I nodded to let him know I understood.

I looked at my dad in a different light as I walked back into the kitchen. I sat down at the table to open the carrier bag that Jabber had left on the table. My dad was chopping onions to cook.

"Cyrus, I've known that man for nearly 20 years, you know?" my dad asked.

"Really, I didn't know that you two would know each other."

"Cyrus, he's a fairly big drug-dealer. I know anyone he speaks to is dodgy; so if you talk to him, I know you are dodgy, and you are up to stuff," my dad continued. There was no way I was going to try to insult his intelligence. He was having a man to man with me, reasoning with me, it would be nothing short of disrespect to tell him he was wrong or had the wrong end of the stick. "So, whatever business you and Jay have, be careful; and remember, anyone in the drug game has only their own interests at heart, and only their own interests, so be careful and know what you are doing at all times," my dad said as he continued to cook, occasionally stopping to look at me to check I was listening properly, and he had my full attention.

"Yes, I understand," I agreed. I started to rip the bag of money open that I had taken my hands off when my dad had started talking to show listening to him was my primary concern.

"So, how many cigarettes did you steal?" my dad asked as he looked at the almost phonebook-sized pile of cash on the table.

Jabber had put the money into thousand-pound piles with a £20 note around each thousand, then put a pile of 5,000 stacked high next to an identical pile. He had then wrapped Clingfilm around both piles, so it looked like a book made out of money wrapped in Clingfilm.

"Well, after Chris' uncle comes to buy some, I'll have £35,000, but I should have some left still, so I'm not exactly sure." I said trying not to sound too happy and let him know I was aware of the risks.

"What are you going to do with your money?" my dad asked.

"I'm going to give it to Mum to look after for me, and I've promised to give her some for you both," I said which I knew would make him happy. He earnt £400 a week at work, so I knew any large contribution of cash would be more than welcomed and appreciated.

"Okay, just be careful of what you are doing. I don't want to put myself into trouble because someone wants to hurt you," my dad said as he looked at me with a look that told me 'you know what I mean', and I did. What he meant is, 'don't make me raise my gun over your bullshit, Cyrus'.

"Dad, I will make sure that doesn't happen," I said as I tried to reassure him.

"Do you know anybody that has good weed? I know any 16-year-old who has 30 grand of illegal money and knows big Jay has weed to sell; your dad is not an idiot," he asked. I had to respect him. He wasn't nagging me or having a go at me. He was reasoning with me. I smiled as I thought about what Jabber had said. *He's a fucking gangster!* I thought as I was left quietly sitting at the table in our kitchen.

"I will call Chris and tell him to drop a 20 bag off to the house," I said as I smiled, being totally honest with him. He just stopped chopping vegetables and looked at me as if to say 'don't forget I shot you out the end of my dick, little man...don't ever forget that'. My dad had earnt so much respect from me for how he had treated me; the only criticism had been about my safety and well-being, and I couldn't exactly knock him for that. I felt like more of a man at home then I had ever felt in my house as I took my phone out to call Chris. "Yes, Chris, could you bring a 20 bag of weed to my house, please, as soon as possible," I said as he answered.

"Yes, but I will have to pop to the McBride's house to get it because I've got nothing left here," Chris explained.

"Yes, go there now then. I need it in the next ten minutes, and call your uncle; it's 2:00 in half an hour," I ordered.

"My uncle will meet me outside your house. I've already spoken to him. I'll be there in ten minutes, we will speak then," Chris said before hanging up.

My mum came from the living room into the kitchen with Trish and put on the act of looking shocked at the money on the table, purely for my dad's observations. "Cyrus, you are not going to take that money out with you, are you?" My mother asked, knowing my dad was in earshot. I'd have to give her a sensible suggestion to what my plans were for the money.

"No, don't be silly. I'd like you to look after it for me please, then I'll have £25,000," I said calmly and with no hint of being cheeky or arrogant.

My mother approached the table and picked up the piles of money I had just counted and returned to the living room with Trish. I got up from my seat to watch my dad cook. Always having a love of good food made me naturally take a keen interest to good cooking. I studied my dad as he browned onions in hot oil, turning them every 10 seconds. "You have to keep moving the onions and make sure you get to the bottom of the pot, so none of the onion sticks," he had said when they had started to brown slightly.

"Hi, Calvin," Chris said to my dad as he entered our kitchen.

"Hi, Chris, you all right? How you doing?" my dad replied as he turned to acknowledge Chris.

"Give that 20 bag of weed to my dad, Chris," I said much to the shock of Chris.

Chris didn't even flinch as he put his hand in his pocket to get the two £10 bags. "Here you go," Chris said to my dad who had turned to face him. My dad took the two bags from Chris and lifted them to his nose as he looked Chris in the eye.

"Is this the same weed that you and Cyrus are selling?" my dad asked. My dad had said it in a way that would have led Chris to believe I had told him everything. It was blatant manipulation, especially because I had just told Chris to give him the two bags of weed. *Cheeky bastard,* I thought as I stood watching with mixed feelings of shock and admiration. I couldn't believe what I had just witnessed. My dad was using *my* manipulation skills on Chris. *I thought I was the only manipulator around here!* My dad had just watched me tell Chris to give him the weed, then took the weed from Chris as he looked Chris in the eye, put the weed to his nose while still looking Chris in the eye and said, "Is this the same weed that you and Cyrus are selling?"

The cheek of it, I thought; and worst of all, there's nothing I could say or do. Anything I could do or say would be instantly accepting defeat, unless of course Chris was to say 'no…what are you going on about?' which there was more chance of a leprechaun knocking on our front door riding a unicorn.

"Yes, that's the same stuff, isn't it, Cyrus?" Chris asked as he looked at me for confirmation. As he did so, Chris looked a bit confused, like he assumed I had told my dad I was getting Chris to drop 'our' weed off, instead of 'some' weed off, Chris assumed! Just like my dad had wanted him to, I wasn't worried about the repercussions because my dad wouldn't have asked if he didn't already know; and if he already knew, he wouldn't have wanted to get angry. He just looked at me and winked as I looked back at him in defeat. *Yes one—nil, Dad,* I thought as my look of defeat turned into a cheeky smile. My dad winked once more at me while maintaining a poker face and taking in every morsel of self-praise.

"One second, I will be back. I'm just going to tell Mum to grab the cigarettes for Chris' uncle. Have a seat, Chris," I said as I remembered his uncle would be here any minute.

As I walked towards the living room, it dawned on me, I had given Jabber 256 sleeves of cigarettes for £10,000, he had been given six for free. I couldn't expect my mum to carry 500 sleeves of cigarettes from Trish's. "Chris, call your uncle and tell him to make sure that he has room in his car because it's a lot of sleeves," I said after turning around in the tiny passageway at the bottom of the stairs in between the kitchen and living room behind the front door.

"Okay," he said breaking his concentration from being admonished by my father.

"Oh, and I need you to come over the road to carry some of these over here," I said signalling him to get up. I walked back to the living room this time with Chris behind me. "Mum, Trish, I need to go over the road to grab 500 sleeves of cigarettes for Chris' uncle," I said with the same pleading tone that seemed to instil some urgency and importance to any question I asked.

"Yes, come on then," my mum and Trish said as they got up.

"Chris' uncle would be here in ten minutes," I said to let them both know why I was in such a rush. It was only about 30 paces or footsteps from our front door to Trish's back door, so the four of us were inside Trish's living room in under a minute.

"No way, Cyrus! Look how many cigarettes you have got!" Chris said in amazement. He was right; there were loads of cigarettes left. Trish's living room was still half-full, still brown boxes full in towers, still towers of sleeves six per level over shoulder height tall. The big boxes were stacked on top each other three boxes high in each tower.

"You see, Cyrus, there is still loads left. In fact, we haven't sold that much," my mother said as Chris and I looked around.

"I'll count them and pass them towards the sofa, and you three, box them up and recount them," I suggested. I counted up to 100 by counting two sleeves at a time slowly and meticulously. When I had finished, I started again until I had counted five separate piles of 100 sleeves. I assessed what I had left after counting Chris' uncle's pile. The pile that I had left was slightly bigger than the pile for Chris' uncle. After counting the first 100 sleeves, I abandoned the idea of passing them towards the sofa through lack of space and delegated a section of the room just for Chris' uncle's cigarettes. "Let's take these over the road than," I said as I picked up a box full. We made just shy of three trips each to retrieve all the cigarettes for the sale.

"Cyrus, look how much you have stolen," my dad said as he scanned the kitchen floor, realising the scale of the robbery.

"I know. I was only going to take 100, 200 sleeve, but I changed my mind," I joked; my dad just shook his head at me and fought back the urge to smile.

"Can I roll a joint?" Chris asked realising the need to hide anything had passed.

"Yes, but you should smoke it after your uncle has been; you should always do business before pleasure," my father advised. As Chris took out his cannabis and utensils to start constructing a joint, his phone rang.

I only heard half of Chris' conversation as I listened to what he said, but from what I heard, his uncle had arrived.

"One second, I will go and bring him inside," Chris said before getting up and heading out of the back door.

He returned a few minutes later with his uncle. "This is my uncle, Arthur. Arthur, this is my friend Cyrus and his dad, Calvin," Chris said as he gestured with his hand to show who was who. Not that there was any chance of him not being able to work out who the father and who was the son.

My dad extended his hand to shake Arthur's hand. *I would wind Chris up later about Arthur's name,* I thought to myself as I stood up to shake Chris' uncle's hand. Arthur was the same height as Chris at roughly 5'10", which was slightly shorter than my dad. He was white and a little Irish looking, he was wearing a shirt and jeans, and he was fat with his shirt tucked in at the waist but over-hanging slightly where his belly stuck out over the top. He had a red-and-white chequered shirt on and light blue jeans. His head was big and rectangular-shaped like a big chubby block. Arthur had light brown hair all the same length. He was standing holding a big blue shopping bag in his hand like a sort of reusable shopping bag. "Arthur, here are the cigarettes you wanted," I said pointing at the unmissable piles of cigarettes that were taking up a third of the kitchen floor.

"How many have you got there for me, my friend?" Arthur asked as he scanned and opened boxes and looked inside of bags.

"I've gave you 500 sleeves here for you, and then 10 separate sleeves for free, because you are Chris' uncle," I explained. Arthur stood and looked at the piles for a moment before picking out a sleeve randomly and opening the box to check its contents. He opened the sleeve, ripping the clear plastic from the outside of it, then opened the cardboard up and took out a packet of 20 cigarettes; then he opened that up and took out a single cigarette.

"Is it all right to smoke in here, my friend?" Arthur asked looking at my dad for approval.

"Yes, carry on," my dad said as the three of us watched on. Chris and I were sat at the dining table; my dad was leaning against the kitchen side where he had been cooking. Chris's uncle lit the cigarette and took a big pull.

"Here you go, this is your money," Arthur said as he exhaled and walked over to place the bag of money on the table.

I picked the bag of money up and put it on the ground in between my feet to look inside of it. It was almost full to the brim with bundles of notes laying on their sides the whole length of the bag; the bundles had little red paper binders on them. I picked one of the blinded wraps of money up for closer inspection.

"A thousand pounds exactly, all in new notes inside the little red binders with £1,000 written on them."

"Okay, thank you, Arthur," I said as I picked the bag of cash to take it into the living room.

"Could you count this money, please, Mum," I asked as I put the bag on the seat next to her. Not even waiting for a reply, I walked back into the kitchen. "We will give you a hand to your car," I said to Chris' uncle.

Chapter 11

Two months had passed since I had spent the night at Holly's house. I had no cigarettes left; between Chris' Uncle Arthur, Jabber and my mother selling my stolen haul, the cigarettes were gone. The money I had earnt through the robbery combined with the money I had saved from my drug dealing business meant that I had saved £80,000. My mum had £50,000 put away for me, and my auntie had £20,000 put away for me. I had £10,000 in a carrier bag at my feet on the passenger side foot well of Chris' car, and I had £250 of brand-new notes in my left-hand jeans pocket. We had been on the motorway for almost 30 minutes when I saw the first sign saying 'Northampton'. The satnav stuck to the dashboard told us we were five miles away from our destination. John and Tom's cousin was in the back of Chris' car—a skinny, spotty kid called 'Kieran'. He was the same age as Chris at almost 19. After following the satnav for another eight minutes, we arrived at our destination. It was a brand-new housing estate. All of the houses on this housing estate looked similar; they all had yellow bricks with white windows. *Definitely, people with good jobs around here,* I thought as I waited for Chris to call the man he had been speaking to. "Hi, mate, I'm outside number 24," Chris said politely. A skinny, white middle-aged man came out of the house we were parked in front of. The man looked intelligent but somewhat nerdy. He wore a white short-sleeved shirt that was tucked in at the waist and had his hair gelled pointing up at the front. Chris and I got out of the car.

"Wait here, please, Kieran," I said quietly to the McBrides' cousin as I climbed out of Chris' car. Chris had on a dark blue tracksuit, and I was wearing a new pair of designer jeans with a designer T-shirt. I had got the items from my most recent shopping trip with Chris. Two thousand pounds I had spent in the designer clothes shop, it was my own treat to myself. I figured I deserved it for robbing the Kosovos/Turks. They had moved out shortly after I had robbed them.

"It's in the garage, I will just get it out," the nerdy-looking 30-something-year-old said. I had treated myself to £2,000 worth of clothes, but I had made roughly 65,000 from the cigarettes. The contents of this nerdy guy's garage was my main treat.

I watched as the nerdy guy pressed a button on a fob attached to his bunch of keys, and the garage door started to lift. The red high-performance Japanese rally car bonnet was shining. It had little vents in the bonnet that made it look aggressive and angry. I had fell in love with it as soon as Chris had showed it to me. "Look at this monster!" Chris had said showing me a picture of the car on the screen of his phone.

"I'm buying that; call whoever owns that, I'll buy that tomorrow!" I had said leaving Chris gobsmacked. Tomorrow was now today. 'Pop, pop, pop' was the sound the car's engine made as the man edged it slowly out of the garage. It had black wheels that shined in a gloss-finish immaculately, bucket seats and a big spoiler and a big round exhaust, 400 bhp just like Chris had said 'this was a monster!' It was exactly the same as one I had seen in a movie that I had watched.

I had picked my carrier bag up with £10,000 in it as I got out of Chris' car. I walked over to the car's driver side door and said, "You want £10,000 for this, don't you, my friend?" I asked. The man turned the car off.

"Yes, mate, it's only four years old, it's worth £12,000 at least. I just need the money quick, that's why I'm letting it go for £10,000," he said sounding a bit upset at the prospect of selling such a sought after road/rally car.

"Well, here you go. There's £10,000 here, I counted it myself," I said while handing him the bag of money.

We had only been on the make motorway for 25 minutes when we indicated to come off the motorway back into Coventry. We had left Kieran far behind us as we drove out of the nerdy man's housing estate. We imagined he was probably only half his way into his journey back to Coventry. Chris was driving my new car, he had a face like a kid in a sweet shop. As soon as he touched the accelerator, the car would ferociously pin us back into our seats as the turbo would kick in.

The car growled and snarled as we drove. I had only brought the car because the feelings of restlessness and anxiety were becoming too much to bear. I was having trouble getting to sleep at night and constantly feeling tense. The cigarettes had all been sold, giving me no more days of earning £20,000 or £30,000 in a single day. Not that I was ungrateful for the amazing luck I'd had; I just wanted more.

Business was good. I was earning between £600 and £900 a week from the McBride's, and the new cannabis Jabber had given me to sell was even better—'Lemon Haze', Jabber had said it was called. Light in weight, which made our deals look bigger, and it was covered with THC crystals from being dried perfectly, which made the THC look like minute pieces of frost. It had the strength, the look and the taste.

Chris and I were going through 50 ounces every five days minimum. I knew this was doing well, but I didn't feel like I was doing well. I had made £30,000 in one day when I had stolen cigarettes to sell; so after that, it made £1,800 a week feel like I had won the battle but was losing the war.

Whenever I was just sitting down and trying to relax, the feeling of restlessness would come back. I was like an adrenaline junkie that was clucking for his next fix of adrenaline. I had brought this rally car to try to feed this urge and relieve my constant need to feel major excitement once and for all. I was hoping that the novelty would never wear off with this car like it had with Holly, or my business with John and Tom or the business with Chris. It's not that I wanted Chris to stop selling drugs for me, or that I wanted to close my shop at the McBride's any less than I wanted to stop sleeping with Holly. It was just none of that excited me anymore.

I didn't look forward to any of it anymore. I felt like I was missing something, and I couldn't put my finger on it. "I love this car, Cyrus," Chris said, eyes glued on the road.

"It's ferocious, isn't it, mate?" I said agreeing with him.

"Where shall we go?" Chris asked. The time on the dashboard said 7:15 in the evening.

"Go to that nice restaurant I took you the other day," I told Chris in the hope to show off my new car somewhere nice.

"Okay, sound," Chris said as he changed direction and started to drive towards the restaurant. I didn't let Chris drive ridiculously fast when he started to be excessive in terms of speeding. I'd say 'calm down, Chris' or 'stop ragging my car!' I knew I had to learn to drive properly soon. I knew the basics, how to change gear and reverse. I had driven on the main road twice before, once joyriding with other underage kids when I was 15 and once driving sensibly with one of my mum's friend's husband.

Walking towards the restaurant with Chris, I looked back at the shiny red rally car. I told myself I'll be driving that soon. It was a Thursday evening, and there were families everywhere as we sat down to eat. I got Chris to order two cocktails. "That's all the alcohol you are drinking while driving that car," I'd said to him as the waitress left the table without questioning my age. I had put my phone and car keys on the table in front of me as I sat in my £200 T-shirt with matching jeans and trainers. We took our time to eat, mainly talking about girls and business. We spoke about what my dad was going to say when he saw the rally car, or my brother's face when he saw the car. I wanted to say 'I wonder what Jason will think when he's watched me go from getting four-and-a-half ounces of cannabis on consignment to having £70,000 and a rally car', but I didn't. I kept my reserve and held it in. I felt comfortable around Chris, as comfortable as I felt around anybody; but even then I had to keep some things guarded and to myself. I didn't tell Chris who Jason was, and I was never going to no matter how much I let my hair down. As far as Chris knew, it was my aunt's boyfriend who gave me the cannabis. One thing I've learnt is that people believe what they hear if it's backed up with what they've seen.

For instance, I told Chris when we got our first batch of weed to sell to drop me to my auntie's, so I can discuss getting weed to sell in bulk with my uncle. Me telling him I needed to speak to my uncle to get the weed was the first step to him believing, the second step was him coming to pick me up from my auntie's and seeing me come out with the weed. So, in Chris' head, he had worked out it was my uncle supplying us, and, of course, he was wrong.

We finished our food, and I felt just as stuffed as the first time I had ate here with Jason and Jabber. I had steak and shrimp, and Chris, who was putting on weight by the hour, had a mixed grill. As we drove back towards our area of town, I noticed that people were looking at us. People looked as they heard the car's engine as we drove past and smiled or put their hand up to say 'nice car'. Total strangers were acknowledging us with respect, purely judging us on the car we drove. It was the same change in acknowledgement I had received through my recent change of dress sense. I was smart enough to know I was the same person in Chris' car, or my shiny rally car. The only difference was I got no recognition in Chris' car, and in the rally car, everyone seemed to take an interest. *Shallow bastards,* I thought to myself. Admittedly,

I liked the fact I would now turn heads in my new car, and I planned to take full advantage of that.

"Chris, go to my house, please, mate," I said as we entered our area. It was starting to get dark outside. Tomorrow would be Friday, Friday had become the biggest day of the week for me. It was the day we sold the most drugs! Presumably because the majority of people get their weekly wage packet on a Friday afternoon. I planned to get Chris to drive me around in the rally car all day on Friday.

"Let's go and show Tom and John, Cyrus," Chris suggested as we pulled into my street. I think he wanted to continue driving the car as much as he wanted to show John and Tom if I'm honest.

"We will show them tomorrow, Chris, let's park this up outside my house and have a joint while we wait for Kieran to bring your car back," I replied much to the disappointment of Chris. As we parked outside my little cardboard council house, I had mixed emotions. My brother would jump with joy when he saw my new car, but I knew my dad would not be as pleased. I imagined the things he would say. 'Cyrus, that car is going to attract the attention of police and people' or 'how the fuck are you going to explain buying that car at 16' or the almost certainty of 'Cyrus, you haven't even got a fucking driving licence'. Chris and I sat in the car smoking our citrus-flavoured skunk while listening to my favourite song at the time. I felt relaxed, partly because I was now high and partly because the restlessness had gone. The excitement of sitting in the monster that was my new car mixed with the fact that everyone was going to be talking about it fed my need for excitement. This solved my anxiety and feelings of missing out momentarily.

Fifteen minutes after we had parked up, Kieran finally pulled round the corner onto my road. He had gone home to wait while Chris and I had went for dinner. The almost silent tiny engine rumbled quietly around the corner. Chris and I watched as the car approached. Chris' car looked small and puny and slow, especially in contrast to the car we were sitting in. "I guess this is goodbye, my friend," I joked as I turned to shake Chris' hand.

"Okay, I will see you tomorrow, Cyrus," Chris said as he pulled himself out of the bucket seat.

"Chris, because it's Friday tomorrow, you want to do something tomorrow night?" I asked as the feeling of not wanting to go inside my house returned. It was a feeling I always got before I went into my house, but if I had something to look forward to, it made it that little bit easier.

"Yes, of course, what were you thinking?" Chris asked happy in the knowledge he would almost certainly be driving my car.

"I just want to drive around and see who's about at night time," I suggested not knowing what else we could do. We could have went to pick up Holly and Charlie, but I couldn't be bothered with them. I wanted to see someone new, to me 'new' meant 'exciting', and 'exciting' made me 'happy'.

"Yes, I don't mind after I've done all of our sales. We'll definitely do something," Chris replied.

"Cool," I said as I fist-pumped him and got out of the car and locked it with the fob.

I waved at Kieran as I turned to go into my garden through the back gate. He just waved back with a face full of shock, Kieran had always thought I was mental. He was as normal as normal was, whereas I was as different to everyone else as a cat is to a dog. I amazed Kieran, and he was scared of me. Unpredictability scares most people and rightly so, unless it is a quality you personally possess; in which case, it's just admirable.

I spent the next morning pottering around my house, bored. I was tempted to drive my rally car somewhere, but I had nowhere to go. At least nowhere important enough to justify driving. Traffic law states if somebody drives a car with no insurance then that car is liable to be impounded instantly until the owner can collect it with valid insurance after paying the cost of roadside removal and impound fees. Since I had put my dad's name on the logbook when I had purchased the car, I concluded it wouldn't go down too well me saying, 'Dad, could you get my rally car out of the police compound for me, please'. In fact, that would go down like a lead balloon.

Instead, I tried to entertain myself otherwise, sending text messages to Holly for a while, then talking to my brother and showing him my car, starting my car and leaving it to warm-up before revving it, which seemed to send vibrations through about 20 of the cardboard houses it was parked near. I called John and Tom to check on the day's business, I called Chris to see how he was getting on. "Everything is good, I've got three people waiting to see me now," Chris said. My brother had left the house after spending at least an hour inspecting every crevice of my car while maintaining a big smile on his face. The problem with selling drugs and being the boss was that most of the time, your job is to do nothing. If someone were to ask me how business was, a truthful answer would be, 'we are busy, so business is good', but what really annoyed me was Chris was busy. John and Tom were busy; even my brother, Daniel was fairly busy. I, however, was bored shitless. I'd done everything that could be expected of me, calling all my employees to make sure they were 'on job'. I had made sure I knew my money was as safe as humanly possible. I worked out how much drugs I had at each location and estimated when I would need to restock those locations. It all involved making a few phone calls or doing a few calculations on my phone or a piece of paper that I would burn after reading and digesting. All in all, everything I had to do took me no longer than 20 minutes. Yes, I earned more for my 20 minutes then an average Joe would for his eight hours, but at least the average Joe had something to do. I would have happily sacrificed a little of my income for having something to do to stop me being 'so fucking bored'. I decided to sit outside my house with the group whose ages ranged between 18 and 24. They had congregated on the little wall by the stumps outside my house. "Cyrus, that car is absolutely amazing," they had said, and, "you're creaming it, you are, lad." It had made me feel happy as I sat looking at my car in the warm afternoon sun. The weather wasn't hot; just warm enough to feel a slight heat on your skin. The warmth made the air seem that little bit thicker as you breathed. All the people around my estate respected me. If I was a pushover, they would certainly have tried to pick on me; they would have probably forced me to take them for a drive or let them take the car for a drive. Or even made me give them weed for free. They were older than me and physically stronger, but they didn't have the balls or mentality that I had. They didn't even ask for any of the above. If they had asked me to take my car for a drive in jest, of course I would have laughed it off. After all, that would be a funny request, and I'd like to think I had a good sense of humour, but anything serious, for example, 'I'm taking that for a drive', would have ended in bloodshed. If any of these divs ever tried anything funny, I'd go in my house and get my dad's 'machete' from behind the bedroom door and make the person in question eligible for the para Olympics faster than my car could go from 0 to 60mph. These were the thoughts that ran through my head as the six strong adolescent guys laughed and joked with each other around me while drinking beer and talking nonsense.

One of the guys outside my house had a girlfriend with a little blue car similar to Chris', so four of us decided to give her money to go and get us fast food. We sat outside on a two-foot wall eating burgers and chips. I was purely there to pass time out of boredom. Being bored all the time gave me a lot of time to think about expansion. The £2,000 I'd earn in a decent week wasn't the flies around the shit when I made £30,000 in a single day. In comparison, it was like being given a house like Holly's one day then being given a £30 tent the next. 'More was the only cure' in order to stimulate my mind and keep active enough to get rid of the anxiety, boredom and restlessness. I sat eating my food, I thought about possibly opening another shop, just like the one I had turned Tom and John's house into. Also, I considered doubling Chris' workload or perhaps getting more hands on myself. Milling the figures over in my head, I eventually came to the conclusion I was never going to make the sort of money I wanted selling cannabis. That left me with few options, which having already been thinking for so long. I decided not to think about what the options were at this precise minute. The fact that I had come to the conclusion that I needed to think about different options meant I had done enough productive thinking for one day.

Chapter 12

The warmth of the day had completely gone, leaving the cool night air filling the expanses of darkness. It was 9:30 at night; I was leaning against my car's front wing, with the side of my thigh to stop the metal badge on my jeans scratching the paintwork. The phone held against my ear had Holly on the other end mimicking every girlfriend I had ever had. "Cyrus, I really want to see you," Holly had said. It was exactly these type of statements that caused my repulsion, I was a man that wanted what I didn't have, not the things I did have and were begging/pleading for my attention; and at this point, it dawned on me; Holly had become one of those things.

"Baby… I'm going to collect some money in, and the second I'm finished, I'm all yours, I promise," I had told Holly a blatant lie and as empty a promise as any.

Chris walked around the corner from the entry he had cut through to get from his house to mine, which walking probably took him six or seven minutes. Chris was smartly dressed in his jeans and jumper. His legs looked thick, like the trunks of trees where his thighs sat in his jeans. "Babe, I've got to go now, I will call you soon," I said to Holly as Chris got closer, and I terminated my phone call.

"Cyrus," Chris said as he put his hand out to fist pump me.

"Christopher," I replied as I smiled at him and handed him my car keys. Our car doors shut almost simultaneously.

"Where to then, Cyrus?" Chris asked. I didn't have anywhere to go. We were only going somewhere because I was bored; where that somewhere was, I had no idea.

"It's totally up to you, mate," I replied. Chris looked at me in amazement.

"Cyrus, I thought you had somewhere to go, you madman," Chris said frowning slightly as if waiting for me to tell him I was joking.

"Yes, I have got somewhere to go, but it's too early," I lied.

"So where do you want to go?" I asked again in a voice that said I was being truthful. Chris sat to think for a second before starting the car that made growling noises as he reversed it from in front of my garage.

"Where are we going?" I asked as he turned left at the top of my estate onto the main road.

"To the McBride's to get at a bag of weed," Chris replied. We were at the McBride's in under two minutes. Chris held the clutch in and revved the engine as we parked outside the front of the McBride's house. The car sounded loud and aggressive, like somebody was letting off a machine gun. John was at his curtains instantly, looking at what was making the noise. As he noticed it was Chris and me, his smile lit his face up through the square, double-glazed windows. John and his younger brother Tom were outside on the driveway within seconds of us parking up. Chris turned the car engine off, and we got out. Seeing people's reactions to the car made me feel special; it made me feel important.

"Is this your new car, Cyrus?" John asked with a face full of happiness.

"Yes, mate; it's nice, isn't it?" I replied smiling.

"It's great!" John said as he gave the car a visual inspection from wheels to roof and from front to back.

"Go and grab a bag of weed, and then you and Tom come for a drive," I said, "These two lads worked their arses off for me from morning till night. They had been there from minute one. If I was up then so were they, it was only fair they experience the pleasure I was feeling."

"Whatever sales come in can wait 15 minutes," I said as they locked their house door and jumped in the back of the car. "Chris, go to that nice restaurant I like, but let it rip all the way there," I said as I pointed forward at the road, letting Chris know he had no more speed restrictions in place. I watched as the power of the rally car slammed the two McBride brothers into the back seat as Chris accelerated, rendering them both speechless. Tyres screeched as Chris was power-sliding around roundabouts. The car stuck to the road, like glue, and seemed to grip the tarmac from under the tyres as it constantly demanded traction. None of us spoke a word while Chris raced to the restaurant.

Chris' facial expression was serious and fixed on the road as he negotiated straights and corners. "This is the fastest car I have ever been inside, Cyrus," Tom said as Chris slowed down to pull into the restaurant car park.

"I know, it's ridiculously fast," I said agreeing with him.

"We will have a joint in the car park, lads," I said letting everyone know why I had chosen to come to the restaurant. It was better scenery than smoking weed in the McBride's living room; plus that was something we did every day, so the change was nice.

While standing in the car park, we began to speak about our business and families. I was still thinking about expansion, but I didn't mention it as I didn't know how or when this was going to take place. Well-dressed women with boyfriends and husbands walked past us after parking their cars or returning to them. Absolutely everyone paid us some attention, either looking at the car or looking where the smell of the cannabis was coming from or both.

"Nice motor," some guy had said. The man had just parked up a brand new German car similar to Delma's boyfriend, Mervyn's. When the man had said it, I thought to myself, *I wonder what Mervyn will think when he sees my car.*

We had been in the car park for half an hour when my business-brain kicked in. It was a Friday night and instead of my shop being open for business, I had both of my shopkeepers smoking weed in a restaurant car park, so using my better judgement, we got back in the car so I could take the McBride brothers home.

Chris and I had been alone, driving around for nearly an hour after dropping the McBride's home. We had spent the time driving around our city, going from area to area to see what we could find people doing with their Friday nights. Although there were cars on the road, because it was night, they were just passing headlights. All the shops were shut apart from the odd off-licence, and even a lot of the pubs were closed.

"Chris, this is dead out here, mate," I said realising there was nothing to do or see.

"Cyrus, that's because everybody will be partying in clubs in the city centre," Chris replied. *Of course they are,* I thought. The fact everyone would be out clubbing had completely slipped my mind due to the fact I was too young to partake.

"Go to town then," I said excitedly at the fact I wasn't going to have to accept defeat just yet.

Chris stopped driving erratically as we drove closer to the city centre. The noise the car made when accelerating would have almost certainly attracted police attention, and we didn't want that. We decided to go to a car park that was outside of all of the main clubs in the city centre. Chris was right about where everybody was. The place was alive with people; the car park was full of cars as we pulled in. All the car park spaces were to our right, and all the clubs were to our left.

"Pull up here," I had said to Chris, telling him not to pull into where the car park spaces were. Instead I wanted him to park by the kerb that was ten metres away from the clubs and bars. There were girls in short skirts and dresses. Everywhere I looked, all different types of girls—white girls, mixed-race girls, Asian girls, short, tall, brunettes, blondes, redheads; there was literally eye candy for all tastes. The bar to our far left had dark windows and looked the least lively of the four venues we were near. We were parked outside the main bar, and it was buzzing with people. It had giant glass windows along the whole front of the bar, music was blasting out of the two open doors which was the entrance. Outside the front of these bars was illuminated with bright lights, the lights on the top of the buildings and from lampposts had lit up outside the front of the clubs, like it was the middle of the day. Two 'doorman' or 'bouncers', as some people call them, stood either side of the club's two open double-doors. Chrome poles with red rope attached to them ran the length of the front of the place that stopped either side of the doorway. It was used to separate the people standing on the club's side of the rope, smoking cigarettes, from the people on the public walkway side of the road passing. It also allowed the bouncers to police who came onto the other side of the red rope into the smoking area or the bar easily.

This place was 'doing it', I thought as I stared at everything there was to see. Next door was a similar bar, but its doors were closed with bouncers standing outside front. It had older people outside in their late 30s and early 40s. Although this place looked as busy as the place that had my attention; the crowd was less appealing to me. 'Sugar house' had 19-year-old-looking girls and girls in their early or late 20s in and outside. Next door, but one to the right was a big club, but it was inside a complex, so there was nothing to see in terms of what was happening there, other than the 60 to 70 people that were outside on the walkway smoking. Chris was right though—this is where everybody was. "Chris, this bar looks amazing," I said without even taking my eyes off the place.

"Yes, it's meant to be really good in there, Cyrus," Chris said while texting away on his phone.

"Have you been in there before?" I asked eager to get more of an insight.

"Yes, I've been in there twice, but clubbing is not really my thing, Cyrus," Chris replied basically drip-feeding me information.

As I sat thinking how I could incorporate some of this club into my life. I saw a group of people heading towards the door from inside to come outside. One of the guys in the group caught my eye for two reasons. Firstly, he looked different to everybody else; he was wearing black for one thing. I estimated the man was about 5'11" tall and I could see his chain flickering in the light as he reached the entrance; it was sitting on top of his black T-shirt. It didn't look like a thick chain, but it was sparkling as the light hit it, illuminating what I assumed to be diamonds into an array of colours. Behind the Asian man wearing black was a 'stocky' white guy with dark hair. The Asian male did not have a heavy build, he wasn't skinny either. He had a hundred-metre sprinters physique rather than a long-distance runner or a heavyweight boxer. His hair was shaved at the sides and looked about 3" in length at the top. He had a light skin complexion, although his skin was clearly brown, and his straight black hair and facial features told me he was Asian instantly. The man had on a black leather jacket that looked expensive. His whole appearance was just 'glowing'. The Asian man took one step out of the club, and the doorman turned to greet him, shaking his hand and smiling at him respectfully. I could see that this man had a lot of respect in and around these clubs. Following the Asian male outside was the stocky white male in a white T-shirt and blue jeans who had a bright and cheerful smile as he shook hands and seemed to be joking around with the doormen. The Asian man and the stocky white man were also with two girls. These two girls looked like glamour models. The Asian man and the stocky white man were holding champagne flutes, and the girls behind them had a bottle in one hand and their champagne flutes in their other hands.

The girls looked like card girls from a boxing match, both wearing short dresses. The blonde girl wore a black dress, and the brunette had a silver sparkly dress on; they were both gorgeous. The Asian guy had put his champagne glass down and was lighting something to smoke, while the white guy was doing something on his phone. The two girls were just hovering around them. "Chris who are they?" I asked as we both sat staring at the people outside the clubs and bars.

"Who are you on about, Cyrus?" Chris asked as I pointed out the Asian guy and his stocky white mate with the two girls. They looked like celebrities I hadn't seen them before.

"Them two in the smoking area with the sexy girls?" Chris asked, not quite sure who I was looking at.

"Yes, in the black. Asian guy standing next to that stocky white lad in the white T-shirt with the girls," I said making it crystal clear who I was referring.

"I don't know, Cyrus, they look like drug dealers to me, mate," Chris replied as he dismissed the conversation and started to look elsewhere.

"You know what, Chris... That is exactly what I thought," I said while eyes still fixed on the group of four. Chris didn't reply; he was too busy looking at girls and had no interest in some smartly dressed Asian man with his mate standing with two girls that we had absolutely no chance of pulling. But I did.

"I'm going to talk to them," I said while still studying the group.

"What?" Chris asked in surprise.

"I'm going over there," I said again.

"Why, you don't know them, Cyrus," Chris replied as if it was a stupid idea.

"You just wait here," I said as I opened the rally cars passenger side door, took a deep breath and walked towards the group trying to remain composed and confident—inside I felt nervous. Chris was right I didn't know them. I didn't even know what to say to the group. I decided not to walk directly to the entrance because I had seen the doormen turn people away from the club and the smoking area, so I didn't want to look stupid by not even making it past the red security rope. I chose to go to the rope nearest to the Asian guy but remain on public property. I figured that way we would be standing right next to each other with only the red rope separating us below our waist. As I got closer to the Asian man, he turned and looked at me in the eyes; he was obviously very aware of his surroundings. After making eye contact with me, he turned to face the white guy to speak to him. It wasn't until I got very close to the red security rope that the Asian man realised I was actually coming to see him, and he turned to face me before I was too close. His chain had been sparkling so much because it was a diamond chain, and it was the first thing I noticed now that I was close enough to see him properly.

"Are you okay, little man?" the Asian man asked. He had an accent that wasn't from our city. I had met a lot of Asian people from our city, and this guy spoke differently.

"Are you all right mate, my name is Cyrus," I said as I put my hand out to shake the Asian man's hand. The man looked at me for a moment and was slightly puzzled as to why I was talking to him; but by looking at his face, you couldn't tell he was puzzled as he gave nothing away. After a few seconds of thinking time, the man extended his hand and shook my hand. As the Asian male extended his hand, his rectangular-faced watch became visible; its bezel displaying all of the colours of the rainbow at once, flashing orange and pink and blue—it was beautiful. The chain and watch this guy was wearing were flashing like a crowd of paparazzi but with an array of different colours.

"Hi Cyrus, how can I help you?" the Asian man asked. The way the man had asked the question had an underlying question; 'what the fuck do you want?' was what the Asian man had really meant.

"Well, mate, basically I'm from Coventry, and I don't come to town much at night, but I'm going to start soon. I just brought a new car so I told my mate to drive it here, so I've been looking around at all the girls and what's going on. You look like you have a lot of respect here, so I wanted to come and introduce myself," I said trying not to ramble on too much but at the same time convey the information I wanted to share.

I hadn't planned what I was going to say, it had just come out from the heart. The Asian man with the expensive chain and watch and perfectly gelled hair just looked at me as his brain digested what I had said. "How old are you, Cyrus?" the Asian man asked still no facial expression to speak of.

"I'm 16 and a half," I replied.

"And that's your rally car?" the Asian man asked.

"Yes, I brought it yesterday," I said calmly and confidently. The Asian man's facial expression finally changed as he began to smile in disbelief; he had found my reply funny.

"You brought that rally car, yesterday?" the Asian man asked still smiling.

"Yes, from Northampton." I replied trying to stay calm and composed.

"That's not your mate's car? The guy who is in the driver seat?" the Asian man asked; he had stopped smiling.

"No. It's mine, he is driving it because I told him to drive me around in it, and he's got a cheaper and smaller car," I replied starting to wonder where he was going with all these questions. I was happy to answer anything this man wanted to ask within reason. I was actually answering truthfully and with respect.

"Who is the guy driving then?" the Asian man asked.

"Oh, that's my mate Chris…he works for me," I answered.

The Asian man started smiling again once more. "He works for you? Doing what?" the Asian man asked.

"He sells ounces of weed for me," I answered.

"So, Cyrus, that's your rally car and not your mate Chris'. Chris works for you and has a shit car," the Asian man summarised.

"Yes. That exactly right," I concluded. The stocky white man started listening to our conversation halfway through and had been smiling as he looked at me finding what I had said funny, just as his Asian friend had.

The two girls were just standing there bored and talking amongst themselves. "Luke, wait here for a second. Cyrus and I are going to go for a walk; I will be back in two minutes," the Asian man said to his stocky white friend, as he started to walk towards the gap in the security rope. I watched as the Asian man walked out of the bars private area onto the pedestrian's pavement where I waited.

"Cyrus, I hear a lot of bullshit in the job I do, but if you're being truthful about what you have just told me, you'll have my respect," the Asian man explained. At hearing this, I smiled at the thought of this man respecting me.

"How can I prove it is true right now?"

No sooner had I thought this than the Asian said, "And here is how we are going to prove the truth. You and I are going to walk over to that rally car, and I'm going to get in the passenger seat; and you are going to get in the back behind the driver, so the driver cannot see you. I am going to ask your friend Chris some questions, after you tell Chris to answer every question I ask truthfully? Okay?" The Asian man said in a way that told me instantly this guy was on the ball. I just gave the Asian man a cheeky smile and thought, *that's perfect.*

"Yes, okay, that's fine," I said.

"Unless what you have said to me is a lie, and we will just forget all about it. I will go back in the club with my friends, and you and your friend can continue whatever you lot are doing," the Asian man said giving me the option to back out.

"No, come over to my car; you seem like the type of person I need to know," I said confidently.

"Okay, let's go, you just get in to the back seat and tell Chris to tell this man the truth and don't lie about anything," the Asian man said sternly.

"Okay," I agreed.

We walked over to the waiting car, and I got into the back. Chris looked to his left into the passenger seat as the Asian man got in beside Chris, presumably confused Chris was about to turn around to face me in the back seat. "Stay looking forward," the Asian man said in a firm and serious tone. It was an order, not a request.

"Chris, this guy is going to ask you some questions. I want you to answer his questions truthfully, okay?" I said in a firm tone.

"Chris, who owns this car?" the Asian man asked.

"Cyrus," Chris replied.

"Chris, when did Cyrus buy this car?" the Asian man asked.

"Yesterday," Chris answered.

"Where did he buy this car from?" the Asian man asked.

"Northampton," Chris answered.

"What car do you have, Chris?" the Asian man asked.

"A small shit car, nothing like this," Chris answered.

"And what do you do for money?" the Asian man asked.

"I sell weed," Chris answered sounding intimidated.

"Who do you sell weed for, Chris?"

"I sell weed for Cyrus," Chris answered.

"Have you got any weed on you now?" the Asian man asked.

"Yes, I've got two 20 bags," Chris said.

"Let me see them," the Asian man asked. Chris put his hand in his pocket to take out the two £20 bags of light green 'lemon haze' and handed them to the Asian man, covered in diamonds, sitting in the passenger seat. "Here Chris, take this back," the Asian man said as he opened one bag to smell it. "Is this the weed that you two sell? It's lemon haze," the Asian man asked.

"Yes, it is," Chris replied.

"You can stop answering questions now; and Chris, here, take this weed back and roll a joint for Cyrus and me. We are going to have a chat," the Asian man said as he put his hand out to shake Chris' hand. They shook hands before the Asian guy grabbed the door handle to open the door. "Come on, Cyrus, let's have a chat," he said, as we got out of the car and stood at the back behind the boot. The Asian man was smiling at me and shaking his head in disbelief.

"Nice to meet you, Cyrus, I'm B," B said as he put his hand out to shake my hand.

"Nice to meet you too, B," I replied as I smiled back. "Can I ask you a question? Well actually, can I ask you two questions?" I asked.

"Yes, go on. What's up?" B replied.

"The first question is what kind of watch have you got on, and the second is where did you go to pull girls like them two?" I asked. B looked puzzled.

"The watch is an AP, and the girls are strippers who work in my mate's club in Birmingham—we go there sometimes. Because they have heard about us, they want to spend time with us," B explained before smiling and glancing over at the waiting girls at the bar.

"Oh okay," I replied as I made a mental note.

"Cyrus, how much weed do you sell in a week; it must be a lot to buy a car like that?" B asked, still coming to terms with the fact that the car was mine.

"Well, Chris sells 50 ounces a week for me, and my other friend sells between nine and 13 ounces a week, but he sells them in 10 and 20 bags for me, so about 60 ounces a week," I explained as I worked through the figures out loud.

"How long did it take you to save the money for the car?" B asked.

"I didn't. I robbed a garage full of cigarettes and sold them," I explained.

"What, robbed a garage? Like a petrol station, you mean?" B asked looking even more confused.

"No… I mean a house garage with £80,000 worth of cigarettes in. I had enough money to buy the car already though," I explained.

"Okay, I understand," B said as he opened the car door to get the spliff that Chris had rolled for us. B closed the door, so Chris could not hear our conversation. B put the cone-shape joint in his mouth and lit it and took two big pulls that created a giant cloud of smoke in the dark night air. "So what can I do for you, Cyrus; because you obviously want something, or you wouldn't have approached me?" B asked. Truth be known I hadn't thought that far ahead, so I thought it best just to be honest.

"B if I'm going to be perfectly honest, I want to make more money. I make £2,000 a week now, but when I had stolen the cigarettes, I made £30,000 in one day. After making that in a day, £2,000 a week doesn't do it for me anymore. I need help to make more," I explained. B just puffed on his joint while staring at me with no facial expression to speak of.

"Twenty thousand pounds is a lot of money to make every week, and you should be happy; you are only 16," B said as he gave me a look that people gave me when I was being unreasonable; and they wanted me to see sense. It never worked before, and it wasn't going to work now.

"B, it's just… You look like a man that could definitely help me get closer to the £30,000 a day I want to make. I'm not expecting to make that much in a day. I'd be happy with £10,000 a week after paying all my workers," I compromised and rationalised.

"Here I've got to go back inside now. I said I'd only be two minutes, and I've been out here nearly 15 minutes. Take my number and call me tomorrow at 2:00 in the afternoon, and we will sort something out. You're a good kid though, Cyrus; don't give this number to anybody. And whatever you and I speak about, do not even tell your best friend. Do that, and I'll make you £10,000 a week if you fly straight," B said as he keyed his phone number into my phone and gave me the half-smoked joint back.

Chapter 13

I watched B walk all the way back through the glass doors of the club we were parked outside of. I had feelings of contentment and hope. I didn't know what I had hoped for as I had no clue what the future had in store for me. All I knew was my gut feeling was telling me that things were going to be okay. B had disappeared back into the loud music of the lowly lit bar. His stocky white friend, Luke, and the two sexy girls had gone back in when he had been sitting in my car. I stood and looked at the busy pavement for a minute full of clubbers wearing their 'glad rags'. Gelled hair and short dresses and tight jeans everywhere I looked. Turning around, I opened the passenger side door to get back into my car. "What the fuck was that about, Cyrus?" Chris asked as I sat in the car next to him. He seemed more disgruntled than scared or angry.

"That's my new mate, B," I replied as I grinned psychotically while looking through the windscreen; my imagination running wild with possibilities.

"What do you mean, you nutter? What did you say to him, Cyrus?" Chris asked as if I had lost my mind.

"Chris, that guy is going to be my friend, and we're going to do some work with him," I replied as I thought about the future results of mine and B's new friendship.

Earlier in the day, I had been thinking about expansion, or what I could do to make more money. Something about meeting B and having a talk with him felt right in my heart of hearts. The sequence of events meant 'dots were being connected'. After all, I didn't want to talk to the Asian guy with the diamond watch and chain because I wanted to meet him to play football on Sundays. I had approached B because I could tell he must make a lot of money, and I want to make a lot of money; that was our 'common ground', and it was this common ground I wanted us to walk on together. "What work?" Chris asked with a confused facial expression on his big, round face full of chub.

"I don't know that yet, I'm going to see him tomorrow," I said hoping I would get to see B the following day.

The clock on the dashboard read 12:16 after midnight as I realised I had lost all interest in staring at drunk clubbers any longer. "Chris, let's grab some food from somewhere," I suggested feeling as though I had already achieved as much as I could hope for parked outside a bunch of bars and clubs I couldn't go inside.

"Come on then," Chris said as he turned the key in the ignition, always willing to eat at any given opportunity. I felt good inside as the car turned around in the car park. I looked at the club, wondering if I could get one more glance at my new friend B. One thing about Chris was that he always knew where to get good food from at any time of the day or night.

The city centre was surprisingly busy, considering it was after midnight. We stopped outside what looked like a type of Turkish-style grill place. Memories of my mum coming home after a night out with chicken or lamb *kebabs* from places like these came to mind as we walked in. I ordered a lamb *kofti* with salad on the side and some toasted Pitta bread. Chris ordered the same as me but chose to order a double portion of lamb. As we sat down to eat our food, my mind started to wander, and I didn't really have much to talk about as I didn't know where things stood in terms of what we were going to do yet. It was hard for me to have a proper open conversation with Chris about business. I couldn't say to him 'do you think is possible to earn £10,000 a week' because he only earned £750 a week because he thought I paid more for the weed than I actually did. So every time I made £1,250 profit, Chris only made £750 profit, so I really had to guard myself in conversation with Chris.

Even though Chris was probably my best friend, I could not be 100 percent honest with him. My brain was tired during the drive home. The thinking I had been doing all day had left me mentally drained. The roads on my way home were deserted; all the people that weren't sleeping off a long week of work were in town drinking, and the rest of the city seemed to be tucked up in their beds.

My housing estate was desolate and empty as we pulled into the dark dead end. Chris parked my car outside the garage next to my dad's Volvo and switched the car off. We said goodbye to one another and made plans to meet the following afternoon. I didn't have any worry of having to wake anybody in my house to get in, as the £5,000 I had given my mother and father for helping me sell

161

the cigarettes had earnt me my own house key. Using it, I quietly crept into my house and up the stairs to bed. I folded my jeans and T-shirt up and placed them in a tidy pile after taking out my £500 pocket money and cheap work phone. As I did, I scrolled through my contacts until I reached the name B. I stood staring at the phonebook contact for a moment while wondering what he was doing, and whether he would even remember me in the morning. Chris had said as we sat eating *kebabs* that he looked like 'a big drug-dealer', as he had the finest Italian designer clothes on, shoes and jeans and leather jacket, Chris continued, "He was wearing about £10,000 worth of clothes and about £60,000 worth of jewellery." I wondered what B did for a living to be able to afford stuff like that. I sat on my bed with the hope that when B had found me to be truthful, I had gone as far up in his estimations as I had hoped. Well, one thing life had taught me was 'time will tell'; it always does, and it always will. The quicker I go to sleep, the quicker I will be awake, the quicker I will know if B is going to help me break the £2,000 a week wage's barrier.

"Cyrus, don't be driving that car and crash it and hurt yourself, you know?" my dad had said the following morning as I walked into the kitchen.

"No, I won't. I don't drive it; I let Chris drive it... Slowly," I replied trying to reassure my dad and get him off my case at the same time.

"Yes, of course, you don't!" my dad said blatantly calling me a liar. I didn't reply; there was no point. My dad was as stubborn as me when he had a view on the subject. He said I drove the car, so in his head I drove it; 'end of'. My mum was dressed and ready to leave the house to go and do her usual visitations to family, and most likely a trip to the supermarket or grocer.

"Mum, wait five minutes, and I will come with you," I had said sensing my dad's mood and wanting to get out of the house. My dad was always bitter and angry about a job he had lost years before. He had said some guy fucked him over because he was black.

He had practically planned to kill the man in question, but in the end had used his better judgement to maintain a stable family life and decided against the idea. In sparing the man in question, he had not forgiven or forgotten, so quite often he would just be in a foul mood at home for this very reason. I think I would have preferred if he would have killed the man, at least then he would have been able to move on; or if not killed the man in question, at least forgiven him or forgotten about it.

Tracksuit now on and outside the house, I told my mum to drive my car. She was going to my nan's sister's street, which is also my Auntie Delma's street and Jason's street. I could show them my new car and kill some time before I called B. "This car is very loud, Cyrus," my mother had said as she touched the accelerator to begin to reverse.

"I know, and it's very, very fast, so be careful," I replied as I smiled at my mother.

The car jerked slightly as my mother drove; she was clearly not used to the power of the car. The engine gave off a low grumble as she made it idle in two high of a gear for the speed we were doing. All in all, my mother liked my new car though. I convinced her to put her 'foot down' a little bit, but as soon as the power kicked in, she quickly changed her mind and said, "No, no, that's enough," after experiencing about ten percent of the cars actual potential. We were on my Auntie Delma's street in under the usual ten minutes. My mother went into the house she parked outside of, and I headed 15 houses up the road to where Jason lived and crossed the road to go to see my Auntie Delma.

Lifting the letterbox twice and letting it slam back down, I knocked the door. No answer. I knocked again, still nothing. My Auntie Delma's car was on the drive, so she must be in. I thought as I looked at the shiny, electric blue German car on the drive. Just as I was about to turn to go back across the road, the door opened. "Hi, Cyrus," Delma said with what I can only describe to be a false tone. I could just tell it wasn't genuine. Delma looked like she had rushed to answer the door but was making out as though she hadn't. The pure fact I been standing outside for nearly five minutes meant she hadn't rushed to the door.

"Can I come in?" I said as I wondered why she was still standing more or less in the doorway like I was a stranger.

"Of course," Delma said as she moved away from the doorway as if she didn't realise she was standing in the doorway. I took one step inside the house, and Delma walked back towards the living room that led through to the kitchen. "Oh, Jason is here, he came to ask if you have any cigarettes left," Delma said as she walked in front of me towards the kitchen. Delma lied. *Why the fuck would Jason come to see you about cigarettes when he has got my fucking phone number, hasn't he?* I thought.

163

"Really?" I said as I walked through to the kitchen. I found Jason sitting on a chair at the dining room table, smoking a cigarette.

"Yes, Cyrus," Jason said as he forced a smile at me that looked pressured and rehearsed.

"Jason," I replied with no facial expression. I couldn't see my little cousin in the house or Mervyn, so alarm bells were calling in my ears.

"What's up, Jason?" I asked as I tried to remain calm, although I felt like stabbing Jason to death.

"Oh, I just popped over to ask your auntie if you've got any cigarettes left for sale. I've got someone that wants to buy some?" Jason asked. He tried his best to act convincing but it fell on deaf ears.

"No, I've got none left, I told you that two weeks ago!" I said in an annoyed and pissed-off tone.

My Auntie Delma had left the room after our exchange of words. She looked nervous, and Jason was starting to see from the look on my face that I wasn't buying his bullshit. "Sorry, Cyrus, I thought you might have had some more or something?" Jason said. I didn't even reply or entertain his lies. I just stood there looking down at him, looking straight at him. I knew as I looked at him, *I would eat this rat for breakfast.* I told myself, and his face was full of fear and shock.

"In future, if you want me, then call me. Don't knock this door again without calling me. I need to talk to my auntie now, so if you don't mind, I will call you later," I said in a constant emotionless tone with the same look on my face. I stepped to the side to let Jason leave without shaking his hand or smiling or anything; I just let him leave feeling like the piece of shit he was. Jason left the kitchen, looking like a dog that had just pissed on a new carpet that he had been told not to 100 times. I heard the door shut behind him as I turned to go into the living room where my auntie was sitting down, smoking a cigarette.

Delma's body language looked like her whole world was going to end. She had on her grey valour tracksuit with the zipper almost all the way up. Delma didn't look like she had taken a long time to get ready, as could usually be expected. My instincts were telling me to ask her where her daughter was, or where her long-term partner was, but I already knew the answer—they weren't here. Instead of asking the questions I knew the answer to, I said, "Delma, how long has this been going on for?" I asked the question in a tone that was more disappointment than anger—how could I be angry with her? She was my favourite auntie. It was Jason who was the rat, not her!

I stood staring at Delma as she sat with her head held low, like she was being told off by a parent. "Nearly three weeks. When I picked that money up from your house, I met Jason at a bar. It's the worst thing I've ever done," Delma said as she started to sob with her head in her hands. *It wasn't that bad, or else you wouldn't have been fucking him in your house, you fucking idiot*, I thought.

"Delma, don't worry, just put a stop to it before you lose Mervyn over some drug-dealing little twat," I said trying to give her advice and hope that things were not as bad as they seemed. I was subtly telling Delma that I was not going to tell anybody, namely Mervyn, and she got the point.

"You're not going to tell, Mervyn, are you, Cyrus? Please don't!" Delma pleaded with the same crocodile tears that women have used throughout history; and like every man throughout history, I consoled her. I put my arm on her shoulder.

"Stop being silly, everyone makes mistakes, it will be okay," I said in a soft, caring and compassionate tone.

I was still thinking about how Jason had violated my trust and our friendship. I sat down on the sofa next to Delma and smoked a cigarette. I had about an hour left before I intended to call B, but catching Jason practically having sex with my auntie red-handed had me feeling like I needed a joint. I wasn't going to let Jason's actions impact on my day though; when I rang B, I wanted to have a clear head. After seeing that Delma had pulled herself together and another 15 minutes had passed, I decided to say goodbye. I reluctantly spared Delma the usual kiss on the cheek more for psychological reasons. If I acted normal with her, she would think everything is normal, therefore she would worry less; and I did love Delma. I didn't want her to worry, especially because of Jason.

The whole reason I had decided to go with my mother was to show-off my new car to my Auntie Delma and Jason; now I felt like running Jason over in the car, and I had no interest in what my Auntie Delma thought about it. I left Delma's house and went back across the road. I walked past Jason's house and knocked my mother's elderly auntie's door to see if my mum was nearly ready to leave.

After the same procedure I had been through over the years of visiting this street—which was leaving Delma's house, coming to the house I was now at, saying hello to the elderly old Irish lady and hurrying up my mother—we were now back in the car and on the way home. I decided to call B. My mum had accepted the fact I was a drug-dealer, so I had nothing to hide from her. The phone rang and rang and rang and rang some more, until finally, the voicemail picked up 'your call has been forwarded to the…' I put the phone down and stared through the windscreen in disappointment. Leaning to the side, I slid my phone back inside my pocket and stared forward at the road. "Are you okay, Cyrus?" my mother asked sensing the change in my mood. Chris was my best friend, but nobody knew me better than my mother.

"I'm all right, Mum, I'm just thinking," I replied; then my mother gave me the best advice anybody could have ever give me as long as I live. And much to my demise, I brushed it off as if she had said nothing.

"Just remain patient, Cyrus, you don't need to rush anything," my mum said. I ignored that advice, but it was that advice that would have made all the difference in more ways than I could ever begin to explain.

The phone started to vibrate and play the cheap version of the factory-set call tone. I took the phone out excitedly. B flashed in the middle of my screen. Not wanting him to hang up, I answered as quickly as my little thumb would allow me to. "Hi mate," I said in the most mature and calm business voice I possessed.

"Who is that?" B asked in his noticeable out of town accent.

"It's me, Cyrus, from last night," I replied in the same tone.

"Oh, yes, the little lad with the rally car?" B asked.

"Yes, that's me, mate. Are you still able to meet?" I asked trying to sound relaxed.

"I was just about to leave Coventry now to go back to Birmingham," B explained.

"Well, my mum is driving my car. I can ask her to bring me somewhere to meet you," I said trying to think of any solution.

"Okay, give me your postcode, and I'll meet you," B said. I gave B my postcode without hesitation before we both hung up.

"Who was that?" my mum asked as I put the phone down. She could clearly see I had been speaking to this guy different than I spoke to other people.

"Oh, it's just my mate B," I said as I smiled. My mum stopped at the grocer, and I waited in the car as she said that she only needed a few bits. I asked her to try and be quick as my friend was now on his way to our street to meet me.

My mum got back into the car and started the engine. My phone rang again.

"Yes, B," I said as I answered.

"Cyrus, where are you? I'm in some crappy estate in a dead end," B said sounding a bit unsure to where I was and where he was.

"Yes, that's outside my house. I'm two-minutes away. My mum just stopped at the shop, but we are two minutes from our house now," I explained.

"Okay then, try to be quick, please," B said as he cut the phone off. As we pulled into our housing estate, I had butterflies in my stomach, and a slight feeling in the bottom of my stomach that was like needing to go to the toilet—excitement, mixed with nerves and anticipation. We turned left into the estate, then straight down to the bottom of the road before turning right at the bottom, so I wouldn't know if B was actually there until we took that right at the bottom of the road. It took longer than ever to get to the bottom of the road; well, it seemed longer especially as my mum practically let the car just tick over in contrast to 'flooring it'. We took the right to see a shiny, brand-new, German hot-hatch sitting outside of our house. B had positioned his car so he was facing the way out; we got closer as B moved to allow my mum to park.

I watched as B got out of his car. He had reading glasses on, or what I'm guessing were reading glasses as he hadn't worn them the night before. His head was shaved at the sides, and the hair on the top of his head swept to the side with gel on the top. He had on a dark grey tracksuit with little metal tags on the chest and leg. My mother and I got out of my car, and B waved at my mum and smiled at her. His car was a spectacle to look at. "Mum, I'm going to chill out here with my friend. Pass me my car keys, we might go somewhere," I said as she got her two shopping bags out of the back of the car.

"Okay, just be careful whatever you do, Cyrus," my mum said as she looked at B and went in through our back gate.

"Nice to see you, B," I said with a big smile as I shook B's hand. I could see the metal tag on his jumper, and I knew that these clothes were very expensive. B had the same logo on his tracksuit bottoms and trainers.

"Yes, Cyrus with the red rally car," B said in his Birmingham accent which was distinctive due to the fact he had a slight lisp.

"What kind of car is that? It's much better than mine," I said as I stared over to the small, white German hot-hatch that was probably the best small car I'd ever seen.

"Oh, it's a special edition, that one is a 45," B had said which had meant nothing to me. "So, Cyrus, this is where you live then?" B asked.

"Yes, that's my house, and my mum just went inside," I explained.

B then went on to suggest going for a walk around the block. He said everywhere he had seen in Coventry looked posh apart from my estate. He told me he liked the look of my area though, as this was the type of area he spent most of his time in. B asked me about my business, and I explained about the McBride's and my brother and Chris. I told him what Jabber was like. I left Jason out of the conversation as Jason had pissed me off badly. B asked me, "Are there many dealers that are big drug-dealers around your side of Coventry?"

I went on to explain that, "Jabber has been around for years, and I know a lot of people. My brother knows some big drug-dealers, and Chris' cousin knows a lot of drug dealers, so yes," I had explained, but I wondered why he had asked that.

"Cyrus, have you ever thought about selling cocaine?" B asked.

"No, not really, I wouldn't know who to approach to get it off. Also, because it's just a white powder, I wouldn't know how to tell if it's any good," I had explained as I thought about what I was saying.

"Well, Cyrus, you said you'd like to make at least £10,000 a week, you are not going to do that selling weed," B said frankly.

B was right though, and this was my train of thought over the last few days. I had already ruled out expanding my current business. "Well, who can I get good cocaine from?" I asked willing to do whatever it takes to get where I wanted to go.

"Me," B said with a slight smile. "Cyrus, do not tell anyone who I am, and get a phone just to call me and me only. I will show you how to make money, but once I do, you have to stay working with me. I'll make you £20,000 a week if you can sell drugs properly," B said seriously as we stepped back near to our cars.

The cars looked out of place in the shit-hole street they were parked in—a brand-new red rally car with black wheels, and big black spoiler next to a white hot-hatch with black wheels and black spoiler—and us two, a dodgy Asian guy covered in Italian clothes talking to a young mixed-raced kid in a tracksuit and the latest trainers. Yes, we looked dodgy, but we also looked dangerous, like people that you don't fuck about with.

"B, I'll get a phone for you; and if it's possible to make £20,000 a week, I'll do it. When can I start?" I asked keen to get the ball rolling. B took a deep breath of air in as he looked up at the sky thinking.

"Get your mate, Chris, to drop you to Birmingham tomorrow at 6:00 in the afternoon. I'll get you a lift back home to Coventry, okay?" B suggested.

"Yes, that's good with me. How long does it take to get there?" I asked.

"About half an hour to 40 minutes maximum," B answered.

"Okay, I'll be there, I will call you tomorrow for a postcode before I leave," I said realising that our conversation had resulted in a verbal contract. Worst still, I didn't even know the details of the contract.

"Okay then, don't eat before you come because I will take you to get some food. I'm going to go back to Birmingham now because I've got things to do when I get back," B said as he pressed the fob to unlock his car which made the indicators flash. I wanted to ask B if I'd definitely be okay if I come over there, or if I can bring my big brother; but all that would do is make me look like a pussy, and I was 'in it to kill it', so there was no 'pussying out for me'. I just walked to B's door to say goodbye and shook his hand.

"I will become one of your best friends in time, and we are going to make a lot of money together," I said as I looked at B in the eye.

The eyes never lie. If you look into someone's eyes, it's almost like looking into their soul; and I knew when B looked into my soul, he saw the good and the bad. The good being the friend I could be, and the loyalty I possess with in my heart; and the bad was the fact that I would blow his brains all over the leather head rest his head was resting on if he ever hurt me, my family or my money.

I respected B though, because when I looked him in his eyes, it was like looking in the mirror. "Cyrus, you know what, mate; if you listen to me and work how you should work, we will become best friends and make a lot of money together. I wouldn't be here if I didn't think that. I'll see you tomorrow, my friend," B said as he shut his car door and started his engine.

I watched him put his reading glasses back on and drive slowly out of my street. B had given me a lot to think about. He had said cocaine was the way forward, the problem with this was that I didn't know much about cocaine. I had chosen to sell weed because it was something I did know about. All in all, my meeting with B had gave me a lot of things to deliberate and not of lot of time to make decisions. No longer prepared to stand in the middle of the street thinking about how I was going to sell cocaine; or if I was going to sell cocaine, I decided to put the whole thing to the back of my mind for the time being. After all, whatever would be would be.

The insult of Jason sleeping with my auntie was something I was not prepared to put on the shelf. Jason hadn't even called me to explain, or at least try to offer some sort of apology. I stood outside my house and devised a plan to teach this piece of shit a lesson. "Daniel, come outside the house please and bring a big kitchen knife," I said as my big brother answered the phone.

"Are you out there now?" my brother, Daniel, asked.

"Yes, I am, and bring a big kitchen knife with you," I said as if I was telling him to bring a cigarette out.

"Okay, two minutes," Daniel said before hanging up. I loved Daniel; he was always ready to do whatever is needed to be done. The fact he hadn't even asked what the knife was for made me smile as I put the phone back in my pocket.

Daniel walked out of the gate with no knife visible in his hands as he scanned the surrounding area as he said, "Are you good, Cyrus?" Daniel said as he continued to scan our surrounding area.

"Yes, I'm good," I replied as I approached Daniel to talk to him. My body language told my brother that the threat was not in close proximity to where we were standing.

"What do you want the knife for? Daniel asked realising we were the only two people in our deserted street.

"Come with me, I will show you exactly what I want the knife for," I said as I pressed the 'unlock button' on the car's fob in my hand.

My brother and I got into the car. I sat in the driver seat and reversed before starting off out of our estate. I drove slowly, giving the road my full attention as I explained exactly what Jason had done to disrespect me. "I need to set an example," I told my six-foot brother who sat in the passenger seat. People stared at us as we were two 'black guys', in tracksuits, driving a red rally car. We definitely looked like drug-dealers. We arrived back on Jason and my Auntie Delma's road ten minutes later, and I parked the car outside Jason's house, being careful not to scuff my alloys on the high kerb. Daniel had agreed with me that Jason had taken a step well over the line. When he had got in the car, he had taken the kitchen knife out of his waistband and put it on the floor at his feet. I slid my phone back out of my pocket to call Jason. The car was grumbling quietly as the phone rang in my ear.

"Cyrus," Jason said as he answered before the phone call almost went to answer phone.

"Jason, come outside your house. I want to have a chat with you," I said calmly and in an attempt to disguise the fact I wasn't happy with him. Having still not admitted his guilt, anything other than compliance would have proven his guilt, little did Jason know, he had already been found guilty by me in his absence; and the reason I was here was to carry out his sentence.

"Is everything all right?" Jason asked in the hope I would give him some insight into the reason for my unannounced visit.

"Yes, of course, come outside; and I'm parked in a red rally car," I said before cutting the phone off before Jason started digressing any further.

Daniel and I sat outside Jason's house with the engine running for a full five minutes before we saw the door open. Jason appeared from the doorway in a blue tracksuit that made him look skinny. He looked like a man that had a lot of stress on his shoulders; and little did he know, he had good reason for it. Jason walked to my car and made eye contact with me. I gave him a nod to acknowledge him. I wanted him to feel at ease enough to get into my car, which he did.

"Are you okay, lads? Is this your new car, Cyrus?" Jason asked seemingly bubbly and cheerfully.

"Yes! Do you like it?" I said as I started to pull off from outside Jason's house.

"Cyrus, I can't leave here now. I'm waiting for somebody," Jason said as the car started to move. It was his attempt to stay in his comfort zone. My brother hadn't said a word to him. Daniel had just sat there without moving an inch, listening and observing.

"I will bring you back in two minutes. I only wanted to take you around the block in my new car," I said convincingly.

"Oh, okay then," Jason agreed as I pulled off. I didn't turn the car around. Instead, I drove straight down Jason's street, then turned off the street into the section of a small car park that had garages in a row, facing more garages.

I stopped the car and pulled the handbrake up.

"One sec," I said as I got out, not wanting Jason to try and run away. As I got out, so did my brother after picking up the big, shiny kitchen knife out of view of Jason. We were out of the front seats and standing either side of the two backdoors, with them open, faster than you can say 'that was very fast'. Jason's eyes widened as his whole body filled with terror and fear.

"Cyrusssss," Jason stuttered.

"Shut your fucking mouth! You little prick, you think you can shag my auntie and get away with it?" My face was scrunched up with anger, and now I was practically snarling at him.

"Cyrus, please," Jason said again as he raised his hands to protect himself from whatever assault we were going to launch against him. I was leaning into the back seat of my car with my fist clenched, filled with rage. He had his back to my brother, but more against the back of the seat; and his face looked like he was close to bursting into tears.

"Get this rat out of my car, Daniel," I said as I looked over the roof at my brother. My brother reached in viciously and grabbed him by his neck and jumper and ripped him out of the car, like he was a rag doll. By the time Jason was out of the car, I was already around the car. I ran around the car to find Jason's face exposed by his attempt to stop Daniel from strangling him as he pulled him from the car. I punched Jason as hard as I could in the nose with my right hand. I felt the bone crack in his face as he winced in pain and groaned. I punched him three or four more times as hard as I could until he lay on the floor trying to protect himself.

"Cyrus, please stop, please," Jason pleaded while he curled up in a ball on the floor. Hearing Jason speak only intensified my anger as I kicked him hard in the face. His hands were in front of his face, but it still must have been excruciating.

"Arrgghh," Jason screamed as my brother stamped on his kidneys as he lay on his side trying to protect his face. I picked up the kitchen knife from the floor and knelt down over Jason. As Jason saw the blade through the gap between his hands in front of his face, I looked into his eyes—he was terrified.

"Cyrus, please don't, please!" Jason pleaded as he sobbed and begged for his life.

"Shut your fucking mouth; you ever even look at my auntie again, and we will come back and cut your fucking throat. Either that or we will kick your door off and shoot you and your whole fucking family! Do you understand me?" I said as I held the knife pressed firmly against Jason's throat.

"I'm sorry, I won't, sorry," Jason sobbed. I stood up and kicked him in the face one last time before saying.

"Good, you just let me hear you've forgotten, and we will come back and fucking murder you!" I threatened as I threw the knife back into the passenger side and walked around the car to get back into the driver's seat.

Jason just lay curled up on the floor as Daniel got back into the car next to me, and I started to drive off. "The cheeky, skinny little twat, I felt like cutting his throat," I said still angry.

Daniel laughed as he said, "I thought you were going to at one point," Daniel said as he sat laughing. I was Daniel's little brother, but he always found it funny to see me lose it and fuck somebody up. I had never understood why.

"The only reason I didn't cut Jason's throat was because I liked his uncle, otherwise I would have probably stabbed him to death," I had explained as we drove back the way we had come.

Three things had been achieved on this Saturday afternoon: one was I had spoken to B, the second was that Jason would no longer think he could sleep with my auntie, like I'm some sort of 'punk'; and the third thing was I had plucked up the courage to drive my rally car. It drove really well, it cornered well, and it stuck to the road and was genuinely very easy to drive. "Light a cigarette, please, Daniel," I said as I parked back outside of our house. I turned the key to turn the car off. My hand started to hurt around my knuckles. *At least it can't hurt as much as Jason's face,* I thought to myself as I tried to stretch it off by extending my fingers, then clenching back my fist. I decided to sit back and have a talk with my older brother. I felt like a big weight was off my shoulders. The anger and violence I had just subjected Jason to had relieved so much tension and stress from my body and left me feeling relaxed and content. I still owed Jason for 59 ounces of weed, which came to £8,850. I had intended to pay it tomorrow after Chris and the McBrides finished selling; then I was going to pay my workforce. I wished I hadn't met Jabber, because keeping the money and not giving it to Jason would have been a surety; but as I knew it was Jabber's money, it would be in insult to him more than to Jason. It wasn't fair to punish Jabber for Jason's actions. This didn't have to affect my relationship with Jabber unless he wanted it to. In which case, Jabber would get shot, and I would be nearly £9,000 richer, so in a way I hoped that he would be stupid enough to make mine and Jason's grievances personal.

I had saved a lot of money up and had a nice car, also I would hopefully be starting a new business venture with B, so what had happened with Jason was not about robbing him—it was about hurting him. For want of something to do, we decided to go for lunch. While my brother and I sat waiting for our food in our local restaurant, my phone rang. I had barely heard it over the noise in the restaurant and Portuguese music playing in the background. "How are you, Jabber?" I said as I answered my phone, not fazed in the least by his phone call. I was ready to play this however he wanted.

"Cyrus, I've just spoken to Jason; he has told me what happened," Jabber said in his low and slightly scary tone. It didn't scare me though; I had seen him turn to putty around my father.

"And?" I replied, as if to say 'what's your point?'

"Jason has told me that you and your brother broke his nose and threatened to cut his throat; what is going on, mate?" Jabber asked not angrily; he was calm as he spoke.

"Did he tell you I gave him money for you, and he arranged to pick it up from my auntie at a bar, and he's been sleeping with her?" I asked in an emotionless tone.

"Yes, he did, and I told him he is bang out of order for that. I just want to know that it's finished now," Jabber said, which was as good to me as backing down.

"Yes, that's the end of it as long as he doesn't think he can do it again, and he can delete my number because I don't want to talk to him anymore," I said in the same tone I had used since answering my phone. The voice I had used had let Jabber know from the start of our conversation that I wasn't bothered in any way about him calling me.

"Yes, I'll tell him that. He said you've got some money for me though?" Jabber said in a way that told me he was anticipating my refusal to pay.

"Yes, I'll be finished with what I have tomorrow night, but where am I going to get some more from, now that I'm not talking to Jason?" I asked leaving the ball back in his court as to where we go from here.

"I will give it to you from now on, if you want? There's no reason for us to fall out, is there?" Jabber said. I had hoped this is how our conversation would go. It was inevitable that we were going to have to talk, it was just a question of what would be said.

"Yes, that's fine with me; and another thing, I'm going to have some cocaine for sale tomorrow. I will show you if you are interested?" I said as I remembered what B had said to me. I liked Jabber; he had spoken to me like an equal. He had spoken to me like I was his age, and he respected me.

"Okay, if it's good, I will buy some; and I have a few mates who buy big bits of cocaine, so bring me some to look at tomorrow," Jabber said.

"Okay, I will catch up with you tomorrow," I said before hanging up.

My brother, Daniel, had sat looking at me to trying to get a feel for how the conversation was going.

"What did he say?" Daniel asked as he watched me hang up and place the cheap phone on the dark wooden table we were sitting at.

"Oh, that was that dickhead's uncle. I like him though, and we do work together. Oh yes, he said we broke that Jason's nose," I told Daniel as I smiled and fist pumped him to congratulate a job well done. A thin white guy in a black uniform brought food over. I had ordered us identical meals—half a grilled chicken medium spiced, peri chips and garlic bread with a special mayonnaise dip—it was a well-needed meal after the morning I'd had.

Being a drug-dealer meant I had started my day later than most. I had my breakfast at lunchtime and lunch at dinnertime, it was nearly 5:00 in the evening, and I was eating my first square meal of the day. Due to the events of the day, I wasn't particularly hungry as Daniel and I had walked in through the restaurant doors. Having now spoken to Jabber, I sat and got everything off my chest to my brother over dinner; 'a problem shared is a problem halved'. I allowed myself to talk almost freely to my brother, more so than with Chris. Blood is thicker than water, and the natural bond between siblings made it easy for me to share my thoughts and views with Daniel.

Expansion was my main issue; by that, I mean increasing my earnings tenfold. I told Daniel, if this Asian guy I've met comes through, I'm going to need him to work a lot harder; but for doing so, I would pay him £2,000 a week.

Chapter 14

'1.2 miles until we reach our destination,' the satnav that was stuck to the dashboard read. It had been a fairly quick journey, partly because I had told Chris to 'floor it', which would throw us back into our bucket seats as Chris accelerated along almost every expanse of open road, and partly because there was little or no traffic on the roads we were travelling down. The motorway had been more or less deserted, which was strange for 5:00 in the afternoon. I guess it was because everybody was in their local pubs getting drunk or sat at their mother's dinner tables, eating their Sunday lunches. That is exactly where Chris and I would have almost certainly been, had it not been for me telling him he had to make this trip with me. Chris had made his face up a bit when I told him I needed him to drive me to Birmingham, but had changed his tune when I told him I wanted dropping there, and he could drive my car back to Coventry alone.

"Crash my car, and I will crash your face," I had told him as he tried not to smile as he knew I wouldn't be giving him unsupervised access to my car if I had a choice.

The day had been bright but very cool. It felt more like spring than summer as the air was crisp. We had spent the day having lunch, getting the car cleaned and collecting in all of our money for the weed, ready to pay Jabber when I returned to Coventry. I had asked Chris if he'd be happy to sell cocaine if I got some, and his answer was exactly what I would have expected from the podgy spoilt 'shithead'.

"How much money will I make though?" Chris had asked as he stuffed his face and smiled. He always made me laugh, always so predictable.

"At least £2,000 a week if you do a good job; so with selling cocaine and weed, you will be earning £3,000 a week," I'd explained. I watched as Chris' brain rushed to do calculations before he looked up at me.

"Okay, I'm on it," Chris said with a big smile before giving me a fist pump to signify his sincerity. Birmingham is the second biggest city in England. It is split into different areas, and each area has different types of people that live within them. Some areas are 'rich and posh', like 'Solihull', and some areas are poor like 'Chelmsley Wood'. In addition, some areas are filled with predominantly one ethnic group, for example, 'Alum Rock' is predominantly an Asian area, whereas, Handsworth is predominantly full of Caribbeans. The area the satnav had brought us to was an area called 'Aston'. The area has a lot of gun crime in and is mainly occupied by a mixture of blacks and Asians. The satnav was now showing 0.2 miles as we entered streets that seem to be exclusively Asians living within them. I slid my phone out of the pocket of my best jeans and called B.

"Hi, B, I'm here now. I'm just about to take the last turn onto Normandy Road, I think it's called," I explained as I read the screen on the satnav.

"Yes, Cyrus, drive down that road, and you will see my car parked behind it," B said before he put the phone down. Chris and I drove slowly up the road to avoid missing the white German hot-hatch due to the amount of cars parked outside of houses on our right and left. The houses were very moderate. They looked like three or four bedroom houses; old brick houses all joined together with the occasional entry every 10 or 20 houses along. We drove halfway along the street before I spotted B's white car that had been outside my house the day before. As promised, there was a space behind that we pulled into. I began to slide my phone back out of my pocket when the driver's door of B's car opened, and B got out of the car. I waved at B and said, "Chris, go back to Coventry, and don't drive my car fast because if you break it, I will kill you," I said to Chris as I opened the passenger side door to get out.

"Nice to see you, Cyrus," B said, as he shook my hand.

"Nice to see you too, B. So this is your area?" I asked as I looked around at my unfamiliar surroundings.

"Yes, this is my area. Come on, jump in my car because we have got things to do," B said as he walked back to the driver's side of the white German hot-hatch with the black spoiler and wheels. I walked to the passenger side and got into B's car. B's car was pure luxury—black leather and chrome trim everywhere I looked, everything made to the highest quality. The car had that new car smell of brand new leather.

"We will go and get some food, then take care of business after," B said.

"Okay, I don't mind," I replied. We drove through streets that mostly looked identical to me. I felt a little out of my comfort zone. Not knowing B at all really, mixed with the new surroundings, was a bit overwhelming; I couldn't give in to these feelings of nerves.

Jason was right about one thing he had said, "If you can't swim, stay out the sea," or something to that effect, so as I was already well and truly in the ocean. I had to just stay calm and keep 'treading water'.

"B, I've had a think about what you said," I said to start some sort of interaction with him. He had Asian music playing fairly quiet on the stereo, but since I had got in the car, he hadn't spoken much.

"Cyrus, wait until we get out the car, I don't like talking in the car, and it's a good habit if you don't talk in cars either," B said dismissing my invitation into conversation.

"Why shouldn't I talk in cars?" I asked as I wasn't a hundred percent sure as to why he had made the statement.

"Because dirty police officers like to plant listening devices in them, so never talk about anything dodgy in a car, not that we've got anything dodgy to talk about," B winked at me and touched his ear. He had basically said he thinks the cops may have bugged his car, so that's why he doesn't talk in the car. It was a lesson duly noted by me.

B and I pulled into the restaurant car park; the car park was nearly full of cars. "What is this place like?" I asked again trying to start conversation.

"Have you never been here before?" B asked.

"No, is it nice?" I asked.

"You will find out in a minute," B said as he parked the car. The entrance to the restaurant was raised from the car park floor with big, white tiled steps. I walked slightly behind B as he opened one of the two big glass doors.

Inside, the restaurant was carpeted throughout with a thick floral design covering the carpet from the entrance out onto the restaurant floor. "Bob, how are you doing?" The entrance employees asked as they saw B; the maître d's eyes lit up like he was B's biggest fan.

So, B stands for Bob, I thought to myself. *B looks as much like a 'Bob' as Santa Claus looks like a 'Mr Singh',* I thought as I watched the restaurant waiters shaking B's hand and smiling at him. The restaurant smelled of Asian food, and as I walked, I looked at people's plates on their table. This was not your usual curry house or *Balti* hut on a side street, this was more of a posh restaurant. The waiter seated us in the back corner of the room, giving us a good view of the whole restaurant. The restaurant was almost completely filled with Asians, consisting of mainly families in small groups of 12 or less people per gathering. B and I sat and spoke about our plans. I told him I had put a few feelers out about the cocaine to see if it was something I could work with; also I told B about the positive feedback I had received. The word that kept cropping up was 'quality' or 'is it good'; so I summarised to B that if the product was good, then we would more than likely be onto a winner.

Regardless of what the future held, life had progressed massively in the last few months. I had gone from dossing around on foot with nothing, to having money put away and having a nice car and meeting serious drug-dealers for dinner in their local posh restaurants. These were my feelings as I tucked into the tender lamb chops the waiter had brought over with our starters. "Yes, Cyrus, when we leave here, I'm going to show you how to make money," B said.

"That sounds perfect to me…is there anything else I can call you other than B?" I asked. Saying B seemed so detached in terms of us being friends.

"Yes, most of my friends call me Bob. Either B or Bob, it's totally up to you," Bob said.

"Okay, Bob," I said as I chuckled at his funny but strange name. Over dinner, Bob went on to explain what he wanted from our arrangement.

"Cyrus, I'm going to make you one of the biggest drug-dealers in Coventry, but what I show you, do not even tell your shadow. It's got to be an absolute secret, because if you tell anyone, it could fuck my work up and yours," Bob stressed. We sat and talked over our quality meal surrounded by posh Asian decor. As we sat finishing our meals, I noticed the same stocky white guy that Bob had been in Coventry city centre with walking towards our table.

The stocky white man was with a slim, light-skinned Asian male with a big beard that came down to his chest. The Asian guy with the white guy called 'Luke' had on jeans and T-shirt similar to mine; and Luke had a grey tracksuit on, that looked fresh and new. Bob noticed them at the same time I did and put his fork down to wipe his hands with his napkin and smiled at them. "About time," Bob said as he smiled at his two friends and shook their hands in turn. Bob's two friends then said 'hello' to me and shook my hand.

"Everything is there for you; are you sure it's a good idea?" the white guy called Luke asked as though he was concerned about something.

"Don't worry, I'm never wrong about things like this," Bob said to reassure Luke. I had absolutely no idea what they were talking about, but I knew it was not something I should ask about either. "I'm going to be about an hour and a half after we leave here, so I'll call you to drop my friend here home when we are finished," Bob said to his two friends. The two men hadn't even sat down; they had walked in and stood beside the table.

"Here," Luke said as he took out a single key and gave it to Bob.

"Make sure Bubbles is at the spot when I get there; we will be there in ten minutes," Bob said as he took the key and placed it straight into his pocket. I just sat there trying to act as though I wasn't listening to their every word. They were not talking to me, so it would have seemed rude to just stop eating and listen to their conversation. I did listen to every word—I just did it subtly.

The Asian man with the big beard and Luke walked off back through the restaurant in the direction they had come after saying goodbye and shaking both of our hands once more. I could tell they were close to Bob; possibly even work colleagues, their relationship reminded me of mine and Chris'. The difference being, these guys were further up the chain than Chris and me. "Who is the guy with beard?" I asked Bob as we finished eating.

"Oh, that's my mate, Yax," Bob said. The name meant nothing to me. I had never heard it before. "Are you ready to leave, Cyrus?" Bob asked as he picked up his drink and tipped the glass just over horizontally to finish its contents.

"I don't know what I am ready for, but if it's business, then I'm ready," I said as I smiled at him in jest.

The two of us got up from our dinner table. As we did so, I put my hand in my pocket to get the £300 I had brought with me out to pay for our dinner. As I pulled the money from my pocket, Bob saw the money. "What are you doing?" Bob said as though I had annoyed him.

"I was going to pay," I replied.

"Cyrus, that is very disrespectful. I have brought you for food, put your money away," Bob said as he frowned at me. It was an order not a request, just as he had told Chris 'not to look behind him at me' in the car outside the club when we had met. I didn't argue the point of wanting to pay any further, as I could tell he was genuinely annoyed that I had thought it was necessary in the first place. We stepped back outside into the cold Sunday late evening air.

"Haven't we got to pay?" I asked in a voice that just let Bob know I was curious and not suggesting that I wanted to pay.

"Cyrus, that's my friend's restaurant. If he heard I had paid, he would go mad and fall out with me," Bob said as he pressed the fob on his keys to open the luxurious white hot-hatch. With my belly now full and feeling revitalised, we turned out of the car park. "Turn your phone off, Cyrus," Bob said as he took out the two phones he had on him as he drove and switched them both off. I didn't ask any questions as I remembered the no talking in the car policy and assumed it was for good reason.

Ten minutes later, we arrived on the street that was predominantly Asian and resembled the road I had met Bob on. "Put this on, I will explain when we get out of the car," Bob said as he gave me a black eye mask—the type of eye mask that people wear to bed to block out the light. The mask had an elastic strap that goes around the back of your head. I had seen people wearing the same masks on the plane when my mum and dad had took me to Jamaica years before. Again, I didn't ask any questions; it was self-explanatory. He was taking me somewhere that he didn't want me to know the location of. It was his place, therefore his right, and who was I to argue. I put the double eye-patched elastic thing on willingly with the thought he must be taking me to see something good, or he wouldn't care if I knew where it was. When I had put the eye mask on properly, Bob pulled off again and began to drive. The world went black with darkness as I sat rocking as the car turned left and right. Bob seemed to be driving quicker than he had before. I could feel the power of the car holding me in place in my seat as Bob sped down straight roads. I had confidence in Bob's driving ability; he seemed like a man that knew what he was doing. My eyelashes rubbed against the nylon feeling material on the inside of my blindfold. The car stopped quickly, and I felt the powerful engine grumble as we parked up. The engine turned off. "Cyrus, when I say 'now', take that blindfold off and follow me quickly. Okay?" Bob said clearly making sure I understood perfectly.

"Okay," I replied.

"Now," Bob said. I lifted the eyepatch causing me to squint due to the dramatic change in lighting. I heard Bob's driver's door open. Bob got out and walked around the car towards my side, which was closest to the row of houses we were parked outside of. I got out and followed Bob closely. He walked quickly to a door which was no more than four houses up from where we had parked. The street had the same brick houses on it—they looked no bigger than four-bedroom houses. Each had a small brick wall outside with a little gate. They were average houses on an average street. I could tell we were still in an Asian area. Bob walked to the front door of a house with me closely behind, and using the single key Luke had given him, Bob opened the door. In through the front door took us into a reception type room. A kind of tiny living room Bob ushered me in quickly and locked the door behind us. The reception room had a sofa and a few pictures on the wall of buildings and nice sceneries. The room also had a brown cabinet with a little table the same colour in front of the small two-seat leather sofa. "Cyrus, I have never brought anybody here before, you're only here because you're going to work with me, and I want you to understand how things work; but you do not tell a soul about what I'm going to teach you, okay?" Bob said in a serious tone.

I could tell that Bob was nervous and unsettled. I had never seen Bob look nervous before, which told me whatever Bob stored in this house was very significant. So significant that this house unsettled Bob as soon as he entered the front door.

The door to leave the reception room and continue on into the house was closed—a cheap white wooden door. Bob walked past me and opened the white wooden door to walk through. I followed Bob to find the strangest layout for a living room I had ever seen. As I walked in through the white wooden door, there was a window in the left side of the wall opposite me. It had a long blackout blind all the way down, covering any view from outside. There was a doorway directly in front of me leading through to the kitchen. The floor in the living room had been carpeted, but that looked cheap and was hard due to the fact it had no underlay. There was a large wooden workbench in front of the window with the blackout blind. The bench ran from the front of the window along the wall at just over waist height and was over two metres long. The room had a three-piece sofa against the wall immediately to my left as I walked into the room. On top of the workbench was what looked like a pair of industrial weighing scales. They looked like the type that people have in their bathrooms, but this pair of scales was much thicker, with a big square silver surface on the top. The scales had a little digital screen underneath the weighing surface. Also on this large workbench was what looked like four big blenders. I could see an extension lead on the workbench with the four blenders plugged in and the scales.

"Welcome to my office," Bob said as he looked around the room. Bob had walked in through the white wooden door and taken three steps forward, then turned left and walked to the wall, putting the sofa on his left and the giant work surface starting on his right. He was kneeling down in front of a rectangular, red metal-frame type thing. It had a circular gauge on the top of it, and a platform in the middle of the frame with a big thick steel black plate resting on top of the platform. It was roughly waist height, and it had a lead coming from just beneath the gauge on the top. The lead was connected to what looked like a large pump that was red and cylinder shaped, as thick as the fat part of a baseball bat. The pump was resting on the floor with a lever above it to pump.

"Do you know what this is?" Bob asked as he turned from the machine to look at me.

"No, what is it?" I answered truthfully.

"It's a 10-ton hydraulic press," Bob answered. It had the words 'strong arm' written on it, and a thick cylinder that is moved using the hydraulics that comes through the middle of the frame to squash whatever is resting on the thick black metal plate on the platform. It is operated hydraulically using the pump. Bob levered the white handle up and down three or four times, and the arm-sized cylinder in the middle started to move down towards the platform with each pump of the lever. I understood the concept, but what the fuck did he want that for? Also, why was he so happy with it? Bob stood up in front of the '10-ton press' and opened the door next to the sofa that presumably led upstairs.

"Bubbles! Yoooh, Bubbles!" Bob shouted as he put his head around the corner of the door. I heard movement upstairs before I heard someone coming down the stairs.

"Didn't you hear me come in?" Bob asked the guy he called Bubbles.

"Yes, of course, I heard you come in, but I thought you were busy," Bubbles replied; he was a white guy in his late 30s or early 40s. He was slightly overweight and bald; he looked a little scruffy and a bit greasy.

"Get a case of 'nose' and three cases of 'Benz'," Bob said to the fattish man he called Bubbles. At this, Bubbles started back up the stairs. "Sit down with me, Cyrus, while I explain what's going on," Bob said as he pointed to the three-piece sofa.

Bob then went on to explain. "Cyrus, I buy kilos of pure cocaine. I buy it from my Albanian friends, or I buy it from my Dutch friends, depending on who has got better cocaine at the time. I pay £35,000 per kilo. What we are going to do now is turn one kg into four kg. Cyrus, how we are going to do that is we are going to blend one of our kilos of pure cocaine with three-kg of benzocaine.

Benzocaine, or as I call it 'Benz', has no taste. It's white and causes a slight numbing if you put it in your mouth. It's perfect for mixing with cocaine. Cyrus, what we are going to do now when Bubbles comes back downstairs is sit here while Bubbles blends one-ounce of pure cocaine with three-ounces of benzocaine. Cyrus, we are going to sit here until he has done that 36 times, because there is 36 ounces in a kilo as you know," Bob went on to explain that he blends the cocaine and benzocaine mix in small quantities as it ensures an even mix.

The fattish white guy called Bubbles came back down the stairs with a black drawstring bag with writing on it 'a sports bag'. Bubbles walked over to the big work surface and emptied the contents onto the workbench.

"Can I watch?" I said to Bob as I began to stand up.

"Yes, of course, just don't get in his way or distract him, because he ain't the brightest crayon in the colouring box, are you, Bubbles?" Bob said clearly mocking him. Bubbles didn't even reply; he just looked behind him at the sofa and grinned at Bob.

I stood up to position myself with a clear view of the work surface without impeding Bubbles' work. There were three giant clear bags of loose white powder that looked finely blended. There was also one rectangular block, the block was about an inch and a half thick and roughly the size of an average book; maybe half an inch wider and longer, like an old videocassette box. "Is that a kilo of pure cocaine?" I asked trying not to disturb Bubbles too much but still acquiring the information I wanted.

"Yes, mate, that's a case of pure," Bubbles replied. The word 'case' being street terminology for a kilo, 'case, box, square' are all words used to describe a kilo of cocaine, or anything else that weighs a kilo. I stood watching as Bubbles used a Stanley blade to slice along the long edge of the kilo of pure cocaine. It was covered in a brown tape. Bubbles was pressing hard as he ran the blade slowly along the corner from one edge to the other. "You've got to press hard because under the brown tape, there's a rubber jacket and clear plastic," Bubbles said as he offered an explanation for his method.

"Oh, okay," I said, showing appreciation for the knowledge. Once finished with the long edge, Bubbles ran the sharp blade along the short edge that met where he had just cut and repeated the procedure. Bubbles then opened the flap and pulled the packaging off using force, but not recklessly. A white rectangular block emerged from the packaging, over an inch thick and as big as an old videocassette case.

"Smell it," Bob called out from behind Bubbles and me. I turned around momentarily to see Bob sitting on the sofa, smoking a cigarette. Bob was clearly enjoying watching me receive my education.

I leaned over and carefully put my nose near to the giant block of cocaine. "That absolutely stinks," I said as a whiff entered my nasal passage that smelt like I had just sniffed high-octane petrol. It had a strong chemical smell. Bubbles put the block of cocaine down and walked into the kitchen, returning quickly with a big plastic lid, and what looked like an ice cream scoop. Bubbles put his instruments onto the workbench and went back to the kitchen. Bubbles came back into the room with a blue and new-looking, large washing up basin. He placed the large washing up basin on the floor underneath the workbench. *Bubbles knows what he's doing,* I thought as he placed the clear tray on the big metal scales and turned them on after. He placed the block of pure cocaine from the brown package on the scales along with all of the bits that had gotten stuck in the packaging.

"One thousand and twelve grams, Bob," Bubbles said as he looked behind him for Bob's approval.

"Good, three grams over, just throw it in the blend, mate," Bob said as he sat looking a mixture of bored and proud of himself.

I stood and watched as Bubbles broke off 28 g from the block of pure cocaine and threw an equal piece, weighing exactly 28 g, in each of the four blenders. Bubbles then opened one of the big see-through bags of benzocaine and weighed out 84 g; and through a pile of benzocaine, weighing 84 g into each of the four blenders. Bubbles then turn on all four blenders. The noise was almost as loud as a broken hoover. Bubbles picked each blender up and manoeuvred it around, making sure it had blended all of its contents properly. A minute or so later, Bubbles turned all four blenders off, took out the big blue washing basin from under the table and emptied the contents of all four blenders into it. A small cloud of white powder rose into the air as he would take the top off each blender. "Will that get me high?" I asked Bob pointing at the cloud of white powder.

"Yes, if you sniff it, why do you think I'm sitting here," Bob replied as he smiled widely. I stood and watched Bubbles repeat the process another eight or so times. By the time Bubbles had finished, the large blue basin was practically full of the cocaine-benzocaine mixture. The blenders were all caked in white powder.

"Finally," Bob said as he watched Bubbles empty the last batch of blenders into the large blue basin. "Get my metal tin now, please, Bubbles," Bob said to Bubbles. As Bubbles disappeared back upstairs, I stood and looked at the drugs factory that this living room had been converted into. That is when it dawned on me, *I am fucking small fry.* What I had just seen was another level.

"Now, this is where the fun starts, Cyrus," Bob said as he rubbed his hands together excitedly. *Starts?* I thought. What was all of that if that wasn't the fun?

"What do you mean?" I asked reluctantly.

"Well, Cyrus, you can't sell cocaine in large quantities in powder. People will think it's shit if it's in powder because anybody could throw anything into it. Cyrus, people mainly like cocaine in block form, so what we are going to do now is turn that powder into a 'rock hard' block. Well, not rock hard, but almost rock hard," Bob explained. Bob had pointed at the large blue basin filled with the benzocaine/cocaine mix. *How could you turn that into a block?* I thought.

Bubbles came back into the room with a metal box with thick metal walls. It was the size of a rectangle cuboid made out of DVD covers with one of the larger surfaces missing. It was made of steel. Just off cubed-shaped, a rectangular-shaped box with one side missing.

"Cyrus, this is my favourite toy," Bob said excitedly as he held the metal box. "Pass me some latex gloves, Bubbles," Bob said. Bubbles walked into the kitchen and returned with a pair of latex gloves and gave them to Bob. Bob picked up the metal box and wiped it down. "Come here, Cyrus," Bob said. Bob turned the box upside down on the workbench as I stood close and examined his favourite toy. When the box was turned upside down, two thick pieces of steel fell out of the middle of the box, making a distinctive thud as the heavy steel hit the workbench. They had been resting in the bottom of the box, two thick pieces of steel that fit into the box almost perfectly because they were smaller by a couple of millimetres around the edges.

I looked into the bottom of the box. Now that these thick pieces of steel had been removed, I could see the base of the box had a coin-sized hole in the bottom of the thick steel that was the base of the box. I was confused. Bubbles had a big clear plastic bag in his hands. Shall I do them in half kilos?" Bubbles asked Bob.

"Yes," Bob answered as he turned the scales back on and weighed 504 g of the cocaine-benzocaine mix. The half a kilo was put into a clear plastic bag. A kilo is meant to weigh 1,000 g, but a kilo of drugs typically weighs 1,008 g. Reason being, one ounce weighs 28 g, there are 36 ounces in a kilo, and $36 \times 28 = 1,008$, so the half a kilo Bubbles had put in the clear plastic bag weighed 504 g. "You ready to see my magic trick?" Bob asked as he smiled at me, holding his metal box with his tight latex gloves on.

"Yes, ready as ever," I replied as if I was watching the best chemistry/physics lesson ever. Bob placed the metal box onto the platform of the metal frame within the 10-ton hydraulic press.

Bob then placed one of two thick sheets of metal that fit inside the box back inside. There was just enough room for it to slot back inside of the box falling to the bottom with the slightest of nudges. Bob then took the bag of cocaine benzocaine mix from Bubbles containing the half a kilo of powder. Bob placed the bag of cocaine/benzocaine mix inside of the metal box as it rested on the platform. Then he took the second thick sheet of steel off the workbench and placed that on top of the half of kilo that was now in his metal box. Bob had effectively made a kind of 'steel cocaine sandwich'. Bob then knelt down and started to pump the lever by the side of the machine. I watched as the small fist-sized arm moved slowly with each pump of the lever towards the top piece of steel. As the hydraulic arm reached the top piece of steel, it began to push the lid further inside of the box as Bob pumped the lever almost effortlessly. The gauge on the top of the machine had started to move as the pressure increased. I stepped forward to read it. It was a pressure gauge reading in tons. Every time Bob pumped the lever, the gauge went up as the hydraulic piston squashed the cocaine into the box further. "Five-tonnes, Cyrus, what I do is put five-tonnes of pressure onto it, then wait for a minute; the pressure will fall back to just over 4.5 tonnes, then I pump it a bit more back up to five tonnes, that way it will stay solid," I could clearly tell that Bob took pride in his work, and the knowledge he had when operating his machinery.

I watched as Bob completed the procedure he had explained, pointing at the pressure gauge to show me the pressure had fallen just as he had anticipated. He then turned a switch on the side of the pump to release the pressure making the hydraulic arm lifted back up and out until it was clear of the metal box. The last piece of steel Bob had put into the box was now pushed far inside the metal box.

Bob lifted the box off the platform and turned it upside down on top of the work surface. 'Clunk' was the sound made as the top sheet of metal hit the work surface. I looked inside and could see the bag containing the half a kilo of cocaine was squashed into the shape of the box—a slab of cocaine stuck inside a thick steel box. Bob then looked at Bubbles who handed him a coin-sized cylinder that was slightly shorter than a pen, but a lot thicker and made from heavy-duty metal. Bob placed the box back on top of the platform of the hydraulic press, this time upside down.

Bob had placed the cylinder Bubbles had given him into the coin-sized hole in the bottom of the box. *He's clever,* I thought as I watched on. The cylinder piece of metal was perfect to put in the hole at the bottom of the box and push the last loose sheet of metal out, releasing the cocaine. Bob then used the same method by pumping the lever, but this time the hydraulic arm was pushing the cylinder into the bottom of the box. Bob released the pressure to lift the arm as the cocaine hit the platform, preventing it freeing the box completely. Then using rectangular blocks that Bubbles had given him, Bob put them under the thick rim of the box giving the cocaine room to fall onto the platform. Bob then released the pressure for the last time and removed the box from the machine. The cocaine block was still stuck in the box, but it was half out and half in. The edges of the cocaine block were square and hard, like a piece of white slab stuck inside a steel cube. Bob held the box over the large workbench while Bubbles hit the cylinder with a loose piece of metal from the platform of the machine. 'Clunk,

clunk' was the sound made as the giant rock-hard rectangular block of cocaine hit the table, closely followed by the thick sheet they had used as the base of the box.

"Have a look, Cyrus," Bob said as he placed the empty box on the work surface.

I picked up the block of cocaine; it was rock-hard and the size of a small slab of concrete. "That's crazy," I said as I examined their work.

"No, that's not crazy, that's how you make money, Cyrus," Bob said as he corrected me.

Remembering what everybody had asked me, I asked Bob, "Is it any good?" I asked curiously.

"Yes, Cyrus, it's very good; and for the price you are going to sell it for, it's great," Bob explained.

"Let's sit down and have a chat for a while. Bubbles is going to finish pressing the rest of this cocaine. I don't pay him to do his job for him," Bob said as he took his gloves off and put them in his pocket.

"Cyrus, I pay £35,000 per kilo of pure cocaine, so I'm going to charge you £45,000 per kilo of pure cocaine," Bob said as we sat down next to each other.

He wants £10,000 profit, I thought. I didn't say anything, but that was my initial thought. "Cyrus, each kilo of cocaine I make cost me £8,750. I am going to sell you each one I make for £11, 250. I want you to sell each kilo for £20,000. When you have sold four kilos, I will have made £10,000 profit; and you will have made £35,000 profit," Bob explained. My eyes were now gaping.

"How long will it take to sell four kilos of what you've made roughly?" I asked trying to gauge how long it would take me to earn the £35,000 profit.

"Well, I don't know that, but you should be able to do it every ten days at least," Bob replied. *No wonder he's got diamond chains and watches,* I thought as I remained silent. I wanted to take in all the information that Bob had given me. "So, what are you saying then, Cyrus?" Bob asked as I hadn't said much since sitting down.

"I will take two kg, as long as you can guarantee they are worth £20,000 each," I couldn't believe what I had said. *My greed and my balls knew no boundaries.* I thought as my ears and brain interpreted what I had said without a second's thought. Bob's face was full of surprise. I was just as surprised with what I had said. Bubbles continued compressing cocaine using the metal box as we spoke. When Bubbles had heard me say I want two kilos, he had turned around to look at me. Fuck it though; 'in for a penny, in for a pound' was my logic. The way I looked at it was; if I'm going to dip a toe in the pond, I might as well shout 'cowabonga' and do a cannonball. My days of playing games were long gone. I wanted what Bob had, in fact, I wanted more.

"Cyrus, it's a lot of money. I'd never give someone I've just met two kilos on trust, and you should never do that either, in fact don't give someone an ounce on trust," Bob said as he followed his head and not his heart.

"I don't want it on trust. I will pay cash," I replied quick for a solution to any problem. Then the thought of parting with £22, 500 hit me, that's when I decided to follow *my* brain and not my heart.

"Well, give me a little piece as a sample to show people. If it's as good as you say it is, I would buy two kilos for cash," I said after having time to think. The smile Bob had when I said I'd buy two kilos for cash had turned back into a plain facial expression. Bob was thinking.

"Cyrus, I'm going to give you a kilo. I want to see how you get on, that's best I think," Bob said. Bubble had stacked up four blocks in the time it had taken Bob and me to make one. They were all piled up on top of each other, like concrete slabs, but as white as the driven snow.

I sat looking around at my surroundings. It was the strangest living room I had ever seen. Windows blacked out, giant workbench, shit thin blue carpet, four blenders and an oversized-pair of industrial scales with a hydraulic press and ice cream scoop trays. Washing basins and some fat guy sweating, absolute madness, but I loved it; and the best bit was, if I could sell four kilos a week, I'd make £35,000 profit every week. I turned to face Bob and smiled. "I'm on it, count me in."

Chapter 15

The leather in the back of Yax's jeep was cold against my back as I rested against it. Feeling the temperature through my thin designer T-shirt was soothing. Bob had dropped me back to the restaurant. We had drove back here to meet his two friends that would drop me home to Coventry. We had driven into the car park and then into the far corner next to Yax's black jeep that was waiting for us. "Cyrus, don't forget, do not tell a soul what I showed you, and don't let me down!" Bob said as I opened his car door to get into the black jeep. I threw the 'sports bag' on the floor of the jeep and climbed in after it. The sky had changed from light to dark in the time I had spent in the house that Bob had taken me to mixed drugs in.

Inside the jeep was so bright in contrast to the darkness of outside. Cream, leather-covered all the surfaces perfectly, beautiful cream leather stretched over all the upholstery, leaving creaseless bright surfaces wherever I looked. The driver of the black jeep was the Asian man that Bob had called 'Yax'. Yax had typed my postcode into the car-satellite navigation system which was positioned inside a big screen in the dashboard.

During our drive back to Coventry, the stocky white man called Luke asked me questions about Coventry and about the other drug dealers in my area. Luke had told me that him, and his business partner, Yax, 'graft' for a living. The term graft, Luke went on to explain, meant that he and Yax tie up drug-dealers and rob them for a living. This did not worry me as I got the impression Bob was the boss and the brains of this organised crime gang.

I was Bob's friend, so I felt safe in their company. "How much do you make from the average graft," I asked as we drove down the more or less empty M6 motorway.

"Well, we've had £100,000 in cash. We've had five kg of pure cocaine, it varies, but we do any work where there is at least £50,000," Luke explained.

Luke seemed like a really nice guy. He had olive skin and dark hair on the top with the sides shaved. Luke had perfectly white teeth and a bright smile, it would be fair to say I liked Luke from our first conversation. The driver, Yax, was a lot quieter than Luke. Yax just drove and added that odd 'yes' or laughed as Luke told jokes.

"Let me know if there's any work around your way, Cyrus, we will come and do it and give you a nice cut!" Luke said as we neared Coventry.

"Yes, I'm going to find you two some work," I said. I liked the prospect of getting free money, and I liked the prospect of getting anybody who pissed me off tied up and robbed even more. *Any rival drug-dealers better be careful,* I thought as I sat reflecting on what I had been told.

I looked down at the sports bag at my feet. It was identical to the bag I had received when I had brought my latest pair of sports trainers; however, this bag had a kilo of cocaine inside. As we neared the exit to leave the motorway near to my house, I called Chris and my brother, telling them to meet me in my street. Bob had told me he wanted £11,250 for the kilo of cocaine I had at my feet. If I sold it for £20,000, I would make £8,750, and this is what Bob had suggested. I, however, had other plans. I worked out that selling it for £20,000 meant I would be selling each of the 36 ounces for £550. I would not be doing that. I wanted to sell each ounce of cocaine for £600, and that would bring me back £21,600. This extra £1,600 would be Chris or Daniel's profit, leaving the full profit Bob suggested exclusively for me. The blacked-out jeep whistled as it accelerated along the main road at the top of my estate. "This left here, lads, then straight down to the bottom and take a right," I said as I directed Yax towards my house. Almost as soon as we took the last right into the dead end, I saw my red rally car parked up, with my brother and Chris sitting in the front.

"Is that your car, Cyrus?" Yax asked.

"Yes, I brought it last week," I answered as I picked up the sports bag and put the string over my shoulder, like it was a pair of football boots or new trainers.

"You are doing it, Cyrus, keep up the bad work!" Yax said as he parked next to my shiny red car. I exchanged phone numbers with Luke and shook their hands. "If you get any trouble, call us, and we will be straight down here, armed and ready for action," Yax said as he made a gun gesture with his two fingers and his thumb.

Yax looked more dangerous than Luke. I put that down to his shaved head and long shiny black beard. He had light brown eyes and the occasional Asian 'twang' that slipped into his English every now and again. I felt like a mob boss as I jumped out of the big, black, brand-new, blacked-out jeep in my Italian jeans with matching trainers and T-shirt. Both the sets of eyes in my car studied my arrival. Both Daniel and Chris smiled as I approached my car. I heard the jeep purr as it pulled off and out of our street behind me.

I opened my car door and jumped into the back of my car without hesitation. I had promised Daniel and Chris £2,000 a week earnings if they both worked hard. I wasn't intending on selling one KG a week; this first batch was a trial run, so to speak. So, paying them £2,000 each a week would be out of the question. I had already decided I would pay them £1,600 for every kilo they sold; and at the end of the month, I treat them if we'd had a good month collectively. I would be making nearly £9,000 profit for every kilo of cocaine they sold after paying them and Bob, so I was onto a winner. Suddenly, the £10,000 profit Bob would be making per kilo of pure cocaine seemed fairer than ever. "Yes, Cyrus, that jeep was wicked, who the fuck were they?" my brother asked.

"Just some lads that I work with," I replied trying to play the whole thing down.

I was more excited than Chris and Daniel were put together, but I kept all my excitement concealed. "Cyrus, is that how you're going on? Getting driven home in brand-new jeeps like that?" Chris asked as he smiled showing his approval.

"That's nothing, I've got a present for you two," I said as I continued to play the whole brand-new jeep thing down. I removed the drawstring bag from my shoulder and opened the top by loosening the string that held the bag closed. Reaching inside, I pulled out the two slabs of cocaine weighing half a kilo of cocaine each. Bubbles had wrapped them tight in Clingfilm 'for presentation', as he had put it. "Lads, each one of these is half the kilo. Every time you sell a whole kilo, I will pay you £1,600, and rightfully you should be able to sell two s a week each," I assumed in a bid to motivate them. I hoped that they would be able to sell two KGs a week each, that way I would make my £35,000 a week, and that would be after they have been paid.

"I want you both to sell no less than an ounce, and you are to sell ounces for £600, 4 ½ ounces in bulk gets sold for £2,700, and a 'nine bar' gets sold for £5,400 and so on," I explained. 'Nine bar' is street slang for nine ounces.

"Is the stuff any good though?" Chris asked as he took one of the slab-sized blocks from me and examined it.

"Yes, of course it is. I'm giving you both half a kilo each, so sell it for 10,800 and give me 10,000," I said as Chris and my brother both examined their packages. Bob had explained in the house with Bubbles that if Chris is going to sell drugs for me, he should never keep drugs in his house.

"If he gets stopped by police, and they find two bags of weed in his pocket, they will go and raid his house and find a kilo of cocaine, Cyrus; then Chris is going to jail, and you will have just lost over £11,000," Bob had stressed adamantly. I had conveyed this information to Chris. Of course, I didn't let Chris know that someone had gave me this information. Instead, I led Chris to believe it was a product of my own intelligence. I had saved just over £70,000, my mum had £40,000 in cash for me, which I demanded be hidden at a relative's house that wasn't my Auntie Delma. My Auntie Delma had £30,000 in cash hidden for me already, and I had nearly £2,000 under my drawers in my room. *Shit,* I thought. All of the excitement of the day had made me forget to call Jabber.

"Chris, have you got the money for the weed; and Daniel, have you got the money for the weed from the McBride's?" I asked the two of them.

"Yes, I got the money for 50 ounces, plus your profit is at my house," Chris replied.

"The money for the nine ounces the McBrides have sold is in our house, Cyrus, plus your profit," Daniel replied.

"Okay, Chris, you take the two half-a-kilos to your house for tonight only. Tomorrow, Daniel will come and collect one back from you. I want you to find a girl to look after it for you. Oh, and bring the money back here for the weed. I want you to walk though, because I know it's only around the corner, but I don't want police seeing a red rally car driving around at 11:00 at night; there's no cars on the road," I explained. Chris opened the driver's door, and I handed him the drawstring bag with the two bricks of cocaine inside. "Oh, Chris, weigh out one gram and bring it back to me with the money. Make sure you break the gram off as a rock; people don't like dust," I said as I looked at him and Daniel to make sure they understood my 'no dust' policy. "Daniel, go and grab the money from the house, please," I said trying not to sound too bossy. Silence fell in and around the car as Jabber's phone began to call in my ear.

"Yes, Cyrus, I was beginning to think you forgot about me," Jabber said in his deep voice playfully. I think he hadn't called me because he wasn't sure I was going to pay him because my brother and I had beaten his nephew, Jason, up.

"Don't be silly, Jabber, you've looked after me from day one; I could never forget about you," I said happily; I did like Jabber. He was the opposite to me in a lot of ways. He was quiet—I was loud. I was brown—he was white. He was big—I was small in comparison... but our common interests were massive—drugs and money. I think we both liked the fact that we both refused to take any shit from anybody.

"So, what are you saying then, Cyrus? Did you want me to come and see you tomorrow as it's late now?" Jabber asked. I could tell from his tone he was at home, probably sprawled on the sofa or in bed.

"Well, not really. Is there any chance you could come to my house now. I've got the money here for all 59 ounces, and I need more tomorrow afternoon, and I've got a sample of that sniff," I explained. 'Sniff' meaning cocaine.

"Go on then, Cyrus. I will be there in 15 minutes, where shall I meet you?" Jabber asked.

"I'll be parked outside my house, my friend," I replied.

"Okay, see you in a minute, Cyrus," Jabber said before putting the phone down.

Daniel arrived back at the car first. The distinctive squeak made by the gate opening could be heard even though the windows of my car were closed. I counted out £1,350 from the bundle of cash Daniel had given me which was Jabber's money, leaving me £930, which was my profit. I gave my brother, Daniel, £130 extra as a little bonus—he was my brother after all. "Roll a joint, look at it like I'm buying a joint off you for £130," I said as I smiled at my brother. Without another word, Daniel started to do as I'd asked. Seven minutes later, and the rally car now filled with smoke, I sat checking my rear view mirrors for Chris. My eyes had been busy all day checking rear-view mirrors and scanning my surroundings. I was happy that I spotted the chubby track-suited figure that was Chris far in the distance. As Chris got closer, I saw he had the drawstring bag over his shoulder. I watched as Chris stepped nearer and nearer. I was happy with myself; as Chris had not even taken two steps into a place, I could have seen him without me spotting him.

Being a drug-dealer had taught me to practice my observational skills. If a police officer saw me while I was driving or in a car before I saw him, that was a slap in my face. If I spotted a police officer, and he didn't see me, then that was a slap in his face. So, the very fact that nobody could sneak up on me or walk into the dark street I was parked in without me seeing them meant there was no chance of a police officer getting close to me without me seeing him or her.

Constantly testing myself to see whether 'I'm on the ball'. Chris opened the rear car door after he had walked through the concrete posts and gave me the same drawstring bag I had given him. "There's the money for 50 ounces and your profit," Chris said as he sat in the back seat, clearly aware the car was filled with smoke. "Since when have we started smoking weed in this car, Cyrus?" Chris asked, probably remembering how annoyed I had been when he even suggested lighting a joint in my car.

"Since we decided to step things up," I replied as I loosened the string, keeping the bag closed at the top. I opened the 'sports bag' to see the usual bundles of cash. Four individual bundles of cash, each containing £2,000 held together with elastic bands, and a little pile of notes on the side, which was the extra £750. As far as Chris knew, the £750 was my profit, and the rest was Jabber's. However, that was not correct, because £1,250 was my profit, and the rest was Jabber's. It had been almost 15 minutes since I had spoken to the big bald white man, Jabber, so I assumed he would be turning around the corner into the little dead-end any second. "Daniel, take Chris into the house while I speak to my friends; and, Chris, give me that gram of 'sniff'," I said as I turned to look at them awkwardly, due to having too much money in every pocket and on the floor, and money all over my lap. The two of them opened the car doors and began to get out of the car. "I will come inside when I'm done," I said as they both got out of the car and went in through our brown gate that made the squeak sound as you open or close it. I locked the car doors before I reached inside the bag Chris had given me and counted out £1,250. I then put the money in my right-hand jeans pocket. My left pocket already had my money from the profit off the McBrides, and my day's £300 spending money. All I could think about as I sat in pitch darkness with the doors locked was, I hope this 'cocaine venture' takes off. *Shit,* I thought as I remembered I had not added the money from my brother, Daniel, to the money from Chris. Daniel's money was still sitting on the floor between my feet. I did so while still looking around, making sure I had complete awareness of my surroundings.

"I'm just pulling in now, Cyrus," Jabber said as he answered his phone. His headlights lit the street up before he took the last right to head towards where I was parked. Jabber's headlights shone bright on the houses he was driving towards before turning and illuminating me and the car I was sitting in.

I got out of my car, holding the sports bag and walked slowly towards Jabber to stop him having to drive right outside my house. I didn't want my dad to hear another car in the street, especially one with Jabber inside of it. Jabber got the message and stopped short of my house. "Are you all right, pal," I said as I smiled at Jabber. We shook hands firmly while smiling profusely. Jabber shook his head as he smiled at me as if he was condoning what had happened with his nephew, Jason. His body language told me that he would have expected nothing less coming from someone he now knew as 'big Calvin's son'.

"Cyrus, you had to do what you had to do, but leave him now, please, my friend. He's shit scared and very, very sorry, Cyrus," Jabber said as he called a truce between his nephew, Jason, and me.

"That's fine, it's forgotten about," I replied as I gave him the sports bag that had started its journey hours before in a drug factory, with a kilo of pure cocaine inside of it. It was now being handed over again, this time with nearly £9,000 in cash inside of it.

"Thanks, Cyrus," Jabber said as he loosened the drawstring on the bag that had been keeping the bag closed, before asking, "How much money is here, Cyrus?"

"That's the money for 59 ounces, there's £8,850," I replied as I pointed at the bag on Jabber's lap. I reached in my little jeans pocket to get the gram of cocaine Chris had given me.

"Here, there's a gram there," I said as I gave Jabber one of our £10 weed bags with a green, pea-sized, little rock of cocaine inside of it.

Jabber took the bag from me and opened it. He put it to his nose to smell it. "It smells strong," Jabber said as he sniffed at the bag. Then Jabber carefully, just about, got his little finger inside the bag to get some powder onto his finger. He rubbed the powder between his index finger and his thumb.

"If it's pure cocaine, it will disappear into oil," Jabber said explaining why he was rubbing it into his fingers. "It's a bit mixed, but it's really oily," Jabber said. I didn't say anything… It's not like I could have said anything.

"Jabber, it was pure before we put it in a blender with benzocaine," that would have went down like a lead balloon. Jabber put some more powder onto his finger and tasted it.

"It's strong though," Jabber said as it met his approval. "How much is it?" Jabber asked as he went to hand me the bag back.

"Twenty one thousand pounds per kilo, and you can keep that as a sample," I replied as I declined taking the bag back from him.

"Cyrus, my mate buys kilos, and I do a bit as well. Let me go home and try it, and I will give my mate some to look at and let you know the verdict tomorrow," Jabber said as he put the small bag of cocaine into his jacket pocket, and his bag of money on the floor behind the driver's seat.

"Okay, I'll let you go then, mate," I said as I shook Jabber's hand once more before getting out of his car.

"Oh, Cyrus, is that your motor?" Jabber asked pointing at the red rally car outside my house.

"Yes, do you like it?" I asked.

"Yes. That's fucking awesome. I will drop your weed tomorrow. Take care, my friend," Jabber said before starting his engine and shutting his door.

Chapter 16

I need a new bed was my first thought as I rolled over the following morning; feeling the metal from my bed frame through my thin mattress was horrible. Me, Chris and Daniel had stayed up until 2:00 in the morning discussing business. Daniel and Chris had wanted to talk about the prospect of making £3,000 a week each, I was more interested in the logistics of money transportation and storage, in terms of stash houses for their cocaine. I had agreed to give them both £100 each a week for storage. Daniel's £100 would be given to Trish, who already looked after his cannabis—and as of this morning, his cocaine. The hundred pounds given to Chris would be given to our long-time friend, Charlene. She would, as of this morning, look after Chris' cocaine. Charlene was Chris' and my brother's age; she lived with her sister and her sister's younger child. Her house was perfect for a 'stash house', as she lived a five-minute walk from my house and Chris' house, and nobody apart from Charlene had access to her bedroom. Also, for her age, Charlene was very 'clued-up', and best of all, Charlene did not have big mouth. Nobody is going to suspect the young girl who keeps herself to herself of having half a kilo of cocaine in her bedroom. Well, it is a lot more unlikely than it would be to suspect me or Chris of having half a kilo of cocaine in our bedrooms.

I had planned to meet Holly for the day and take her out for food. She had complained that since I got my new car, she hadn't seen me. I planned to tell Holly today I was going to be busy all the time from now, and we should keep things casual—the last thing I need is more stress in the form of girlfriends. I had just got out the shower when my phone rang; 'Jason' flashed on the screen. *What the fuck does this dickhead want?* I thought as I looked at his name on my phone screen.

"What?" I answered ready to tell him where to go.

"Hello," a female voice said on the other end. I didn't recognise the voice.

"Who is that?" I asked puzzled as to who this girl was.

"It's Jason's girlfriend. Is this Cyrus?" she asked.

"Yes, what up?" I asked as I wondered what she was calling me for.

"Jason has gone to the shop, but I want to meet you to talk to you," she said as she spoke quickly.

"Yes, okay, where do you want to meet?" I asked. I remembered what she looked like—blonde, big tits and about five years older than me at least.

"I'm going to take your number out of Jason's phone. Meet me at the shop around the corner from Jason's in ten minutes if you can," she said.

"You mean the corner shop?" I asked, as there was two shops equal distance from Jason's in opposite directions.

"Yes, that's the one. And my name is Emma," Emma said before hanging up. I stood in my room wearing only my boxer shorts looking at my phone, thinking *what the fuck was that about?* when I remembered how fit she was. It had completely slipped my mind to ask her what the fuck she wanted to talk about. Judging from her tone, it was important. It crossed my mind to call Jason's phone back, but I didn't want him to answer.

I got ready slowly, in the hope Emma would call back, but she never did. I left my house wearing a pair of dark-blue expensive jeans, with matching jumper and blue leather trainers, with white trim. *Holly will have to wait,* I thought as I slowly pulled off out my street. Fifteen minutes had passed as I neared my Auntie Delma and Jason's street. I was two or three minutes away as an unsaved number call my phone. "Hello," I answered as I continued to drive.

"Hello, it's Emma, I'm standing near the shop," she replied.

"Okay, what's up, Emma?" I asked as I continued to approach the shop.

"It's about Jason, and what I think he's been doing," Emma replied.

"Oh, okay, I'm one-minute away from the shop. I'm in a red car," I said before hanging up. My immediate thought was that she had caught on to Jason sleeping with my auntie. *If he has been back near my auntie since his beating, I would be putting a bullet in him,* I thought as I placed the phone into the centre console.

The blonde girl in the tight blue jeans and white vest top walked towards my car as I pulled up at the side of the shop. She had her hair down straight. Emma hadn't seen me as I approached the shop because she was facing the other way. Emma's bum looked round in her tight jeans; she was super sexy. I kept a plain facial expression as she approached my car. I didn't want to make it obvious that I fancied her.

"Hi," I said as Emma got into my car.

"Hi, you," Emma replied in a friendly tone.

"Let's move from here. I don't want Jason to see you in my car," I said as I pulled off.

"Okay, is this your car?" Emma answered and asked.

"Yes, why?" I asked like it was the first time anybody had asked the question.

"It's a really nice car," Emma answered as she smiled. She was flirting with me. She had given me the same smile I have received from every girl that I had been intimate with—flirty but subtle. I still understood the sign clearly, so clearly it was as if she had wrote it down and stuck it to my forehead. I acted as though I hadn't read her body language. I wasn't even sure if she had realised she had done it. The thing about studying people's body language is that their mannerism or speech mean something more than the action done or word said. Sometimes the person knows what they are doing and understand their own body language; for instance, a mother waving her index finger in anger at a naughty child, or a girl that sees the man of her dreams and plays with her hair. The mother knows she's doing the finger waving, the girl plays with her hair because she is nervous, and she does it without even being aware. I think Emma replicated the girl who plays with her hair by saying, "It's a really nice car, this is," and smiling at me like an idiot.

Still, I just kept an expressionless face while I asked, "What did you need to talk to me about?" I said in a concerned voice that told Emma I had no clue what this conversation was about.

"Cyrus, I think you're going to get angry," Emma said as her face looked a little worried.

"I'll tell you what, I will tell you what I know about Jason, and you tell me what you know about Jason," I said as I thought how best to play this situation out.

"Okay, you go first," Emma said as she sat back in her seat. *It definitely suited her… Being next to me,* I thought as I looked at Emma in my passenger seat.

"Okay, I will go first. But I'm only prepared to tell you over a cocktail," I said as I looked at her with my best poker face. Emma smiled as I looked her deep into her eyes.

"Jason will be back in about half an hour though. He thinks I'm at his house," Emma said. "A cocktail, Cyrus?" Emma said as she looked at me smiling, like I was crazy.

"Just tell him you've gone out for an hour," I said as I floored my rally car on the straight road which ripped us back in our seats viciously. The speedometer jumped from 30 mph to 130 mph in seconds.

"This car is too fast!" Emma said as her eyes widened as adrenaline coursed through her body. I slowed down, not wanting to scare her. "I will text Jason and say I've gone to see my mum; my mum doesn't like Jason, so he won't check," Emma said as she tapped buttons on her phone. I had liked Jason a lot before our fallout. But I liked Emma more; she was more mature than the girls my age.

I made a call to Chris as I drove to make sure he was taking care of business.

"Put them things away and go to see your cousin. Ask him if he wants that sniff," I said as he answered.

"Yes, will do, I'm just going to meet Charlene now to put that away; then I'm going to see my cousin," Chris replied. Now that Bob had brought it to my attention, if Chris got stopped by the police for any reason, and they found any drugs or money on Chris, resulting in the search of his house, I'd be pissed off. I put the phone down after talking to Chris and placed it in the centre console while I continued to drive.

"Where are you taking me, Cyrus?" Emma asked as she turned her gaze from the road in front of us to me.

"I fancy a daiquiri while we have a chat if you don't mind coming?" I replied trying to sound confident but hide the fact I had any other ulterior motive.

"Yes, I don't mind, is that a cocktail?" Emma asked.

"Yes, have you never had one?" I asked to keep the conversation flowing as we drove.

"How old are you, Cyrus? Emma asked. *Fuck my life,* I thought, *how can you answer this without putting her off you?* I screamed at myself internally. I knew I only had milliseconds to think and answer before that in itself would be off putting to her.

"Nearly 18," I lied, calmly, hoping she wouldn't detect the deceit. "How old are you?" I asked to change the conversation direction.

"I'm nearly 23. I feel old now I know you're only 17," Emma said.

"I feel older than I am though; I've got a life like a 35-year-old," I said as I pulled into the restaurant car park. As we walked towards the restaurant, I felt confident; I looked good, my hair was freshly cut, and I was wearing an almost brand-new designer outfit—all Italian. We looked good together; she was stunning, she had long blonde hair that came down just below her nipples, her tight blue jeans complemented her figure, and she had absolutely huge breasts.

"Cyrus, what do you do for a living," Emma asked as we walked through the car park.

"Emma, I'm not going to lie to you, but I got this car and all of my money as payment for the hard work I do for the community," I said as I smiled mischievously.

"You mean selling drugs?" Emma said quietly as I opened the door for her to enter the restaurant ahead of me. When she did so, she smiled and looked at me in the eyes. Emma's gaze sent tingles through my body. She liked bad boys, I could tell that for sure. *Therefore, she was going to love me,* I thought as I walked in behind her, slyly checking out her round bum and curvy hips.

"Can we have a table for two, please?" I said to the young man who was tasked with seating diners. We followed the waiter up to a booth not too far from where me, Jason and Jabber had once sat. I gestured a girl to come to our table; she wore the same attire as always—little black skirt, red shirt and little piny with all of her waitress utensils inside. I ordered Emma and me our cocktails. I spoke confidently and using a mature tone. I was also holding my car keys in my hand, so she could clearly see them. I didn't want her to ask me for identification that would have pissed on my bonfire before I had even lit a match.

"Okay, guys, are you two eating?" The pretty brunette waitress asked.

"We will have a look through the menu and let you know when you come back," I said as I took a wad of cash from my pocket and went to hand the waitress £20 from the £500 I had. Her eyes widened as she caught sight of the wad, like she was surprised I had so much money in my possession.

"That's okay, you can pay when you're leaving," the pretty waitress said as she left to get our cocktails. The dining room was practically empty; it was spotlessly clean, dark wood and chrome spotlights everywhere.

"So, what have you got to tell me then?" I asked Emma in a concerned voice. I didn't care what information she had. I just wanted to take her for a cocktail because she was fit.

"Well, Cyrus, I know you and your brother beat Jason up for swearing at your auntie," Emma said. I just looked at her, thinking, *so that's what the piece of shit told you.*

I didn't say anything; I just rose my eyebrows to say, "Wow."

"Well, I don't think he did swear at her. I found text messages on his phone. I think they slept together," Emma said as she began to sound annoyed and betrayed.

"When were these text messages sent?" I asked as the brunette waitress placed the two decorative cocktails on our table. "Could you bring me two more, please; we've got two more people coming to meet us," I said to the waitress, partly because I wanted her to go away, and partly because I wanted to get Emma drunk.

"The text messages were sent two days ago," Emma explained. I picked up my cocktail and took a sip.

"Try some of your cocktail, these are the best," I said as I sipped my cocktail thinking about how best to handle this; by this, I mean the manipulation of Emma, not the situation of Jason texting my auntie. As the text messages were sent before I gave Jason a beating, I didn't care. "What did the texts say?" I asked as though I was oblivious to what she told me.

"They said, from Jason, I think you're fit and a few naughty things, and she had told him to come over, but I didn't read them all; he makes me sick! I was only at his house today to finish with him," Emma ranted.

"The rat bastard, you're too good for him, he's a fucking snake," I said as I pretended to be fuming with this 'new' information.

"I know I'm too good for him. I can't believe he's done this," Emma said as she sipped her drink.

"Do you like your cocktail?" I asked.

"Yes, thank you, it's really nice, Cyrus," Emma replied pleasantly.

"Are you hungry? I haven't eaten anything today," I asked.

"No, I'm all right, I don't feel like eating." Emma replied.

"Let's just have cocktails and figure out what to do about this dickhead," I said as the pretty brunette delivered two more cocktails to our table.

"Cyrus, who is coming here?" Emma asked as she looked at the two fresh cocktails sitting at the opposite ends of the table.

"Oh, nobody, I just said that because I wanted her to go away while we spoke." Emma and I sat talking about Jason, my auntie, and how all this started. I told her about when I had given my auntie £12,000 for her to give to Jason for his Uncle Jabber. He must have used my money to act like a gangster thinking he's the big I am to chat her up.

"I can't believe them two," I said. "Drink up, Emma, I'm leaving you behind," I said as I finished my first cocktail, seeing she was only just over halfway through hers. I felt my phone vibrate in my pocket. I slid it up and out of my jeans to see 'Holly' flashing on the screen. "One second, it's my brother," I said to Emma as I got up and left the table. "Hi, Holly," I said as I walked off towards the exit.

"Hi, Cyrus, are you on your way yet?" Holly asked.

"Holly, I've just had to meet my mate to collect some money; he's going abroad tomorrow and he owes me £20,000. I will be with you in the next hour and a half after I drop this money where it needs to be," I lied to gain some time with Emma.

"Oh, Cyrus, I'm ready; can't you come and pick me up and then do it?" Holly asked impatiently.

"But I'm here with him now; we are just waiting for his mate to bring the money here," I lied.

"Okay then, try to hurry then please, Cyrus," Holly said.

"Okay, gorgeous," I said as I put the phone down and walked back inside to Emma. "My brother is always bugging me about the silliest of things," I said as I sat back down. The gorgeous Emma and I continued to talk about our families, where we both lived, and what our plans were for the future. I was very careful not to disclose any sensitive information.

We finished our second cocktail which left me feeling very tipsy. I knew if I drank any more, driving my car would be suicide, but we were getting along so well. I liked Emma a lot—her maturity was refreshingly new for me.

"If we do have another cocktail, I will not be able to drive," I said reluctantly.

"Yes, I know. I should get back soon as well," Emma replied.

"Either that or we get drunk together and go and book into that hotel behind this restaurant," I joked with a hint of seriousness. Emma just laughed and blushed.

"Maybe another time," Emma said as she looked at me shyly and smiled.

"Come on then, let's go; the quicker we go, the quicker this 'other time' will come around," I joked as I stood up feeling slightly lightheaded. I put the key in the ignition, feeling slightly disorientated. "Emma, we should definitely meet up again sometime."

"Yes, I would really like that. I think you are nice, Cyrus," Emma replied. I turned to face Emma and leaned slowly towards her. She looked deep into my eyes and leaned towards me. Meeting in the middle, I kissed her passionately; our tongues deep inside each other's mouths. I couldn't help but caress Emma's breasts tenderly. The sensation in my body made me feel like ripping her clothes off, but we were in a restaurant car park in the middle of the day. I pulled away and fought the urge, sitting back in my seat.

"Emma, you are amazing!" I said giving up the charade of not being interested in her.

"Cyrus, you are pretty hot yourself," Emma replied as she smiled and bit her lip erotically, which made me want her in my bed even more.

"What about Jason?" Emma said remembering the whole situation.

"Forget about that clown, you're mine now," I said confidently.

"What would Jason say if I start seeing his mate though? I can't do that," Emma said.

"I am not Jason's mate anymore, and he can't say a thing. I think you're gorgeous; and if you want to, I would like to start meeting you?" I said as I started my rally car.

"Yes, okay, but keep it just between us for a while. I'm going to tell him I know what he's done, and I don't want nothing to do with him anymore," Emma said. I stopped at the exit to the car park before pulling out into the main road and kissed Emma again. The second kiss was better, less passionate, but better because this time Emma was mine. We pulled out onto the main road, turning left. Inside, I was bubbling with excitement. "Cyrus, I know you are a bit younger than me, but you are so mature for your age; you are more mature than Jason and all of his friends that I have met," Emma complemented.

"Thanks," I said as I pressed my foot down onto the accelerator pedal, ripping us back into our bucket seats. My car made a phenomenal sound as I redlined it and changed gear.

"Be careful driving this car; it's too fast this thing is!" Emma said with face full of shock after realising how powerful the car actually was.

"I only drive fast once in a while, not all the time. Emma, do you want to meet later to go for food and drinks?" I asked as I drove back towards the side of town I had picked her up from.

"Yes, I don't mind, as long as you are not busy with work. If you are, I will meet you another day," Emma said.

"Emma, now that I have spent a little bit of time with you, you are now my top priority," I said as I glanced at her and then back at the road.

"Oh, that's so sweet, Cyrus," Emma replied.

"Shall I pick you up at about 8:00 tonight?" I asked.

"Okay, but what shall I wear?" Emma asked.

"It's up to you. I'm going to take you somewhere nice though," I explained.

"Okay, pick me up at 8:00 then," Emma said. As I parked outside Emma's house to say goodbye, I gave her a kiss.

"Make sure you tell Jason you don't want anything to do with him anymore," I said as she began to get out of the car.

"I will, I don't want to see him ever again," Emma replied as she smiled at me and turned to walk up her blue brick driveway. Her house was nice; it was similar to Chris' parents in size. It had a new-looking wall outside; the house was on the corner.

I watched Emma walk up her driveway, staring at her bum. Still parked outside of Emma's house, I called Holly. "Hi gorgeous, I'm ready now, where are you?" I asked trying to sound excited to finally be available to see her.

"I'm at home, Cyrus," Holly replied. Holly was pissed off; I was already nearly two hours late.

"Okay then, ten minutes, I'm sorry I'm late," I said with no sincerity. Holly's house was at least a 15-minute drive from where I was parked. Putting the phone back in the centre console, I sped every time I had open road towards Kenilworth. Holly was sexy, and I liked her. I liked the fact she didn't come from a poor background and had a great standard of life.

Holly had opened my eyes to the possibilities if I became successful. It was now time to spend my time trying to achieve my goals. Her constant need for my attention was a hindrance—it was like a hurdle. I would keep needing to negotiate every time she wanted to see me. Holly wanted a boyfriend, and I wanted to make money and have sex when I felt like it.

I stopped my car just short of the turning to Holly's house. Her mum and dad had returned home from their holiday, and I had declined the offer of meeting them. I knew it would only involve her dad questioning me, almost certainly about qualifications and long-term aspirations. I didn't blame him; I'm sure I would do the same if I was him, but I had enough stress entertaining his daughter's bullshit before I'd even consider a quick-fire round of questioning in his oversized living room. After calling Holly and telling her to walk to the end of her driveway, I called Chris to check on his progress.

"Yes, Cyrus," Chris said happily.

"What are you so happy about?" I asked sensing the joy in Chris' voice.

"I am on the way to sell this half a kilo now, so I'm going to need another one; or in fact, get me a whole kilo, please, Cyrus," Chris explained.

"Don't lie, have they tested the quality though?" I asked eager to know if they had already had a sample and agreed to buy it.

"Yes, Cyrus, I gave them a sample, and they want to buy it for £10,800, so I've made £800 today," Chris said as he sounded happier than I had heard him for a long time.

"Okay, good, call me the second you get back with the money, and I will get you some more," I said as I realised the second Chris calls me, I will have made £4,000 profit. I put the phone down and called my brother. "Daniel," I said as he answered.

"Cyrus, we need more weed, mate, for the McBrides," Daniel said.

"Okay, what about the cocaine; have you sold any?" I asked.

"No, but I've put it away until I sort the weed out for John and Tom," Daniel replied.

"Okay, I will call you back five minutes, and let you know where and when you will be receiving your package," I explained before putting the phone down. Jabber's phone rang in my ear.

"Cyrus, how are you doing?" Jabber said in his usual deep grunt.

"Jabber, I need another 59 ounces of weed as soon as possible," I said in a voice that let him know it was of great urgency.

"Okay, I'll drop it to you now, but have you got a kilo of that cocaine there?" Jabber asked. I couldn't believe my ears.

"What? Do you want to buy a kilo of that sniff?" I asked.

"Yes, have you got one there now?" Jabber asked.

"I've got half a kilo; I can get you more tomorrow. I'm getting two kilo's tomorrow," I explained. "You can pick the half a kilo up when you drop the weed off if you want; will you have the money for it?" I asked as I tried to close out the deal.

The phone went quiet while Jabber thought about my proposition. As Jabber was thinking, Holly approached the car and got in. I didn't even look at Holly as I was hoping that Jabber would say yes. "Okay, Cyrus, get me the other half a kilo tomorrow. I will give you £10,500 when I drop your weed off," Jabber said in his deep, almost husky, voice.

"How long are you going to be getting to me though, Jabber?" I asked.

"I will be there in 25 minutes. I just have to go and pick the money up from my place," Jabber said.

"Okay, my brother, Daniel will meet you exactly where I saw you last night by my house," I explained before putting the phone down. "Yeaaahh," I said as I sat with my cheap phone in my hand, rocking forward and back in my seat with excitement.

"You are happy to see me," Holly said as she looked at me.

"Oh, shit. Sorry, babe. I just had some really good news, give me a kiss," I said as I leaned over to kiss Holly on her lips with far less enthusiasm than I had kissed Emma with half an hour before. I called Daniel back while still sitting outside the entrance to Holly's driveway. I explained to my brother that Jabber was going to meet him outside our house in 15 minutes.

"Daniel, my mate is going to meet you outside the house in 15 minutes. He wants to buy that half a kilo of cocaine I gave to you; he will give you £10,500 for it, and he will also give you the weed for the McBrides and Chris' weed. So, put that all away at Trish's house and put the money from the cocaine in my bedroom after taking £500 for yourself," I explained.

"Why am I taking £500?" Daniel asked.

"Oh, I'm selling it for £10,500, you can have the £500 for yourself," I said calmly.

"Thank you, Cyrus, I love you," Daniel replied.

"Just make sure you put the weed away safe, and count the money for the cocaine, and hide the money in my bedroom. Call me when it's done," I said clearly to make sure he understood every word. Daniel put phone down. I wanted to call Bob and tell him the good news, but I decided to wait until I had confirmation that both Chris and Daniel's transactions had been completed.

"You are busy, Cyrus, aren't you?" Holly said as she gave me a half-smile.

"I know, gorgeous, I'm sorry, let's go," I replied as I began to drive.

"So, this is your new car? It's nice, Cyrus," Holly said as she looked around at the black interior of the car. The seats were black suede material and hugged your body as you sat in them. As I drove, Holly and I spoke about our weeks, and about her parents returning home from holiday—nothing that interested me. All I could think about was business, and the fact that when Chris and Daniel complete their one transaction each, I would have made £8,750 profit—practically a new rally car.

I put my foot down to stimulate my excitement. The car roared as it accelerated before slowing down again. Holly smiled, obviously impressed by the power of my car. I considered taking Holly for a cocktail where I had just taken Emma, but I didn't want the waitress to 'drop me in it'. 'Prevention being better than cure', I chose another restaurant. Holly looked gorgeous as she got out of the car; she had a light blue summer dress on and had her dark wavy thick hair down. I must admit, we were a good-looking couple.

We had been sitting in the Italian restaurant for ten minutes when Chris called. "That's done," Chris said sounding happy with his work.

"Give Daniel £10,000, and go and get your 50 ounces of weed from Daniel. He has that waiting for you," I said talking into the bottom of my phone so none of that other people in the restaurant could hear what I had said. I put the phone down before Chris could even reply.

A minute later, Jabber called me. "I'm here, Cyrus," Jabber said a little nervously, presumably due to the fact he had a black bag full of weed and £10,500 on him parked in a shit council estate in a dead end.

"Okay, two minutes," I said as I put the phone down on Jabber. "Daniel, my friend is there—a white guy. Give him the cocaine, and get the money and the weed from him. Call me when you have put everything where it needs to be, and get my money off Chris and give him his 50 ounces of weed, please." I put the phone down before my brother could even say a syllable. Holly just sat looking at me, like she didn't know what to make of how I was acting.

She wanted all my attention, but loved the fact I was a bad boy and a boss. "I want to stay with you tonight," Holly said as the waiter poured us both a glass of white wine from the bottle I had ordered. I don't know why I ordered a bottle as I only wanted a glass. I thought I'd look cheap ordering a glass. I had ordered garlic butter king prawns and scallops to start, and then a seafood linguine main course. Holly had ordered garlic mushrooms to start with and spaghetti Bolognese for main course. I had heard people say white wine complements fish dishes, as I dipped my prawn into the garlic butter sauce and ate it and then sipped the wine, my taste buds went crazy. I repeated the process, this time sipping the wine and then eating seafood. *The finer things in life,* I thought as I cleaned my fingers in the finger bowl, then dried them with the napkin.

"Holly I'm going to take you somewhere nice tomorrow night," I said. I was trying to drop the hint that I would not be spending the night with her tonight.

"Where?" Holly asked as she smiled and looked at me with surprise.

"Maybe to a nice hotel with a steam room and Jacuzzi or something," I said as I made it up as I went along.

"Why not tonight?" Holly asked as the penny finally dropped that we would not be spending the night together tonight.

"Oh, Holly, I've got to have a meeting with some people that want to start working with me," I lied.

"Why do they need to see you; can't you just see them tomorrow? I want some alone time with you tonight," Holly said as she attempted to change my mind.

"Holly, I would much rather be making love to you than talking to these people. They have travelled far to see me, and I am lucky that they even want to talk to me, so I can't let them down. Tomorrow, I am all yours, I promise," I said as I answered my phone that was now calling again.

"Daniel," I said as I accepted the call.

"Cyrus, you have got £20,000 in a carry bag under your bed, and Chris has got his 50 ounces of weed. I'm just going to John and Tom's to 'bag up' for the shop," Daniel explained.

"Good lad, thank you, Daniel. I will catch up with you later. I am just out for dinner with my sexy Holly before I go for the meeting," I said purely for Holly's benefit.

"What meeting?" Daniel asked.

"No, I'm not hungry, Daniel, and I don't like chocolate cake. Anyway, I will speak to you soon. Bye, Dan," I said before hanging up. "You see, Holly, I'm all go at the minute; that was my brother on the phone telling me not to be late to the meeting," I explained.

I had told Holly I would be back in 'one second' as I left the table to use the bathroom. I had been sure to slide my phone back into my pocket before doing so. The dining room was littered with the odd rich or old couple wearing shirts and suits and dresses, mostly businessmen and business owners with their well-kept wives.

I felt slightly out of place due to my appearance. I was different to them and much younger; my skin colour and occupation made me somewhat their opposite. I didn't feel nervous or ashamed to be sharing a dining room with upper-class people. I could afford to eat in these restaurants, so if they didn't like it, they should eat elsewhere. I looked at these upper-class people as inferior, vulnerable antelope that could be eaten any time one of them was stupid enough to cross me or offend me.

In the toilet, I called Emma. She had been the only thing I could think about apart from business. "Hey, beautiful," I said as Emma answered her phone.

"Cyrus, it's not 8:00 yet," Emma replied cheerfully.

"I know, but I've got you on the brain, haven't I?" I joked.

"Oh, Cyrus, you are so cute," Emma replied.

"I just wanted to make sure that you are okay, and that Jason isn't bothering you, and we are still on for later?" I asked.

"Oh no, I told Jason I want some time; and yes, as long as you are not busy, I could do with a drink to relax," Emma said.

"Okay, 8:00, and I look forward to it," I said before saying goodbye and handing up. As I did, I realised I had made a crucial mistake. I had put pleasure before business. I didn't mind as Emma was almost worth it due to how she looked and acted—it was an easy mistake to make.

The fact I had realised that I had put business before pleasure meant that I was 'on the ball'. The business call I should have made first rang in my ear as I stood in the posh restaurant's bathroom. "Yes, Cyrus," Bob said as he answered his phone.

"Yes, Bob," I replied.

"What's up, mate?" Bob asked wondering why I had called him.

"I've sold that kilo already; you want to come and get your money, and I need some more," I said trying not to sound as happy as I was inside.

"You have sold that already?" Bob asked with his voice full of excitement. "How much do you want?" Bob asked.

"I want two kilos, but I'm going out with this girl tonight. She's a little older than me. Do you want to bring a girl over with you and come for a drink with us? That way, you and I can talk business?" I asked.

"What I will do is, I will get Yax to follow me over to you to pick the money up. I will ask one of my lady friends if they want to come out for a drink. What time were you thinking?" Bob asked.

"Seven thirty p.m. outside my house, because I've picked this girl up at 8:00, so that will give me time to pay you and put the cocaine away," I explained.

"Okay, Cyrus. See you at 7:30 p.m.," Bob said before he put the phone down. I turned and left the bathroom without using the facilities.

I walked back over to the table where Holly was waiting, and our main courses had arrived. "That wine has gone straight through me," I said to Holly as I sat back down opposite her.

Chapter 17

A moment of content was the relief I craved to cure my anxiety. Since I had met Bob, the feelings of restlessness had completely disappeared. I watched as the people working in the car wash used their 'rags' to shine my car as they dried it. I had dropped Holly home and planned to get my car cleaned inside and out before going home to get a shower while I waited for Bob and Yax before meeting Emma.

I had dropped Holly home. I concluded that telling her that I wanted space would only make her want more attention. So tonight I had left things as they were. It was easier that way for the time being.

As I pulled into the estate and turned right towards my house, I could see Chris' car. I parked next to it and got out of my car. Chris and my brother got out of the small grey car.

"Cyrus, I need another kilo. I'm going to have sales for it tomorrow," Chris said before I could even say hello.

"Guys, don't worry, I'm getting you both a kilo each at 7:30 p.m. today. So Daniel, make sure you are around to put it away, and Chris, you too," I said as I pressed my fob to lock my car. "Roll a joint someone," I said as I looked at them both, seeing who was going to adhere to my request.

"Yes, boss," Daniel joked as he opened Chris' car to sit in the passenger seat. I sat outside my house with Chris and my brother for nearly an hour, talking about work and Holly, and how their days had been. Chris told me he had sold his cocaine to one of his cousin's friends, and that they had promised future business. Daniel told me about some girls him and his mate, Lee, had met that had no inhibitions, which made us laugh. I didn't tell them about Emma, but just explained how I was getting bored of Holly. Chris rolled his eyes as if to say 'I had seen that coming'. I had smiled at him and shrugged my shoulders.

"Cyrus, you get bored of every girl after you have slept with them," Chris said as he laughed and shook his head in disbelief.

With an hour and a half before Bob and Yax were due to arrive, I opened our back gate to go into our house.

"Hi, Mum," I said as I walked over to kiss her on the cheek.

"Are you okay, Cyrus, have you eaten?" My mother asked.

"Yes, I took my old girlfriend to the new Italian restaurant near town," I replied boastfully.

"What are you doing now, are you staying in for the night?" My mum asked.

"No, I'm taking my new girlfriend out for a drink," I replied while smiling proudly. My mum just looked at me and shook her head, neither condoning nor condemning my actions.

I carried on through the kitchen and turned left to go up the stairs and left again into my room. I sat on my bed for a minute to evaluate my current situation. *Things were moving along nicely.* I reached under my bed to get the carrier bag full of money from under it. I emptied the money out onto my bed and counted it. The piles of money covered a large proportion of the middle of my bed. I counted out £1,000 and put it in a neat pile in one corner of my bed, then another and placed it next to it and so on, and so on. When I had finished the last thousand, it was £40 short. I reached into my jeans pocket and added two £20 notes to the last pile. *Twenty thousand pounds exactly.* I picked up eight of the piles and took them downstairs. "Mum, here you go, this is the day's earnings," I said as I placed the two large piles of notes onto the kitchen side.

"Cyrus, you earnt that today?" My mum asked as she looked at the colossal amount of money.

"Yes, that is today's profit," I answered somewhat arrogantly.

"Cyrus, whatever you are doing, please be careful," my mum replied.

"Mum, take £500 for yourself, then you've got £47,500 for me," I explained.

"Okay, I'll go and put this away when your dad gets home," my mum replied.

I returned to my room and counted out £750 and put it in my pocket, leaving £11,250—this was Bob's money. I also had just over £3,000 under my chest drawers and nearly £1,200 in my pocket, plus my Auntie Delma had £30,000 of my own money. I put the £1,250 from my pocket under my drawers. There was no way I'd spend more than £750 during my night out, plus having too much cash made my jeans look silly, like I had a pair of football socks in my pocket. I arranged the outfit that I would be wearing on the bed next to my £750 spending money and my cheap work phone. *I need a nice watch,* I thought as I looked down at my empty wrist. As I stood in the hot shower, my brain was clouded with thoughts about my new cocaine business and my weed business. I was already thinking about the women troubles that I knew were sure to come when I started to distance myself from Holly. I had decided to just let things play themselves out and not stress too much.

Once dressed and back outside the back of my house feeling fresh, I knew I looked good. White T-shirts and dark blue jeans had always suited me. I figured it was because the white worked well in contrast to my almost reddish-brown skin. I headed out of my back gate to find Chris and Daniel in Chris' car smoking weed and drinking milkshakes. I nodded at them to acknowledge them as I took my phone out to call Bob. After confirming Bob's arrival time, I decided to kill a few of the minutes I would have to wait talking to Chris and my brother. I approached Chris' car which had both the front doors open, with Chris and my brother lounging on the two front seats listening to music.

"Daniel, go into my bedroom and get the carrier bag off my bed and throw it in my car boot, please," I said as I handed my brother my car keys. Daniel got out of the small grey car, and I got in next to Chris. "Air this car out. You are going to have a kilo of cocaine in here in a minute; you don't want it stinking of weed," I said as I reached across to take the joint Chris was smoking from him. Daniel came out of our back gate holding the carrier bag in his hand in plain-view, like it was his dirty laundry. Daniel opened the boot of my rally car and threw the bag of money inside before locking the car using the fob. "Thanks, bro," I said as I slid my car keys back into my pocket. I could hear loud music coming from a car driving down my street. Chris, my brother and I, all turned to face the corner of our street. Whatever car was playing the music would have to turn around this corner to come into the dead end. As the white car turned the corner, the music stopped playing as Bob drove towards us. I could see a girl in Bob's passenger seat; then I saw the black Jeep pull around the corner behind Bob.

Most of the people on my estate either had shit jobs or no jobs. There were now two cars on my street that cost more than the houses. The big black jeep with Yax and Bob's mate, Luke, stopped next to the white hatchback with Bob and the dark-haired girl inside of it. Bob got out of the driver's seat as I started to walk towards his car. "Yes, Cyrus," Bob said as he smiled and shook my hand firmly.

"Yes, Bob, look how you lot are moving," I replied in reference to the two top of the range cars moving in convoy.

"The white hatchback looks nice next to the black jeep, doesn't it?" Bob said as he turned and looked at the two cars. As I did the same, I nodded and waved at Yax and Luke as our eyes met. I turned around to get the money from the boot of my rally car and handed it to Bob. "Give it to Yax, he's got your cocaine," Bob replied. I walked to the window of the black jeep on the driver side; Yax wound down his window.

"Are you okay, Cyrus?" Yax said as he gave me a friendly smile.

"Yes, I'm okay, guys," I replied as I gave him the carry bag full of money through the driver's side window. Yax looked inside the bag as I shook Luke's hand who gave me the usual bright smile of acceptance.

"Give Cyrus that bag, Luke," Yax said as he handed Luke the bag of money. Luke reached to the floor between his legs and came back up holding a 'sports bag'. Luke handed Yax the bag, who then gave it to me through his driver-side window. "There is two kilos of cocaine, Cyrus," Yax said as he handed me the bag.

I put the bag over my shoulder as I walked away from the jeep; I could feel hard slab shapes. I took the bag over to Chris' car and opened it—four slabs in brown tape. "Here, lads, take two slabs each. Then you both owe me £20,000 each, plus the weed money," I said as I left the bag on the floor at my brother's feet in the passenger-side foot well where I had looked inside of it. "Okay, I will see you both later, keep that stuff safe," I said as I turned to walk back to the white hatchback. Bob was talking to Yax and Luke through the driver-side window. Bob had on black jeans and a black jumper; the jumper had white stars on it, and he had his rectangular diamond watch on. The girl in Bob's passenger seat had olive skin and looked tanned with long, straight dark hair and big lips that were in good proportion with her face; they looked natural but sexy—she was exotic. Bob turned from the jeep that started as he walked away from it.

"Jump in my car, Cyrus," Bob said.

"Oh, I thought you were going to follow me?" I replied.

"There is no point in taking two cars, Cyrus," Bob replied as he got back into his car. Bob's car smelt of a mixture of perfume and aftershave. The black leather seats had red stitching. I directed

Bob towards Emma's house. On the way, I called Emma to let her know I would be five minutes. "We will have a good talk when we get out this car, Cyrus," Bob had said as he drove. We pulled up outside Emma's house. The three of us were all speechless as Emma appeared from her front door; she looked amazing. She had on a ribbed mini-skirt that came just below her knees and matching ribbed sweat top that came just below her belly button. Her whole outfit was in the pale pink colour; she had her hair down—blonde and wavy. She looked beautiful.

"Cyrus, is this your girlfriend?" Bob asked as he stared at Emma.

"Yes, mate," I replied as I smiled inside.

"So, you have got a nice car and a nice girl then, my friend," Bob joked with admiration.

I leaned across to open the back door next to me for Emma. Emma got into the car, and I made the necessary introductions. Bob helped with the introductions, as I didn't know his friend 'Cara's' name. I leaned over to give Emma a kiss. "You look beautiful," I said as I kissed Emma.

"So do you," Emma replied. She smiled at me, and I held her hand as Bob drove.

"Have you got any weed on you, Cyrus?" Bob asked.

"No, I haven't, mate," I replied. Bob suggested that we go and get some weed, so I directed him back towards my area to go to the McBride's. John McBride opened his front door and ran to the white hatchback with three £10 bags of weed and a handful of rolling papers. "Thanks, mate, I will call you later," I said as I closed the electric window.

"Shall we go for food in Birmingham?" Bob asked as we pulled off.

"How are Emma and I going to get back to Coventry though?" I asked as I didn't have any transport. We decided to stay in Coventry, as Bob told Cara to have a look online for a hotel suite for them to spend the night in. They found a suite at the football stadium. The hotel was built on the football stadium grounds. Cara showed us a room called 'the water room' with a giant Jacuzzi in the middle of the room. Two 60-inch flat screen TVs and a queen-sized bed with a minibar and eight-seat dining table.

"Book that for me," I said as I stared at the pictures on Cara's phone.

"Book the same suite or one like it for us," Bob said.

We drove towards my favourite restaurant to eat and have a drink.

"Cyrus, the room that you want is £190 for the night," Cara said as she turned to show me the price on her phone.

"That's okay," I said as I looked at Emma, hoping she didn't mind me arranging to book us a hotel room for the night.

"Emma, you haven't got to go home tonight, have you?" I asked.

"No, I've got to go out tomorrow with my mum, but that's not until tomorrow afternoon," Emma replied.

"Bob, your room is £150," Cara said as she showed Bob the price on her phone.

"Cara, we are not bothered about the prices. You can't put a price on spending time with the people you care about," Bob added smoothly. As Bob parked the car outside the restaurant, Bob gave Cara £100 and said, "You two go in and order some drinks and get us a table, we will be inside in ten minutes," Bob said. I reached into my pocket to do the same. "Cyrus, what is it with you and paying for things? At least let me get us the first round of drinks; you can get the next round when we go in," Bob said just as annoyed as when I had offered to pay for dinner. I couldn't believe my luck as I watched Emma walk off towards the restaurant—tight skirt and her curvy figure. "Cyrus, let's smoke a joint, then sit outside the restaurant smoking it while we talk," Bob said as I got out of the back of the car and into the passenger seat. Bob and I did not speak about anything illegal in Bob's car. Instead, we spoke about the hotel rooms we had booked, and how pretty the girls looked.

I told Bob that I had only just been out for dinner with my actual girlfriend. We laughed and joked. Bob told me he was married to a quiet Asian girl, and that Cara was his 'out-on-the-town piece'. We got out of Bob's car to sit on the outdoor tables and chairs where Jason and I once sat on together. This time, I was with Bob, smoking a joint, and Jason's once girlfriend Emma was inside ordering me a cocktail. "Cyrus, you sold that kilo fast," Bob said now willing to talk business, now that we were out of earshot of the car and the girls.

"Yes, I could have sold another half a kilo, but I didn't have it," I explained.

"Build your money up, then buy it for cash; it's easier for both of us that way," Bob said as he smoked his joint.

"Well, what I want to do is sell the two that you have given me, then get another two; then buy either two or four kilos for cash up-front," I suggested.

"Cyrus, I don't mind however you want to do business," Bob said as he threw the half-finished joint on the floor.

"Come on, let's go in before someone steals our girls," Bob joked as we walked into the restaurant. We found Cara and Emma sitting at the table drinking cocktails. Two more cocktails were at the empty table spaces opposite the girls. I explained to Bob that the cocktails were Bahama Mammas. Bob had already had them before and told me his stocky white mate Luke loves them.

We sat and joked between the four of us as we ate our meals of steak and shrimp and fish while we drank our cocktails. I decided to take my time with the alcohol; as this was the first time I had been out Emma and Bob, there was no way I would be making a fool of myself. "Bob, I want a watch like yours," I said as I looked at his wrist which was glistening with orange, blue, pink, red and green as the lights hit the diamonds that were encrusted all over the large rectangular bezel.

"Yes, I've got another one; you can have this one for £20,000," Bob said seriously. *Twenty thousand pounds for a watch?* I thought.

"I will buy it in a month. I just want to save up some money first," I replied.

We left the restaurant to go and check into our rooms before going out to town. Bob wanted to leave his car outside of the hotel and catch a taxi to a bar to avoid drunk-driving. *Bob didn't mind having a drug-factory, but wasn't prepared to drunk drive,* was my initial thought. I didn't question Bob, as I knew he would have a perfectly good explanation for his actions.

Bob parked up outside the hotel on the grounds of the football club. I gave Cara £190, and Bob gave Cara the money for their room. We let the girls go into the hotel reception together to pay and collect our room keys. "Cyrus, I bet you cannot wait to get Emma back to that hotel room," Bob said as he watched the two women walk off towards the electric doors into the reception.

"You know what, Bob? You are not far wrong," I said as I smiled and reached into the front to fist pump him.

Just over five minutes later, we saw the two girls coming back towards the car. We got out of the car to wait for the taxi we had told them to ask reception to call after getting our room keys. "Cyrus, I cannot believe you have just paid all of that money for one night," Emma said as she gave me a plastic card which was the room key.

"Why? I would have paid double!" I said as I smiled and slid the room key into my back pocket.

All four of us spotted the hackney carriage taxi turning off the main road into the hotel car park. The air was cool and the sky was beautiful as it was just starting to change colour to get dark. By the time we got out of the taxi, it was dark; we decided to go to a bar instead of a club. We wanted to find somewhere that wouldn't have hundreds of drunken arseholes, so we chose a popular bar on High Street. The two big doormen shook Bob's hand as he led the three of us in behind him. We walked through a dim-lit alleyway before coming out into the courtyard. Music was blasting out from behind a set of double glass doors. We followed Bob through them; then up a set of winding stairs, there had been a room downstairs that had people drinking and music playing, but Bob had just led us straight upstairs. We entered a room upstairs that had a DJ playing house music; summer songs that were new and current. There were a lot of pretty girls in this place, mostly with white guys with skinny jeans and gelled hair.

The music was loud and vibrating my chest as I stood near to the speakers. Bob walked over to the bar to speak to the barman. I watched as Bob leaned over the bar, being careful not to let his expensive jumper touch the surface of the bar. "Come on, let's go out into the garden," Bob said to me as he turned to walk back out of the room. We followed Bob back through the door we had used to get in, then through a door opposite which led to the garden area—it was the first garden I had ever seen that was upstairs. It had leather sofas and chairs and a big gazebo that would stop any rain falling on the gardens occupants. The garden had spotlights that housed powerful red heaters underneath them; the leather sofas were cream and had big glass tables in front of them with miniature tree-looking plants in expensive-looking pots here and there. In the middle of the garden area was a square-shaped bar which was smaller than the one inside, like a type of cocktail bar. We all sat on a leather sofa—Emma and me on a two-seater, and Bob and Cara on another.

"Shall we get a drink?" I shouted over to Bob to try and be heard over the loud music and other 60 or 70 people in the garden.

"No, we don't go to get drinks; they bring the drinks to us," Bob said as he sat forward. As he did so, I spotted the guy Bob had spoken to at the bar walking towards us. "Cyrus, I'm going to get a bottle of rosé champagne, it's £180 a bottle. If you don't want that one, then get a cheaper one for £80 a bottle," Bob suggested as the barman stood awaiting our decision.

"It's a special occasion, I will have the rosé as well," I said. Bob and I both sat back in the leather sofas to make access easier to the wads of cash in our jeans pockets. I counted out £180 and gave it to the waiter as Bob did the same.

"Cyrus, I cannot believe that you do not have a girlfriend if this is how you treat girls," Emma said as she squeezed my hand. I leaned over to give her a kiss.

"I don't treat girls like this; I want to treat you like this," I said before I kissed Emma again.

"Save that for the hotel room, Romeo," Bob said jokingly; Emma and I laughed as Cara smacked Bob on the leg.

"Leave them alone, you," Cara said in my defence.

The sky was still visible at the side of the gazebo. Considering we were outside, it was quite warm. I put that down to the heaters and all the people blocking the wind with the big glass walls around the garden at waist height. I spotted flashes of light coming from inside as they court my eye; my looking in that direction made Emma and Cara look in the same direction. It was the same waiter followed by another waiter, they both had big white buckets sitting on big shiny platforms balancing on their shoulders. In the buckets were our bottles of champagne with a giant sparkler for presentation.

I smiled as the waiters walked over and placed the two buckets on our table, the buckets had the names of expensive champagnes written in black letters on the side of them. Bob was expressionless as the two waiters placed the buckets down on the table in front of us. The two waiters took a bottle each and opened them, then carefully filled four champagne flutes with the pink coloured champagne, handing the girls a glass each first and then Bob and me. Bob nodded at them to say thanks before they left. "Cyrus, you can say a toast," Bob shouted at me above the music. I had never said a public toast before, but I was never short of something to say either.

"Here's to the best of people, sharing the best of things, making the best of life," I said cheerfully and merrily.

"Cheers."

"Cheers."

"Cheers," we all said as we 'clinked' our champagne flutes together.

I could feel the eyes of everybody in the beer garden looking at us, and I could tell a few people were talking about us. It felt good though, like we were celebrities.

The four of us sat drinking our rose champagne and listening to the music while talking and laughing joking. We sent the girls inside to dance together while we smoked weed in the garden. The door staff had come upstairs and took one look at who the weed-smoking culprits were and shook our hands, signifying their respect.

"Watch the manager with the weed—he's a dickhead," one of the big butch doormen had said before going back downstairs. *This is the life,* I thought to myself as we sat talking.

The girls returned after 15 minutes. "Cyrus, you are the best. I'm so glad I met you," Emma said as she sat down and kissed me. I could tell Emma was tipsy; I was closer to drunk than tipsy.

We finished our champagne, and Bob ordered us all a double vodka and lemonade. "We will drink these, then go," Bob said as the waiter delivered our drinks to our table.

"I want you to be my girlfriend," I whispered into Emma's ear as we all climbed into a waiting taxi.

"Do you mean that?" Emma replied as she captivated me with her amazing gaze.

"Yes," I replied.

"You're my boyfriend then," Emma replied as we passionately kissed in the back of the taxi.

The four of us staggered into the hotel reception and into the lift. "Where's your room?" I asked Bob.

"I have got no idea, I will find it to though," Bob said before laughing at the fact he had no clue where he was—the champagne had definitely made Bob lightheaded. Emma and I said goodbye to Bob and Cara as we headed off in opposite directions to look for our hotel suites. I read the door numbers as I walked... '48', '50'... 'water room' was in the place where numbers had been on other doors.

I took the key from my back pocket and opened the door. "Wow," Emma said as she stepped into the suite in front of me. It was amazing; there was a large bathroom immediately on the left behind a brown door. In front of us was a large brown table, positioned to the right; and behind that, at the back of the suite, was a queen-sized bed with a giant Jacuzzi to the left of the bed. It was a big circular tub, easily able to fit six people inside. The suite had a sitting area behind the bed to the right. It had two large flat screen TVs on the walls. One was in front of the sitting area, and one on the opposite wall, both visible from the Jacuzzi or the bed. The floor from the entrance to the bed area had dark wooden flooring, and around the bed had carpet that stopped just before the Jacuzzi. The room was amazing.

"I will fill the Jacuzzi up while you call room service to bring us a bottle of rosé," I said as I began to fill the tub.

Emma and I soaked in the Jacuzzi, drinking wine and making love. *This is the life,* I thought as I sat back to let the powerful jets massage my back. Emma was the most beautiful woman I had ever seen! Her body was perfection—round bum and bright round eyes—absolutely stunning. From the Jacuzzi to the bed, we enjoyed each other before falling asleep.

Chapter 18

It had been three years since Emma and I had officially became boyfriend and girlfriend. Well, we were official in the sense that Emma told everybody she was my girlfriend, and I confirmed this to anybody that would ask me. We were also official in the sense that I knew if she ever caught me taking the odd girl to a hotel, she would chop my dick off and put my head on a stick.

I had come a long way from the 16-year-old wanting to make a few quid. I was almost 20 years old now, and my mentality had evolved completely. I was no longer interested in £10 bags of weed. I had given my whole weed-selling operation to my brother, Daniel. Chris had also given my brother all his bulk cannabis customers. Jabber was happy to deal with my brother, Daniel. After all, it was money.

I now had ten very good customers from different parts of the country that bought kilos of cocaine and heroin from me. Bob and I had spoken every day, and we were as close as Chris and I had ever been. Bob had taken me back to his drug-factory at Bubbles' house. This time, without the blindfold, and showed me how to mix heroin; it was basically the same process to mix and press as cocaine. The only difference was instead of using cocaine, you would use heroin; and instead of using benzocaine, you would use mannitol. Mannitol is a white powder that, once heated, liquefies and would run down a piece of tinfoil as a liquid that was either red or clear. People would blend heroin with mannitol, and the drug-addicts would know the 'gear', as they call it, has been mixed. So some bright spark brought out a new type of mannitol that runs clear, so when the drug addicts put it on the foil to heat it, it will just look like heroin is supposed to look.

A heroin-addict would get a flat piece of tin foil and make an indent along the length, then pour a £10 bag of heroin at the top of the indent, roll a tube out of foil and put that in their mouth to suck the vapour. Then they use a lighter to heat the powder from underneath the tin foil and suck the fumes and smoke from the pile of liquid heroin as it runs down the foil. Addicts would sit down and follow the pile of molten heroin with the tube in their mouth up and down the foil until the last bit frazzled away to their despair.

Once the pure heroin had been blended, it would be compressed exactly the same way using the metal box. More pressure was needed to hold the heroin/mannitol mixed together. Bob gave me kilos of heroin for £17,000, and I sold them to my Scottish friend for £25,000.

Chris did the majority of my logistical work. He was happy to; he had brought my red rally car and crashed it not even a month later while drunk-driving. He had ran away from the car where he had left it practically attached to a lamppost.

I had invested £400,000 to buy a car rental company with Bob. My half of the business was in my mum and dad's name, it had cost me another £80,000 to legalise the money, so it could be deposited into my mum's bank account. Bob had got his friend who lived in Dubai to send £400,000 to my parent's bank account, in exchange for a bag containing £480,000 being dropped to Birmingham to an Arab family. Our business was doing very well; we had top of the range German and Italian prestige cars, and we planned to spend another £400,000 each in a year or so to buy a few Italian supercars.

Chris was our first customer, and he practically claimed a brand-new, white, six-litre German saloon. Bob and I didn't care. Chris had been warned if he drinks and crashes the car, he best either have the money, or be ready for his mum and dad to re-mortgage their house.

I had just woke up in my new flat in town. Emma had spent the night with me. I had picked Emma up late on the night before, after getting back from a meeting with a major cocaine-selling firm from London. Bob had forced me to get a driving licence. I had spent five days in a city called Blackpool doing an intensive course. I slipped the manager a £1,000 tip on the first day, which more or less guaranteed a pass. I got out of bed and put my dressing gown and slippers on and walked into the kitchen to get a drink. It was a Friday afternoon,; my plans for the day consisted of going for breakfast with Emma, then dropping her home, then collecting money from Chris and the people we trusted enough to give work to them on our 'pay later' policy. Finally, I would have to go put the money away in a safe place. Chris and I would sit down in the evening to do a stock take of how much cocaine is left; then maybe chill out back at the flat if we didn't have any 'skirt' that tickled our fancy for the night.

I had just sat down in my favourite café with Emma. Having literally just sliced my toasted muffin and was in the process of dipping a small piece into the yoke of my perfectly poached egg when Chris called.

"Cyrus, that fucking prick, Morris, has robbed £40,000 from us," Chris rambled angrily down the phone. I could hear his blood was racing.

"Who has done what?" I said calmly, not wanting to alert other diners as I got up slowly and started off out of the café door.

"One second, gorgeous," I said to Emma as I signalled the call was important and not to be had in a public domain.

"Cyrus, that cunt, Morris, has gave me a bag with £40,000 in fake notes," Chris explained angrily. I didn't doubt what Chris was saying; he was fuming.

"Are you sure the money has come from Morris?" I asked, needing to be sure, as I know Chris received a lot of bags full of money from a lot of different people.

"Yes, I'm sure, Cyrus. I just picked it up from him in the supermarket car park. I gave him two kg, and that bastard gave me this bag of fake notes," Chris explained as the devastation started to sink in.

"Well, call Morris back and tell him to bring my stuff back, or he is fucked," I said as I looked at my glistening wristwatch. The tiny letters that read 'AP' were barely visible due to the amount of diamonds in the face of the watch that I had bought from Bob.

"Chris, it's 1:00 now. If that cocaine isn't back by 2:00, he's a fucking dead man," I said before hanging up. I wasn't angry; all anger does is cloud judgement. *If he doesn't bring that cocaine or my money back today, he is getting shot,* I told myself as I walked back into the café to finish my eggs benedict with no bacon or sausage.

"Is everything okay, Cyrus?" Emma asked as I sat back down.

"Yes, of course, my mate has just spilt some milk," I replied, which let Emma know no further questions on the matter were warranted.

Twenty-five minutes had passed by the time I dropped Emma home. When Emma had gone into her house, I got out of my white German jeep and called Yax. "Yes, my brother," I said as he answered.

"Yes, Cyrus, how are you doing, mate?" Yax asked.

"Not good! Someone has just had my worker's pants down for £40,000. How long will it take you to drop two handguns over to Coventry?" I asked.

"I can get them to you within the hour, mate. I've got a Glock and a Desert Eagle. My mate would probably want £3,000 each," Yax explained.

"Okay, send them both over to me, I have the money here." Next, I rang Chris. "Have you got our money or stuff back yet?" I asked sounding pissed off at Chris for his stupidity.

"No... Have I fuck, Morris has switched his phone off," Chris said sounding as though his world was slowly ending.

"Okay, we are going to 'blast' this fool today. My mate is bringing two handguns over, so get a location on this clown," I said before putting the phone down once more. I stood outside of Emma's house feeling violated. It wasn't the money, it was the principle that made my blood boil.

I looked at my phone as it rang. "Yes, Bob," I said as he answered.

"Cyrus, Yax has just told me what's happened," Bob said in a concerned tone.

"Yes. I'm not having that, I'm going to show this clown today," I said angrily.

"I agree, but don't do anything today, and do not do anything yourself," Bob advised.

"No, he has ripped me off, so I want to do him myself," I replied stubbornly.

"Cyrus, are you a businessman or a cowboy? These things happen, so does this mean we are going to throw away all of our hard work? The boys said they will shoot or stab him and just keep the two kg. You don't have to give them anything," Bob said as he pleaded with me to see sense. He had a point though, the only thing stopping me from accepting the deal was my pride.

"Okay, tell them to come over now, and tell Yax I still want both of them handguns. I want to 'park them up' (meaning put them away)," I reluctantly agreed to let the lads deal with Morris.

Morris was about 33 and a big lump of an Irish-looking guy. He was English not Irish though, he had a big square head and dusty-looking brown hair, and his skin was bad due to his cocaine-abuse almost daily. A few of Morris' mates were pretty big cocaine-dealers; and quite often, he would get their money and buy cocaine from Chris. Morris would consequently make £1,000 or £2,000 commission. Morris was known for fighting and being a hard guy; his big hands were like sledgehammers when clenched into fists. I definitely wouldn't like to fight Morris, but I would happily meet him anywhere with a 9mm Glock fully loaded; and after seeing him, he would be in urgent need of medical attention if he was lucky enough not to need processing in the local morgue.

A Glock is a handgun that a lot of police officers use in America. They are light and accurate and very reliable. I had always wanted a Glock ever since I knew what a gun was. Still standing outside of Emma's house like I had lost my car keys, I got back into my jeep to call Chris. "Come to the McBride's house, I will be there in 10 minutes," I said before hanging up. Chris had pissed me off with his stupidity massively. I could have made Chris pay for the loss, and rightfully so, that would have been the smart thing to do, but I felt as Chris worked for me. Morris had directly insulted me and everything I stood for. If I didn't deal with this matter now, what would stop the next guy who wants a few kilos of free cocaine from robbing Chris? I parked my jeep outside of the McBride's house. I didn't feel like going in, as I knew John and Tom's gentle nature would only cause me to calm down, and I was not prepared to calm down until I had my cocaine back, or Morris' head on a stick. I heard the roar of the car Chris had leased from mine and Bob's business as he pulled into the McBride's street.

I had my windows down and had been looking in my mirrors at the road behind me. Chris pulled in behind my jeep as I got out of it and jumped down onto the pavement. "How the fuck did you let this happen, son?" I said to him as I looked at him in annoyance.

"Cyrus, I'm sorry. If we can't get the cocaine back, I will have to pay for it," Chris said as he walked towards me, holding his head in his hands.

"Chris, find out where this piece of shit lives in the next half an hour. I'm going to send my mates through his front door," I said as I pointed at him in anger.

"Cyrus, I know where his mate lives that he usually buys stuff for, but he probably won't say where Morris lives. I know he definitely knows though," Chris explained. I leaned against the side of my white jeep while I assessed the situation. Chris just stood looking at me gormlessly while I devised a plan to clean up the mess he'd made.

I took my phone out and called Yax. "Yes, my brother, I have spoken to Bob," I said when Yax answered the phone. I wanted him to know I was aware he had spoken to Bob after I had spoken to him.

"That's good, Cyrus, I had to call Bob because you sounded hot-headed, and we all don't want you to do something stupid, that's why I had to call Bob," Yax explained, letting me know his intentions were clean.

"Yes, Bob said that you and Luke want deal with it?" I asked

"Yes, that's our job, Cyrus. We are just getting ready to come over there now," Yax explained while laughing at the fact he would finally get to prove his expertise.

"Okay then, I need to get this prick's address, so what I want you to do is send them two handguns over now; then you and Luke come over as soon as I get the address. Then I want you to do this guy!" I explained.

"Cyrus, I will send the handguns over now, but you have got to promise me that you will not do anything silly. Bob will never forgive me if I give you a gun, and you go and shoot someone and get locked up," Yax explained compassionately.

"No, I am not going to do anything stupid. I just need to have them close by, and I need them quickly, mate. I'm not going to throw all my hard work away for some dickhead; you and Luke can fuck him up later," I said calmly and using the exact terminology Bob had used to put Yax at ease.

"Okay, a woman will be in your street in a black hatchback in exactly half an hour, give her £6,000 and take the laptop bag out of her boot," Yax explained.

"Okay, thanks, Yax. I'm here waiting now," I said before cutting the phone off.

"Are they going to sort it?" Chris asked, full of self-pity.

"No, you idiot! I'm going to sort it!" I snapped back at Chris as I turned around to climb back into my jeep.

"Get in," I said as I started the jeep. Chris pressed the fob to lock the car behind me as he climbed into my passenger seat.

"Have you got £6,000 at your house?" I asked Chris as I slowly drove out of the McBride's street.

"Yes, and I got £80,000 at my grandad's in the safe, and I've got £8,000 at my mum's around the corner," Chris replied.

"Is the £6,000 at your house out of the business, or is it your own money?" I asked as I drove slowly towards Chris' parents' house.

"No, the £6,000 at my mum's is mine; the business money is in the safe at my grandad's," Chris explained.

"Okay, I am going to use the £6,000 at your mum's to buy something," I told Chris. I was annoyed at the fact that he hadn't told Morris to give him the money first, then checked the money, then finally and only then gave Morris the cocaine. That was standard operating procedure; Chris had probably pulled up high from smoking too much weed, thinking he was the dog's bullocks in my brand-new white saloon and got his fat arse robbed, the Wally. "Chris, if I didn't love you so much, you know I would bust your fucking skull for this; don't you, you fucking retard?" I said emotionlessly. I meant it. If he was anybody else, he would have been in as much trouble as Morris was sure to be in very soon.

"I know that, Cyrus, and I'm sorry, mate," Chris replied as he walked up his mum and dad's driveway to get the money I'd sent him to retrieve. Chris was obviously upset, and he deserved to be upset. He had completely ruined what would normally be a good Friday afternoon. I sat with my car windows up and air-conditioning on until the air was cold and crisp. *You have to get Morris today, Cyrus. If tomorrow comes, and he has not bled, you hang your criminal boots up and get a job at the local supermarket,* I told myself as I turned the air-con off again. Chris appeared from his parent's front door holding a designer clothes bag. He looked demoralised and deflated due to the day's events as he walked to my car. Until Morris was bleeding, Chris would receive no pity from me. Chris got back into the passenger seat of my jeep and threw the bag with the money onto the passenger side foot well. I didn't say anything to Chris as I started the two-minute drive from Chris' parent's house to my parent's house. I parked outside the garage at the back of my house and got out of my jeep to sit on the wall and wait. Chris also got out of my jeep and sat on the wall beside me.

I could tell Chris didn't know whether to talk to me or not. "What is the plan, Cyrus?" Chris eventually said.

"We are waiting for two handguns, Chris," I replied calmly, like I had said we were 'waiting for a pizza'. Chris' eyes opened wide with shock—he knew I was serious. What Morris had done was inexcusable, and Chris knew I would not let it go until I had my reprisal. Fifteen minutes later, I had wound myself up more, I had also given Chris a stern telling off while smoking two cigarettes.

I decided to call Yax back to see how long this girl was going to be. "Any progress, Yax?" I asked as Yax answered.

"Yes, Cyrus. That woman's going to be with you in the next ten minutes. Don't tell her what's in the bag though; just take it out of the boot and open it when she has gone," Yax explained.

"Okay, nice one, Yax, have they both got bullets with them?" I asked, as a gun with no bullets is as useful as a house brick.

"Yes, of course they have; there's 30 bullets for the Glock, and 20 bullets for the Desert Eagle," Yax replied.

"Okay, thank you," I said before putting the phone down.

I sat watching the corner of the road, hoping this girl, whoever she was, would hurry up. I hated waiting, patience had never been *my* virtue. Chris just sat, patiently awaiting my next move. He occasionally would look at me, but wouldn't say anything out of fear. He was waiting for me to have another go at him. After all, it was his fault that this whole situation had arose. Ten minutes later, a shiny, new, black hatchback turned the corner slowly. Clearly, the driver was unaware with their surroundings. I waved as I stood up to signal the driver that I was the person they had come to meet.

The Asian girl who was alone looked at me suspiciously before stopping and picking up her phone. As I got closer to her, I could see her speaking on her phone. I stopped short of her car while she finished her call to allow her to feel at ease. When I could see she was no longer on the phone, I approached the driver-side window. "I'm Yax's friend," I said as she wound down her window electrically.

"Oh, okay," she replied. She was Asian, and she looked like she was in her late 30s. She had a baby-booster seat strapped into the back seat.

"One second, I've got to give you something," I said as I turned around to go to my jeep to get the money from the passenger side foot well.

I gave the Asian lady the bag of money through the driver-side window, at the same time as asking her, "Is the boot open?"

"Yes, it is now," she replied as she pressed a button to unlock the boot. I walked to the back of the small black hatchback and lifted the badge to open the boot. There was a laptop bag sitting in the middle of the boot. Leaning in, I unzipped the bag and peered inside. Two handguns, surrounded by bullets that were loose in the bottom of the bag. My heart started to race with excitement as I zipped the bag shut.

"Tell Yax I said thanks," I said to the Asian lady as I walked back towards Chris and my big white jeep.

"Get in the car," I said to Chris after placing the black laptop case on the passenger-side foot well where the money had been two minutes before. I didn't want to drive my jeep with two firearms inside of it, but I didn't want Morris to steal £40,000 from me even more.

"Cyrus, are there two guns in that bag?" Chris asked as he pointed to the bag at his feet.

"Yes, I've just brought a Glock 18 and a Desert Eagle, both with bullets, and the Glock is full auto," I said as I drove back in the direction of the McBride's house.

I parked the white German jeep in front of the German saloon Chris had left when he'd got in my car. "Go into the McBride's and get me some gloves," I said to Chris as I turned the car engine off.

I knew what I was about to do was a madness. It's common sense, but I had to put all rationality to the side. *Fuck the police, fuck the law; and most of all, fuck this big lump of shit Morris, because he is a dead man.* I didn't want to be driving around with firearms, but I had to. So, my mentality was to treat the situation like doing anything else in the world; for instance, going for a game of pool. By this, I mean, I'd have to drive to the place, parked the car, get out of the car and go and play pool; no stress and no hesitation, simply just do it. That was exactly how I intended to play this out, calmly and calculated, but I was just going to do it. The more I thought about it, the more I would not want to do it; so as I said, 'rationality had to sit this one out'.

Chris came back to the jeep and gave me a pair of black woolly gloves. They looked small but stretched to fit any sized hands. *Magic gloves.* I put them on and gave them a quick inspection to make sure they had no holes in them. It would defeat the object of wearing gloves in an attempt to leave no fingerprints on a firearm if my gloves had holes in them. "Pass me that bag, Chris," I said as I pointed to the passenger-side foot well. I put the heavy laptop bag on my lap and unzipped the zipper. The two firearms were loose in the bag with two clips that were also loose, having been ejected from the handles of the firearms; they were not loaded. There was also dozens of bullets loose at the bottom of the bag. I picked out eight of the smaller bullets, as there were two sizes of bullet, one fitting each gun. The Glock used 9mm rounds, and the Desert Eagle used .45 calibre rounds, which were slightly bigger in width. The Glock was lighter and easier to conceal, so I chose this as my weapon of choice, plus I knew it was more than capable of killing with one-shot. I picked up the black handgun and rested it on my lap. Then I picked up the clip and held it in my left hand, pushing down on each bullet I pressed and slotted 15 bullets into the magazine carefully. I then inserted the clip and pulled the slide back to put a bullet in the chamber. Finally, I ejected the clip once more to put the final bullet into the magazine, this firearm was now loaded to max capacity. I had loaded my dad's handgun before, so I knew exactly what I was doing. I then placed the loaded gun on the floor between my legs and then zipped the laptop bag closed.

"Take this into John and Tom's house and tell them I will get it moved within the hour," I said to Chris as I handed him the bag containing my Desert Eagle .45. *Look what this dickhead has got me doing on a Friday fucking afternoon. I should have shot Chris and Morris,* I thought as I sat waiting for Chris to come back to the car.

Chris came back out of the McBride's house as I got out of my jeep and locked it. "Come, let's go," I said to Chris as he walked towards me. I could see the confusion on Chris' face as I locked my jeep. "What? You didn't think I'm driving my car around with a gun, did you? Open your car, you fucking idiot," I said as I walked towards the passenger seat of the 6L saloon. Chris got into the driver's seat and started the engine. I told him, "If police try and stop us, take them on a straight road and blow them. Then turn a corner, so I can throw this gun out of the car," I explained. The German saloon we were in was powerful enough to lose any police car on a straight road. 6.5L of German engineering.

"Okay, where are we going though?" Chris asked as he pulled off the kerb from outside of the McBride's house.

"If you don't know where Morris is, then take me to his friend's house," I said angrily. I had picked the Glock up and tucked it under my waistband before getting out of my jeep. Having a loaded Glock in a 6.6 V 12 supercar, I felt untouchable. I had not a care in the world; the adrenaline having a loaded gun on me made me know, if I saw Morris, I would not hesitate to shoot him three or four times without a seconds thought.

We drove past a police car, and the police did not even look at us. *Idiots,* I thought as I watched them disappear in the rear view mirror. Ten minutes later, we drove into the council estate that Morris' friend lived on. Morris' friend was a mixed-race guy in his mid-30s called Mark. Mark sold a kilo of cocaine every week and had bought that kilo of cocaine from Chris, he'd also bought drugs off Chris before through Morris, who was Mark's very close friend. "Chris...all I want you to do is knock the door. I will do the rest!" I said as I prepared to get out of the car. I could feel my heart rate increase as I fought to control my nerves. My stomach turned, but I wasn't scared; it was more anxiety. Turning back hadn't even crossed my mind. "Come on, let's go," I said as I opened my car door. "Hurry the fuck up," I said to Chris as he walked towards the door at his normal pace. Chris knocked Mark's door. I kept my hands in my pocket, so nobody would see I was wearing gloves.

Mark looked out of the living room window to see Chris and me at his door. Mark came to the door and opened it. "Are you okay, lads?" Mark said as he tried to remain calm, like he had no idea in the world why Chris and I were at his front door.

"Are you okay, Mark? Could we have a little chat?" I asked pleasantly.

"Yes, what's up?" Mark asked.

"Can we come inside, I don't want to talk on your doorstep," I asked as though he had been rude not to invite us inside.

We followed Mark through to the living room where he had one of his friends waiting for him. As Mark sat on the sofa, I reached into my waistline and pulled out the 9mm-loaded Austrian pistol. "Don't you move, or I will blow your fucking head clean off," I grunted as I pointed the gun at Mark's face. Mark's jaw had dropped into his lap in shock as his eyes widened in terror. "Or you! You just stay there, or I will paint the walls red with the contents of your fat head," I snarled as I flashed the gun from Mark to his friend's face and back to Mark. "Cyrus, why are you doing this?" Mark pleaded as he sat looking into my eyes terrified.

"Where's that fat cunt, Morris? If you can answer that correctly, I might only shoot you both once each; if you can't, then I'm going to empty the clip in you and your mate, then I will wait for your missus and children, and do the same to them," I growled at Mark.

"He was here earlier to drop some stuff off, but he's moved house recently, and I don't know where his new house is, but I can find out," Mark pleaded.

"What stuff?" I asked.

"A kilo of cocaine," Mark replied. I walked over to Mark and pressed the barrel of my gun firmly against his eyebrow.

"Where is the kilo of cocaine now, Mark?" I asked slowly putting emphasis on every word.

"In the kitchen drawer, next to the sink," Mark answered.

"Chris, go and get my cocaine," I said as I nodded at Chris to get his fat arse moving.

"Where is my other kilo of cocaine that Morris stole from my worker this morning, Mark?" I said while still holding the gun pressed firmly against Mark face.

"I don't know, mate. If I had it, I would definitely give it you. I don't want to get shot," Mark replied. I pulled the gun back six to eight inches and thrust it forward into Mark face with all my might. It was a calculated vicious attack, as it was a precise blow to Mark's eyebrow. The flesh that had been Mark's eyebrow split instantly as the barrel of my gun ripped through his flesh, exposing the bone above his eye. Mark screamed in pain as he cowered up to protect himself.

I didn't smile as Chris waved one of our stolen kilos of cocaine at me. I was too zoned-out to smile; Morris still had one! "Mark, show me where Morris lives, and I will let you and your mate stay alive. If you don't, then you both are dead," I said angrily.

"I will show you, Cyrus, just tell me what you want me to do?" Mark pleaded as the blood started to drip onto the laminate wooden-flooring from the gash above Mark's eye. The severity of the blow had made a third of Mark's face deformed with the swelling instantly—a flap of flesh was clearly visible.

"You two are coming with Chris and me; then when you show me where Morris lives, you can go. If any of you two try any funny business, I give you my word that I would murder the pair of you! I also give you the same word; if you show me where this cunt lives, I will let you both go without injuring either of you any further," I said while still pointing my gun at Mark, then his friend and back at Mark.

"We will not try anything, Cyrus," Mark replied in compliance.

"And what about you? Are you feeling brave?" I said as I aimed the pistol at Mark's friend's face.

"It's nothing to do with me, mate. I just came to get a gram of cocaine," Mark's friend said as he looked at me full of fright.

"Okay, let's go then. Mark, you sit in the back with me, and I'll sit behind your mate who will be sitting in the passenger seat," I said signalling everybody to get up. I was the last person to leave Mark's house, and I locked the door before following the group to the car.

I opened the car door and slipped my phone out of my pocket. I still had the loaded Glock in my right hand. I didn't care about Mark's neighbours or anyone else that had anything to say. I was in 'act first and think later' mode. "If any of you two makes a sudden move, I'm going to start squeezing this trigger; so everyone, stay calm and relaxed," I said as I held the gun in my left-hand facing towards Mark, who was on my right in the back of the car. In my right hand, I held my phone to my ear. "I'm with a guy who knows where this Morris guy lives. I've got a kilo of cocaine back; so if you want to go come over and fuck this guy up, then I am happy to wait for you and L to come over," I said to Yax as he answered. I didn't want to use Luke's name, in case Mark told the police, or his friend told the police.

"Yes, we will come over, has the guy still got a kilo of your cocaine?" Yax asked.

"Yes, the guy who stole two kilos still has one, you and Luke can keep that if you get it. I just want him stabbed up or shot," I said still annoyed at the fact I hadn't caught up with Morris yet.

"Okay, text me a postcode, and we will be in Coventry in half an hour," Yax said in his Birmingham/Asian accent. I cut the phone off and placed it onto my lap.

"So, where does Morris live then, Mark?" I asked as I sat next to Mark, pointing the gun at his midsection.

"I will have to call him and ask him. I know it's in an area called 'Coundon' somewhere, but I'm not sure where exactly. I would have to call him," Mark replied. I believed Mark; he was holding his eyes to stop the bleeding, and I could tell he just wanted to comply and get himself out of this situation as soon as possible. "Cyrus, Morris is not my friend if he is going to get people coming around my family house with guns. I don't even want anything to do with him ever again after this," Mark said as he sat bleeding and scared. We devised a plan for Mark to find Morris' address while we drove to a public park's car park.

The plan was to wait for my friends from Birmingham (Yax and Luke), then Mark would called Morris and say he needs another nine ounces of cocaine. If Morris asked him if he's heard anything from Chris or me, Mark would tell him 'no'. When Morris gives his location to Mark, my mates will make forced entry to the house or flat. When Morris is bleeding to death, I would drop Mark and his friend home.

"Sorted then?" I asked Mark.

"Yes, deal, I don't want any trouble with you, Cyrus. You are driving around in a £50,000 saloon with a loaded handgun. I am not stupid, and Morris deserves whatever he has coming to him for messing with you," Mark said as he analysed the situation.

"Yes, Mark, I would rather be out shopping or having a cocktail or a joint somewhere, but when people start trying to rob £40,000 from me, I have to put the cocktails down and pick the guns up, my friend," I explained still holding the gun pointed towards Mark as I rested my hand on my lap. We had sent the postcode for the car park we were sat in to Yax. The four of us sat waiting. The adrenaline I had in Mark's house had faded from my bloodstream, leaving lactic acid that was now making me feel somewhat at ease. I didn't allow myself to relax too much though, as I still had a loaded gun on my lap, pointed at one of the two hostages in my car.

Having been so angry in Mark's living room had taken a lot of energy from me, and I almost felt like leaning back on the seat and going to sleep, like the calm after the storm, but I couldn't do that yet as the storm hadn't passed. I decided to stay one hundred percent alert with the knowledge that Morris would soon be dead or fighting for his life, then I would relax. I watched as a black saloon turned into the car park. I had been keeping a close eye on the coming and going of any car, in case the police turned into the car park. The black saloon drove around the car park before parking next to our white saloon. Luke was driving, and Yax was in the passenger seat. I opened the car door to get out. "You lot stay in the car," I said as I got out to speak to Yax. There was a big black guy in the back that was dark-skinned and built like a house; he looked scary. I stood by the black saloon and explained the whole scenario, leaving nothing out, from Chris giving Morris two kilos of cocaine, to taking Mark and his friend hostage, ending with the plan of Mark calling Morris.

"Okay, when you get the address, we will follow you there; then leave it with us," Luke said.

"What do you want us to do to Morris after we take whatever money and cocaine he has?" Yax asked.

"I want him either shot or put in a wheelchair for the rest of his life; so if anybody even thinks about doing anything like this again, they will think thrice first!" I said as I turned to get back into my white saloon.

"Make the call then, Mark, and make it good," I said as I sat back down, gun still in hand.

"What phone number are you calling, because his phone has been off all day?" Chris asked

"He gave me a new number today," Mark replied as he began to make the call. The car was silent inside as Mark held the phone to his ear. He had dried blood smeared over his cheeks and chin, blotches of blood had dripped into Mark's T-shirt, leaving coin-sized circles of dry blood soaked into the material.

"Yes, Morris…"

"Morris, I need another nine ounces if you have got them; my friend wants to buy them now."

"No, I don't want to give it out of my kilo. I will not make any profit, because my friend only wants to pay what you charged me."

"Morris, I don't want him to know that I've got a kilo of cocaine because he owes me one ounce; so if I get him to get the cocaine from you, he will have to give me the ounce he owes me."

"No, Chris hasn't called me. Why?"

"Okay, give me the address, and I will get my friend to drop me to your house." This was the side of the conversation I had heard before Mark put the phone down. "It's 180 Hall Green Road," Mark said as he put the phone back into his pocket.

"Is he there now?" I asked.

"Yes, he said to come now," Mark replied. I got out of my white saloon to relay the message to Yax and Luke and the abnormally big black guy in the back.

I had been told that when we get near to Morris' house, I should park around the corner. Luke would go to the door with Mark, then Yax and the big black guy would go straight in after Luke had pushed Morris back inside his house. "He is a big guy, Luke," I said at the thought of Morris being pushed back inside his house.

"I will shoot him in the head if he messes about," Luke said as though me thinking he couldn't handle Morris was ludicrous.

"Okay, follow us," I said as I turned to get back into the white saloon.

"Chris, drive to this silly bastard's house," I said as Chris started the powerful saloon. On route, I told Mark what I wanted him to do.

"Morris is going to kill me for this," Mark had said in reply.

"Morris will be lucky if he can walk after this; and like you said, it's his fault you are here. You're just making sure you get home to your family safely," I explained.

180 Hall Green road was a flat in a five-storey block of flats. Flat 180 was on the top floor, which as Luke said, makes it impossible for Morris to escape 'unless he can fly', Luke had said before laughing hysterically.

Luke and Mark walked into the flats, closely followed by Yax and the big black guy, whose back was the size of a small dining room table. They planned for Mark to knock the door, and Luke barge his way in at gunpoint. By the time Luke was in, Yax and the big black guy would also be inside Morris' house. Mark would then return to the white saloon, so Chris and I could drop him and his friend home. The time was 4:30 p.m. on a Friday afternoon, not the best time for this sort of thing, but Morris' violation had made us throw caution to the wind.

Chris and I sat with Mark's kidnapped friend silently as we waited. We were parked at the side of the block of flats in case Morris looked over the balcony or out of his window and saw the white saloon that Chris had drove to meet him earlier in the day. I kept my window open to listen for gunshots. I heard nothing.

Ten minutes after getting out of the car, Mark came running back to our white saloon. Mark looked just as scared as he had been when he had first had my gun pointed at him in his living room. Mark had ran to the car and opened the back door and jumped in.

"Drop me off, it's done," Mark blarted out as he waved his hands towards Chris to drive.

"Did they get him?" I asked calmly.

"Yes, Morris is in a bad way; they said drop me off and then meet them where you arranged," Mark said as he panicked profusely. Chris started the white saloon and pulled off slowly.

"Are you sure that they got him?" I asked again.

"Got him? I think that they have killed him," Mark said as he sat looking at me shaken by what he had just seen.

"Calm down, and tell me exactly what happened," I said slowly.

"I knocked the door. When Morris answered his door, that stocky white guy came from behind me and punched Morris in the face with a knuckle-duster; then the other two ran into the house, pushing me into the house with them. They then beat the shit out of Morris and tied him and his girlfriend up. I saw that black guy stab Morris; then they told me to go," Mark explained as he visualised what he had just seen.

"What did they tie him up with?" I asked.

"Zip ties, the black guy had them, and a Rambo knife," Mark replied as he held his head in his hands.

As I smiled widely, I felt a large weight lift from my shoulders. "Do you see what happens when people fuck with me, Mark?" I asked as I smiled, realising Morris had got his comeuppance before the sun had set.

"Yes, I know, Cyrus; he is mad for trying to rob from you," Mark agreed.

"How do you know the black guy stabbed Morris?" I asked eager to hear all the information I could.

"Because I saw him do it; that black guy is evil," Mark replied. Chris parked the car back outside the house that we had kidnapped Mark and his friend from.

"You both were not with us today. If I hear different, you know what will happen. Next time you want a kilo of cocaine, call Chris directly, okay, Mark?" I said as I warned them both before they got out of my car.

"Chris, let's get this gun out of the car now," I said as we pulled off once more. The relief of knowing Morris had now been taught a lesson had brought me back to reality. It was like my ego had been fed, my pride had been restored, bringing me back to rationality. "Let's go back to my car, and I will leave the gun in this car while we go and meet my mates by my house in the jeep," I told Chris as we drove from Mark's back towards the McBride's. I left the loaded handgun under the passenger seat of the white saloon and got back into the driver's seat of my jeep.

"Cyrus, do you think that they killed Morris?" Chris asked as we started the short drive to my parents' house.

"I hope so," I replied emotionlessly. If I'm honest, I did hope they had killed him, as long as I wouldn't get arrested for it. As we made the right turn into a dead-end outside of my parent's house, I saw the black saloon was already parked outside my parent's house.

I parked quickly and got out, as I did, three of the four doors opened on the black saloon. Chris and I walked towards Yax, Luke and the big black guy. "Did you get him?" I ask Yax, who was wearing a black tracksuit with a black skullcap.

"Yes, he is finished. My mate stabbed him and sliced his Achilles tendons, so he will never walk properly again. It's at the back above your ankle," Yax explained as he smiled, clearly impressed with his friends handiwork.

"And we got a kilo of cocaine and £10,000 from him," Luke added as he smiled with his usual bright smile.

"Yes, good, you lot keep that. Thanks, guys," I said as I shook their hands firmly.

"We are going to go back to Birmingham now, Cyrus. The car has got false number plates on it, so we want to get back and park it up. Get us some more jobs though, Cyrus; you have seen how we work now," Yax said.

Chapter 19

I had become the most feared man in my city overnight. I was also known and feared throughout the whole of England. My connections in the drug world, combined with my violent reputation had made my name spread throughout the country, like wildfire. The West Midlands was my playground. I had now turned 25 years old and felt more of a man than ever before.

I had given Chris one of the two guns I brought from Yax to store at a safe location near to his house in case anybody tried to harm him or my bank balance again. I had also paid for a builder to put a secret compartment into the wall in my bathroom at my flat. This is where I stored the other handgun I had brought from Yax. If the police ever found it, I would tell them I didn't know the compartment existed. I had it all figured out. Also, I had been out in our local town to do some shopping with Emma, and I had saw people's faces when they saw me. There were mixtures of feelings displayed on people's faces as they'd notice me, or their friends would tap them on the shoulder and say, "Do you know that is? That's Big CY." People's faces that would spot me as I walked through the town would be filled with fear or respect or admiration or an unsurety. Even people I have known for years had started to treat me differently, everybody seemed to be humble in my presence. The older kids that used to doss outside my parent's house at the time I started selling drugs were now almost 30 years old. I had seen a few of them in town on a Saturday afternoon. "Yes, guys, long time no see," I had said happily.

"You okay, Cyrus?" they had replied with forced smiles on their faces. Almost seven years of selling drugs had made me an expert at reading people's body languages. I would have to be able to read people without them uttering a word, or how would I know when somebody is lying or trying to pull a fast one or hiding something from me?

So, when the people that were once my superiors in my childhood replied to my happy greeting with 'you okay, Cyrus?' I read into that like it was an open book. It wasn't that they weren't happy to see me; it was that they were scared of me. Just my presence alone had them 'walking on egg shells'.

"Yes, I'm good, lads. How are you lot?" I replied to their sheepish question. It saddened me to see people I had known my whole life to be scared of me and not able to treat me normally.

"Cyrus, we have got to go because we have someone waiting for us," they had replied as they made a quick but polite getaway.

It did upset me. The average person that knew my reputation was scared of me. I accepted it though; it had to be that way to ensure the smooth running of my business.

Girls loved the fact that people feared me. I had never imagined in my wildest dreams it could be so easy to 'net new skirt'. Girls practically threw themselves at me. I would walk into the club in the city centre, and wherever I went, the doormen would shake my hands. "Are you all right, big fella?" or "You all right, Big CY?" They had said as they extended their hand to shake hands with me. Why these giant doormen called me 'Big fella', I would never understand.

I would walk into the club wearing either Italian or French designers with my big diamond watch on, and I would feel hundreds of eyes gravitate towards me, like I was glowing. It got to a stage that I got sick of guys coming up to me to say 'hello' and shake hands. I would just give them a fist pump and say, "You all right, lad?" or "Give me a minute. I'm busy if you don't mind".

They would always reply, "Sorry, mate, I just wanted to say hello." I didn't go to a nightclub to shake hands with a bunch of guys I don't know. I knew that these people only wanted to talk to me so that they could be seen to be friends with the local gangster or impress a girl by proving that they know me. I would go to a club more often than not after a long day. I would tell Emma I was busy working or out-of-town working. I would walk around the club and meticulously find an extremely sexy girl that tickled my fancy. I would then go to the bar and order a bottle of champagne if I had located a target. I would tap the nearest idiot who had been claiming to know me on the shoulder.

"Oi mate, do me a favour, please," I would say as the shocked nine-to-five worker would turn to look at me, as if to say 'what could this guy possibly want from me?'

They would almost certainly reply, "Yes, CY, what's up?" As they would try to stay composed, with no idea what I wanted, "Go over there and tell that girl with the brown hair to come over here;

244

tell her I need to tell her something." I would say with an expressionless face.

I would pour the girl in question a glass of champagne and wait. Nine times out of ten, I would wake up in a hotel suite to see the very same handpicked girl asleep on the pillow next to me. It was almost too easy—a few well-polished chat-up lines, or a bit of good humour, combined with my reputation and expensive clothes and jewellery had women eating out of the palm of my hand. My favourite approach was to engage them in gentle conversation before saying, "I need to drop some money to my mate around the corner." I would talk to the girl in question for 15 minutes or so to make sure that they were comfortable in my company before I would say, "I've had four glasses of champagne, and my mate keeps bugging me to drop some money off to him. Would you mind coming for a drive with me; it will only take ten minutes to go there and come back." If a girl sits in my passenger seat, I am less likely to get pulled over, and I'd lose my license. "You'd be doing me a big favour," then I'd give them the 'butter wouldn't melt' facial expression.

As soon as we would walk outside, and the girl would see I had an Italian supercar; it was practically a done deal.

I would usually go to the McBride's house to get some weed, then ask the girl if they want to go somewhere a bit better than where we had left. This would of course be my hotel suite, swiftly followed by room service and a dip in the Jacuzzi.

Life was good, social life and business life was good. Chris was doing his job properly; and since that palaver with Morris almost three and a half years ago, I had not heard much on the matter. Morris' cousin had got my number and called me saying, "I know that had something to do with you, Cyrus," almost in tears.

"Piss off you, Wally," had been my reply before putting the phone down. I had always said I would make an example out of the first person that crosses the line. Morris chose to be that person—nobody had forced him.

It was a Saturday night when I pulled outside the nightclub in the city centre in a top of the range German supercar that Bob and I had bought. We had decided to invest further into our prestige car rental company 'CB Prestige' by buying 12 top-of-the-range motors. I liked the car I had chosen to drive. It was white, with red leather interior and had big glossed alloy wheels. Even people that had no interest in cars would look at this piece of machinery in admiration. I had told Emma I was taking a new business associate out for dinner, but I had actually done that hours before. I planned to pop into the busy High Street bar to have two drinks and find some light entertainment in the form of a sexy girl to spend the night with. It was all about the chase for me; it excited me to know that the girl I'd chosen would have no idea my every move was premeditated. She would think I just wanted to have a friendly chat, but the reality was that I had already planned where she would be spending the night. Intellectual manipulation! At its finest.

I didn't use somebody to call the girl I wanted tonight. She had looked at me two or three times as I stood talking to the guy behind the bar while he neglected people waiting to be served. She had observed my presence and the way people treated me, practically like I owned the bar. I used a 'come here' gesture with my hand as she looked at me with a friendly smile. She joined me at the bar, and I gave her the old 'I feel stupid here on my own. My mate was supposed to meet me here, but he's had to work late', followed by convincing her to have a drink with me so I don't look like a loner. Two hours later, I slid the key card for my hotel suite through the sensor to open the door. "After you, gorgeous," I said as the girl walked into the room ahead of me. The room I had for the night had a large bathroom on the left as soon as you enter the room. The bathroom had a whirlpool Jacuzzi tub in it. When I had purchased the room before going to the bar, I had sat and made a few business calls. While making my business calls, I waited for room service to bring a bottle of rosé inside a bucket of ice. After paying for the bottle of wine, I left it on the table in the room and went to find tonight's conquest. "Pour us a glass of wine each while I finish filling up the Jacuzzi," I said after kissing the girl passionately and putting my car keys and phone on the table.

The two of us got into the Jacuzzi and sipped our wine in the lowly lit bathroom. It was always the perfect end to a long day; soaking in the tub being massaged by the powerful jets propelling water into my back. I enjoyed listening to a beautiful girl ramble on about stuff I had no interest in. It was stimulating for me to indulge in senseless conversation with a girl that I'd taken to my room. It relaxed me not to talk about business or personal problems. I decided to drink some more wine before having sex. 'Click', the sound was unmissable to my acute sense of hearing. I had heard a key card activate the lock in my hotel suites door! I was always aware of my surroundings, even in the most relaxing of situations. My brain was still moving at the speed of light as I heard the 'click'. I had instantly thought, *who the fuck is that?* And *I haven't ordered any room service.* Before I could even put my glass down, the door burst open.

"Police, armed police, police, armed police," the voices screamed as the officers ran into the hotel suite. I looked to the doorway in shock as four armed police officers in full tactical clothing ran into the bathroom and switched on the light. They had marksman hats on, like miniature black baseball hats with a black and white chequered pattern on them with the word 'police' on the front. All four police officers in my view had sub-machine guns pointed at me as I sat in the Jacuzzi.

"Don't move, or we will shoot," the closest officer had said.

I believed him. I just sat, staring at them in shock. I didn't even look at the girl opposite me in the Jacuzzi.

"I want you to stand up slowly. And step out of the tub, slowly; any sudden moves, we will shoot, do you understand!" the same officer shouted at me angrily. I knew he meant it. He was standing perfectly still with one foot in front of the other, like he was practicing at the shooting range.

I stood up slowly. "Any sudden moves, I will shoot!" the officer shouted again. I was completely naked, still holding my glass of wine. "Drop the glass of wine, do not put it down; drop it! Do you understand!" the officer shouted angrily. The situation had sobered me up instantly. It was almost surreal, like a bad dream. I dropped the glass without even looking where it had landed. "Now step out of the tub one foot at a time, and lay face down on the floor!" the firearms officer instructed me aggressively. I was under no illusion that this man was ready to fire without a seconds' thought. His finger was on the trigger, and his gun was definitely loaded.

I felt the pores on my forehead open as I started to sweat as adrenaline started to course through my veins. I wasn't scared, but I was definitely concerned for my welfare. I hadn't even realised that I was holding both my hands in the air in surrender. I stepped out of the tub one foot at a time as instructed.

I began to kneel before lying down on the bathroom floor. As I did so, I was bombarded with officers pinning me to the ground. "Put your hands behind your back," the officers shouted as they zip-tied my hands securely behind my back.

"Are you expecting anybody else here?" one of the police officers asked.

"No," I replied feeling deflated.

"Cyrus Johnson, I am arresting you for conspiracy to murder David Morris. The time is now 1:40 a.m.," the armed officer said as he took me by the arm. "Could you find his clothes?" the same officer asked. *How the fuck are they arresting me for this now?* The voice in my head screamed as I put my jeans on one leg at a time, with my arms still bound behind my back.

"We are going to take these plastic cuffs off now, Cyrus, to put metal handcuffs on you. If you move or resist, we will use deadly force, do you understand?" one of the armed officers shouted.

"Yes, I am cooperating," I answered as they performed the swap of arm restraints. Now out of the bathroom and back in the hotel suites' main room, I watched as what looked like 30 officers searched the room, leaving no cubic centimetre untouched. My T-shirt and jumper were thrown over my head. Pushing my head down to waist height in front of me, while two officers either side held my arms up with one hand, and the back of my neck down with the other hand to stop me lifting my head, I was marched out of the room and then out of the hotel. Having been taken outside, I could now see the scale of the police's operation mounted against me.

Police vehicles filled the hotel's car park with cars, vans and jeeps. There must have been 30 vehicles, all with silent, flashing blue lights. They had kept their sirens off to avoid alerting me to their arrival. I was put in the back of a police car with three police officers inside. We were being followed by several police cars as we left the hotel. *How are you going to prove this? It happened over three years ago,* I thought as we drove. Worry really started to settle in when I realised the police were not taking me to our local police station; instead, we were leaving town via the motorway.

We arrived at Boyd House Police Station, Birmingham city centre, 20 minutes later. On the way there, the driver had broken almost every traffic law known to man—speeding, driving through red lights the lot. *Just because you are a police officer, you can break the law,* I thought to myself as I watched the driver doing as he pleased. The big electric blue gate to enter the police station opened as we drove in, followed by three other police cars. The officers that had transported me asked me if I understood why I had been arrested, but I didn't answer. I just remain silent.

"If you get arrested, don't say a word. Just ask for Mr G from GQZ solicitors, he will sort it out," Bob had said after making me repeat what I had been told back to him. As I walked into the custody suite to confirm my name, the 'desk sergeant' read me my rights and confirmed the reason for my arrest.

"You are being charged with conspiracy to murder David Morris, with the following people. He then said Bob's real name, Yax's real name, Luke's name and the big black guy's real name. I couldn't believe it. "Do you wish to make any comment to this allegation?" the sergeant asked.

"Yes, could you get me Mr G from GQZ solicitors, please," I said as calmly as I could, considering my current circumstance.

"Yes, that shouldn't be a problem; your mate (Bob's real name) asked for the same guy," the sergeant said informing me Bob was already in the same police station. "Could you put Mr Johnson in cell number five, please," the sergeant said to one of the officers. *No fucking way... I have to beat this and get the fuck out of here,* I thought as I followed the officer to my cell.

Sitting on that thin blue plastic mattress, if you can even call it a mattress, gave me a lot of time to think, but the stress of what had just happened made thinking impossible. I didn't know what evidence the police had to arrest me. Why had they arrested Bob? Most importantly, what was going to happen now?

The End...

Book two is fast-paced from page one as Cyrus is 26. It is the conclusion of Johnson's journey.